PRAISE FOR THE AUTHOR

'With her fast-paced mysteries set in the tumultuous reign of Henry II, E.M. Powell takes readers on enthralling, and unforgettable, journeys.'
— Nancy Bilyeau, author of *The Crown*

'Both Fifth Novels are terrific. Benedict and Theodosia are not merely attractive characters: they are intensely real people.'
— *Historical Novels Review*

'From the get-go you know you are in an adventure when you enter the world of E.M. Powell's 12th century. Peril pins you down like a knight's lance to the chest.'
— Edward Ruadh Butler, author of *Swordland*

The
Lord
of
Ireland

ALSO BY E.M. POWELL

The Fifth Knight

The Blood of the Fifth Knight

E. M. POWELL

A Fifth Knight Novel

This is a work of fiction. Names, characters, organizations, places, events, and incidents are either products of the author's imagination or are used fictitiously.

Published by Thomas & Mercer, Seattle
www.apub.com

ISBN-13: 9781503951938
ISBN-10: 1503951936

Cover design by Jason Anscomb

Printed in the United States of America

For my father, the late Patrick C. Powell.
I hope he's proud of Maggot.

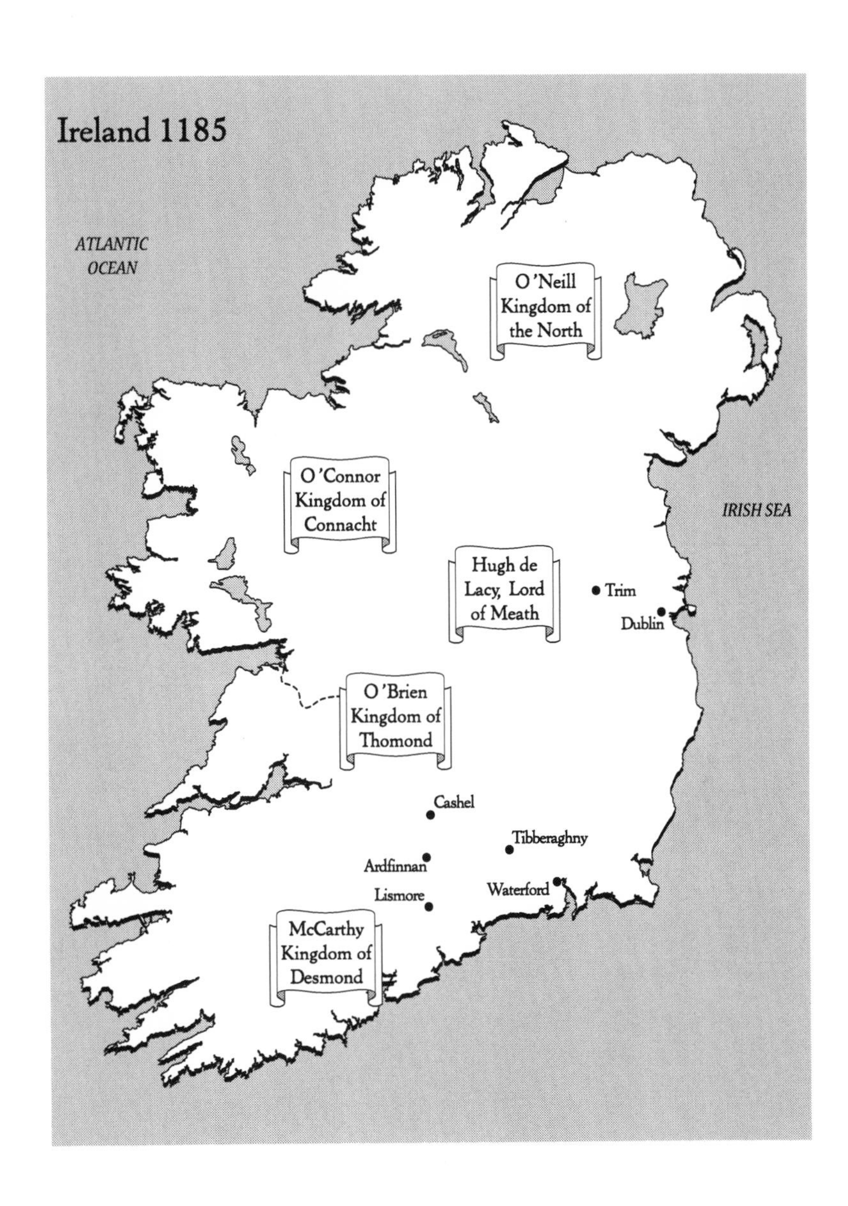
Ireland 1185
ATLANTIC OCEAN
O'Neill Kingdom of the North
O'Connor Kingdom of Connacht
IRISH SEA
Hugh de Lacy, Lord of Meath
Trim
Dublin
O'Brien Kingdom of Thomond
Cashel
Tibberaghny
Ardfinnan
Waterford
Lismore
McCarthy Kingdom of Desmond

Every tree, as a lordly token,
Stands all stained with the red blood rain
War that demons might wage is woken,
Wails peal high as he raves again

From: *Heroic Romances of Ireland*
by A. H. Leahy

Chapter One

The Priory of the Order of St John of Jerusalem, Clerkenwell, London
18 March 1185

Today, he would receive his crown. As the youngest son, John had heard so many scoff at the idea that he would ever have a kingdom to call his own. Even his own royal father, the great Henry: siring child after child, boy after boy, by his mother, Eleanor. She whelped them out, year on year, leaving them to jostle like too many puppies for too few teats. As the last son, there was nothing for him. Nothing for Lackland.

Lackland. Henry's mocking, dismissive name for him as a boy, taken up with glee by so many. Worst of all, by his older brothers, who used the humiliating taunt until he would cry with rage, setting about them with his small fists even as they laughed at his feeble attempts. *Lackland.* Its shame had never left him, with the crumbs of territory that Henry had granted him only whetting his appetite for power and never close to sating it.

But from today, he'd be Lackland no more. He would have his crown. And what a crown.

'Pray rise to welcome Heraclius, Patriarch of the Holy City of Jerusalem!' The cry of the grand master of the Hospitallers came from the high doorway, echoing up to the curved and vaulted stone ceiling of the candlelit chapter house.

The dozens of barons and abbots seated on the dais around the circular room rose to their feet in a rustle and clink of their ceremonial raiments.

John stood up too, glancing to the highest seat of all. Of course, Henry didn't stand. The King sat in his carved wooden chair, straight as his ageing spine would allow.

The grand master strode in, his flowing black robes emblazoned with the white cross of his order.

Heraclius followed him more slowly, weighed down by the sumptuous, gold-embroidered vestments of Jerusalem. The small party filing in behind him bore padded cushions of scarlet silk on which a number of items rested, the sight of which made John's heart race.

The keys to the tower of David. The standard of the Holy City. And, most precious of all, the key to the Holy Sepulchre itself, its metal dull against the glow of the silk but which he could swear heated his flesh by its very presence.

He pulled in a long, calming breath as Henry inclined his head to the Patriarch. 'We welcome you to our holy priory, Heraclius.'

The narrow-faced Patriarch bowed deeply. 'Truly it is a sign from God that you have summoned me to a place that is dedicated to the Holy City.'

And a place that bore the name of John. Yes, this was a sign. The sign for which John had waited for eighteen long years. His hands quivered now that his prize was so near, and he slid them out of sight beneath his fur-trimmed cloak. *Lackland no more.*

Henry waved to his court to retake their seats.

John did so too, arranging his visage into a mask of noble serenity, the better that those present should marvel at the glorious moment at which a man became a king.

'I offer you the warmest of welcomes to my council, Patriarch Heraclius,' said Henry. 'I have considered your request for a number of weeks.'

A number? Six, to be precise. Six impossible weeks since the Patriarch's arrival at Henry's court in Reading. How the man had gone on about the Holy Land and its being in danger. How leprosy consumed its ruler, Baldwin. How the sacred land was in danger of falling into the hands of the infidel. On and on, the man's impassioned pleas reducing the whole court to tears. Well, not the *whole*: John had had trouble stifling his yawns. The only thing that had kept him awake was wondering which parts of Baldwin had dropped off and in what order. But he'd sat bolt upright at the Patriarch's conclusion: could Henry send an Angevin prince to assume the crown of Jerusalem?

Henry had nodded sagely and said he would convene a council to give it grave consideration and issue an answer.

Then John had known. Known what his father planned. His eldest brother, Henry, had been dead for almost two years. The King was still embroiled in reassigning lands to John's uncooperative older brothers, Richard and Geoffrey. It only left him, John. He would have Jerusalem.

He had of course been excluded from the council. For that he was truly grateful. Listening to this room full of wrinkled old men puff and blow for the last week about a matter to which they already had a conclusion would have had him dead with boredom.

The Patriarch smiled. 'I am humbled and grateful for your grave consideration, your Grace.'

'We have our responses for you,' said Henry. 'I have asked all at my council to advise me for my soul's safety, and I will abide by their wise opinions.' He nodded to the baron seated nearest the door. 'You may speak.'

John swallowed hard and prepared himself for the first momentous confirmation of his new power.

'My answer is guided by God,' said the old baron, toothless, but clear as day. 'And it is that his Grace needs to attend to his realm here.'

Stunned, John grabbed for the ornate wooden arms of his seat.

The Patriarch looked as if the baron had slapped him across the face.

The baron went on. 'His Grace, full of charity and holiness, will send money to the aid of the Holy City.'

John's glance flew to Henry. Surely his father would let loose his famous wrath at the ridiculous suggestion of the dithering old nobleman? But no. No. *No.*

'I thank you for your gracious consideration,' said Henry, 'and praise God the Almighty for guiding your decision.'

Henry nodded to the next baron, who cleared his throat before announcing: 'My answer, guided by God, is that his Grace needs to attend to his realm here. His Grace, full of charity and holiness, will send money to the aid of the Holy City.'

The same words. The exact same words. John's grip on his chair tightened to hold in his shout of disbelief, the Patriarch's expression matching the shock surging within him.

Henry appeared as calm as a man enjoying a garden walk and sought the next response with a grave nod.

An abbot this time, opening his wet mouth to trumpet the words like a sermon. 'My answer, guided by God . . .'

Rage pounded in John's chest as baron, baron, abbot, baron – the whole infernal circle – continued to spew out the same reply.

His father listened to each one as if it were a real opinion instead of something he had imposed upon them.

John could only stare and stare, fearing his building fury would choke him.

'. . . to the aid of the Holy City.' The last man finished to a silence disturbed only by the roar of the blood in John's ears.

Henry turned his gaze to the Patriarch. 'Truly, an answer guided by God. I shall make sure your armies are well funded.' He gave a magnanimous smile.

Heraclius did not return it. 'Guided by God, your Grace? By *God*?' His voice climbed in his displeasure, the colour rising in his face to match. 'Does God wish that his own city should fall to the infidel?'

Henry's expression darkened to a frown. 'You would question my judgement? That I fight for Christendom?'

'You fight only for yourself! Like when you had Saint Thomas Becket, your holy archbishop, murdered when he would not bend to your will.' Heraclius's sharp accusation brought forth a stream of outrage from the council.

'Shame on you, sir!' cried a baron.

'The King has received God's forgiveness.' An abbot waved an angry fist in the air. 'He does not need yours!'

John leaned forward in a rush of renewed hope. Becket's murder was a stain on Henry's reign, his soul. The Patriarch's rash speech would surely sway the King.

Henry's expression did not change as the black-robed master stepped closer to the Patriarch. 'Enough. You forget your place.'

Heraclius thrust him to one side. 'I forget nothing. I remember in my prayers every day that Becket's sacred head was sacrificed to his martyrdom. You can take mine too. I will not be silenced. You condemn us all to the infidel's sword.' He pointed a finger at Henry. 'You may as well be a Saracen.'

The horrified clamour at Heraclius's words drowned out John's gasp of delight. That would do it. He looked at his father, waiting for the roars in response to the goads, the insults. The capitulation that would follow.

Henry raised a hand and silence fell, broken only by the Patriarch's fast, enraged breathing. 'I forgive you, Heraclius, for your harsh words. Becket's death still brings us all to grief that is near madness.'

A subdued chorus of 'Amen' met his words.

Henry continued. 'God has called my son Henry back to Him, but I have my remaining three sons, Angevin princes all, to hold my kingdom and to serve me. Now it is time for my son John, whom I have asked here today, to undertake a venture of the greatest difficulty and importance.'

John inclined his head at his father's words, renewed certainty hot within him now. Henry liked to create a spectacle. All of what had gone before had been just that. Now was when he would make his announcement.

'One I have clear in my mind.' Henry stood, and all rose with him.

John stood too: tall and proud. And ready.

'For the time has come.' Henry paused.

Now. Finally. John held in his smile of triumph as he met his father's eye. He needn't have feared. All was as he'd surmised. The Holy Land was his. *His.*

'Today,' said Henry, 'I make the solemn and proud dedication of my son to assume' – he opened his hands – 'the Lordship of Ireland.'

John's mouth fell open. The most meagre crumb of them all. 'Ireland?'

'Ireland?' repeated a stunned-looking Patriarch.

'Ireland.' Henry gave a firm nod.

'But, Father.' John thrust himself from the dais and stepped before Henry. 'I should be defending Jerusalem. The Holy Land. Not an island that is of no consequence in the world.'

Henry's fists clenched. 'No consequence?' came his instant bellow. 'It is within my realm. Mine! And as ever it remains in need of pacification. Its lordship has been in your name for the best part of ten years, and the day has come when you are of an age to deal with it. You should be honoured to serve me, boy.' Henry jabbed a finger at him. 'Honoured!'

'Of course I am, Father, but I would be better to take the crown of Jerusalem than the crown of Ireland, for God would want that, and He would . . .' John stuttered to a halt, lost as to what God might want. He fell to his knees on the hard stone of the floor and joined his hands, aware of how noble a sight this public humility would make. 'I beg you, your Grace.'

Henry's expression softened a little.

Yes, that was it. Beg – make his father feel powerful, generous. 'I beg you, implore you, with all my heart, and my – my soul.' But dread grasped at him as Henry shook his head slowly.

'John, there is to be no crown of Ireland sanctioned by Rome.' Henry's voice tightened in his anger. 'The Pope refuses to allow it. Refuses me.' His hard eyes bored into John's. 'So you remain Lord of Ireland. Under my superior lordship.'

'What?' John shot to his feet. 'No crown? Father, you cannot—'

Henry held a hand up. 'Remember to whom you speak. And the decision is that of the whole council. Guided by God.'

John looked left, right, behind, the better to meet every eye, to view every impassive face. No one uttered a word, but they might as well have clamoured a chorus of humiliation to the high ceiling: *Lackland, Lackland.*

'Guided by God,' repeated Henry as John met his gaze once more. 'My council.'

'Your council?' He glared at his father. 'That is what you would call this assemblage of – of nodding know-nothings?'

Henry drew breath to speak but John's shout stopped him.

'Fools! You're all fools!' Shocked gasps broke out as he shoved his way past the Patriarch, dashing the key of the Holy Sepulchre to the ground in a ring of metal on stone. He made for the closed entrance, unheeding of Henry's roars to remain.

'Fools, I tell you!' One hard blow from his hands drove the door open, sending the monks guarding it staggering back as he burst out.

He didn't care. His steps echoed hard in the stone cloister as he marched away, the door closing on his father's continued shouts and bringing silence to the near-darkness of evening.

His fool of a father too. And that meddler in Rome. Leaving the cloister, he spurned the tidy gravelled path that led to his apartments, cutting instead across the lawn. He needed to get to his rooms as quickly as he could, to let out some of this rage. Rooms to which he had bidden farewell as a man on the brink of his great destiny, and which he should have re-entered as a king. Instead – *nothing.*

He halted in the coolness of the gathering dusk, the race of fury in his chest threatening to break out in tears.

Worse, a nothing that had been planned. Every simple-pate in there had rehearsed and sung Henry's tune. The Patriarch could have been talking to seats taken by donkeys for all the notice taken of his excellent proposal. John kicked and kicked at the soft, neat grass, sending clods of earth and dirt into the air. He could wring every neck in there: scrawny, muscled, flabby. They all denied him his greatness, the power that was his by birth. By right. Who were they to deny him?

He booted up another sod of earth, then set off across the dark lawn. Lights shone from his grand accommodation, as they did from all the other buildings. The savoury smell of roast meat came on the cool air: final preparations for tonight's celebration to honour the Patriarch. A feast where all the nobles would gather and sate their appetite with the best food, the finest wines, joined by their wives. The whole court turning out to witness the humiliation of Lackland.

As if hearing his thoughts, a peal of female laughter came from a half-open window shutter. That's what they would do later, all of them, when they were alone together. And the barons' women would reward their husbands' loyalty with loyalty of their own, legs and mouths opening for their brave masters. Everyone would receive his reward tonight, even the Patriarch. The man might depart without a new owner of Jerusalem's keys, but he'd be weighed down with gold and silver. Only he, John, the son of a king, would have nothing, such was the travesty of the council's decision.

The laugh sounded again. A woman's silhouette was visible in the lamplight, her hair loose as a maid braided it in preparation for its covering veil.

John halted. He could not allow it. He would not slink back to his rooms as if he were a cur of no worth, then sit meekly at the feast. He would have one solace tonight. At the woman's door in moments, he entered without knocking. He had no need to so do.

He was of royal blood.

'You have no need to weep.' John did up his braies as the woman lay on the floor where he'd taken her, her white-faced maid cowering speechless in the corner. 'I have taken only what is my due.'

Powerless. Both of them.

Just as he had been so rendered by his father and the council before the Patriarch. He allowed himself a small sigh of satisfaction. Now someone else shared a little of how difficult life was for him, day after ceaseless day. Yet he carried that burden with noble fortitude. He would carry on that wearisome journey tonight and join his father's feast with smiles and platitudes.

As he walked to the door, the maid crept to her mistress with a whisper.

'Oh, my lady.'

He threw the woman a coin, and it rattled to a stop on the floor next to her.

Neither woman acknowledged it, the baron's wife clinging to her servant as she continued to weep.

John shrugged and left the room. He was the one who really had something to mourn. He'd lost Jerusalem, no question.

As he walked down the corridor, the woman's sobs faded away, mercifully no longer interfering with his thoughts.

If Henry thought he'd won today, if he really thought his son would be content with merely clearing up the mess that was Ireland, then the old man had made a grave mistake.

John took the stairs to his rooms, possibilities presenting themselves with every step. He marvelled at his speed in changing strategy.

That was what came of having a brilliant mind.

Chapter Two

The Palace of the Bishop of Salisbury, Sonning, Berkshire
28 March 1185

'My wife and I wish to gain entry. On orders of the King.' Sir Benedict Palmer held up the letter marked with Henry's seal so that the monk at the gatehouse could see it, praying the man wouldn't ask him to read it. Despite Theodosia's best efforts over the years, Palmer still took an age to make sense of the written word. Yet his pride meant he didn't want to have to pass it to her and make himself look less than the noble he appeared to be.

'Of course, sir.' The monk moved immediately from the small window to open up the gates with a clatter of bolts.

'We're in.' Palmer let out a long breath of relief.

'Yes, but in to what?' Theodosia's face was drawn, not only in tiredness from the many days she'd spent in the saddle but also from the strain of not knowing.

'I'm sure we'll find out soon enough.' Palmer collected their tethered horses as the monk pulled open the gates. A stable hand already waited in the quiet, sun-filled courtyard.

'Welcome to our holy house.' The monk waved to the man to take their mounts. 'Pray follow me; I am sure you will need refreshment after your journey.'

Theodosia went to speak. 'Good brother, we would like to—'

'Thank you.' With a warning shake of his head to her to say nothing else, Palmer slipped Theodosia's arm through his as they walked after the monk, the departing horses' hooves a loud clatter on the cobbles.

She shot him a fierce look out of the monk's sight and slowed their steps. 'I do not want refreshment,' she murmured. 'I want to know what is going on.'

'You must eat something or you'll fall sick.' Palmer kept his voice low in response. 'That worries me far more than the fate of a king.' He lowered his voice further. 'Even if that king is your father.'

She opened her mouth to protest.

He put a hand to his chest in an overdone, pompous apology. 'I utter treason. I know, my lady.'

Finally, he got the smallest smile.

But he didn't know what this might be about either. The last time they'd seen Henry had been nine years ago, when he'd granted them the security of a dead lord's estate. The King had kept in occasional contact through a secure system of letters to check on their well-being and to let them know of his.

Then, without warning: this. The crackling parchment, safe again in Palmer's belt pouch. A message of few words that had pulled them back out of the contented peace they'd come to take for granted.

Theodosia had been frantic, sure that it meant something terrible had happened or was about to happen to the King. Her pale face showed him she thought that still.

Palmer was more concerned that the letter had ordered that she come to this place too, so far from their home in the north, with no explanation.

The monk led them up a flight of stone stairs, opening the heavy door onto what Palmer assumed was the bishop's hall. Fresh with the scent of the floor's clean rushes, the fine room's carved and waxed wood shone in the light from the tall windows. But neither bishop nor king awaited him and Theodosia.

Instead, to his shock, there stood a tall woman of the Church, whom he and Theodosia knew from their past.

Theodosia gave a soft gasp.

'My lady,' said the nun. 'Sir Benedict. It gladdens my heart to see you again.'

'Abbess Dymphna.' Theodosia's stunned glance met Palmer's.

Palmer gave a polite bow, unable to find words. 'Abbess.'

The Abbess of Godstow Nunnery came to greet them with a broad smile, clasping Theodosia's hands in welcome. 'God has been treating you well, my lady, in the years since we last met.' Her soft voice still held the traces of her Irish birth.

'He has, Abbess.' Theodosia returned her smile, though with bewilderment clear on her face as to what the Abbess could be doing here at Sonning.

'You have moved here from Godstow, Abbess?' asked Palmer.

The ever-shrewd Dymphna met his query as he would expect. 'You mean, why on earth am I here at Sonning to greet you, Sir Benedict?'

'I sought to be polite, Abbess.'

'Of course you did, Sir Benedict.' Dymphna's mouth twitched in a smile. 'I am still Abbess of Godstow. But here at his Grace's invitation, the same as you. He must be the one to tell you why. I cannot.' She gestured to a linen-covered table along one wall, laden with fine-looking meats and wine. 'Now, please. Restore yourselves. The King is expected soon.'

Palmer knew he'd get no more from her and did as she offered, the food calling to his stomach after the long journey.

Theodosia hung back. 'Abbess, I have far more hunger for knowing why we are here.' She wouldn't meet Palmer's eye as he poured water from the full aquamanile into the washing bowls. 'I beg you: has something happened to the King?'

'The King is hale and well, my lady.' Dymphna's words brought a bit of colour back to Theodosia's face.

'You see?' Palmer pulled Theodosia's chair out with one hand as he took a large bite of venison from the knife in his other. The gamey meat brought a delicious iron tinge on his tongue. 'You have worried for nothing.' He wouldn't show Theodosia his own unease.

Dymphna came to the table with a swish of her long dark skirts as Theodosia took her seat too.

'You have no injuries that need seeing to, Sir Benedict?' Dymphna raised a knowing eyebrow.

Palmer held up a hand at the memory of Dymphna's efficient if robust healing. 'Not this time, Abbess.'

Thumping footsteps from outside could only mean the arrival of one man: Henry.

Palmer dropped his knife and scrambled to his feet even as Theodosia was halfway to the door.

'God smiles on me!' The King burst in, dressed for hunting, his splattered clothes telling of a recent hard ride as he flung his arms wide to greet Theodosia, the daughter whom he could never claim.

'Father.'

As Theodosia returned his hard embrace, Palmer was thrown by how old Henry had become since he had last seen him. The passing of the best part of a decade is kind to few: Palmer knew his own dark hair was now mixed with grey in places, and he had to weigh up a sack before he threw it onto a cart without help. Theodosia's pale skin, still beautiful, showed threads of wrinkles when she laughed or frowned. But Henry had fared badly. His eyes had the rheumy look of an old man, and his sure stride of old had gone; he swayed instead in a cruel limp as he made his way to the table with Theodosia.

'Palmer, my boy.' He clapped Palmer hard on the shoulder and acknowledged Dymphna's bow. 'Abbess. Sit, all of you.' The relief to be off his bad hip showed plain in his face. 'It is so good to see you. It has been too long since the last time we met.' The King shook his head. 'A great comfort that we do not gather in grief today.'

The Abbess poured him a generous measure of wine into a finely worked goblet.

'We do not,' said Theodosia. 'But I think of you and pray for you every day.' The joy in her face at being reunited with Henry shifted to sadness. 'And Mother.'

'As you know we pray at Godstow, your Grace.' Dymphna's voice softened as she looked from Palmer to Theodosia. 'We pray for you both every day of every year, pray for everyone the King loved. Everyone.'

Her meaning was clear: Theodosia's mother had been laid to rest at Godstow, but a woman whose life Palmer had not been able to protect had too. The old regret at his failure came back, piercing him as if new.

'I offer my eternal thanks that my wife lies in a place of such great holiness, Abbess,' said Henry. 'I miss her sorely.' He sighed. 'It gives me great comfort to think we will be reunited in heaven.' He splashed water over his hands and scrubbed them hard. 'And God in His greatness offers us other comforts in this life. Those who gladden our days.' His shrewd look met Palmer's. 'I assume you have followed my orders and not brought your children?'

'Yes, your Grace,' said Palmer. 'They are safe at our hall, as you instructed.'

'Good.' Henry nodded in satisfaction. 'While I would have dearly loved to have seen them, the risk is too great. They are well, Theodosia?'

'Very.' Her face lit with the glow that always met any word of them.

Despite the many questions he still held, Palmer smiled inside. Their son and daughter were her life. As they were his. He and Theodosia had come so close to losing them forever. He shook off the grip of the past.

'And they have left childhood behind,' continued Theodosia. 'Tom is almost fourteen, Matilde eleven.'

'God's great mercy spared them.' Dymphna gave her a quiet smile.

'Then they are ready to start lives of their own, eh?' said Henry.

'Not yet.' Theodosia's glow snuffed out as she met her father's eye in instant challenge. 'Father.'

Palmer tensed. The idea that the King might have plans for their children had not even crossed his mind. Theodosia would likely take one of the eating knives to Henry if he dared to suggest it.

'Fear not, Theodosia.' Henry picked up his goblet. 'Your children are not the reason I summoned you both here. Not at all.' He took a deep draught. 'Abbess, you have brought what I asked?'

Dymphna nodded. 'I have, your Grace.' Her hands went to her belt pouch, and she drew out a small casket made from what Palmer guessed to be bone, and carved so finely it could be lace. She placed it on the table in front of Henry and blessed herself.

Henry opened it up and removed what it contained. 'Now, this.' He placed it on one open palm. 'This is the reason.'

Chapter Three

Palmer could only stare as Theodosia caught her breath in wonder.

A thick gold ring rested on the King's hand. Palmer couldn't even guess at its value. The metal alone would be worth a fortune. But that would be nothing compared to the jewel set into it: a huge emerald, greener than any grass and catching the light from the windows as if it were lit with flame.

Yet he was at a loss as to what it meant. He'd never seen it before, and Theodosia's questioning glance to him told him she hadn't either.

Henry picked it up with the fingers of his other hand. 'The Pope gave me this ring many years ago, when I first ascended my throne.' He turned it slowly, the gem sending specks of reflected light across his face. 'Not our current Pope' – the dawn of a scowl darkened his features – 'but the great English Pope, Adrian.' He turned the ring again. 'Along with his blessing to take the land of Ireland. My own mother persuaded me not to act on it.' He gave a quiet laugh as he gazed into the jewel's depths. 'Was I ever so young? But of course my reach has now extended there.'

'A reach which has greatly benefited the Church's reforms there, your Grace.' Dymphna gave an approving nod.

Theodosia still looked confused. 'Father, Benedict and I have no links with Ireland.'

'None, your Grace,' said Palmer.

'You do now.' Henry's eyes met his. 'That is why I have summoned you, Palmer. I am sending you there to defend my realm.'

Theodosia drew in a shocked breath.

Palmer put a hand to her shoulder. The King wasn't including her. Palmer didn't care about anything else. He bowed, relief sweeping through him. 'As your Grace orders. I will make prep—'

'No, no.' Henry interrupted. 'You will be travelling there with forces I am assembling. It is a land in sore need of pacification.' He scowled. 'Yet again.'

'Also in our prayers.' Dymphna gave a regretful sigh.

Henry went on. 'As Ireland was the year I first went there.' He pointed a finger at Theodosia. 'The year Tom was born to you and Palmer.'

Theodosia found her voice. 'Father, you have no need of Benedict for such a task. He is needed—'

Now Palmer interrupted her. 'Your Grace, you know the depths of my loyalty. But I need to stress that I'm no longer your best choice to fight for you. I'm past my prime. You need young, strong men. The best of fighters. That's not me.'

Henry snorted. 'I'd wager that you could still hold your own in a brawl, Palmer. I have a very specific task for you: assisting the man who is leading my campaign.' His eyes bored right into Palmer's. 'The Lord of Ireland.'

'The Lord of Ireland?' Palmer's fists clenched, unbidden. 'But that is your son, John, your Grace.'

Theodosia nodded, aghast. 'It is.'

Palmer went on. 'Your Grace, so much of our past, of your past, has been clouded by your sons from your wife, Eleanor. Thomas

Becket's murder.' He fought to keep his tone polite. 'The rebellion which nearly cost you your throne.'

'Which almost cost us our lives also, Father.' Theodosia's mouth set in a firm line that could have been Henry's own. 'Those of our children. How could you send Benedict to help John?'

'I understand your concerns. God knows, I have walked much of that road with you.' Henry shook his head. 'But so much of what was done was done in John's name and not by the boy himself. He was only four when Becket died, not even into two digits when the rebellion took place. Which is why I made sure I took him from my wife's corrupting influence.' His mouth turned down. 'Made sure he was fostered at the most loyal household too. I could not have him polluted like the others. He has not been.' Henry's face relaxed into a fond smile. 'He is now eighteen, a handsome prince, as I once was. It is time for John to prove his worth to the world. He will prove it as Lord of Ireland.'

'Then let him prove it, Father.' Theodosia rapped her knuckles on the table to make her point. '*Him.* He does not need Benedict.'

Henry ignored her protest. 'As I have said, John is young. Or, to be more precise, he's young for his years.' His gaze went to the ring again, and he sighed. 'I fear the boy has been too coddled. Oh, he's sharp enough, but he's not a naturally gifted warrior like his brother Richard. So gifted, Richard needs bringing to heel by me.' He snorted once again.

'So much to attend to, your Grace.' Dymphna refilled his goblet in an attempt to soothe him.

'Indeed.' Henry passed a weary palm over his face. 'I want John to go and take control of Ireland, just as I did. As I had to.' He leaned in close to the table. 'The Ireland I went to had noblemen from this land who thought they could steal it from me. Men who should have been loyal to me. Fighting the native Irish kings, who fought back, as well as waging war with each other. And all sides making and breaking alliances. So I landed there and demanded submission from every single one of them.' His hand closed on the ring in a tight fist. 'And they gave it. The men who had settled there gave me an oath of homage. The native Irish kings gave me an oath of fealty. I brought stability and order. Without resistance. Me.' He jabbed his fist for emphasis.

For a moment, the years fell away, and Palmer saw the force to be reckoned with that Henry had been.

Then the King shrugged. 'Perhaps my army and my siege equipment helped too.' He gave a short laugh. 'Which is why I am giving John the resources he needs to succeed. I have assembled a large fighting force for him, assembled every type of support for his mission. I am sure his show of strength alone will achieve it, as did mine.'

It still didn't make sense to Palmer. 'Your Grace, if that is so, I can't see that I would make any difference to your son's military campaign.'

'I cannot see it either,' came Theodosia's firm confirmation.

'Yours is a different task, Palmer. It concerns my biggest threat in Ireland.' Henry's look darkened in fury. 'Hugh de Lacy, God rot him.'

Palmer shook his head, meeting Theodosia's glance. 'The name means nothing to me, your Grace.'

'Nor do I know of him,' she said.

'Hugh de Lacy is my own Lord of Meath,' said Henry. 'I have given him much land and power in Ireland since he accompanied me there. He has taken oaths of homage to me. The trouble is, he is too talented. Not only can he win the bloodiest of battles with a skilled sword, he has the wit to know when the time is right for diplomacy. For compromise. But, by the blood of the Virgin, he is ambitious.' Henry shook his head. 'Relentless. He's like a hound constantly straining at the leash, ready to break free when his moment comes and devour all before him.'

'It is believed that such a moment may already have come,' said Dymphna.

Despite his deep misgivings at Henry's proposal, the King's words intrigued Palmer . 'How so?'

'De Lacy has married Eimear O'Connor, the daughter of an Irish king.' Henry's hands shook in barely contained rage. 'The Irish High King at that, Rory O'Connor. O'Connor, who rules much of the west in Connacht. De Lacy has huge tracts of the east. With his second bride, de Lacy has his sights set on stealing the whole island from me. I feel it in my very bones!' He pulled in a breath to calm himself. 'But I have no proof. Which is where you come in, Palmer.'

'Father, you are already sending my half-brother to Ireland with military might.' Theodosia's voice tightened. 'Let John find the proof you need.' She looked at Benedict. 'And we can go home to our children.'

'No, my dear.' Henry shook his head hard. 'I have shared my concerns about de Lacy with John. But' – he held up a finger – 'and this is for your ears only: John is not yet a match for him. My son needs to concentrate all of his energies into taking hold of the place again. I need someone who can get to the bottom of what de Lacy is up to. Someone in whom I have absolute trust. Most important of all, someone who is de Lacy's equal. And that's you, Palmer.'

Pride rose in Palmer's chest even as he saw the anger flare in Theodosia's eyes. 'Father, the last time Benedict and I were parted, we almost lost our lives.'

'I know, my child,' said Henry. 'Which is why I could not summon him on this occasion by messenger. I wanted you to hear the truth of what I am asking of him from my own lips.'

'I will of course serve your Grace, as was my vow to you.' Palmer bowed.

Theodosia clutched the table. 'What about your vows to me, Benedict? What about our family?'

'There is no danger to you this time, Theodosia,' said Palmer.

'But there is to you! We promised each other that we would not be parted again. At least let me go with you.' She turned to Henry. 'There will be a place for me with John's court in Ireland. I am sure of it.'

'No, Theodosia.' Palmer shook his head as Henry held up a hand in refusal.

'A dangerously disordered Ireland is no place for you, my dear,' said Henry.

'Then it should be no place for Benedict either.'

'Theodosia, I will allow your disrespect to me because I realize this has come as a shock,' said Henry. 'Unlike my last summons, you have some time before you part. You have the bishop's palace at your disposal until I dub John Lord of Ireland at Windsor in three days' time.'

Theodosia stared at him, her eyes hard as stone. 'Three days?'

'A privilege for us all to witness it, my lady.' Dymphna tried to distract her.

'I am to lose my husband in three days?'

'Thank you, your Grace.' Palmer stretched a hand out to halt Theodosia. 'I'm going to watch over someone who's your blood.'

'And are clearly happy to shed your own as you do so.' She shook off his touch and stood up from the table. 'I am going to pray in the chapel. For our family. Our real blood.'

'Theodosia—'

'Do not even try to keep me from it.' She strode to the door.

Dymphna rose too. 'I shall go with her, your Grace. It may help her to let some of this out with me.'

Henry nodded his approval, and the Abbess hurried out.

'I should probably go to her too,' said Palmer.

'Let her be for now. She'll come round.' Henry held the ring up to the light once more. 'I know she worries about you, Palmer.' Then he placed it back in the protection of its little carved box, closing the lid. 'As I do about my son.' He gave the box a thoughtful pat. 'You know, I received a request to give John the crown of the Holy Land.' He returned his gaze to Palmer's. 'God's eyes. The Saracens would have strewn his bones across the desert by Christmas.' Henry blessed himself swiftly. 'Yet Ireland is also an endeavour of great risk. I only hope I have made the right choice.'

'I'm sure you have, your Grace.'

Henry drew in a long breath, and every year of his age showed in his face once more. 'I thank you, Palmer, for coming to my aid. I am in your debt. Once again.'

'As I'm forever and deeper in yours, your Grace,' Palmer said, mortified at the King's humility.

The thought of being parted from Theodosia and his family again hurt like a blade in his chest. But he had her and his beloved children only because of Henry's generosity. Palmer was the one in debt and always would be. Refusal had never crossed his mind.

Chapter Four

Windsor Castle
31 March 1185

It is a sin to hold hate in your soul for anyone.

Theodosia berated herself with every beat of her anxious heart. She stood in the splendour of Henry's chapel at Windsor with Benedict, in a packed assembly of the noble and the holy. With the bishop now reciting the final prayers of the lengthy, solemn Mass, the time for John's knighting ceremony drew near.

Even graver to hate your own brother.

No, she reminded herself yet again, pulling in a deep breath of the incense-scented air. She did not hate John. She did not. But she hated what he stood for: the reason Benedict was being taken from her.

Unnoticed by her husband, her gaze moved over his face, his dark eyes, still so utterly beloved to her. She cared not for the finely woven black cloak he wore, edged with exquisite bright yellow embroidery. Nor for her own wide-sleeved silk gown, pale as a meadow flower, with its lining deep as a rose.

She had loved him just as much when they had shared a poor cottage in the early years of their marriage. When they had been blessed with Tom and Matilde, and all of them dressed in patched linen and the roughest of coarse wool. The lives as nobles they had later been granted by the King could have brought them great ease. Yet Benedict strove as hard as he ever had, bringing prosperity and justice to those who worked his lands.

A great 'Amen' rose up at the bishop's concluding prayer.

It was time.

'My good people!' Henry's voice, ringing with expectation.

Though right at the other end, she could clearly make him out, as he sat high on the altar and a pillar gave a convenient break in the crowd. A heavy-set abbot moved to one side. Then she could see John too, kneeling in humility with his head bowed, his curling red hair a stark contrast to his white silk clothing and ermine robe in the glow of the hundreds of candles.

Henry went on. 'Today, my heart is filled with joy. I knight my beloved son John Lord of Ireland. He has taken this responsibility as part of his humble service to me. I have been to that isle, and I know that there are great challenges to be faced. Yet my son has agreed to face them and to bring glory to my name.'

A rumble of approval met Henry's words.

'Before I bestow this honour upon him, I want to remind him – to remind us all – of the magnitude of what he is undertaking. My royal clerk, Gerald of Wales, learned in the ways of the Irish and of the land itself, will impart that knowledge to us all.'

An angular monk stepped up to the altar, his sparse lips compressed in readiness below a hooked nose. He bowed to Henry, then to John.

'Gerald, let us hear of what awaits my son.'

And my husband.

'Your Grace, my Lord John.' Gerald's voice sounded as clear as if he stood next to her and Benedict, ringing with authority. 'The great Saint Columbanus, his wisdom echoing down the centuries to us, wrote of the Irish that they are the dwellers at the edge of the earth. Such a true description must have been guided by God. They cling to that rock, for beyond it there is no habitation of man or beast.

One looks from the western horizon there, knowing that there is nothing beyond. Nothing except the flowing ocean in boundless space.' He let the word resound to the lofty height of the arched roof far above before continuing. 'At such extremes, nature provides wonders, and there are some on that island. But' – his tone hardened – 'nature also indulges herself in freaks there: distant and secret abominations that make my soul quail.'

A rustle of whispered concern passed through those present.

Theodosia's mouth dried. Henry had not mentioned any of this. She shot Benedict a look, but his fixed gaze remained on Gerald.

'Such abominations will have to be met with valour by the King's son, of which I have no doubt.' Gerald sighed and shook his head. 'But there is a far greater threat: that of its native people.'

A greater threat. Theodosia's heart tripped faster in anxiety.

'A people who are wild.' Gerald's thin lips turned down. 'Inhospitable. They live on beasts only, for they live like beasts.' He clenched his fist and beat time with the steady flow of his own words. 'Filthy. Wallowing in vice. Adulterous.'

Shocked gasps began to break out.

Gerald's voice rose over them. 'Incestuous. Carnal with beasts.' His eyes scanned the assembly as he let his scandalous words sink in.

Theodosia put a hand to her mouth. What was Benedict going to?

Gerald held a hand up and received instant silence. 'But for all of their enormous vices, the Irish possess one that dwarfs all the others.' His eyes narrowed. 'Treachery. Above all the peoples of the earth, they prefer wile to war. They always carry an axe in their hand, like a shepherd might carry his crook, ready for when the right occasion presents itself. And when it does . . .' His voice dropped.

Those present craned to hear him, necks bent like a field of wheat in the wind. Theodosia too. She could not help herself.

'They raise that axe to afflict a mortal blow!' His words thundered forth to calls for God's help for John.

Henry's shout silenced them in a heartbeat. 'It is time!' John lifted his arms and looked up at his father.

The bishop stepped forward, holding a gleaming sword and a belt of finest ox-blood leather.

Henry took them from him and bent to fasten the weapon around his son's waist. With a tender kiss to John's cheek, he straightened up, taking his own sword from the bishop.

As Henry raised it, Theodosia crossed herself, as did every other right hand of those around her and throughout the crowd, their number making a rustle that could have been the stirring of leaves.

The blade met John's shoulder to a murmured prayer from Henry.

And it was done.

Take your acclaim, my son.' The King's voice shook with his emotion. 'My most holy and noble servants, I present to you John, *Dominus Hiberniae*, Lord of Ireland!'

Cheers met his words as John stood up to turn and face the assembly, his stature surprising Theodosia. He was only a few inches taller than her; Benedict would stand head and shoulders above him.

Henry beamed in adoration at his son. It was clear he saw himself in John. His young self: powerful, able to subdue a country with his very arrival.

Disquiet knocked at Theodosia. John was Henry's son, no doubt. But though his face matched Henry's own, with his heavy brows and small mouth, his expression did not. His visage held no compassion, and his lips pursed in a superior arrogance.

Yet the King's indulgent smile remained as he gestured to his court to strengthen their support, and the ovation swelled. Finally, he signalled for silence. 'Speak. Your first words as Lord.'

'Your Grace. Father.' John bowed briefly to Henry before he faced the court again. 'Good people.' A brief cheer met his greeting and the tight smile that left his eyes cold. 'I have been chosen for this endeavour, and I approach it with solemnity and singularity of purpose.' His confident gaze swept the room. 'It is clear from Gerald's account that there is much to be done.' He lifted his chin. 'So much. It is God's work, which I welcome. It is clear to me that Ireland has a black heart of sin. Of adultery.' His eyes narrowed. 'Of debauchery. Which must be duly punished, and—'

A lone female voice rose in wordless cries.

John frowned as he sought the source of the interruption.

A clamour of conjecture broke out as the woman's cries increased, loudened.

His clamped lips showed that John had located her. 'Take that woman out!' His cry came shrill, insistent. 'Now!'

Theodosia grabbed for Benedict's arm. 'What's happening?'

Benedict strained to his full height. 'It's the wife of one of the barons,' he said in surprise. 'Her husband is trying to control her.'

'Has she lost her reason, God help her?' said Theodosia.

Benedict shrugged. 'No idea.'

Henry's face remained impassive as John's voice echoed out again. 'I have faced adversity in my life too. But I have prevailed!' He nodded vigorously. 'As I *will* prevail! My lordship will be an example to the world. The world!'

He raised both arms, and cheers and claps broke out, Henry applauding with greater energy than anyone.

Conscious that Benedict clapped too, Theodosia joined in as a great chant rose up: '*Dominus Hiberniae! Dominus Hiberniae!*'

But the cheers did nothing to lessen her apprehension.

Theodosia looked to Benedict. 'You heard the clerk's words?' she whispered. 'How dangerous this is?'

'Men of the Church scare easily.' Benedict gave the suspicion of a smile. 'I don't.'

'Neither do I. But you would be foolish not to heed the clerk's warnings.'

He caught the edge in her voice. 'I'm sure the man exaggerates.' He took a quick glance around to make sure no one had observed their exchange. 'Theodosia, Abbess Dymphna told us she's travelling with John's court to Ireland. The King would never allow it if he thought she wouldn't be safe.'

'Perhaps you are right.' The Abbess had indeed spoken of the pilgrimage she was making: to the abbey of her own brother, an abbot of great reputation.

Yet Benedict's reminder brought scant comfort to Theodosia.

For in Ireland, a land fraught with sin, with danger, Dymphna would be secure in the arms of the Church.

There would be no such protection for Benedict.

Theodosia knelt in the deserted church at Sonning, finishing her pleas in prayer once more for Benedict's safety.

He was gone. Benedict was gone. And she could not follow him.

The shafts of sunlight from the narrow windows had moved across the floor, marking yet another day's passing as reliably as the monastery bells.

'Keep my husband from bodily harm, I beseech you, O Lord. Let him have the strength to protect his soul from peril on this journey he makes. Amen.'

She should be journeying also. Sonning should have been but one stop on her long road back home, protected by some of the bishop's armed men.

Home, to the security and comfort of their manor at Cloughbrook, where her children awaited.

Tom, not as tall as Benedict, but with a fierce strength and a restlessness of spirit to match Henry's own. Matilde, unfazed by her brother's noise and muscle and completely devoted to him, her young mind already sharp as a blade and always seeking to know more.

They were not merely at home, they *were* Theodosia's home, as they were Benedict's. She should be making her way to them, like any mother would.

But she could not take the next steps that would put her farther and farther from Benedict.

So she had pleaded an illness to the riders who accompanied her, suggesting it a delicate matter, which had ensured that no further query came. She had remained here for twelve days.

Her disobedient act would anger Benedict as well as her father. She cared not. Neither of them was here or knew what she had done.

Her legs cramped from kneeling for so many hours, and she shifted to ease them.

Twelve days. She'd witnessed the passage of John's court from the roadside, hidden amongst the crowds that cheered as it went by. Three hundred knights, according to rumour. So many. An impossibility to pick out Benedict. Yet she'd seen him, though he'd not seen her. One glimpse, through the clouds of dust kicked up by the huge procession on the dry road, swirling around him as he sat astride a fine horse, talking to an unknown knight who rode alongside him.

Benedict!

He'd not heard her call, though she'd hurt her lungs with the effort she made to be heard above the cacophony of cartwheels, horses, hooves, shouts.

Then the crowd shifted, and he had disappeared from her sight in the throng.

Gone. And that might be the last sight she ever had of him, turned away from her, not knowing she was there. Gone to Ireland, the land of which Henry's clerk, Gerald, had given such a terrifying account. A destination to be deeply feared. No wonder that poor baron's wife had become so distressed: Theodosia could have cried out too.

She stood up to ease her legs further and paced the floor, arms folded tight across her chest.

Try as she might, she could not banish the images Gerald had planted in her head. Ireland was a land of sin, of violence, of betrayal. A land where Henry feared treachery from one of his own greatest lords, de Lacy of Meath. A land at the very edge of God's earth, the last solid ground before the eternal ocean. Where Benedict might fall, an axe buried in his head or a sword in his chest, never to return to her, to lie next to her in life, then together for eternity.

Theodosia joined her hands and faced the gleam of the gold cross on the altar once more. 'Devoutly with trust I pray to Thee, implore Thee for Your protection.'

Into the silence came a deep roar, like the advance of a huge wind. But the sun on the floor still shone bright.

The roar echoed and rumbled into a boom of loudest thunder.

The ground beneath her feet lost its substance in a heartbeat. She grasped uselessly at the air in abrupt dizziness, falling to the ground.

Every bell, near, far, rang out in a clamour of jagged jangles as mortar pinged down on her from the ceiling.

The whole world shook, creaked, rattled in terrifying sound as the contents clattered and smashed from the altar.

She tried to get to her knees, but the flagstones beneath her were soft as a swamp.

The bells pealed louder in a chorus that could not be being rung by human hand. Judgement must be upon the world. God was returning.

Theodosia gabbled a paternoster in terror, then half another.

A stone crashed from the roof, then a second.

She ducked her head beneath her arms with a shriek. *Tom. Matilde. Benedict. Let us meet in Paradise.*

Then the world stilled. The bells slowed, their last peals giving way to shouts, calls, screams from outside. Fine dust filled the air, dimming the sunlight from the windows.

Coughing, Theodosia sat up, every inch of her body trembling. The chapel looked as if it had been sacked by marauders.

'All to the gatehouse! Quickly!' A monk's command echoing from the cloisters. 'The earth may move again!'

Theodosia got to her feet, the stone flags beneath her shoes solid and cold as if nothing had happened.

But something had. No apocalypse, but a sign from God to her, shaking the earth beneath her to remind her that Benedict had gone to its perilous edge. She could not remain here.

She knew what she had to do.

Chapter Five

The Port of Waterford, Ireland
25 April 1185

'A good crossing and still half the daylight left. God smiles on us, eh?'

Palmer nodded in agreement with the young, heavy-set man next to him on the deck of the docking ship. 'Still prefer dry land every time.' He gave different, silent thanks to the Almighty. Seasickness had been his curse for many years. Though he no longer suffered as badly, he still couldn't wait for the moment that his boots met a surface that stayed in one place.

He'd heard on the voyage how much Henry favoured this sheltered port, with the King placing it under his rule during his first visit, in the year Tom had come into the world. It was still far finer than Palmer had expected, especially after witnessing the ravings of the royal clerk, Gerald. A rounded stone tower sat high above the well-built city walls, with many wooden quays reaching far out into the quiet water and lining the muddy lip of land outside the defences. Despite its good size, the number of vessels that had transported John and his men filled every landing space, while many other ships waited, all needing to dock and unload.

The low, grey cloud brought a damp coolness to the day as seagulls clamoured for the waste being thrown into the water. With whistles and shouts, the men on the quays threw ropes to the sailors, bringing ship after ship to rest. The arrival of so many in the name of the Lord John couldn't fail to send a message to Ireland, just as Henry had planned.

Four men approached Palmer's vessel, carrying the long, heavy, dirty wooden gangplank, and it finally thudded into place.

Palmer walked off with the others, his bundle of possessions heavy on one shoulder. Beneath his boots, wicker panels had been laid over the ground to provide dry passage. Even so, the wet oozed through from the clay underneath.

The man he'd docked with nudged him and pointed to a small group along the quayside. 'Looks like they're buying ale from that barrel.'

'You were right about God smiling on us.' Palmer made his way there with the man, taking with thanks the cup from the woman selling it. The wooden cup of ale went down sweet and cold, and he paid for another.

A small, dirty boy ran past, hitting the barrel with a stick as he ducked through legs.

The ale seller saw him off with a swipe and a stream of interesting threats.

Palmer grinned. 'We might have to step in if she catches the lad.'

'True,' the man replied. 'She sounds like my wife.' He took a drink with a long, satisfied sigh. 'You married?'

Palmer shook his head. 'Only have myself to worry about.' The beer soured in his mouth with the ready lie. But he needed to stick to it. Theodosia was safe. No matter that he wished with every inch of his being that he could get straight back onto a boat to sail for home.

'Well, I'm going to find a whore,' said the man. 'It's been weeks since I've cooled my loins. You joining me?'

'Happy with my beer, my friend.'

'Suit yourself.' With a wave, the man was off.

A group of monks hustled along the quay from the direction of the town gate, making for one of the ships that had pulled up. Of course. They had come to greet Abbess Dymphna as she led her group of nuns off onto one of the best landings. Greetings floated on the still air as bundles and baskets were stacked off to one side, ready to be brought with her to the abbey that was her place of pilgrimage.

One of the nuns went to the pile and bent to untie a string that held two bags together, her pale hands working steadily in her determination to unknot the thing. For a moment, the nun could have been his Theodosia, as he'd first encountered her all those years ago, robed in the dress of the Church. His Theodosia, who'd claimed his heart and who still stirred desire in him with a look, a touch. He smiled to himself, even as tears stung his eyes. He took a huge gulp of beer to banish them. Any more feebleness and he'd stick his face in the seaweed-filled harbour instead.

Dymphna walked over to speak to the nun, who turned to answer.

Half the beer shot down Palmer's nose. *Forcurse it to hell.* The woman didn't only look like Theodosia: she *was* Theodosia.

Palmer thrust the cup back at the beer seller and marched over to his wife and Dymphna, careless of whom he pushed aside.

'Can I help you with anything, sisters?' His question came through clenched teeth.

Dymphna wouldn't meet his eye. 'I don't think so, sir.'

'No, thank, you, sir knight.' Framed by her dark veil, Theodosia's pale face flushed at his discovery of her even as joy lit her grey eyes. 'We have all the assistance we need.'

'Sisters.' Palmer kept his tone low, polite, desires waging war within him. All he wanted was to pull her into his arms, crush her to him. Let loose a string of oaths at her foolhardiness. 'If you don't tell me what's going on, I'll put you over my shoulder and row you back to Milford Haven myself. And you will be with her, Abbess. King's pilgrimage or not.'

'You do not have to threaten me like a barbarian, Benedict.' Theodosia's voice came steady with defiance. 'Or the Abbess. It is perfectly simple. I am not going to be left behind this time while you run into peril on behalf of the King, leaving me frantic with worry and not knowing if you are alive or dead, day in, day out.'

'What of our children?' A low blow, and he knew it.

She levelled her chin. 'They are out of harm's way and are surrounded by the most loyal protectors. And Tom knows how to wield a sword.'

'Then your plan is to – *what*?' he hissed. 'To ride out for the Lord John, a holy sister on horseback, with a blade at the ready?'

'Oh, *Jesu Christus*!'

The scream cut through every noise on the dockside, interrupting Theodosia's response.

'Who in God's name is that?' said Dymphna.

Palmer looked too.

A familiar robed figure writhed at the foot of the nearby gangplank, yelling out a stream of pleas to God for help.

Theodosia grimaced. 'It is the King's clerk, Gerald.'

Gerald yelled louder. 'My arm! Oh, Blessed Virgin and the choir of saints! My arm!'

One of the dockers bent to help him, but Gerald shoved the man away with his good hand. 'Stay away. It was your plank that turned under my feet and sent me tumbling. Away, I tell you, away! You'll not get the chance to harm me more.' He shrieked again.

'You there!' He stretched a hand out to a group of open-mouthed knights who had stepped off another ship. 'Protect me, bring me to the safety of Regnall's Tower. Quickly.'

The knights complied, accepting an offer of an old sail from the docker. Manoeuvring a still shrieking Gerald onto it, they bore him away and headed off for the town gate.

Dymphna crossed herself. 'The poor man. We shared his ship, and it could so easily have been one of us who fell and hurt ourselves.'

'See?' said Palmer to Theodosia. 'What if it had been you?' His heart quailed even at the thought of her injured, but he'd not show her. 'This is no place for you.'

'As I feel about you being here,' said Theodosia, her response firm.

'Theodosia will travel with me to my brother's abbey at Jerpoint,' said Dymphna. 'She will be perfectly safe there.'

'More importantly,' said Theodosia, 'I can get news of you, Benedict, and can be with you in a short time if I have to be.'

Dymphna nodded. 'She can travel from monastery to monastery, if necessary, to follow your progress with a prayerful one of her own.'

He would love for it to be so, but he couldn't allow it. 'This is some of the greatest bilge I've ever heard,' said Palmer. 'You'll stay at the abbey only until I can arrange to get you home. And that's my final word.'

Theodosia's cheeks flushed again, and he braced for her attempt at refusal. Then all colour left her face, as he knew it did from his own, at a male voice raised in query.

'Which of you is Sister Theodosia?'

For a wild second, Palmer thought he could spirit her away through the crowd, but a monk walked up to them.

'I am she,' Theodosia replied with a panicked glance to Palmer.

'Who makes such bold enquiries of this holy sister?' He took a step in front of her.

With a wary eye on Palmer, the monk bowed to her. 'Not merely enquiries, sister. The royal clerk, Gerald, demands your presence. Immediately.'

Palmer grabbed Theodosia's bundle of belongings to add to his own. 'Then let me carry these, so she can hurry.' It was the first thing he could think of. An argument in this large crowd would only turn curious faces towards them.

'You will wait for me, Mother?' Theodosia asked Dymphna.

'Indeed I shall.' The Abbess turned to address the monk. 'I am her superior, and I want to know what reason Gerald might have to seek her out. My permission for any requests he might make is not to be taken for granted.'

'Of course, Abbess,' said the monk. 'Please, sister, make haste and come with me: the King's clerk is in no fit state to be kept waiting.'

Palmer didn't care what state Gerald was in. All he cared about was getting Theodosia away from here to the security of the abbey and then home. They'd humour the clerk and then Palmer would make sure Theodosia left with Dymphna. At once.

Ushered in by the monk, Palmer followed Theodosia into Regnall's Tower. It should have been quieter in there, but Gerald's screams filled the large, circular stone room.

'God release me from my agony!' Henry's clerk still lay on the sail in which he'd been carried, placed on a large chest as a makeshift bed. 'My torment!'

'May God grant you courage.' Theodosia moved to his side with a hasty sign of the cross.

The monk who'd summoned them wrung his hands. 'Others are out trying to find a barber-surgeon as we speak. But it's so crowded. It could take much time.'

'Make sure they do not bring me one who is from these shores. They will not be skilled unless it be in the dark arts.' Gerald twitched, then howled again. 'Mother of God, even to breathe is pain!'

'That arm needs to be set as soon as possible.' Palmer put down the two bundles he carried. 'Theo— Sister, do you have some linen in your belongings that I can use?'

'Yes, let me get some.' She bent to her task as Palmer grabbed one of the stools set before the large lit fireplace. He bashed the stool against the stone hearth and freed two of the legs, stepping back quickly to Gerald's side with the pieces of wood in one hand.

'Make a move and I'll have your head.'

The hard-voiced threat came from behind him.

Theodosia took a step to Palmer as the clerk shrieked still louder. Palmer turned to see a shorter, muscular, dark-haired knight advancing on him, sword ready in one powerful hand, face drawn in a scowl. Or rather half his face. The right side was tight and red and shiny from a large, hideous scar.

The monk dropped to his knees in terror as Palmer's free hand went for his own blade. 'I mean the clerk no harm.'

The knight halted, appraising Palmer with his one good, dark, deep-set eye. His other eye would be no use, blank as a fish's, with the red and watery lower lid pulled down by his scarred flesh. 'Word reached me of an attack on Gerald.'

'Let the man be, de Lacy,' came Gerald's sharp, breathless reply. 'He is trying to fix me.'

De Lacy. Hugh de Lacy, Lord of Meath. Henry's man in Ireland. The one Henry suspected of treachery. The very reason Palmer was here. He released his grip on his sword.

'Fix you? Why?' De Lacy strode to Gerald's side, sword lowered but still in a ready grip.

Theodosia helped the monk back to his feet, linen clutched in one of her hands. Her look to Palmer as she passed it to him showed that she recognised the name too.

'My arm,' moaned Gerald. 'Broken by an ambush.'

'Such a fall from the gangplank.' Theodosia's quick tact made Palmer proud.

'We need to stop the bone from moving as soon as we can.' Palmer bent to Gerald, aware of de Lacy's stare on him.

'You don't look like a barber-surgeon to me, sir knight.'

'Sir Benedict Palmer, my lord. And no, I'm not. But I've fixed enough bones on the battlefield in my time. Including my own wrist once. The more bones move, the more chance of inflamed flesh. We need to act quickly.' Palmer held up the stool legs. 'These will do for now.'

'In the name of God's love, stop delaying him, de Lacy,' said the clerk.

'Then do your work, Palmer,' said de Lacy with a jerk of his head.

'The more help, the better, my lord.'

De Lacy sheathed his sword as Palmer laid the wooden pieces next to Gerald.

Theodosia went to stand by Gerald's head, trying to soothe him, with de Lacy clicking his fingers to the monk as he joined Palmer. 'Go and fetch wine for the royal clerk from those upstairs. Tell them the Lord of Meath orders it.'

'Yes, my lord.' The monk scuttled over to the spiral stone staircase and clattered up it.

Palmer bent to Gerald's injured arm. 'First, I need to cut off your sleeve.' He went to pull his knife from his belt.

'Use mine.' De Lacy already had his own blade in his hand. 'It's a sharp one.'

Palmer took it from him with a nod of thanks. His flesh prickled. The man had been standing right next to him, and he hadn't noted his movements.

He quickly completed his careful cutting as Gerald called for the saints' aid.

'It will be over soon, brother,' came Theodosia's soft words. 'Soon.'

'Seems as though you were unlucky in how you fell,' said de Lacy. 'Rather than an attack, as I'd heard.'

'Unlucky?' Gerald ground out a low groan. 'If it wasn't an attack, then it was a sinister portent for the Lord John's progress. We did not stop to do penance at the venerable Church of Saint David's as we travelled through Wales.' He groaned again. 'That was one ill omen. And now this.' He launched into another loud lament about his pain.

'I would say you had some luck, brother,' said Palmer as Gerald's pale spindle of an arm lay exposed. 'Your flesh is sound and there's no redness. I'll bind it now.' He drew breath to ask de Lacy to support the limb, but the lord already had his large hands on it.

'I've joined the ends.' De Lacy had to raise his voice above Gerald's howls.

Palmer strapped the clerk's arm with swift movements, then splinted it with another layer of linen. 'We're done.' He straightened up as de Lacy did too.

'You could have had much worse,' said the lord.

'Praise God.' Gerald's face matched the white sail beneath him, but the relief in his voice told of his lessened pain.

'I will pray for your recovery, brother,' said Theodosia, 'as I will ask all the monks at Jerpoint to do.' Her words were meant to smooth an exit; Palmer could tell.

He picked up her bundle, but Gerald grabbed her arm with his good hand.

'Stop,' said the clerk. 'I summoned you here for a reason. I saw you writing something on the ship.'

De Lacy's ruined, questioning gaze went to Theodosia.

Palmer's grip slid round the handle of his knife, readying for action. He could overpower the slight, injured Gerald with a modicum of his strength, but de Lacy would be a tough foe.

'Indeed I was writing, brother,' Theodosia responded quickly. 'As well as joining the Abbess on her pilgrimage, I will be having schooling from the monks in producing sacred texts. That is all.'

'Then you can wield a quill. Good.' Gerald winced as he sat up. 'My broken arm is the one I use to record.' He pointed at her with his uninjured hand. 'Sister Theodosia: you will scribe on my behalf until I have healed.'

Palmer's shoulders stiffened in disbelief.

'The wine, my lord.' The monk hustled from the staircase, jug and goblet in hand.

De Lacy took it from him, briefly distracted in pouring the drink for a pleading Gerald.

Palmer met Theodosia's shocked glance and drew breath to argue, but Theodosia gave a swift answer.

'I am deeply honoured, brother,' she said, 'but I believe I should follow God's path to Jerpoint.'

Palmer stepped forward. 'I'm sure there must be others that could carry out this task for you, brother.'

'You think there are many who can carry out a task appointed by the King?' Gerald lowered his goblet to glare at Palmer. 'Report on the progress and the actions of his son? You think it will be easy? That you could perform it?'

'I wish I could, brother,' said Palmer, shame hot within him, 'but I'm no scribe.'

'No.' De Lacy's full attention was on him again, curse it.

'I can see you are not employed for your intellect.' Gerald shook his head. 'And I need someone who acts as the quill in my hand. Not someone with . . . ideas of their own.' Gerald drained his drink and shoved the goblet at Theodosia to dispose of. 'The sister will perfectly suffice.' He shifted to prepare to stand. 'Now, give me your arm, woman.'

With a swift glance to Palmer, Theodosia moved to Gerald's side.

'I must make haste,' said Gerald. 'The Lord John is about to disembark and lay his first mark on this land of misfortune. I must be present to witness it.'

'As must we all,' said de Lacy.

Palmer hesitated. There must be something – anything – he could do.

Theodosia spoke to him as if he were a stranger. 'Thank you for carrying my possessions, sir knight. You can leave them here.'

She met his eye with the word *leave*.

Palmer lowered Theodosia's bundle to the floor, refusing to break her gaze.

Gerald didn't appear to notice, complaining as he took a few steps.

But de Lacy looked askance at Palmer's reluctance to go. 'Thank you for your actions.'

Palmer could argue no longer: de Lacy already eyed him in mistrust. 'It was nothing, my lord. I'm glad I could be of service.' He picked up his own pack and walked out without a further look at Theodosia, his chest about to split in his anger.

Through the crowds, he caught sight of an agitated Dymphna who must have followed to find out what was happening. He signalled to her to retrace their path back to the quay. As they fell into step, a line of guards blocked their path, preventing them from leaving.

'All assemble outside the cathedral. The Lord John is arriving!'

'And guess who has to be with him?' Palmer fixed Dymphna with a glare as he explained Theodosia's fate.

'Keep your temper, Sir Benedict,' murmured Dymphna. 'You'll not help her by losing it now.'

'This is your doing. Yours.'

'I accept that, and my heart grieves at what has come to pass,' said Dymphna. 'But Theodosia followed us – said she had had a sign from God that she should. She told me that if I refused to give her a habit, then she would steal one.' She sighed in frustration. 'She was so determined, I knew she spoke the truth. I thought that if I agreed to her actions, then I could keep her safe.'

'Safe.' Palmer moved towards the high tower of the cathedral. If he said more than one word now, he'd say a hundred.

His mission was to watch de Lacy and find any proof of the lord's treachery for Henry. But now Palmer had a far more urgent and important task: to protect Theodosia and keep her from harm. Theodosia, who would now be alongside the Lord John as he tried to pacify a warring nation. A wave of dread broke through Palmer. If anything were to happen to her, it would be the end of his life.

Chapter Six

Assembling before a cathedral had to be a sign. It might be the sole, small comfort that Theodosia could draw: she had to find one from somewhere. Her plan had been to travel anonymously, to wait for Benedict in the quiet of an abbey. Now, here she stood at the clerk Gerald's side, high on the steps with the nobles of Waterford, men and women loyal to her father and settled here for many years. That should have been a reassurance too. But Hugh de Lacy stood with them, Henry's disfigured Lord of Meath, the man who could be plotting in his mind right at this moment to overthrow Henry. How could she be at ease with such a man near her?

A stir came from the cathedral doors.

Theodosia looked to see what it could be, all other eyes turning too.

A young woman, barely into her second decade, stepped out, flanked by attendants. Her cloak and dress were of a style unfamiliar to Theodosia. A white silk tunic came to a scandalously short length: the pale skin of her ankles showed between it and her finely tooled leather shoes. Thinly plaited fringes of purple edged her opulent blue and crimson cloak, and a huge, oval, carved gold pin secured it at her breast. More gold adorned every single one of her fingers and even her thumbs. A carved golden circlet held her white veil in place. For all this, her face was the most arresting sight of all: her eyes, the colour of a deep mountain lake, contrasted with pale, unlined skin and gave her a rare and unusual beauty.

De Lacy left his place to walk up to her. 'Eimear.' He gave her a stiff bow.

'Husband.' Her expression remained unchanged. 'I have been at prayer.'

Even deeper unease bloomed within Theodosia. Eimear O'Connor, whom Henry suspected of being married to de Lacy for political gain. Their greetings were not of a nobleman to his cherished wife, but rather of one ruler to another.

De Lacy drew Eimear over to his place among the dignitaries as Theodosia looked away. She could not afford to be obvious in her appraisal of them. Her position was perilous enough.

People filled the wide area between cathedral and the tower where Benedict had treated Gerald's injury. She bowed her head, hoping she appeared modest. She wore this habit as a lie, and now she had to add and add to that untruth to keep from discovery.

'You should not tremble, sister.' Gerald's gaze raked the crowd.

'Oh, I am not afraid—'

He cut her off with a sharp tsk. 'I only mean that you have to keep a steady hand at all times.' He brought his hand to his sweated temple. 'My mind is sharp. Sharp. It remembers all things. Yet with my broken arm, my pain, I may not remember every detail, especially at a time as momentous as this, with so many present. When I need a reminder, you will note it for me. A quill that shakes will mean an unclear account. Are you listening?'

'Yes, brother.'

A cry came from beyond. 'All hail John, the Lord of Ireland!'

A chorus of welcome erupted at the words.

Gerald sighed in satisfaction. 'Praise God for the loyalty that exists in this royal city. Henry chose it well on all counts.'

Then John walked into view, flanked by guards, resplendent in his white ermine robe, with the richest of deep red silks beneath. A group of his men filed in behind, noble knights in gleaming mail and surcoats.

As the King's son greeted the lines of cheering people with a raised hand, Gerald's expression shifted to a frown. 'He should be coming in with the most high-ranking nobles of his court. The Irish are coming to declare fealty to him. Why does he bring his young friends?'

'I am afraid I do not know, brother.'

'I don't expect you to know anything,' said Gerald. 'Neither should you. Move to one side. You have no right to share this great event. You are my scribing hand only, remember?'

Theodosia bowed and moved as ordered. If only Gerald knew what right she did have to stand beside John. She swallowed hard. If John knew. If de Lacy knew.

She joined her hands in respect as her half-brother stepped towards her, with huzzah after huzzah still echoing out. A broad smile spread across his face at the crowds that had assembled for him.

Finally he reached the steps of the cathedral and mounted them slowly.

Theodosia took a step back against the wall of the cathedral as if the grey stone were her living protector. She need not have feared. John's glance passed over her, the better to face out into the crowd.

His guards took up their places in two lines, near to him, but not hiding him from anyone's view.

John's friends climbed the steps too, young men all, not many years older than Tom, to join the mature nobles already gathered.

She could tell by the rigid expressions of the latter that John had snubbed them in not allowing for the correct order. Their disapproval was palpable, except for de Lacy. His ravaged face merely showed interest.

The senior members of the court whom Henry had so carefully assembled for John finally filed in. The guards of the port moved them all back, so a wide space opened out in the big clearing between cathedral and tower. One look at their stony expressions told of their displeasure at being so poorly treated.

John gestured for silence, and the cheers lessened, then died away. 'My good people. I stand before God's house to give thanks for our safe arrival.'

Another loud chorus of rejoicing.

Theodosia offered up a brief prayer of her own for her delivery from his presence.

Then loud blasts of horns and the thud of drums filled the air.

John's face sharpened into annoyance, and Gerald moved to his side. 'Smile again, my lord – smile. The Irish come to give you their oath of fealty.' He matched his own words with a show of long teeth. 'Precisely as they did for your father.'

The King's son produced a beatific beam of his own.

Three figures walked in through the gate, and Theodosia's spirit quailed. Gerald's terrifying description at Windsor had been correct. Each man carried a large axe propped across his body. Unlike the men of Henry's court, they had long, long beards and hair, and their clothes consisted of thick robes wound round their bodies.

Another similar grouping, a dozen or so, followed them closely, but she assumed their position must mean they were of lesser importance. Last, two lines of musicians also marched, their drumming like the beat of an angry heart, with the blare of their horns and the wild skirl of their pipes matching their uncouth look.

The musicians followed the men as they gave tread after deliberate tread towards the steps that led up to the cathedral.

'Gerald' – John spoke through his continued smile – 'what are they doing?'

Though his words were barely audible to Theodosia over the echoing music, she desperately desired to know the same thing. She fought down the urge to run for the sanctuary of the cathedral, scanning the crowd for Benedict. But no, she could not see him.

The three leaders reached the foot of the steps; then each lifted his axe.

'Gerald?' came John's fierce, insistent whisper.

'They are coming to offer you their allegiance, my lord,' murmured Gerald in return. 'They told me it would be allegiance. Fear not: you have your guards with you.'

The music cut in an instant to total silence.

The man on the left, round faced, his beard full and square, took one final step.

Theodosia dug her fingernails into her palms as John flinched.

'From McCarthy, King of Desmond.' The man laid his axe on the ground.

The man on the right, grossly fat with a beard almost to his knees, did likewise. 'From O'Brien, King of Thomond.'

Then the man at the centre, the tallest and oldest of the three, spare-framed with thick, white hair and beard, stepped to the front. He fixed John with eyes sharp as a bird of prey. 'And I come from Rory O'Connor, High King of Ireland and King of Connacht.' He brought his axe up high.

Theodosia's breath stalled as Henry's words echoed from her memory. *'O'Connor, who rules much of the west. And de Lacy has huge tracts of the east.'* The axe and the sword of the King's two great enemies. Here. Now.

Then O'Connor's man lowered the axe on top of the others. 'I come to offer fealty to the Lord of Ireland. As do we all.'

He bowed deeply, the chieftains representing the other two kings matching him, along with the rest of the Irishmen, to new, wild cheers.

Theodosia raised her voice in relieved joy also. She should never have doubted the protection of God.

Palmer joined in too. His calls and whistles were of relief.

'I told you to have patience,' said Dymphna. 'The most powerful kings have sent men, and the others will be important chieftains.'

'Yes, but O'Connor's man had an axe,' said Palmer. 'They all did.' His innards roiled. Though John had guards, the Irishmen stood feet away from Theodosia. As did de Lacy too, with a sword at one hand and the Irish High King's daughter at the other.

Palmer had a place beneath a big oak tree with Dymphna, and he reckoned Theodosia couldn't see him from this angle. But he had full sight of her. Even if Palmer had made a run for it, the Irishmen would have had many heads split before he'd got there. And he doubted if any of them could match de Lacy for speed.

He took deep breaths, banishing the picture of a murdered Theodosia from his mind.

As the cheers echoed on, John drew himself up to his full height, hands on his hips. Finally, he raised a hand for silence.

Every ear strained for his reply to the Irish before him, including Palmer's.

'Your fealty is indeed wonderful to behold.' His voice rang clear. 'First to my father, many years ago. On this day, to me.'

The loudest cheer yet.

The musicians struck up again, this time with a rhythm that had the speed of a celebration, of rejoicing. Every man who had laid down an axe clapped hard with each beat, showing his approval in ringing sound.

Palmer pulled a hand through his hair in further relief. John's repeat of Henry's actions here was going exactly as the King had planned. Maybe his own fears for Theodosia were unsound.

The music finished on a single, crashing note and another cheer.

'And now, my lord.' O'Connor's man went to step forward with the other two who stood in their kings' stead. 'We first offer you our kiss of peace. Every Irishman here will follow.'

Palmer opened his mouth to speak again to Dymphna. But no words came out.

'Stop!' John's voice echoed into the still air.

The men of the Irish kings halted, with unsure looks, at his command.

Other faces showed the same. Theodosia. Eimear O'Connor, her smooth brow creased. Gerald, his toothy smile vanished. Even de Lacy's ruined one.

John pointed at the Irishmen. 'You, or those of your blood, who came to this very spot to greet my father.' He descended from the top step. 'You, who proclaimed your personal submission to him.' To the next. 'You, who agreed the division of lands.' And the next. He halted, his shorter height now equal to theirs. 'Yet as soon as my father's back was turned, every single word from your mouths was as if it had never been.'

Exclamations spread as those who understood his tongue passed his speech on.

'Your word.' A deep flush rose in John's face. 'Your word means nothing.'

'Oh, dear God.' Dymphna's tiny whisper.

Palmer's hand went for his sword, instinct taking over as John continued.

'You will get no kiss of peace from me. I will not give it to traitors like you.'

Then Palmer thought he dreamt.

For John stretched out a hand. Brought it to the beard of the first chieftain. 'You.' And pulled it. Hard.

Palmer's own gasp and hundreds of others told him he was awake.

'Or you.' The same to the next.

John's guards stepped close to him.

And the next. 'You also.'

O'Connor's man recovered first.

'Enough!' He thrust himself back from John's reach.

The guards moved between John and the Irish.

Palmer's jaw set closed as he checked for Theodosia, measuring the gap between them. By all that was holy, he'd get to her fast if he had to.

'Enough to all of it!' O'Connor's man turned to address the Irish. 'We, who have had some quarrels amongst ourselves, came here today to offer our fealty, our personal allegiance to the man whom Henry has sent in his stead.'

John drew breath to speak, but Gerald put a hand on his arm to stop him.

The man went on. 'Yet we find no man.' His white bushy brows drew down in a frown. 'Instead, we find a youth. A stripling.'

Shocked cries came from those whom Henry had settled here. But ugly taunts rose from the Irish.

Palmer tried to catch Theodosia's eye. She should get inside the cathedral. Now. But he couldn't do it.

'A stripling,' said the chieftain, 'who insults us. And, worse, declares our oaths worthless.'

The Irish yelled their approval.

Palmer tensed. *Leave, Theodosia. Just leave.*

Then yelled harder as O'Connor's man picked up his axe, followed the other kings' men and, with a great rattle, all the others who had laid them down.

John flinched, even as his mailed protectors drew swords from sheaths.

'Stay your hand, men.' The man of Connacht's order allowed no action. 'There is no hope of security for the Irish now.' He looked back up at Eimear O'Connor. 'My lady. We leave for the court of your father and of the other kings. They must be told of what has come to pass. Are you coming with us?'

De Lacy went to reply in her stead, but she spoke over him.

'No.' Her voice rang clear. 'My place is with my husband. You can tell my father that.'

'As you wish.' O'Connor's man pointed the axe at her. 'Be it on your head. Now, away, brothers!'

'Away!' chorused every other Irishman, breaking into a stream of angry shouts and threats.

In the noise and dust of their exit, a still-flushed John stood and watched, head high, fists on his hips, legs apart in a wide stance.

Palmer met Dymphna's look.

'What has he done?' she said, the same aghast question being asked in hushed murmurs all round them.

'The opposite of what Henry ordered.' Palmer fought to keep his anger in check, his voice low. 'The Irish were here to make peace. All John had to do was accept that. At least to start with.' He looked to the group in front of the cathedral.

He wasn't the only one angered by John's actions. Eimear fixed John with a look that would have him dead. Yet Palmer could swear he saw the hint of a suppressed smile on de Lacy's face.

Palmer went on. 'And that would have meant Theodosia would've been in a far safer position. As would we all. But now?'

'I don't know, Sir Benedict.' Dymphna's look was deeply troubled.

The rumble of the departing Irish died away, leaving only the buzz of the voices of the many witnesses.

'My people.' John raised a hand once more and received an absolute, immediate silence, broken only by the cry of a lone seabird as it swooped overhead. 'My father has sent me to pacify this land. And I will.'

Palmer wondered if he'd heard right again. The young fool had this minute destroyed an offer of peace.

John dropped his hand. 'But not with empty promises and hollow oaths. No.' His mouth made its pucker of arrogance. 'No, the time for promises is at an end. And the time for action has come.'

Still the silence. The swooping seabird cried on.

'For a savage people understand one thing and one thing only. And that is force.' His gaze swept over every stunned face gathered before him. 'That is their real language. We shall speak it to them. Oh, how we shall speak it to them.' He clenched a fist. 'And they will understand.'

Palmer tensed in disbelief at where John's words were leading.

'They will understand it when they see my castles rise from the land that they claim is theirs. They will understand it when my men pour from those castles and speak to them with the point of a sword. They will understand it when the lands are no longer theirs. My first three castles will be at Tibberaghny, Ardfinnan and Lismore. From there I will push on. And on. That is the path to peace.' He threw his fist in the air. 'The path of the Lord of Ireland!'

Palmer wanted to drop his head in his hands as the loudest cheers yet burst forth, led by John's group of young knights.

Henry had wanted John to take control here. But not like this.

John had not come to make peace. Instead, he was embarking on a campaign of war.

And he was taking Theodosia with him.

Chapter Seven

Tibberaghny, Co. Kilkenny, Ireland
1 May 1185

Palmer sat on the low trunk of an old fallen tree, with his chain mail spread across his lap for checking. He wore his padded gambeson, not only for warmth on this cool, cloudy morning but so he'd be ready for any action.

The site of one of John's castles at this place called Tibberaghny had been chosen well: Palmer would give him that much credit. Near to a fast-flowing river, higher hills rose some way off to the south and the curve of a mountain, covered in the low cloud, loomed even farther off to the north-west.

Chosen well, but it should not have been chosen at all.

Palmer shook the first section of mail hard to dislodge the last of the sand he'd used to clean it. He needed his armour to be ready, like his newly sharpened sword on the trunk next to him.

The creation of the new motte used a natural rise in the low-lying land. Many men laboured with picks and shovels to add to its height with more and more earth, though it was still a way off what it should be. Once the motte was up, work could begin on the keep. Enclosing the bailey could happen at the same time.

Palmer scowled to himself. The pace of building wasn't fast enough. This day would be the third here. Despite the guards that had been posted, the camp of many tents continued to lie exposed to attack on this stretch of flattened ground. Charging at canvas was a much easier task than attacking a well-built wooden fortification.

Canvas that formed the only protection for Theodosia.

He lifted the mail to peer closely at its tight rings, blowing the few remaining grains of sand from them. Dirt and moisture meant rust. And rust meant weakness.

She was here because Gerald was here. John had insisted that the royal clerk should be with him in his chosen base of Tibberaghny. This was the first stop from Waterford, the nearest to that city. The two other castle sites chosen in these borderlands were farther into the territory of the Irish.

Satisfied that the metal was sound, Palmer moved on to the next section. Interesting that John didn't want to go that far. Happy to send others, mind.

He tested what looked like a rust spot with his thumbnail. Only a piece of dried clay. It wouldn't yield so he reached for his knife to work it free.

He'd kept out of the chaos that had been John's assignment of men to castle sites, making sure he'd be in a position to stay with Theodosia. He knew it meant he wouldn't be able to track de Lacy if John sent the Lord of Meath elsewhere. But Palmer had had no choice but to take that gamble.

And he'd won. De Lacy was right here with John.

Palmer nodded to himself. Also interesting.

He moved on to the final section of his mail. His armour was almost ready for any fight.

Truth be told, that fight could well include de Lacy. All well and good for Henry to tell him, Palmer, that he was to find proof of treachery. That might well have to come at the point of a sword. As for whose sword, Palmer would do everything in his power to make sure it was his. No matter who came at him.

A movement at the edge of the camp caught his eye. Mounted men. He straightened up, his heart fast. Normally he wouldn't be acting like a maid. But Theodosia was in this camp.

He let out a breath.

De Lacy, returned from a ride, mounted on a huge destrier, a small group of mailed knights with him.

'Put another man on this patch.' De Lacy gave the order to a guard who had appeared to check on his arrival, spear in hand.

Appeared too late. Palmer's shoulders tightened. Not good enough.

'If I can, my lord,' said the guard.

It was as if de Lacy had heard Palmer's thoughts.

'If you can?' came the Lord of Meath's sharp question to the guard. 'Of course you can find an extra man. One is needed. Had I been an Irish warrior, I'd be in the middle of this camp by now.' He gave a tight grin. 'And you would be missing a head, my friend.'

The guard didn't smile in return, only bowed and went to move off.

'Wait.' De Lacy raised his head to look over the rest of the camp.

The man halted.

Palmer bent low over his work, yet still able to see de Lacy with his upward glance. De Lacy already knew him from Waterford. He didn't want to draw the man's notice again. Not until he decided on it.

'How many men are guarding this camp today?' asked de Lacy of the guard.

'I don't know, my lord.'

'How many tonight?'

The guard shrugged. 'I don't know, my lord.'

'You think those are satisfactory answers?'

'No, my lord.'

'Then what is?'

'I'll find out, my lord.'

'And you will tell me,' stated de Lacy.

'Yes, my lord. At once, my lord.'

As de Lacy dismounted and handed his reins to a groom, Palmer frowned to himself again. What reason would the man have to be so curious about the number of guards at this camp?

He watched as the lord walked towards his large tent, which Palmer knew he shared with his wife, Eimear.

It would probably come to nothing, but he might be able to hear something useful. Though his priority had shifted to Theodosia's protection, he still had orders from Henry to carry out.

Grabbing an abandoned shovel, Palmer went as close to the tent as he dared and began to dig. With so many others doing the same all over the camp, he shouldn't attract any notice.

He could hear murmured voices: one man, one woman. Without doubt de Lacy and his wife, but not clear enough to catch what they said.

Swearing silently to himself, he placed a shovelful of earth off to the side.

Then words. Clear as day.

'But I want to see William, Hugh.' Eimear's voice. No tear-filled plea. Climbing. 'I want to go back to our castle at Trim. To our son.'

'When I say we can. And no sooner.' No softness in de Lacy's tone either. 'I too need to return. I have pressing matters to which I have to attend.'

'How is our son not a pressing matter?'

'Eimear, the Lord John has set events in motion here that no one could have anticipated.'

'Events in motion. Is that what you call it?' Her disdain could burn a hole through the canvas of the tent wall. 'Irish lords, about to be thrown from their lands to the bogs and the mountains. By that stripling?'

Stripling. The same insult used by the spurned Irish at Waterford for John. Palmer raised his eyebrows to himself as he carried on slicing the shovel into the earth again.

'Stripling or not, John is here on the orders of our king.'

De Lacy used it too.

'Henry Curtmantle is not my king.' Her voice lowered in her deep scorn. 'My king is my father. Rory O'Connor. King of Connacht. High King of Ireland.'

Now de Lacy's tone rose. 'You are my wife. Your loyalty is as mine.'

'My loyalty?' Eimear laughed, a terse, bitter retort. 'That still belongs to me, safe in my heart. Whatever else you take from me, you can't take that. As for yours, it's clear to me why you're staying around the stripling.'

'It is, is it? Then why don't you—'

Palmer's shovel hit a mud-covered stone in a loud, sudden scrape.

Both voices went silent, and rapid footsteps came from the tent.

Palmer gave a quiet oath. He couldn't run – he'd be seen. He'd have to lie. And well.

De Lacy appeared at the tent door as Palmer crouched to pull the stone out of the earth with one hand.

'Who's there?' De Lacy's look went to him, then shifted into surprised recognition. 'Palmer, isn't it?'

'Yes, my lord.' Palmer stood up to give a quick bow. 'Not many of these in this ground, thank the Almighty.' He flung the stone he held over to one side. 'Makes progress on the motte much easier.' He wiped his hand off on his gambeson.

'The motte?' De Lacy nodded to the growing mound several yards away. 'The motte is over there. Not here. Outside my tent.'

'I know, my lord.' Palmer pointed to the nearby bushes with his shovel. 'But there's a stream in there, with shallow banks. I'd guess that it'd overflow at the first heavy rainfall. The ground under your tent and those other two would be soaked.'

De Lacy looked from Palmer to the bushes.

Palmer had no idea if the stream posed a threat or not. He offered up a quick prayer that de Lacy wouldn't go to look.

'Moving tents would take time we don't have,' said Palmer. 'So I'm putting in a ditch to make sure they stay dry instead.'

'And why is a fighting man like you digging the earth?'

Palmer shook his head. 'No choice, my lord. At least not for me. That motte isn't going up fast enough. I'd rather be a fighting man with a castle for my use.'

'Hugh.' Eimear's sharp call came from inside. 'I haven't finished.'

De Lacy looked at him for a long moment. 'Then I won't keep you, Palmer.' He stepped back into the tent and yanked the canvas shut.

The voices began again. But this time stayed far too low for Palmer to catch a word.

Palmer thrust his shovel into the earth once more. A useful task, digging a ditch that wasn't needed.

No mind. The exchange he'd heard between the Lord of Meath and his wife might have given him more questions than answers. But it was a start.

Once he'd finished this empty task, he'd go and do what he'd told de Lacy was needed.

Palmer didn't care if he shouldn't be digging. The quicker this castle went up, the better.

Chapter Eight

'Please slow down, brother.' The damp vellum resisted Theodosia's quill pen as she strove to complete her latest word. 'I am not as skilled as you in scribing.' She sat up straight from the small table, capturing a moment's rest for her aching shoulders before she carried on. 'And the ink remains wet for a long time.'

Across the gloomy tent from her, sat well back on a low chair, Gerald gave one of his impatient tsks.

'That we had the comfort of the Church to go to as Abbess Dymphna did.' He brushed a large drip of water from his forehead and glared up at the leaking canvas above him. 'Do the heavens weep at the sinfulness of our endeavours in this land?'

'I am sure we will be housed in dry walls soon. There is progress every day.' Theodosia's words drew another tsk, which she could understand, despite the sounds of shovels, saws and hammers from outside. After more than two weeks of placating him, her words sounded like a hollow promise even to her. Their accommodation at Tibberaghny still consisted of damp, mildewed tents, soaked through with the constant rain. Her only consolation was that Benedict had been posted within this camp. She had not been able to speak to him but had had sight of him. Far, far worse would have been for him to have been sent to one of John's other two castle sites.

'If you don't work faster, I'll have you whipped!'

Theodosia caught her breath at the angry yell. *John.*

The canvas door moved as if someone wrestled with it, the movements causing yet more drips to descend from the ceiling.

'Untie the thing, sister,' said Gerald, 'before he has us both soaked through with his attempts.'

'Yes, brother.' Theodosia hurried to the flap and opened it, only to be thrust to one side as John shoved his way in.

'Gerald, my father has given me useless men.' John did not even glance her way as he flung himself into an empty chair. 'Useless. I need my castles complete, to show the Irish my unstoppable progress. How long does it take to raise a basic fortification?'

'It would be faster if men weren't disappearing by the day, my lord,' came Gerald's testy reply.

'I have put out an order that any who deserts my service will be hanged,' John snapped back. 'That should be sufficient.'

Theodosia went to close the flap, wishing for a cloak of invisibility. She had managed to avoid John's presence since the encounter at Waterford. Now he was closer than ever.

'You. Sister.'

Her mouth dried at the unexpected order. 'Yes, my lord?' She kept her head lowered.

'Leave that door open. I want to keep an eye on those workers. First one I see slacking gets my whip. And get me some wine.' He sneezed. 'My head is fuddled from this ague.'

Theodosia complied, tying the door back before hastening to get the wine.

Gerald withdrew from John as much as his injured arm would allow. 'I fear an ague in my weakened state.'

'Then fear you must.' John wiped his nose with the heel of one hand. 'Most have their humours unbalanced in this place.' He sneezed again. 'How could they not when, at every dawn, the skies throw down rain, which doesn't stop until dusk, then starts again at night?' He took the goblet from Theodosia and gulped down a mouthful with an unsteady hand. 'Nights where no one can sleep, with the sounds of the Irish devils in the woods. Only my wine allows me rest.'

'We are in the midst of their lands, my lord,' said Gerald. 'And they are not,' he cleared his throat, 'well disposed towards you, shall we say.'

As Theodosia placed the wine jug on the table, she slid a blank piece of parchment over her most recent words, words which despaired of John's actions towards the Irish at Waterford. Her careful script might have been dictated by Gerald, but it came from her hand.

Selecting a clean goblet, she began to pour.

A terrible, high scream came from outside.

Theodosia's hand jerked in shock, splashing wine over the tabletop as an unearthly chorus followed the scream: drums, whistles, harsh shouts in a strange tongue.

John leapt to his feet with an oath, even as the hammers and saws stopped dead. 'They're attacking. The Irish are attacking.'

Men with axes, with swords. Theodosia had faced them before, but never on this terrifying scale. Her heart tripped fast, faster as Gerald struggled to stand up. 'Sister, help me.' His usual plea, though a broken arm should not be making him so helpless.

Shouts came from those within the camp, orders to defend, to take up positions.

'Lean on me, brother,' she said. 'We should hide. With all haste.'

'You can't hide. You have to defend this place.' John flung open one of Gerald's chests, rummaging through it and sending clothing all over the canvas floor. 'God's eyes, have you no weapons?'

Gerald's arm tensed under Theodosia's hold. 'I am a man of God, as is the sister who serves Him too. We cannot fight; we rely on others for our protection.'

'Don't you understand?' said John. '*I* am the one who needs protection. I am the highest prize for the enemy. I have to get to those who are armed.' He gestured to Theodosia and Gerald. 'You will help me do that. I can shelter behind you as we make our way there.'

Theodosia stared at him in shock. John, the lord who'd announced a brutal campaign from the steps at Waterford, would use a cleric and a nun as his shield? But she could say nothing; she had to be true to the habit she wore.

Gerald drew breath, and she guessed his view would be the same.

'Let us make haste as much as we can, brother.' Theodosia knew she spoke over him, but any utterance he made right now would only make things worse.

The noise echoing from the woods increased, drowning out the calls of the defenders.

John's eyes widened. 'Hurry up. Before they break through.'

'Take care.' Theodosia took Gerald's weight as his foot caught on the clothing scattered by John and he stumbled.

'I said, *hurry*.' John had to raise his voice over the noise outside. 'Gerald, stay here. You'll only slow us up.'

'None of us should go,' said Gerald. 'It's too dangerous.'

'Please, brother.' Theodosia lowered him to the seated safety of a closed chest, every inch of her aching to do the same. 'You risk further injury.'

'No more arguing, Gerald.' John pulled up his cloak to cover his face. 'Go on, sister.' He fell in behind her and prodded her hard in the back. 'And stand as straight as you can; your stature is woefully short.'

With her mouth clamped shut to try to steady her breathing, Theodosia walked on shaking legs to the door of the tent, John's hand fixed hard on her clothing.

The sounds of enemies, of defenders, echoed even louder in the open air in a buffeting, petrifying din. Men ran past with swords, bows, yelled to each other in a string of panicked oaths. Her hands went unbidden and foolishly to her face, as if she could stop a missile or a blow with her own flesh. She looked in vain for Benedict amongst the shouting mass of men, in a desperate hope that she would see him.

'Stop,' came John's muffled voice. 'Let me see what's happening first.'

Theodosia obeyed, her breath faster as she scanned the thick woods beyond the half-built wooden wall. Yet she could see nothing of the unseen enemy, with only their nightmarish clamour reverberating through her head.

'We will go. When I say.' John again.

'Yes, my lord.'

Then it stopped. Silence from the woods, as if it had never been.

Only the shouts of the defenders floated on the air, suddenly sounding ridiculous in their alarm.

A sharp whistle halted them too.

Theodosia looked to its source.

The scarred lord, Hugh de Lacy, stood there, sword blade resting on one shoulder. 'There's no attack, men. At least not this time. What we need—'

John shouldered his way past Theodosia. 'Are you all hens in a coop?' His shrill shout drew every look. 'Panicking, and, in doing so, panicking each other to worse confusion? Back to work! Now!'

Men acted on his command, many still with weapons in their hands.

De Lacy walked over, sheathing his sword. 'My Lord John.' His one-eyed gaze took in Theodosia too as she stood next to John. 'I didn't realize you were there.'

John hitched his cloak straight. 'I was trying to get the sister to safety. Who knows what could have befallen her should the brutes have attacked.'

De Lacy nodded solemnly as if he believed the obvious lie. 'Try not to fear, sister.'

'Thank you, my lord.' Theodosia lowered her hands, weak with relief that made her shake even harder.

'The danger has passed.' John gave an unconvincing cough. 'I need to get out of this rain before I catch my death.'

'Of course, my lord,' said de Lacy. 'And this rain will stop soon. You can see the mountain now.'

Theodosia followed his point. The dark curves of the distant mount were indeed emerging through the thick clouds.

'The mountain of the women, the Irish call it,' he said.

'They have their women assembling there?' John's face creased in uncertain fear once more. 'Why?'

'Fear not, my lord, they don't.' De Lacy caught back a laugh. 'It's one of the ancient legends of the Irish. One of their heroes, a great warrior named Fionn, wanted to choose a new wife, so he commanded a large group of women to race to the top. He gave the woman he really wanted a secret path, so she would be the winner. That mountain is where the Irish say it happened.' He gave a quick bow. 'Now, if you'll excuse me, I have much to attend to.'

'Yes, yes. Go.' John watched de Lacy leave, a frown deepening. 'Bring me that wine, sister.' He ducked back inside the tent, and Theodosia followed. 'I need it more than ever.'

An ashen-faced Gerald remained seated on the chest. 'What's happening?'

'All is calm once more, praise God,' she said as she prepared John's drink. 'Our prayers have been answered.' She took a long breath, still alert to the threat that was her own brother.

John took the goblet from her without thanks, still wearing his frown.

'You do not look all that relieved, my lord,' said Gerald. 'Sister, I will have wine too to steady my heart.'

'Yes, brother.' Theodosia complied as John drank deep.

'That Hugh de Lacy,' said John. 'My father suspects him of treachery, and I share that view. He knows this land so well, he could be one of them. And how did he know that there would be no attack? He seemed very certain, yet he stands on this side of our wall.'

Heart knocking afresh, Theodosia bent to folding and tidying the cleric's clothing that had been thrown about by John, alert at the mention of de Lacy. She might be able to glean information that she could pass on to Benedict.

'The man even knows their wild tales and mocks me with them.' John related the legend of the mountain in the distance as he refilled his goblet.

Gerald crossed himself. 'The Irish are simple as well as savage. I know of it from my previous journeys.'

'No wonder they need taming. I believe de Lacy does too.' John looked at the bottom of his empty goblet. 'Or maybe he only likes tales of women who would run up a mountain for a man.' He gave an unkind laugh. 'With a face like his, he must only see them run away. That fine-breasted young wife of his, that Eimear, must keep her eyes shut, all night, every night.' His frown returned. 'The same wife he has brought here as part of his group. She's of Irish stock.' He slapped the goblet on the table. 'I need to regroup with my men, examine what has happened today.' He went to the tent door. 'Keep a close eye on de Lacy, Gerald. His wife too. Anything suspicious, I need to know.'

'My lord.' Gerald inclined his head, and Theodosia bowed too, aware that John did not even acknowledge her presence. While his casual use of her for his own protection irked her sorely, she was also relieved. She had no wish to attract his closer attention.

'Close the door, sister,' said Gerald. 'We need to get on with our work. We are behind, thanks to the commotion.'

Returning to her table, Theodosia gasped softly in frustration.

'What's the matter?' asked Gerald.

'It is all ruined.' She held up the vellum that had contained the account of John meeting the Irish. 'I spilled so much wine in my fright. Forgive me, brother.'

'Fret not, sister.' Gerald crossed himself. 'The inks have mixed together, as the Irish have done in the face of John's insults at Waterford, surrounding us here and waiting to pounce. We shall start afresh, no matter how many hours it takes us.' Gerald's mouth turned down. 'But it is an ill omen, sister: an ill omen.'

'Back to work, all of you! Stop standing around like staring sheep!' John delivered his yell as he stalked back to his own quarters, steps clumsy in the sticky mud.

With a shake of his head, Palmer replaced his sword against the nearby tree, ready to grab it again at a second's notice. The King's son should be giving orders about how best to counter an attack. The answer to the Irish had been chaos of the worst kind. This camp needed orders. Direction. A plan. But no. Nothing. Men deserted by the day, with the rumour that the Irish chieftains were paying them the money John was not. And no men came to replace them. Many of those who remained seemed to favour the bottom of a beer barrel. Palmer himself spent all his time on the building work now.

Even with all these problems, all John did was scuttle away like a rat back to its hole.

Palmer picked up the axe he'd been using to strip the bark from a felled tree. He looked towards the tent where he knew Theodosia lodged with Gerald, reliving the horror he'd felt when he'd seen her step outside. It still gripped him, along with the fear he'd felt in defending the half-built encampment. Not for himself. Fighting brought out sharpened senses, faster limbs, a surge of strength. His fear was for Theodosia.

He lifted the axe and brought it down on the tree trunk. He and she had fought together, and he loved her courage, her quick mind. But battle was different. Men ready for brutal slaughter, and so many of them. The wet wood took the force of the blow and split, but did not cut. A woman, nun or not, would be nothing except a special prize. More and worse attacks would follow, he knew that. He had to speak to her, to make her understand the danger she faced. And soon. Pushing the picture from his mind of how Theodosia could be assaulted, he wiped his dripping hair from his face and cursed long and hard.

'You can say that again.'

Palmer looked up to see the heavy-set younger man from the ship at Waterford, no longer looking pleased at the thought of whores and wearing instead the sweat of fear. 'Why? You've forgotten how?'

'No, no.' The man gave a nervous grin at Palmer's terse reply. 'Just thought that we were for it then.' Still holding a blunt-looking, short blade, he held out his free hand. 'The name's Simonson, sir knight.'

Palmer shook it. 'Sir Benedict Palmer.'

Simonson's grin fell as he nodded to Palmer's sword. 'Can use that, can you, Sir Benedict?'

'You can call me Palmer.' He wrenched a strip of tight bark from the green wood. 'And yes, I can use a sword.' Would use it to take the head of anyone who laid a hand on his wife.

'Thank the Almighty.' Simonson blew out his cheeks. 'Sounded to me like the Irish were about to attack. They made the fiercest noise I've heard yet. Even when they make it at night. And the nights are terrible.'

Saints alive, the man looked more fearful than a beaten dog. Palmer raised his axe again. 'They choose the nights on purpose. A tired camp is an unready one. Makes mistakes.' *Like Theodosia was making.* The wet wood squeaked under his strike. 'How's your use of that blade?'

Simonson looked at the poor weapon he held. 'Middling.'

Palmer grunted as he hauled his axe free. 'Like your readiness to work?'

'Sorry, sir.' The man flushed and tucked his blade into his belt. He picked up the small axe he'd flung away at the first sounds of danger. 'Always ready – I got distracted, that's all.' His strike at the wood came at an angle and bounced off, narrowly missing his own face.

'Middling, you say?' Palmer landed a sure blow on the tough wood.

Simonson's colour deepened. 'Maybe better to say that fighting's new to me.'

'Then what drew you to it?'

'Land, sir.' Simonson took another cut, better this time. 'The word went out that the Lord John would pay men to fight for him. It wasn't only me that came from my village. There's at least half a dozen that I can see from where I stand.'

'I see.' Palmer's doubts hardened tight as his neck muscles as he struck the wood yet again.

'We'd get paid for fighting. Even better, the Lord John would reward us with our own lands.' His big, bland face became curious. 'As I'm sure you will get too.'

'I have land.' Palmer went to swing his axe again but stopped dead.

Theodosia.

She had walked out of her tent, jug in hand, headed towards a barrel of water in a quiet corner.

'What I need now is to get some water.' Palmer laid his axe down, pulse surging at this chance. 'Keep at it.' He nodded at the tree trunk. 'It's almost done, and we'll have something to show for this morning.'

'That we will.' Simonson set to, happy to claim Palmer's work as his.

Palmer walked over to Theodosia, holding in his deepest urge to run to her as she struggled to lift the heavy lid. 'Need a hand, sister?'

She looked up and her eyes met his. Delight and relief shone in them as he knew did in his own.

She took in a long, long breath. 'Please, good sir.'

He lifted the lid with ease and laid it on the ground. 'There's no one near?' He kept his voice low.

'No, we're alone,' she said. 'Oh, Benedict. How I wish I could hold you.'

'And I you. You're unharmed?'

'Yes. Though it shames me to say it, when I thought we were under attack, I was so frightened.'

'I know you must've been. But I was watching your tent. You shouldn't have come outside.'

Her gaze dropped like a stone.

'What?'

'Swear to me you will do nothing.' She bent to pick up her water jug from beside the barrel.

'Theodosia.'

She looked at him again. 'John forced me out. He concealed himself behind me so he could get to his men.'

'So the warrior lord is in truth no more than a yellow-braies. The snivelling little snake.' With a low growl, Palmer yanked the jug from her. 'We're leaving. Now. I'll take my chances in explaining why to Henry. I know I can get us home.'

'No.' Theodosia tried to tug the vessel back. 'We must stay.'

'To have you used by John to try to save his own skin?' Palmer held firm. 'Theodosia, the man has no idea of what he's doing. Look at what he did at Waterford, insulting the Irish and estranging them. Proclaiming some wild conquest of his own.' He battled to keep his voice from climbing. 'Here at Tibberaghny is no better. He's brought men who know less about fighting than a dairymaid. And they know even less about building a fortification. We still have only half a wall, and half of that will fall over if there's a gale. He's drinking with his friends every minute he has, instead of leading the men he's got. I'll wager the Irish know it. They're playing this perfectly: I swear they're biding their time, waiting for the right moment.'

'Precisely.'

Her response threw him, and she scooped the jug from him.

'Benedict, John believes Hugh de Lacy is definitely working against him, possibly his wife, Eimear, too. He spoke freely to Gerald of it.' Her hands tightened on the jug as she gave him an account of what she had overheard. 'Which means that my father's suspicions are correct. If I stay where I am, at Gerald's side, I may be able to gather information to pass on to you. Information which you can use far more effectively than John.'

Palmer was glad she held the jug. He probably would've dropped it. 'You mean act as a spy?'

'Call it what you will.' She gave a twitch of a smile. 'After all, that is what you are for the King, is it not?' She didn't allow his answer. 'But if I am also in a position to help you to do what the King needs, what he ordered, then that is what I must do.'

'Theodosia. It's too dangerous. You can't.'

'I can.' She dipped the jug into the barrel. 'This water butt can serve as our meeting place when it is deserted. No one will question our presence here.' She held the full vessel with a look as firm as her tone. 'Now I must return or Gerald will wonder where I am.' Her free hand brushed his for the briefest moment. 'I know you are watching over me, my love,' she whispered. 'You will keep me safe.'

She walked away before he could say another word.

A nearby crash had him turn quickly. A pile of logs had dislodged and rolled across a cooking fire, sending sparks and shouts of blame into the air.

Keep her safe. Here. A difficult enough task, and to which he'd devote all his waking hours. But to keep her safe while she spied on the King's son?

Palmer pulled his hands through his hair. He could only pray that John was too wrapped up in his fool's behaviour to notice. But that behaviour couldn't last. What he needed to do was to get Theodosia away from her half-brother. He just needed his chance. Then to take it. And her.

Chapter Nine

Tibberaghny, Co. Kilkenny, Ireland
26 May 1185

The hours before dawn bring a cold to the bones like no other. Palmer long knew that, but it didn't make it any easier, even on a short, early summer night such as this. Sat cross-legged on the damp ground next to the fire at the centre of the camp at Tibberaghny, he poked the embers back to new life with a stick.

Plenty of life echoed from the high wooden keep on the motte behind him. John had ordered that the building be the first built. Safe within its walls and the high palisade that surrounded it, the Lord of Ireland and his circle of young bucks drank the night away yet again. The rest of the camp remained in damp tents on the churned mud ground.

Palmer rubbed his face hard to push away his tiredness. Unlike the King's son, he'd not fall into bed at cockcrow and sleep off the late night until well after noon. He'd see out the night watch, yet again, then oversee the building work along with keeping a check on the men who watched over the camp by day. He had to. The men who worked for John had to be driven, not led. At least those that remained did. The ranks of the deserters had continued to grow. All who were still here were of the same kind as the sleeping Simonson, who lay with others on the ground near the fire, swaddled in a blanket and snoring fit to wake the dead.

'Is someone wrestling a pig?'

Palmer's hand went to his knife at the unseen voice.

Before he could react further, de Lacy stepped from the shadows to take a seat next to him.

'Easy. It's only me, Palmer.'

'My lord.' Palmer's jaw set in his anger at his own failure. He'd not heard the man arrive.

Fluid as a cat, de Lacy settled and drew out a hunk of bread from his own satchel. 'Food in your belly helps keep you sharp.' He held it out to Palmer, the gesture showing he knew he'd bested Palmer.

'Not for me, thanks.' Palmer pulled a pail containing cuts of meat closer to him. 'So many cattle around here, there's beef for the taking.' He jabbed at a large lean piece with his knife. 'Can I cook you some too?'

De Lacy shook his head. 'Can't abide the stuff,' came his odd reply as he tore off a chunk of bread with his awkward, lopsided bite. 'I must say, I'm impressed with the progress you're making here.'

'There are many men working hard, my lord.'

'I would see it more as a few men being organised to work hard. I've been riding out to see the Lord John's other two sites at Ardfinnan and Lismore, and they are nowhere near as far on as this fortification.'

Palmer shrugged. 'I wish we could work faster still, my lord.' The other sites didn't have a Theodosia to keep protected. He might not be able to take her out of John's orbit, but he could build the most secure encampment he could and guard it with his life to protect her from those outside. Yet the blasted thing still wasn't finished.

As if hearing his thoughts, a chorus of whistles broke from the darkness of the woods.

'And it starts again.' Palmer threw his meat down with a tired oath and stood up to have a look.

The whistles loudened, the men on the ground stirring and muttering in their sleep. Simonson's snores cut out in a snort.

Palmer had his sword ready, looked for any signs of movement from beyond. Nothing.

De Lacy didn't move, carried on eating.

The shrill sounds brought the men to wakefulness, sitting up in bleary unease, swearing death to those that woke them.

'It'll stop,' said de Lacy.

It did, fading back down to silence.

'You can sleep, men,' said Palmer. 'A false alarm.' Another one. But for how much longer?

'Bloody was asleep.' Simonson flung himself back on the ground like a sulky maid. 'That's all I bloody want.'

Similar complaints rumbled from the others as they lay down once more.

Palmer ignored them, retaking his place before the fire. He too ached for rest. But he couldn't give in.

'Such rudeness should be punished.' De Lacy nodded at them.

'Not my place to do it.' Palmer brushed bits of mud and grass off his piece of meat and held it before the fire again. 'My lord.' The fat caught in a sizzle, sending up licks of flame.

De Lacy flinched back, the scarred skin on his face shining red as the glistening beef in the firelight.

No wonder the man didn't want it.

De Lacy's one-eyed gaze went to Palmer. 'So what is your place, Palmer?'

'To serve the Lord John, of course.'

'I see.' De Lacy bit off another mouthful of bread. 'Then you should join his man, Theobald Walter, on the mission into Munster. They're setting off on the morrow. John has decided it's time to attack the Irish, to start putting his mark on these wild stretches of land. No more sitting around waiting for them to come to us, he says.'

Sitting around? Palmer kept his rueful smile in: every aching muscle and bone in his body disagreed with the Lord John on that one.

De Lacy jerked a thumb at the castle, where the sound of revelry carried on. 'They're supposedly setting off at first light, but my guess is it will be later. Plenty of time for you to join them.'

'The Lord John is staying here, so I will be too.' And John was, forcurse him. No attacking for him. Palmer busied himself with turning his cooking meat to avoid de Lacy's continued stare. Theodosia had told him the frustrating news. He'd hoped that if John left, even for a short while, he could persuade her to leave.

'A strange choice,' said de Lacy. 'I had you marked as a fighting man. You told me yourself of your time on the battlefield when you were setting Gerald's arm at Waterford. Yet you choose to stay here to build and guard.' He sniffed, wiping his nose on his sleeve. 'And dig ditches to keep tents dry, of course.'

The man missed nothing. Palmer shrugged, not taking the bait. 'I'm past my best fighting days. I'm doing it for the money.'

The sounds of carousing wafted ever louder from the height of the motte.

Smiling, de Lacy put his head to one side as he considered Palmer's reply. 'You need to hope there's some left after they've finished drinking it.' His smile dropped. 'So what is John paying you?'

The sudden question threw Palmer. With a bite of the hot beef, he named a sum, had no idea if it was right or wrong. Henry's rewards to him had not been ordinary.

De Lacy gave him a long look.

Palmer knew he'd guessed too high. De Lacy had pinned the lie. He braced himself for action.

But de Lacy only gave a quiet laugh. 'Then you may well find yourself needing another employer, Palmer.' He stood up. 'The Lord John and his court of young men drank that two weeks ago.' He hitched his cloak straight. 'And if I were you, I'd get the men you do control to cut some more of those trees down.'

He walked away from the fire, the darkness of the bailey swallowing him up.

De Lacy was proving to be everything Henry feared. The scarred lord knew every move, every plan being made by John. He appeared to be able to guess what the Irish would do too. He'd even worked out that something wasn't right about him, Palmer.

The revelry from the keep loudened, with bawdy songs bellowed in roars of laughter.

Palmer threw his meat into the fire, appetite gone. He still had found no proof of the lord's treachery for Henry. Trapped here, he could achieve nothing, though his work on the castle threatened to fell him with exhaustion.

De Lacy was one step ahead.

And Palmer couldn't tell what that next step would be.

Chapter Ten

'My lord, wake up. You must wake up.'

'No, I must not.' John clung to sleep, his head buried beneath the soothing darkness of the thick bedcovers. 'I'll wake when I'm good and ready.'

'Now, my lord.' The owner of the male voice became more insistent, even daring to shake John by the shoulder. 'You must wake now!'

'Unhand me, you son of a pestilent whore.' John stuck his head out from the covers, cursing as the daylight pounded into his sight and straight into his wine-tortured head.

'My lord.' The voice dripped with disapproval.

John squinted hard and made out the clerk Gerald standing over him. 'What are you doing, man? Leave me alone.'

Gerald's mouth became a thin line. 'There are men approaching the bailey's gate. Many of them.'

'God's teeth, we're under attack!' John flung the covers back. 'My clothes. Quick! I can't escape naked.'

Gerald averted his eyes. 'My lord. Calm yourself. It is no attack.'

'No?' John stilled.

'The guards have identified Theobald Walter and his men, returned from Munster.'

'Returned? Finally?' They'd been gone for twelve nights with no word. 'And?' Gerald's lips parted in a triumphant smile. 'It looks to be victory.'

Trembling hard, John stood on the wide lowest step of the motte and watched as the gate dropped over the water-filled ditch surrounding this privy called Tibberaghny Castle.

He'd ordered up his best ermine robe, shouted at his servants to dress him fast, faster. He'd only had to pause once, to vomit last night's wine long and hard onto the rush floor, an act which had completely restored him.

And there, emerging from the trees, riding into view, proud on the proudest destrier: Theobald Walter, his long-time friend. More brother than John's own judgemental, aloof male siblings, he gladdened John's heart with his loyalty. Walter headed up a group of battle-stained men, on foot and on steeds, who bore the glow of triumph and who, more importantly, carried many spoils.

Walter's gaze met John's as his horse thudded across the bridge, and his fist thrust in the air, confirming all of John's hopes.

'All hail the victors!' John bellowed his order in joyous relief.

Magically, wonderfully, the whole camp responded: cheering, clapping, shouting praise, raising thanks to God for the Lord John.

As if the heavens heard, the sun slipped out from behind the breeze-filled clouds.

Tears pricked at the insides of John's lids. This was it. This was what he was born to do. This was the reward of power.

Walter dismounted and made his way through the hollering assembly to John, falling on bended knee before him.

'Quiet!' John cut the noise with a sweep of his hand. 'Walter. I rejoice at your return. Tell us your news.'

'My lord, we have defeated the Irish in Munster,' said Walter. 'And better, my lord—'

Huzzahs rose up.

John allowed them for a moment or two, then stopped them again with a raised hand. He could be God Himself, guiding the sun through the heavens, such was his complete control.

'Better, my lord,' said Walter, 'we have killed McCarthy, King of Desmond!' Walter reached beneath his surcoat and threw a bloodied hand at John's feet.

No one waited for John's signal. Wild cheers echoed out, feet stamped.

'You killed their king?' John's fists clenched, hot, searing delight tearing through him.

Walter looked up at him, the dirt of his face splitting with the gleam of his white-toothed smile. 'Yes, my lord. That is his right hand. I took it as proof of the Irish loss.'

'My valiant, worthy servant.' John hauled him to his feet and embraced him hard to more waves of loud praise. He loosed his hold, turned Walter to face forward to present him to the crowds, raising his voice to make himself heard. 'This is what a conqueror looks like. A man who fights without mercy in loyalty for his ruler.'

As the sea of faces below shouted their approval, John scanned them, looking for the one that mattered, the hideous visage like melted wax. Now he could show de Lacy that anyone could put these Irish dogs down, with no need for alliances or marriages. The sword did its work better than any agreement: such pacts only got in the way.

But he couldn't see the Lord of Meath anywhere.

'Where's de Lacy?' said John to Walter, who shrugged.

John pointed at a tall, broad-shouldered man who stood near Gerald's nearby tent, leaning on a water butt. 'You there, idler! Find de Lacy and fetch him here. Now, if you know what's good for you.'

The dark-haired man reacted with a stiff bow and disappeared into the crowd.

John whipped up more cheers, more proclamations of his glory, ensuring Walter received his share too. All here would marvel that he, John, could be so humble, so generous in sharing acclaim.

The dark-haired man reappeared, making his way through the crowds.

John's stomach tightened. This was it. This was the moment when de Lacy would realise that this island was not his to claim, the moment when his plans would turn to dust. The moment when the Lord of Meath would have to salute John's victory over the Irish. John waved for silence again. Everyone here should witness this momentous event.

The man bowed before John. 'My lord.' He moved to one side.

But he hadn't brought the swarthy, hideous de Lacy.

Striding towards him, her head held high, her gaze directly meeting his, came de Lacy's wife, Eimear. She wore no modest cloak, only a brazen tunic that kicked up as she walked, showing the smooth skin on her calves. She stopped before him, with her hands bunched in fists by her sides.

John looked at the man he'd dispatched on his errand. 'Are you a fool? This woman is not who I ordered you to bring to me.'

The man bowed again, with a set look that John didn't like. The fellow had a definite air of the usurper about him. 'My apologies, my lord. When I went to the Lord of Meath's tent, I found only his wife. She said—'

'Who are you both to discuss me as if I were a woman of low birth?' Eimear's clear, loud tone cut the man off while her cold stare still remained locked on John's. 'To summon me here as if I were a servant to do your bidding?'

A surprised murmur met her words.

John's shoulders tightened. This woman was spoiling his triumph with her rudeness. 'I did not summon you here at all. I ordered your husband's presence. Or is he such a lesser man that a woman can serve in his stead?'

Walter and his friends laughed at his clever response, and two spots of colour appeared in Eimear's pale cheeks. John permitted himself a smirk.

'I came here to answer for my husband; that much is true.' Her arrogance didn't wane, curse her. She still stared him down.

'Then is he hiding beneath your skirts, enjoying the view?' His quick retort drew a louder laugh.

Her colour deepened, yet still she held her head high. 'My husband has gone to fight.'

The laughter faded away along with John's own good humour.

'To fight? I gave him no orders.'

'He does not need orders from you.' Her voice rang with audacious authority.

'Yes, he does! If he does not heed my orders, then he is a traitor!' It came out too high, too shrill. Damn this woman. She made him a boy in britches.

'Hugh de Lacy is loyal to King Henry. As am I.' Her brows arched. 'My lord.'

Fury swelled within him. She mocked his title, this bitch of the Irish dogs. Her face, her bearing, her words: all spoke of her superiority in this land. And not his, despite his glorious victory. Every single person who stood here, from the noblest knight to the lowliest privy cleaner, could tell it. She needed humbling. And quickly. Inspiration struck him.

He held his hand out. 'Then prove it. Come and kiss my hand.'

She stepped forward, gaze still locked on his.

As she did so, he bent and scooped up the hand of the dead king.

'My hand.' He held the thing before him.

Gasps and muted disgust from those watching met his bold action.

Pulse racing, he waited.

While the colour in her face drained away, she didn't flinch. Slowly, very deliberately, she bent to place a fervent kiss on the corpse hand, the red of her warm, living lips a hideous contrast to the mottling flesh of the King of Munster. Then she straightened up to face down John once more to a chorus of long breaths and conjecture.

Her actions had made her allegiances clearer than a thousand words. He only had one response.

'So you were devoted to him as a fellow Irish noble?' He gave a sage nod. 'What a shame he can no longer return that.' He flicked the hand hard at her breast.

She jerked away in shock, stumbling onto the wet, muddy ground with a suppressed cry.

It worked. Laughter broke out.

He'd broken her spell. The laughs mixed with scoffs as she climbed to her feet, her hands and skirt stained with mud.

'You would shy away from the touch of one of your own?' He flicked it at her again and this time she ducked her head.

Jeers and hoots followed her as she turned and stalked away through the crowd.

Blood rushed fast and hard to his groin at his exquisite humiliation of this woman. He'd made a mistake, allowing her to behave in such a disrespectful way and taking the joy out of his victory. His swift thinking had regained the power, had regained the . . . Oh, this was too, too good.

He waved the hand of the slain King of Munster above his head. 'I have the upper hand!'

A new, hard wave of delicious mirth and cheers broke over him.

'The upper hand! Now, to feast, my men! We have much to celebrate.'

So very, very much.

'Are you ill, sister?'

Theodosia shook her head at Gerald's question. 'I am fasting today, brother.' Ashamed of her own untruth, she gestured to her small piece of bread and goblet of water. She wanted no part of John's raucous feast in the small hall within the keep, where he celebrated with his closest young friends. His proximity to her, as he sat at the head of the long table while she mercifully was at the far end by Gerald's side, gave her deep disquiet.

Gerald sniffed. 'Good. So long as you are not sickening for something. There will be much for me to record. You must be paying attention to it all in case I miss a detail.'

Sickening. A fitting word for this dreadful assemblage. The loud, swaggering knights, swapping battle stories of the rout of the Irish as they crammed their mouths with mounds of the roasted flesh of animals and jug after jug of wine, yet still called for more. She knew of the need for fighting, for war. But to hear the detail of each sword blow, of how wounds were inflicted, of how each man met his end, was terrible to her. She herself had seen such horrors, had even ended lives with her own hands, and knew she could never celebrate it. Yet this was what they did, rejoicing in the carnage they had inflicted. And she would have to relive it all again when Gerald retold it so she could write it down.

'Of course, brother.' She took a mouthful of bread, willing herself to swallow it.

Gerald made an ineffective stab at the haunch of beef before him on his trencher and sighed sharply. 'How I hunger for the riches this meal offers.' He sighed again. 'The burden of my limited capabilities tires me out.' He pushed his trencher in front of her, resting his bandaged arm on the table. 'Chop my food, sister.'

Theodosia took his knife without complaint. The clerk had set her to many tasks other than writing, citing his injury in his plaintive tone every time. Mixing ink. Rolling papers. Arranging his cushions. Washing his gnarled feet. Combing his thin hair. Though sure he could manage many of them, she took the easier course of not arguing. She could do nothing to draw attention to herself, nothing to suggest that she was other than what she seemed. She chopped the meat with care into bite-sized chunks. She certainly had not told Benedict in the times she snatched to be with him. Gerald would probably be nursing another useless limb if she did. Their history with powerful men of the Church was not a good one.

'Is that sister your personal slave now, Gerald?'

Theodosia looked up at John's shout, hand tight on her knife as the knights quietened, their attention drawn too.

With his chair pushed back and his feet crossed on the table, John wore a grin on a face that shone with copious amounts of meat and wine.

Gerald gave a tight smile in return. 'God does not see fit to heal my grievous injury yet. I try to get by as best I can.'

John's grin broadened. 'I have what you need.' He dropped his feet to the floor to lean forward and search amongst the platters and bowls. 'This.' He threw something to the clerk, where it landed with a soft thump in front of Theodosia's and Gerald's trenchers.

A great roar of laughter burst from the watching knights as her sight swam. The hand of the dead king rested before her.

'Remove that foul object from my sight,' Gerald ordered one of the servers, who scooped it up in a linen cloth.

Theodosia's sight cleared, though the sweat of nausea coated every inch of her body.

'Bring it back here.' John clicked his fingers. 'I will preserve it as a trophy for my father. As proof of my success.'

Gerald shot him a malevolent look as he stabbed at a piece of his beef. 'The King prefers wealth to trophies, my lord.'

John waved his remark aside. 'I know. It's only for fun.' He took a deep drink. 'Have fun, Gerald. We've so much to celebrate, thanks to my dispatching of Theobald Walter to deal with the Irish.' He raised his goblet to his friend. 'To Theo.'

The knights joined the toast, the most recent of many.

Theodosia drank some water to steady her resolve. She could tolerate this obscene banquet of John's no more. As soon as his attention shifted elsewhere, she'd tell Gerald she felt unwell and take her leave.

'Theo, the hero.' John slapped the tabletop. 'Hark: I'm a battle poet now.' He rejoiced in his new jest with his fellows. 'You shall have great rewards.' He pointed at his friend with his goblet. 'Great. In fact, I am awarding you lands. You can have five cantreds from Munster. Five. I shall retain crosses and donations of abbeys and bishoprics. But you can have the rest.' He picked up a jug to refill his glass.

Theodosia let out a breath. He'd forgotten all about her. She went to rise.

'My lord.' Gerald's response drew John's attention back.

She froze, fiddling with her bread as if unconcerned.

'Those rights belong to the Crown.' Gerald wore his most sour look.

John reddened. 'God's eyes, Gerald. The rights of the Crown might as well be mine.'

'You may say, "Might as well," but that is not the same as possession,' said Gerald. 'The land is not yours to give. There are many who already have rights to the land, and many more who might stake a claim. Men like Hugh de Lacy—'

'That festering traitor!' John hurled the jug at Gerald, its contents splashing over all it passed. The clerk ducked, and it smashed on the wall behind him.

The table fell silent, the trickling of wine making its way to the floor in small rivulets the only sound.

Theodosia did not dare to make a move now.

John's good temper had shifted with the speed and strength of the very drunk. 'He knew my plans – I'd swear my life on it. So he ran away like the cowardly cur he is. Fighting for my father, his wife says? I believe that as much as I believe a woman would open her legs to him without gold in her pocket. Or a knife to her throat.' He stood up from the table, with a loud scrape of his chair. 'Now he's out there, scheming and plotting and conniving to stop my progress.' He paced and all eyes followed him. 'Waiting to make his strike, the cursed snake that he is.'

Theodosia's gaze locked on him too, tensed for what John might do in a rage like this.

'We could hunt him down, my lord,' said Walter, not obviously less sober than John. 'You could join me. And we wouldn't only take his hand.'

Murmurs of agreement met his words, with feet stamping, and fists and goblets struck on the tabletop in a rousing clamour.

John nodded with vigour, retaking his seat as he held up one hand to silence them again. 'I have much to consider about where we fight next and who we chop to pieces in our victory.' His bloodshot eyes had the shine of fever, but it was a glow stoked by his rage. 'I also have much to consider about what to do with de Lacy's wife.' He chewed his lip, frowning. 'Gerald, you said at Windsor that the Irish have a reputation for treachery and guile?'

'That is the truth, my lord,' said Gerald.

'Well, Eimear O'Connor is one of them. You saw her today, where she would kiss the hand of the King of Munster, even in death.' John spat on the floor. 'She hates our success.'

'As de Lacy will too,' said Walter.

'Precisely.' John helped himself to more wine, slopping it messily as he poured. 'We cannot afford the risk of her sending information to him.'

'Which she may have already,' said Walter.

'Agreed.' John tapped the tabletop with his fingers. 'I'm going to have her brought within this keep and held here under close watch. Then I can take my time finding out what she knows and what she doesn't.' He smiled. 'I can be very persuasive.'

Theodosia stiffened. She knew the terror of a woman who is at the mercy of murderous men, men who would torture for sport in the worst of ways before they killed. She could not sit by while it was planned for another of her sex. But what in the name of the Virgin could she do?

Gerald raised his voice in disapproval. 'My lord, I would advise caution. Eimear O'Connor is of noble birth.'

John rolled his eyes. 'Noble *Irish* birth. A savage spawned by savages.'

'Nevertheless. You do not want to antagonise the Irish any more than is necessary.'

John drew breath to dismiss the argument.

'My lord.' Theodosia used her will to keep her hands, her voice steady. 'May I make a suggestion?'

'Who asked you to speak?' John looked as if he couldn't believe her forwardness.

Gerald gaped at her, appalled.

'I am guided by God, as always, my lord.' Theodosia prayed God did, at this moment, direct her. 'I know from my time in the Church that people will say much when they pray.'

John continued to stare as if she were a cat that spoke.

'I could pray regularly with my lady in her captivity, my lord.' Theodosia pressed on. 'I may find a way of truly knowing her heart while helping her soul on the path to God's forgiveness.'

'God, eh?' John raked a hand through his hair. 'I believe He mocks me right now. Only one woman at my feast, and she's a nun.' He grinned round at his friends. 'And a talkative nun at that. The worst type.'

His reward was more laughter as Theodosia's shoulders tensed at his ignorant jibe.

Theobald Walter pointed the greasy capon leg he held at John. 'Might be worth a try, though.' He interrupted himself with a belch.

'I agree,' came Gerald's swift remark. 'I of course apologise for Sister Theodosia's rudeness. However, I believe there is value in what she says. She may have found a way to get what you want, without bloodshed that could terribly tarnish your noble name.'

'Hear, hear,' said Walter. 'And, John, it means you and I can seek out some real opponents. Like McCarthy.'

A new drunken roar met his words, and John threw a fist in the air, shouting for more wine.

Theodosia bit her lip. Her half-brother had avoided responding to the suggestion that he should go and fight. She felt Gerald's eyes on her.

'You will still attend to me,' he said. 'But a goodly suggestion. Praise God for His intervention.'

'Praise God indeed, brother.' Now she had to tell Benedict. She crossed herself. She would need God's help a little more.

'You've done *what*?' Palmer could scarce believe he'd heard Theodosia's words right.

'Shh. I had to do something.' Theodosia looked around to make sure no one had overheard his angry remark.

For Palmer, the hours that Theodosia spent at John's feast had crawled by. She'd been summoned there by Gerald, and Palmer had only been able to watch in dread as she left with him. Palmer had had no idea of what was happening. No idea except what usually went on at such gatherings. And John hosted this one. Now the relief he'd felt on seeing her descend the steps on the lumpen shadow that was the motte in deep dusk was gone.

She went on. 'I feared for Eimear's safety, even for her life, to the depths of my soul.'

Shaking his head, Palmer lowered his voice. 'John wouldn't dare touch her. She's of royal blood.'

'John does not see her in that light. He called her a treacherous savage.'

'She's no savage. Fierce, more like.' He remembered Eimear's words as he left her at her tent: *'If you dare to fetch me for such shame again, I'll have your eyes. But not before I have your hide as a cloak.'* Palmer's jaw set at the memory of the look with which Eimear delivered her promise to him. 'And she is the wife of a nobleman.'

'A nobleman who is not here, Benedict. John knows that, which is why I intervened to prevent any actions he might take.'

'If I've learned one thing about the King's son, it's that he says a great deal and does very little.' Palmer snorted. 'He's good at drinking and shouting and hiding, but that's about all.'

'He was indeed very drunk, and he sidestepped a request to fight alongside one of his friends.' Theodosia's brow furrowed. 'Then perhaps he will not carry this out. Maybe I did act too soon.'

'Perhaps?' Palmer let out a long breath. 'It's bad enough that you've been trying to get information from John without him knowing. Now you're working for him too.'

'Yet by doing this, I may be helping the King.' Her brow cleared. 'I could discover the proof about de Lacy through Eimear.'

'I would wager that Eimear would allow nothing to be discovered unless she orders it. Theodosia, you're only doing this because you thought that it would help her, remember?' Palmer fixed her with a look that allowed no argument. 'No more plans, no schemes that I find out about afterwards. You pray with her as you've agreed. That's all.'

Her grey eyes met his. 'You think I've been foolish.'

'No. Foolhardy.' He looked around. No one could see them in the darkness. He raised her hand to his and pressed his mouth to it for a moment, drinking in her scent. 'Which is why I love you.' He let her go, his heart hurting. 'But for all that's holy: no more. This is all too dangerous.'

'Sister!' A tremulous call came from the top of the steps. 'I fear a fall in this darkness.'

Theodosia shook her head. 'Gerald. I must go.' She passed Palmer with a whisper: 'You came to save me when no one else would. I love you too. With all my heart.' Then she was gone.

Of course he'd saved her. Would still lay down his life for her in a heartbeat.

Palmer tipped his head back and took great breaths of the damp night air. A gust of wind rustled the dark trees that surrounded the camp, the darkness of nightfall now complete.

The darkness into which Hugh de Lacy had disappeared. To what end, Palmer didn't know. The threat without. Now, with John's rash actions towards Eimear, the threat within.

And him, Palmer, caught in the middle. Worse, far worse, sending a fear that gnawed at his innards: Theodosia too.

Chapter Eleven

Palmer climbed the mud-slicked steps of the wide ladder that led to the wooden watchtower above the bailey gate, careful of his step. The low clouds of the last few days had brought yet more rain, and the soaked treads might as well have been oiled.

A forlorn voice floated down to him. 'The blessings of the feast of Saint John the Baptist to you, Sir Benedict.'

'And to you, Simonson. How goes the watch?' He climbed onto the planks of the floor of the tower as the younger man, hunched against the coolness of the damp, nodded a greeting.

'All quiet, Palmer.' He held a spear but used it as a leaning post. 'Don't think it'll be like that at Ardfinnan Castle. The Lord John's men looked out for more Irish blood when they left.'

'That they did.' Palmer had watched them depart earlier in an orderly formation, sent on their way by an excited John. No question of the Lord of Ireland joining them to swell the ranks at Ardfinnan. John remained secure behind walls, as he always did; his fighting words never more than empty bluster.

'I swear I regret not being picked to go with them. Or with Theobald Walter: he's gone to claim his new lands in Munster.' Simonson gave a wistful sigh. 'Think of the glory they'll bring.'

'Glory? Not always the case, I'm afraid.' But the call of battle had tugged at him too. The mailed knights, the keen horses, the shine of ready weapons, the gleam of polished shields: all brought an urge he'd thought behind him. No mind. His place was here.

'Hard to believe it's summer.' Simonson stamped his feet, a long shiver passing through him. 'Can't wait to finish my watch. My belly's empty. The only thing filling it is cold. Hot food and a warm tent. That's what I need.'

Palmer caught back a smile at the forlorn look on Simonson's big face. So much for the man's urge to go into battle. 'You've only a couple of hours to go. And those fires aren't cooking much at the moment.' From where he stood on high, he could see each sulking pile of wood in the bailey, belching smoke into the wet air. Except for one. One that sent up a stronger plume. Behind a group of tents. He frowned. 'Who's built a fire so close to the wall?'

'Oh. I don't know.'

Of course you don't. Palmer set off along the wall walk to get a better look, Simonson trailing behind him.

A movement in a huge, heavily leafed oak tree a few yards beyond the ditch caught his eye. A branch, moving abruptly, though the rest of the tree stayed still. Then he saw it. A man daubed in mud, his gaze locking on Palmer's.

'Down!' Palmer dropped.

Too late.

A wooden dart flew through the air, its wicked point burying in Simonson's shoulder.

Simonson squealed, his eyes wide in shock as his hands flew from his spear.

Palmer yanked him to the floor, as dart after dart whipped over the wall.

Screams and yells shrilled from the bailey below.

Tibberaghny was under attack.

Theodosia entered the stuffy room high in the keep, her hands clasped, head bowed in respect. 'I have come to pray with you, my lady.'

Eimear turned from the narrow window, her pale skin even paler from the number of days she had been incarcerated by John. 'As you do every day, sister. And I tell you, as I do every day, that I pray in private.'

'As you wish, my lady. Then I shall pray here alone, and for your soul.' Theodosia settled on her knees on the hard floor. The sparse room had no luxuries such as a faldstool, with a straw bed and a small chest the only visible possessions. She crossed herself as she removed her paternoster from her belt.

'And what else do you pray for?'

'My lady?' Theodosia looked up to see Eimear step before her, arms folded.

'Do you pray for the victory of the Lord John's men at Ardfinnan? That they take all the Irish lives, return with hands as trophies to be used for his disrespectful jests?' Her look pinned Theodosia.

'No, my lady. I pray for the souls of those who have perished.'

'The souls of those who would tear this land to shreds.' Eimear said the words as if she tasted poison. 'You can see why I would never pray with you. Sister.'

Theodosia's chest tightened. She would not allow her faith to be dismissed like this. 'No, my lady. I pray for the souls of all who have perished. Including McCarthy, King of Desmond.'

Eimear's eyebrows arched. 'Why would you do such a thing? He is your enemy. You should rejoice in his death, celebrate his body's dismemberment. As did the Lord John.'

'I could never rejoice in such acts.' Theodosia gripped her paternoster hard.

'If you ever fought in battle, even witnessed a battle, perhaps you would.'

Theodosia's tone tightened along with her fingers. 'Believe me, my lady: I have fought.' Taken the lives of others. 'I have witnessed the brutality of murder.' Her Lord Becket, his body carved up before her horrified sight at Canterbury. 'I can only pray for those who have suffered it. All those.' The string snapped, scattering her beads across the floor. She shook away the old grief. 'And I can promise you, I ask God to forgive the Lord John for his wicked treatment of the body of the King of Munster.' She had to stop; she was saying too much. She bent to scrabble for the beads, collecting them into her cupped palm.

Eimear stopped her with a raised hand. 'Listen.'

Theodosia halted. Her stomach turned over. Screams. Yells. And not only the ones from a camp in panic. The unmistakeable sound of those calling for blood.

Eimear hurried back to the window. 'Ah.' She let out a long, slow breath. 'They come.'

Palmer swore hard. The trees, they'd come from the trees. Just like de Lacy had said: *'If I were you, I'd get the men you do control to cut some more of those trees down.'* And Palmer hadn't. Not yet. So de Lacy had known, forcurse him. Known what was going to happen.

'Get under here.' Palmer hauled Simonson back to the shelter of the gate tower as more sharp wooden missiles pelted down.

'It hurts.' The younger man breathed fast, shallow, his eyes fixed on the weapon stuck in his shoulder. 'Am I going to die?'

'No.' Palmer yanked the dart free in one movement to Simonson's shriek. 'At least not at this minute.' He ripped his own kerchief off and thrust it into the injured man's hand. 'Put that to your wound, it'll do until the barber-surgeon can see to you.' He rose and headed for the ladder.

'What are you doing?' Simonson pressed his palm to his wound as blood seeped around it. 'You'll be killed if you go down there.'

'Not if I can help it.' Palmer doubled his cloak over his head and half-slid down the steps in his haste, a dart slicing all the skin from his knuckles as he landed at the bottom. Cursing, he sucked the blood away.

'They're in the trees!' His shouts merely joined the chaos.

Men ran, screamed, yelled, ran for cover, as the sky spat down yet more sharpened darts, the sheer number of their vicious points finding targets in those that fled.

The air above him moved, and he jerked to one side, the sharp wooden missile impaling the muddy ground instead of his flesh.

He grabbed an abandoned leather water pail, tipping out the contents. Propping it over his head with his bent elbow gave him a bit of cover. He ran for one of the tents where he knew arms were stored, the clatter of wood on hide loud above his head.

As he burst in, he saw others had come to find weapons too. But not many. And they grabbed at whatever they could, shouting and arguing with no one listening.

Palmer blew a sharp whistle with two fingers, and all eyes went to him, every man abruptly silent. 'Sir Benedict Palmer. Who amongst you is a knight?' He knew the answer as his gaze swept over untrained bodies and unwise choices of weapon.

'Then I'm in charge of this defence.'

One man opened his mouth to argue.

Palmer drew his sword in a swift movement.

The man shut it again.

'We haven't much time,' continued Palmer. 'The Irish have set a fire at the north wall of the bailey, nearest the forest. They have men in the trees with darts, so they're free to burn. As soon as the wall comes down, they'll be in.' He scanned the group. 'Now, have I any archers?'

Three men raised a hand.

'That's all?'

'The Lord John sent the best fighters to Ardfinnan, Sir Benedict,' said one. 'There are a few more here, but I fear they've been struck down by the enemy's attack.'

Palmer let loose a string of curses. For a brief moment, he was tempted to haul John from the safety of the keep where he no doubt cowered. Haul him out and use him as a shield against the deadly Irish darts.

'Does that mean all is lost, Sir Benedict?' The man who asked had managed to jam a helmet on but hadn't laced it tight under his chin.

Palmer couldn't add to the hopeless terror already clouding the man's eyes. He too tasted the fear of lack of hope, not for himself, but for Theodosia.

'Of course not. Now put your damn helmet on, man. Same for the rest of you. You can't fight with a sharpened stick in your head.'

Theodosia ran to join Eimear at the window, her heart racing.

'Stay well back.' Eimear matched her command with her own action. 'Even this narrow window is a target.'

The clatter of wood on wood on the wall outside confirmed it.

Theodosia started, though Eimear did not react. She peered past Eimear to the camp far below and a sight from hell met her vision.

Smoke covered the whole camp, the shouting figures running through it like spirits trying to flee damnation. She could not make anyone out, could not see if Benedict was amongst the crowd. Then one fell with a wail, sinking from sight, then another and another.

Her hands went to her mouth. 'What is happening?'

'The Irish are using darts, and they possess great skill with them.' Eimear's stare outside remained fixed. 'But we are still safe in here. For now.'

As if brought forth by her words, yet more spines of sharpened wood showered down, some piercing even the roofs of the tents.

People ran from the punctured canvas, making for the steps of the motte and the safety of the keep, clutching whatever they could over their heads to protect themselves from the deadly onslaught.

Then she remembered. 'Dear God. The clerk Gerald.'

Eimear looked at her. 'What of him?'

'He will be in terrible peril. I have to bring him to safety.'

'He is a man, sister. He can see to himself.'

'He is not a fighting man; he is a man of God. And he cannot defend himself. One of his arms is useless.'

'Then he will meet his fate.' Eimear spoke as if Gerald might miss a meal.

'I do not believe in fate, my lady.' Theodosia hurried to the door. 'I believe in doing what I can.'

'Sister!'

Ignoring Eimear's call, she hauled the door shut behind her, praying she still had time.

The wall burnt brightly now, as the wood had properly taken hold.

As he crouched beneath a shell of shields, Palmer's eyes streamed in the smoke, and he rubbed at them hard, cursing his lack of his neckerchief. 'Keep firing.' He called his order to his small group of archers, huddled on the wall walk, doing their best to strike down those in the trees.

One arrow hit home, then another. Two bodies dropped from the branches with a howl.

'And more!' He broke into a spasm of coughing. If they could lessen the onslaught of the darts, they might have a chance at putting out the fire. But he had too few archers, and they had too few skills.

A movement caught his eye. Farther along the wall. Hands gripping from outside. The top of a long-haired head. A climber.

'There!' Palmer's shout and point had the archer spin and fire.

The intruder fell from sight. Hit or not, it didn't matter. They'd driven him back.

Yet another arrow loosed into the trees and fell short, its soaked feathers limp and useless.

The wall shook hard in a loud, deep thud.

'What's that?' said the man next to Palmer.

'They're testing a battering ram.'

Another thud.

Palmer watched the bounce of the wood. 'It'll hold for a bit.'

'And then?' The man's mouth fell open in dread.

Palmer went to reply but a familiar voice interrupted him.

'Palmer, let me in. Quickly.' Gasping in fear, Simonson forced his way into the group, his shoulder bloody and his spear in one hand.

'I told you to stay where you were.'

'I know. But I brought this. I thought it might help.'

'One spear?' The other man's mouth gaped even wider. 'By the blood of the Virgin, we're all dead.' He pushed Palmer aside.

'Stop!' Palmer roared as loud as he could as the man broke from the shields' protection, heading for the ladder in the watchtower.

Too late. A dart pierced his neck, then another his thigh. He fell with a scream to the ground below and lay there twitching as his life left his body.

A ripple went through the group.

Palmer could tell what it was: defeat, taking hold of men's hearts and minds before it froze their bodies like winter ice. He could not allow it. 'Keep firing!' He forced every ounce of power into his order. 'We need to take out those darts.'

A couple of arrows flew. Did nothing.

Palmer's hand went to his sword. Once the wall came down, he'd do what he could here, then head for the keep to protect Theodosia. Thank the Almighty, she went to pray up there at this hour.

Simonson nudged him. 'Palmer.'

'Keep your spear, Simonson. You'll need it.' Palmer focused once more on the archers. 'And again!'

'I just wondered.'

He glanced at the big young man. 'What?' If the man said another word about his spear, Palmer would throw him to the Irish right now. 'Again!'

Simonson's reply sent the air from his lungs.

Palmer stared at him. 'Say that again.'

'I just wondered,' said Simonson, 'why aren't you using the crossbows?'

Chapter Twelve

High on the motte, Theodosia halted at the gate of the keep, holding on to the shelter of the high palisade with sweated palms. Men pushed past her in a blur of yelling forms, running, staggering, not even noticing her as they fought to get into shelter and safety. So many were injured, many grievously, and she knew still more lay in the thick haze of the bailey below.

She could see the tent she shared with Gerald from here. Yet between her and it lay the exposed steps, then a stretch of open ground, shrouded in smoke, soft with mud underfoot and death descending from the skies along with the rain. She would be struck down, becoming one of the huddled forms she could see on the steps and on the nearby ground, twisting in agony, or terribly, horribly still.

Then she saw it, on the muddy slope of the motte, a few steps down, so caked in soil she almost missed it. A shield, still clutched in the hand of a man who lay without moving, his body pierced so many times that he would never rise again.

She had to do this. With a deep breath and a plea to God, she loosed her hold. And ran for the steps.

A few strides. Pain on her face. She screamed and ducked, but it was only the driving rain. Her feet met the first step, slick with rainwater and blood, then the next and the next.

Men still ran up, shoving, pushing, not even seeing her.

She fell to her knees as the rain slashed against her and grabbed the shield, fighting down her bile as she yanked it from the dead man's fingers.

But it was so heavy. Too heavy. No. It was stuck, stuck in the mud.

Another dart swished down, burying itself in the poor dead man with a noise that could be a knife in raw meat.

She tugged hard, then harder.

The shield came loose, sending her off balance. She flung it above her head as a missile hit it in a ringing strike.

Theodosia looked up at the gate to the keep. She should go back. To be out here was insanity, risking her life for a man whom she had only known for a short while, who was neither blood nor friend. But she had to because of what she did know. She knew the absolute terror of helplessness, to have to wait for death in the full knowledge that she could not even defend herself. Shaking hard, she got to her feet. She could not condemn another to that hell while she hid, safe.

May God protect me.

She scrambled down the open flight, staggering, stumbling as the noise of fighting, of death, buffeted her as rain and missiles struck the shield above her. With a renewed burst of speed across the smoke-filled flat of the bailey in a crouching shamble, she was there. She flung herself into the tent, her breath loud in wheezing gasps.

'Get out, you devil!'

Gerald. Her heart surged in relief. But she could not see him.

'It is I, brother. Sister Theodosia.'

A rustling came from underneath the open lid of a large chest. 'I'm down here, God help me.'

'Are you hurt?'

'No.' The clerk's face, pale with terror, showed in the shadow. 'It is a miracle I am not.'

'Indeed, thank the Almighty.' She hunkered down, her legs like water. 'I have come to get you to the safety of the keep.'

'Out there?' If anything, his face paled even more. 'Up to the motte?'

'Yes. I have this shield.'

The cacophony outside increased, with a new wave of yells and shrieks.

'The raiders may be finding their way in.' Theodosia swallowed down a lump of new fear. 'The keep is the only place we will be safe. Brother, we need to hurry.'

'I cannot hurry. You will have to help me to my feet.'

Theodosia laid the shield down with a silent prayer that God would watch over them for a precious few minutes. Flipping the lid of the chest closed, she held out one arm. 'Hold on to me. I will assist you to rise.'

With an array of gasps and objections from the clerk, she got him upright.

'I cannot run.' He shook his head. 'Not when I'm out there. I cannot fall on my bad arm.'

'Then we shall walk as quickly as we can.' Picking up the shield, she stepped beside him.

Gerald clung to her with his good arm, his weight dragging from her as she raised the heavy shield with both hands, her muscles protesting from her double burden. She doubted she could hold both for long. But she had to try. No: she had to succeed.

'As quick as you can, brother. I implore you.' She went to lead him to the door.

And froze.

Entering the tent, axe raised and ready, crept an Irish warrior.

Now it wasn't only darts that fell from the trees. Men fell too.

Palmer loaded his own crossbow yet again, shouting to his men. 'Keep firing. Just keep firing.'

Many bolts went wide and wild, but enough were reaching their target.

He could see the shadowy figures climbing down through the branches, fast and sure, as they abandoned their posts.

The hard click of another bow sounded next to Palmer.

Its bolt hit home, an Irishman sliding down through a tree with a howl that cut off as he loosed his hold and fell.

'Got him!' Simonson bellowed with pride as he balled a fist in triumph.

Palmer didn't stop him. It might be a waste of energy in battle, but this ragged crew were no army. If the man got the miracle of a lucky shot, then so be it. Palmer let loose another bolt, and it hammered into a dangling limb. And he had Simonson to thank for knowing the whereabouts of a pile of crossbows and bolts in one of the stores.

One of the archers didn't need luck. He reloaded rapidly and smoothly and shot with deadly accuracy.

'I think they're withdrawing, Sir Benedict.' He didn't pause, his hands and eyes sure in their purpose.

'My thoughts too. But that wall is still burning.' He nodded to the man. 'I need your cover.'

The man nodded back, increasing his shots as Palmer straightened up with caution to look over the sharply pointed top of the wall, his shield held tight to protect him. For the first time, no clatter of darts landed on or near him.

Below, blurred in the smoke and heat, what looked like a large, hide-backed creature with no head struck a hewn log against the blazing wall again with a muffled shout made up of many voices.

Palmer dropped back, coughing. 'This is what I want you to do.' He gave a stream of rapid orders as the Irish battered the wall again. 'And keep that crossbow going. Aim down too.'

'Yes, Sir Benedict.' The skilled archer kept up his pace, as sure in his shots as Simonson's were wide, while the other men rushed to act on Palmer's command.

Palmer used his own crossbow again, clutching for the top of the wall as it shook again in a massive blow.

The archer swore and Simonson's legs went from beneath him. 'It's not going to hold much longer.'

'Keep firing.' Palmer raised his voice to shout down to where he'd dispatched some of the other men. 'Get a move on!'

'We are, God rot it, we are.' A heavily sweated man heaved himself back up the ladder, rope coiled across his chest and one shoulder, closely followed by another.

They ran along the wall walk to the shelter of the continued firing by Palmer and the archer.

Palmer uncoiled the rope from the first man in rapid movements. 'You do the same,' he said to the second. 'Keep at least three lengths wound round you.' He dropped the rope below.

The unseen Irish struck the wall again, the vibration shaking the wall walk under Palmer's feet. 'Hurry it up down there!'

The call he needed to hear floated back up to him.

'Ready, Sir Benedict!'

'Time to pull, men. On my count. It has to be together.'

The men nodded.

'Now.'

With set arms, they pulled in unison, veins standing out on their foreheads.

Palmer dropped his crossbow to help as another strike landed against the beleaguered wall. 'Again. Pull!'

And another.

'Again.' The sinews in his arms threatened to snap. The other men's faces told him they neared their limit too.

'And again.'

Another blow thudded into the wall, this time ending in a loud crack.

'May the devil take them.' Simonson dropped to his knees. 'They're breaking it down.'

'They're not in yet. One last time, men.' Palmer hauled hard and their prize came level with the wall walk. A steaming iron cooking vat, filled with gallons of water that had sat and boiled unattended from before the attack began.

The wood of the wall walk creaked under the strain of the new weight.

'Palmer, the whole thing's going to come down.'

'Not yet it's not, Simonson.' Sweat trickled into Palmer's eyes, but he had no hand free to wipe it. 'We need your bulk. This thing is red hot.' He nodded to the other men. 'Up and straight over. The whole blessed thing.'

The wall shook and cracked from another loud bang.

'Now,' said Palmer. And grabbed, bracing against the pain.

His palms seared. Scalding water sloshed onto him, the others, as they wrested the thing to the top of the wall.

The vat tottered above them. It was coming back down on top of them.

'Get over!' Whether Simonson yelled it over or whether the man's panicked shove was enough, Palmer didn't know.

All he knew was it dropped from sight onto the Irish below.

The weight, the heat, the water: the screams told him it had done enough.

Palmer picked up his crossbow. 'Time to finish them off.'

He'd done it.

'May God help me!' Gerald clutched even harder on to Theodosia.

The long-bearded warrior stepped farther into the tent, his axe tight in his heavily muscled hold.

Theodosia stared at the sharp-bladed weapon, then him, then it again, terror flooding her veins. 'Please do not hurt us, sir,' she said, lips dry. 'We are no threat to you.' She held the shield with the tightest grip she possessed.

The man answered her in his own tongue.

'I am afraid I do not understand,' she said. 'Perhaps if—'

His axe struck hard against the shield.

She screamed – Gerald too – as it was wrenched from her grasp and landed in a far corner.

The warrior stepped towards them, with a longer stream of words this time, his deadly weapon firm in one hand.

Pain sparked through Theodosia's hands, but she cared not. She could not speak, could not scream, could not even breathe as the man advanced.

'Help! Murder!' Gerald's thin shout did not even fill the tent and would make no impression on the noise outside.

The warrior raised his axe.

Theodosia braced in terror, with a last prayer for her children.

Then he froze.

A sharp voice, issuing a string of words that sounded the same as the man's, came from the door of the tent. A woman's voice.

Eimear marched in, her breath fast, her arm outstretched in an accusing point at the warrior.

Theodosia gasped in a breath as Gerald let out a long cry.

'Now what's to become of us?'

The man lowered his weapon, turning away to face Eimear.

She stood before him, continuing her tirade.

A great trembling took hold of Theodosia. They were saved.

Eimear's words, delivered in a sharp tone, continued to pierce the air as she flung her arm to gesture towards the door.

But Gerald was moving too, silently, his good hand raised.

Theodosia caught the flash of a blade. 'No!'

The man half-turned at her scream. Too late.

Gerald sank his pointed knife into the man's back, and he crumpled from his knees, with a useless swipe at the clerk.

Eimear gave an anguished shout. 'What have you done?'

'Sent a devil to hell.' Gerald waved his bloodied knife at Eimear. 'Stop where you are, or you will join him.' He made for the door with surprising speed. 'Guards! There is treachery within! Treachery!'

'Brother, no.' Theodosia went to halt him. Her legs would not hold her. She sank to the ground, the horror that was the murdered man's lifeless stare inches from her own.

Gerald's calls continued to ring from outside in a dreadful chorus in her head. *Treachery.*

Chapter Thirteen

'The rain's stopped too.' Simonson puffed worse than an old cart-horse as he laboured. 'It's a good omen, isn't it, Palmer?'

'It's making for hot work. That's all.' Palmer dug his spade into the soft soil yet again as the midday sun pounded down, the air sticky in the heat.

'I think it's God. He's smiling on us for our win.' Despite his injury, Simonson still revelled in the victory like he'd done it alone.

'I hope He is.' Palmer brushed sweat and plaguing flies from his forehead with his throbbing hands. 'It's making this job much worse.' He hated the aftermath of battle and the stench most of all. Bodies, blood, men who'd voided at their moment of death: all clogged his nose and mouth. Only burying it all in the earth would remove it.

Around him, others did the same, the men silent as they covered over the faces of those they had journeyed here with. Men who would never return home.

'It is hard in this heat, no mistake,' said Simonson. 'But I don't see why we have to bury the Irish too.'

'We bury all the dead.' Palmer rammed the shovel into the ground again and flung another shovelful onto the grave's mound.

'Well, I think we should leave them to rot,' said Simonson. 'They attacked us, and—'

'Shut up.' Palmer pointed his spade at Simonson. 'What did you think would happen when you joined the Lord John? That the Irish would simply hand over their land to you with a smile and a bow? This is what conquest means.' He finished the grave with a last load of his spade. 'You should be begging God that you don't end up in one of these pits next.'

Palmer walked off without waiting for a reply. Simonson blabbered like a dolt, and he wanted to hear no more of it. The number of dead wrenched at his innards. He could have, should have done more to secure this camp. The victory had been a lucky one, nothing more. He too could have been lying in one of those mounds. As could Theodosia. And if she was, he might as well be. Exhausted though he'd been from the long hours of the battle, he'd not been able to rest for a second until he'd had reliable word that she was safe. By then, sleep had left him, and he'd turned instead to burying the dead, a back breaking task that had taken almost two days.

He passed back over the water-filled ditch and in through the gate under the watchful eye of guards armed with crossbows.

Subdued men slowly restored order to the bailey, repairing the burned wall and mending the damaged tents. Those with bad injuries lay in the shade of one. A small group of Irish prisoners sat murmuring amongst themselves in a space of open ground, their hands and legs in chains.

'Sir knight.' Theodosia stepped from a tent to his left.

Palmer's stomach lurched anew. The sheen of blood stained the skirt of her habit. 'You are hurt, sister?'

She glanced down, then met his look with a shake of her head. 'Praise God, no. I have been helping to attend to those who are and praying with them.' Her gaze went to his hands, wrapped in soiled bandages, and she frowned. 'As I should attend to you. Sit there. I will not be a moment.'

Her order allowed no argument. Besides, he ached to talk to her, to be with her. The time for that could so easily have passed. Forever. He took a place on the ground in the welcome shade of the tent, making sure he kept his distance from any prying ears or eyes.

Theodosia arrived next to him, carrying a bowl of water and some clean linen. 'Let me see.' She laid his hands on her lap, undoing their wraps with care. His heart soared at her living touch against his once more.

She gave a soft gasp. 'Oh, Benedict.'

The wounds across his knuckles where he'd been hit by the dart pulsed with pain. Large blisters had risen on his palms from the scalding water, and digging for hours had broken them open. 'These will heal. I was lucky.'

'This does not look like good luck to me.' She wetted some of the linen and picked up one of his hands, dabbing at his ruined skin with gentle care.

'It is.' He met her gaze with his most serious look. 'Bad luck would have had me dead and buried. And you.'

Reaching into her belt pouch, she drew out a jar of herbed goose fat. 'I know.' She shuddered and glanced over at the group of prisoners. 'I know I had God's protection.' She spread a thin layer of her ointment over his skin.

Palmer frowned. 'The Irish got as far as the keep?'

Theodosia wouldn't meet his eye as she wound fresh linen onto his right hand. 'It matters not.'

'Theodosia, what has happened to you?'

'Pay no heed now. Please.' She moved on to his left. 'Please also believe me when I say that I am completely unharmed.' Her glance flicked past his shoulder and her face changed. 'What is happening?'

Palmer looked around. To his astonishment, men scurried to and fro, setting up tables and laying them with fine cloth and trenchers and goblets.

'What is happening, indeed?' He got to his feet.

'Benedict, I am not finished.' She stood too.

'You've fixed me better than a barber-surgeon, sister.' He gave her a small bow, which drew a quick smile from her.

Palmer tied off the last of the bandage himself as he went over to one of the men, Theodosia matching his quick pace.

'What are you doing, fellow?'

'By order of the Lord John,' said the man. 'He has commanded a feast.'

'A feast?' came Palmer's surprised echo, along with the same from Theodosia. 'Has he lost his wits?'

'You'd have to ask the Lord John, sir knight.' The man carried on with his setting.

Theodosia squeezed Palmer's arm. 'This man does not lie.'

A number of servants processed from the far side of the camp, bearing piled platters of roasted meat. Others wrested in a couple of large barrels.

'Now we celebrate!' John descended the steps of the motte, his red hair reflecting in the sunshine, his fine white robe gleaming in the sun. Behind him walked the few of his inner circle that had not left to fight at Ardfinnan, cheering his name and his victory, a silent Gerald bringing up the rear.

'The clerk seems to be managing better now.' Palmer glanced down to see the flash of disapproval in Theodosia's eyes.

'He does.'

Palmer itched to find out why she looked so annoyed, but too many stood too close, drawn by John's shouts.

'There's ale for all my brave fighters.' John raised his hand to a ragged cheer, then clicked his fingers to a man who opened up the first barrel with a swift blow of a small axe. The cheers became louder. 'And, for my brave companions, a place at my table.' John sat, waving those who'd hidden in the keep with him to their seats. 'Even the injured royal clerk felled an Irishman. That's how good they are at fighting!'

A burst of laughter met his words.

Palmer looked at Theodosia, who stared ahead. 'What's been going on?' he said through clenched teeth.

'Not now,' she whispered.

John joined the laugh, then scanned the faces at his table. He raised his voice again. 'Where is Sir Benedict Palmer?'

The noise lessened as those at the table swapped curious looks. All other eyes went to Palmer.

'He's there, my lord!' Palmer recognised one of the archers' shout.

He went to duck into the nearby tent.

A huge huzzah went up, on and on, with men chanting his name, whistling, clapping.

Palmer wished he still had his spade, that he could shovel earth over himself and hide from view. He didn't deserve this. Too much had gone wrong. Too many had died.

The chorus only died away when John sliced the air with his hand.

'Well, well, Palmer.' The King's son's face had tightened, though he showed his teeth in a smile. 'It seems you are quite the hero. Come and sit. There.' He pointed to the seat farthest from him and in the lowliest spot.

Palmer hesitated.

'You must.' Theodosia breathed her command, not heard by anyone else.

Palmer walked forward to take his seat. His seat at the cowards' table.

Such a reward could only come from John.

John drank deep from his wine. So annoying that Palmer had turned out to be the big man he hadn't liked the look of, the one who'd brought back that treacherous strumpet Eimear when he'd sent for de Lacy that day.

'You are the most gracious victor, John.' His friend Fitzmiles gave him a broad wink and a snigger.

John hid his smile in his goblet. 'I know what you mean.'

The man, Palmer, stood out at this noble-clad table like a pustule on a diseased whore, with his rank, filthy clothing and his bandaged hands. Still, it worked in his, John's, favour. Other wretches would look on in awe and believe that one day they too could sit alongside those of royal birth.

John picked up a haunch of roasted pork and took a bite of tasty crisped skin. They could wish all they liked. He was doing this once and once only. He had heard that the man called Palmer had fought well. Some even said that Palmer had saved Tibberaghny Castle. John had almost swallowed his tongue in rage when he'd heard that. Then he'd had his brilliant idea: all the men would fight harder if they thought they'd win the prize of feasting with the King's son. He chewed hard and shot a glance at Palmer, rising irritation spoiling his enjoyment of the tasty mouthful. If only Palmer would look a bit happier. The oaf hunched over his food, chewing like a horse in a barn.

'Want some?' Fitzmiles raised his voice and waved a bone at the small herd of Irish prisoners nearby.

John frowned. What was his friend playing at?

'Stick that in your beard!' Fitzmiles threw the bone, hitting one of the chained men with it.

John's laugh broke from him, half-choking him in the process as the rest of the table joined him. Except for Palmer. Good God, the man was irritating. Even the miserable clerk Gerald, sitting next to the obnoxious knight, had raised a smile. Perhaps the clerk had gained a taste for fighting instead of the Bible.

'Glad you've taken battle blood too, Gerald?' called John.

'My lord, I have to insist that I had no other choice of . . .'

John stopped listening. Gerald bored him senseless at the best of times. He'd already heard the man's flowery version of something very simple: Eimear somehow had command over the Irish. Gerald had dispatched an Irish savage. But Palmer had brought his frowning gaze to Gerald as if the clerk spoke of the most important thing in the world. How peculiar.

Fitzmiles interrupted him. 'Still, John, two battles and two victories, eh?'

'And Ardfinnan will make it three!' shouted another man.

John waved a hand, as if it were nothing. Inside, he flushed hot and hard. Everything was proceeding exactly as he'd planned.

Palmer's hands still throbbed. But not as bad as his head. His chest.

The clerk Gerald's terrifying account of what had happened with Theodosia battered inside him. He scanned the people milling about for her, but she appeared to be busying herself with the wounded. He needed to get the truth from her. He didn't believe for a heartbeat that Theodosia had fallen at the Irish man's feet, screaming and renting her clothes in the loss of her sense in terror. That was not his Theodosia. He believed even less that a laughing Eimear had urged the man on. Yet all seemed to accept that Gerald had stabbed the man to death. What Palmer didn't know was what

Theodosia had been doing in Gerald's tent in the bailey. She should have been in the keep with Eimear.

Palmer drained his goblet, aware of eyes on him.

'Drink up, Palmer. Plenty more where that came from.'

The stripling spoke to him like he was a dull-witted child. Sore though his palms were, Palmer would love to throttle the speech from the cowardly little toad. 'Thank you, my lord.' He forced the words out.

John still stared.

Then a voice floated from the watchtower. 'Ardfinnan!'

Palmer looked up to see the guard gesturing hard.

'Open the gate!' shouted the guard. 'The garrison are returned from Ardfinnan!'

John leapt to his feet, all at his table following suit. 'More for the feast! More!'

Huzzahs broke out again, louder than ever as he gestured to all present to gather round.

Palmer let go a long breath of relief. John would get lost in his latest victory. Palmer could leave this ridiculous table and go speak to Theodosia. He'd find out what she'd been doing in that tent. And get to the bottom of what had really gone on in there.

Excitement surged within John as he awaited the opening of the gates. He couldn't have asked for better timing of this latest news. Everyone here had already assembled for celebration. He glanced to his left. He even had a group of Irish prisoners to witness the further defeat of their kind. A tremor passed through him. He truly stood on the edge of greatness.

The gates swung open.

John filled his lungs to lead the cheer. But he could only form a soundless word. *What?*

This time, no orderly line of men. This time, no bearing of spoils. This time, no fists in the air, telling him what he needed to know.

Instead, a tiny knot of humanity that Satan himself would spurn from his clutches. Such wounds. So much blood. The few exhausted horses bearing bodies slung across their backs.

The rising chorus of gasps and mutters from those watching the group's arrival reflected his shock. He forced himself to speak.

'What news of Ardfinnan?' Good: his voice sounded calm. In control.

'News, my lord?' The leader of the group, a knight he didn't recognise, his cheekbone visible in a wide gash to his face, swayed on his feet. 'The news is as you can see. We have brought as many of the dead back as we could. Many, many more lie at Ardfinnan. We have been crushed.'

A stunned quiet enveloped the camp.

Fitzmiles nudged him. 'Say something, John,' he murmured.

John opened his mouth, closed it again, his mind foundering at the terrible news.

Fitzmiles again. 'Anything.'

'Are you sure?'

A muffled laugh came from one of the nearby Irish. John could swear it. Fists clenched, he went to react, but his defeated leader spoke first.

'I'm sure, my lord.' The man stumbled over his words, his hand to his stomach-turning injury.

'What of de Glanville?' Fitzmiles's urgent question turned his innards to water. *Geoffrey.* Son of John's own foster father. He'd forgotten.

The man shook his head, gesturing to farther back in the group.

Four men stepped forward, a crude sling strung between their spears. They laid their burden at John's feet. His beloved Geoffrey lay on the cheap cloth, his noble face sightless and unmoving, his body hideously ruined by his fatal wounds.

'How?' John's voice climbed. 'How?'

'The men of the King of Thomond knew we were coming, my lord.' The leader's voice trembled. 'They were ready for us.'

Great sobs heaved from John, unbidden. He didn't care. This grief was too much. 'Ready?' He marched over to a nearby cart and snatched the coiled whip from the driver's seat. 'Are you ready for this?' He ran at the bearded men in chains, the long, heavy lash snaking out, catching one on his gaping face. 'And this?' Another on his hands as he ducked.

'This?' The ear of a third split with a scream from the man, the others shouting and grasping at each other for cover. 'That's it, herd together like the beasts you are!' His fury strengthened his hand, drove each slash with even greater accuracy. He drew blood, cut skin, on and on till his sobs in his own ears became ragged gasps.

He paused for breath, the whip wet and stained in his hand, his gaze moving over his audience.

Every eye was on him, yet no one said a word. Now they knew who had the power. 'Curs like them' – he nodded at the bleating Irish as he fought for breath – 'cannot defeat my men on their own. Somebody is leading them. And I'll wager I know who.' He spat a wad of spittle from his mouth and pointed at a guard. 'Bring me Eimear O'Connor. Now.'

Palmer kept his face an unmoving mask as two man hauled a struggling Eimear down the steps of the motte.

Standing beside him, Theodosia whispered to him, 'We must do something.'

'No. There's nothing.' Palmer put force into his low tone. 'John is like a foaming dog at the moment.'

'Unhand me. I order you. I can walk unaided.' Eimear's angry orders went unheeded as the men dragged her before the King's son.

'Let her loose for now,' ordered John. 'By the time I'm finished with you, woman, you will be glad of any help you receive.'

Eimear shook the men off, glaring at John. 'You would raise the lash to me?'

'The raising of it is harmless.' John pointed towards the cowering, shuddering Irish. 'It's the lowering that causes problems.'

The shadow of fear flicked across Eimear's face as she saw what he indicated.

Palmer could tell from John's look that he'd seen her reaction. And liked it.

'It's time for you to confess to your spying.' The King's son smiled. 'I might leave some of your flesh on your bones if you do.'

'Spying, my lord?' Eimear's eyes widened. 'I have not—'

'Yes, spying!'

Even Palmer flinched at John's yell.

Eimear kept her silence as John continued, stabbing the air an inch from her face with his coiled whip with each charge. 'Who could know I was sending troops to Ardfinnan? You. Who knew when to attack here? You. Who was in my clerk's tent with an axe-wielding warrior? You.' He clicked his fingers at his guards. 'Tie her to that cart.'

'Do not dare to do this!' Eimear slapped one of the guards across the face.

Ugly jeers broke out.

'Benedict,' came Theodosia's anguished whisper. 'It was not—'

'No. Not now.'

The men wrestled Eimear to the cart as she fought hard. 'You cannot do this! I am the wife of a lord!'

'A lord?' John cracked his weapon loud in a test. 'You mean that traitor de Lacy?'

'My husband is no traitor.'

'The husband who has disappeared.' John gave a wide sweep of his hand. 'The husband who wants to hold his own lands and get his hands on even more. The husband who you are spying for, so he can keep betraying us all!' He slashed his whip at her, uncaring that the guards still tried to secure her.

Eimear screamed now. 'I don't know anything!'

Theodosia yelped in pain.

Palmer looked down at her. A red blotch marked her face, and she raised a hand to it. 'My cheek?'

Something pinged at his head in a sharp nip. *'Ow!'*

Eimear's screams carried on as she still fought those who held her.

A goblet shattered on the table. A bowl.

A few exclamations broke out. More.

A small stone bounced onto the table. Another at Palmer's feet.

Then he knew. He grabbed Theodosia by the shoulders. 'That tent. Right now. No argument.'

'None.'

He thrust her from him and ran towards John. 'My lord! Stop!'

John paused, whip raised for another strike. 'What the devil are you doing, man?'

'Everyone get under cover! Now!' Palmer grabbed hold of John, hauling him near off his feet.

Some acted on Palmer's order. Others stared, perplexed.

'Have you gone mad?' John took a swing at him, drew back for another.

'We're under attack!' More tiny pebbles fell, like the first drops of a storm.

'Get your hands off the Lord John.' A big knight stepped forward. Then with a rap like stone on stone, he fell, half his skull no more with the large rock that had broken it open.

'Slingers!' Palmer yanked John under the shelter of the abandoned banqueting table. 'Get down!'

And the deluge of murdering stone broke above them.

Chapter Fourteen

Theodosia knelt in Eimear's room in the keep, praying in silence as always as the other woman ignored her.

Eimear had come through the latest attack by the Irish unharmed, ducking under the cart as the deadly rain of stones had fallen. In the chaos that followed, John had had to abandon his whipping of her and had ordered her secured in the keep again.

But Theodosia's prayers were not for Eimear today: she prayed for Benedict, over and over, for God's protection, and would do so until his safe return. John, incensed beyond reason at the death of his friend in the fighting near the other castle of Ardfinnan, had assembled a party to travel with him there. And he'd ordered Benedict to join him. So now Benedict travelled through this most perilous land, and she had no way of knowing what might be befalling him. All she could do was wait. The helplessness she had felt as she knelt in the chapel at Sonning flooded back, plaguing her. This time, she received no sign from God. She would have to redouble her efforts and beseech Him day and night.

'You look troubled, sister.'

Theodosia's hands stilled on her beads. 'I do, my lady?'

'Sorely.' Eimear, sat on the bed, eyed her with curiosity. 'My prayers have been of thanks. God watched over me when the stones of the slingers fell. Perhaps you pray for the soul of the Irishman murdered by the clerk, Gerald?'

To her shame, she had forgotten. 'I have neglected to do so. I have had many tasks to which to attend.'

'Believe me, I have prayed for him.' Eimear's look hardened. 'Perhaps you need to pray for Gerald's soul. He killed that man.'

'You spoke to the warrior in your own tongue, which I do not understand and neither does Gerald. He believed there was treachery afoot.'

'You do not speak the language of the Irish either, but you shouted to Gerald not to attack that man. You could tell what was happening, yet he could not?'

Theodosia met Eimear's challenging look with one of her own. 'I believe the warrior would have attacked us both had you not arrived, my lady.'

'My fellow Irishman was going to kill the two of you.' Eimear stated it as one might remark that the wind felt cold. 'He told me so. I ordered him not to. I did not want to see you hurt. As for Gerald, I care nothing.'

'Then I have you to thank for my life.' Theodosia swallowed hard. The encounter had brought death as close as she feared. 'Gerald's too.'

'I will not wait for his thanks. Eternity is only so long.'

'You have mine. With all my heart.'

'Yet your face shows doubt.'

Theodosia hesitated, searching for the right words. 'Your actions surprised me, my lady.'

'You wonder why I did not simply let the axeman kill you and the clerk. Am I correct?'

Theodosia nodded.

'Unlike the Lord John, you have shown my people respect with your marking of their passing. You come here to me, day after day, to try to join me in prayer, even though I push you away. Not many people stand up to me. But you have. Then, with no thought for your own safety, you run to the aid of that miserable Gerald. I admire you and am grateful for your attempts.' Eimear put her head to one side. 'All of this from a woman who is not an abbess or a noblewoman, but who is a mere sister. So you intrigue me also.'

'I seek my guidance from my God, my lady.' Theodosia kept her expression unchanged, even as her heart quickened beneath her habit as Eimear edged towards the truth.

'Then you seek well. I do not see much of God's guidance in the actions of others that King Henry has sent here. I see land theft and murder and more.'

'Your beloved husband is one of Henry's men, my lady.' Theodosia's pulse tripped faster still at the chance to steer their exchange to de Lacy. 'Do you not see God in his life?'

'Hugh de Lacy is my husband, yes. As for beloved?' She gave a humourless laugh. 'No.'

'That is indeed a sad situation for you to be in, my lady.'

'Advice on men from a nun.' Eimear shook her head.

'I do not presume to offer advice, my lady. Only to listen.' Theodosia hesitated. To bring up her old life as an anchoress could be a risk, but she had to take it. 'I spent some years in a church's cell, hearing the secrets of the heart from many people. To lay down the burden of unhappiness can be a comfort.'

'Oh, I'm sure it can. For most. But tell me, sister: how many wives came to you to tell you that they had tried to murder their husbands on their wedding night?'

Though the thick canopy of trees and tall bushes in full leaf cut out much of the sun, sweat still coated Palmer's body. The heavy padding of his gambeson under his mail might take the worst of a weapon's blow, but it kept all his own heat in. His soaked hair under his close-fit helmet sent salty rivulets down into his eyes and mouth. Beneath him, his destrier took slow, careful steps along the narrow track that stayed slippery with mud in the green shadows.

He swatted at the flies that loved this mix of wet and heat and shade and perspiring men and horses.

'Hell's teeth! Does the very ground conspire against me?'

Palmer's shoulders knotted at the angry shout. He turned in his saddle as much as he could in his heavy mail and with his shield slung across his back.

Farther back in the column of mounted men, the horse in front of the King's son had slipped to its knees.

Its rider urged the animal back up, with a string of apologies to John.

Palmer pulled his animal from the track, allowing the other to pass. Riding at the front didn't bother him. The unending noise that John made did. So far, their luck on this journey had held. They would soon be at Ardfinnan Castle, but Palmer would wager that those stationed there could already hear him. This group did not need to draw any attention to their progress.

He slipped back into the line to ride in front of John. Distracting the Lord of Ireland might keep the man's loose tongue busy. 'We make good progress, my lord.' He glanced over his shoulder.

'Oh. It's you, Palmer.' John scowled beneath his tightly laced helmet, his face red from the long ride in the heat. 'We'd be a lot faster if this cursed place had decent roads. These woods are barely passable.'

A low branch swished against Palmer's head and shoulder as he passed, swinging into John's path next.

He hacked it down with an irritated swipe of his sword. 'See? Barely passable.'

Palmer held in his command for the man to stop his noise. 'I agree it's not ideal, my lord. But your men have made their way to Ardfinnan. And back.'

'Back with the body of my friend.' John's mouth turned down. 'Back from defeat. Not like my great victory at Tibberaghny. Had I been at Ardfinnan, it would have been a different story.'

Palmer went to laugh but swallowed it back. No, John didn't joke: he really thought he spoke the truth.

'What's more, Geoffrey de Glanville would still be alive,' said John. 'The savages must have had the luck of the devil on their side to vanquish him.'

Palmer noted John's rigid shoulders and the constant flick of his gaze to the thick undergrowth on either side. The attack by slingers had not been luck. Clever tactics, more like. Many of the Irish prisoners had managed to escape while the stones had rained down. At least those that John hadn't whipped to pulped unconsciousness had. He guessed that John spewed his lies through deep fear.

'Indeed, my lord.' He had to try to settle him down. A jittery fighter was more a danger than a help in any battle. 'We'll be at Ardfinnan soon. I'm sure we'll hear tales of Sir Geoffrey's valour.'

John gave a tense nod. 'As I shall inspire them with how the enemy can be defeated.'

'That would be a great rallying speech, my lord.'

'Of course it would. That's why I've thought of it, man.' John's chin lifted. 'And I think you presume to speak to me as if you have been granted that privilege. Hold your tongue until you are asked to wag it.'

'My lord.' Palmer faced forward again. If John also stayed silent, then all was well. He flexed his hands and fingers in his mail mufflers, working out the stiffness of his wounded flesh. Not far to Ardfinnan now.

'Palmer.' A panicked, strangled word from John.

Palmer turned to follow his point to the right. A group of ferns moved. There wasn't a breath of wind in these woods. Something was in there. His hand went to his hilt.

In a flash of red fur, a fox broke from the concealing fronds to a strangled cry from John. It darted under his horse and across the path to the cover on the other side.

John swung his sword at its disappearing tail. 'Stupid creature could have startled my animal.'

But Palmer frowned to himself. Foxes liked to roam at dusk. Not in the full light of day. The shy animals would never run into a group of men and horses. Unless. 'Unless they were disturbed.'

A spear arced through the air to pierce the rump of the horse in front as he said it.

The animal kicked out, squealing.

Palmer's own horse reared beneath him in fright, the high-backed saddle keeping him on. 'We're under attack!' His shout joined howls and screams that broke from the woods.

'My lady?' Theodosia could not be sure if her ears deceived her.

'I thought so. Murdering brides are a rare breed.' Eimear's eyebrows arched. 'More's the pity.'

'But why would you try to carry out such a terrible act?'

'It was my husband or my father. For the fate they imposed on me.'

Theodosia bit her lip. 'Men can indeed be responsible for the ruination of girls' and women's lives.' Her own life, before Benedict.

'Ruination? A good word to describe what they did to me. And such mortal enemies up to then. Hugh was Henry's royal official, using harsh rule and the King's name to grab more and more land. My father, the great High King Rory O'Connor, went to Henry to appeal for help against him.' She snorted in disgust. 'Both of them dangling on the King of England's strings. Real men would have cut loose and fought to the death for victory.'

'Take care, my lady.' Theodosia glanced at the door. 'Those are treasonable words.'

'What if they are? It's only you and I here. Like it would have been when people came to whisper to you in your cell.'

'I did not mean for you to stop unburdening your soul to me. I only mean for you to take care that you are not overheard. It would be dangerous for you.'

'Speaking the truth doesn't frighten me. Scheming like my father and Hugh de Lacy does.' Eimear got to her feet and paced the room, arms folded across her chest. 'Hugh came to my father, suggested a truce so they could both keep hold of the vast lands they already had and not waste energy fighting each other. He'd recently lost his wife of many years. So it was a truce that could be sealed with my hand in marriage. With me.'

The second marriage that had so enraged Henry. 'I cannot imagine, my lady,' she said quietly.

'Of course you can't.' Eimear gave her a pitying look. 'And I'd never given any thought to marriage. Not only was I young, I'd never held such a dream, unlike most of the other girls I knew. I enjoyed boys, then men, as combatants, as people who could teach me the skills I loved, like hunting and fishing and riding. Like my namesake of the legends, I wanted to be a warrior, leading a troop of fierce women. Instead I was forced to become a wife.' She grimaced. 'I saw Hugh de Lacy for the first time on my wedding day. Twice my age, to my chin in height and half a face from a nightmare.'

Theodosia kept her counsel, unable to think of a polite response.

'Oh, you think I'm being unkind. But he strode into that chapel in his huge castle at Trim, the best castle in the whole land, like I should have rejoiced to have been chosen by him.' Her voice lowered, unsteady for the first time. 'I knew what was to come. And I couldn't do it. I just couldn't.'

'Neither should you have, my lady.' Theodosia's condemnation came from her heart, imagining Matilde in that position, her daughter only a few years from it being possible.

'Exactly.' Eimear recovered her strength. 'I got an idea from my wedding clothes, from the gold pin at my breasts. Eimear of the legends had that. She had a glittering knife in her right hand too. So I got mine ready as the servants escorted me to the bedchamber after the feast. Ready for him. For Hugh de Lacy, the Lord of Meath.' She paced on.

Theodosia's stomach tensed. She did not want to hear the rest of this story. But she must hear it out. Refusing to listen would be another injustice to Eimear.

'Do you know what he did first?'

'No, my lady,' she whispered.

'He tried to woo me.' Eimear shook her head. 'He actually thought I would respond to easy words about my beauty, about how he would be gentle. Despite my disgust, it was all I could do not to laugh. I let him lean to me for a kiss. And my knife was up, his heart my target.'

'But you stopped, showed mercy.'

Eimear snorted again. 'No. He moved too fast for me. I don't know how he did it. But he had that blade from me in an eye-blink.' She took a long breath. 'And then.'

'You do not have to tell me, my lady.'

'Nothing.'

'I do not understand.'

'I mean, nothing. He stuck my knife in his belt, said he wouldn't say a word to my father. He didn't even punish me. Instead, he made an agreement with me. One I could tolerate.'

'What sort of agreement?'

'He wanted an heir, to bring the lands of O'Connor and de Lacy together. Once he had one, he would never come near me again.'

Theodosia took in a long breath. 'You have a son, my lady.'

'I do. My William: my beloved boy.' Eimear nodded, two spots of high colour in her cheeks now. 'My husband let me be until I was ready, until I allowed him into my bed. I have all the saints to thank that I conceived very quickly. And Hugh stayed true to his promise. The first time he saw William, his words to me were, "You are done."' Her voice became unsteady once more.

'I am sorry, my lady.'

'You do not have to be sorry.' Eimear shrugged, her composure returned. 'My father told me my loins could be my weapon. That gave me the courage to go through with it.' She pulled in a long, deep breath. 'I thank you for your compassionate ear. You were right: it has helped me.' She knelt before Theodosia. 'Shall we pray for that warrior's soul? Together?'

'Of course, my lady.' Theodosia began the prayer, her blood, royal as Eimear's, surging through her veins at what she'd just heard.

Henry's suspicions were correct. Hugh de Lacy was lining up great power for himself in this land. Power that could challenge Henry for possession. But as she had seen so many times, the hunt for power devoured the blameless to their bones. And could devour her and Benedict still.

She would pray for the soul of the dead warrior.

Then return to those for Benedict.

Palmer forced his heels down to keep his balance. He swung his shield to his left arm, slipping through the enarmes in a tight hold.

'Ready yourselves!' Loosing the reins from his right hand, he pulled his sword free of its scabbard in one movement.

Another spear whistled towards him. He flung his shield up and it bounced away.

'Kill them all!' came John's shout from behind him.

A quick glance saw the man brandish his sword, his face set in terror.

Palmer swung his own blade as movement flicked at the edge of his vision. His blade met a long spear, thrust up at him from an Irish warrior who'd appeared beside him. The spear handle snapped, and the man ducked from Palmer's next strike, grabbing the shortened blade before diving back into the undergrowth.

Another dashed out in his place.

Palmer's sword met his long-haired, helmetless skull in a swift arc. The attacker was down. And another.

His horse spun under him, desperate to be off, as he parried, slashed, stabbed.

Still they came. Below him, next to him, behind him. Bearded warriors breaking from the bushes, the trees, roaring their murderous intent from behind painted, round shields as they held short swords aloft.

He took blows, traded them, his mail and helmet and height on his horse giving him and others the advantage.

For now.

He wrenched his head around to check on John.

The King's son kept a few attackers at bay with his fine sword. A crossbow-wielding horseman saw to the rest.

'Stay on your horses, men!' Palmer roared his order above the melee of squealing horses and yelling men.

A slinger's stone slammed into Palmer's right arm in breath-robbing pain. But his armour saved the bone; a bruise wouldn't kill him. He swore hard, sent another attacker staggering back, the man's hand a mess of blood.

Ardfinnan wasn't far. He and John's men were holding the Irish off. He could ride – any of them could ride – and fetch reinforcements back.

Then a huge, black-haired, long-bearded warrior emerged from the bushes near John, a battleaxe raised in one hand, round shield painted with bright red coils in the other.

'My lord!'

Too late.

The Irishman struck. Fast. Hard. Brutal. Not at John. At the mounted crossbowman who shot so well. The man's mailed thigh could have been dead wood. His severed limb fell on one side of his horse as his screaming, dying body fell from the other.

And the warrior turned next for John.

Chapter Fifteen

'Use your horse, my lord!' Palmer yelled with all the air in his lungs. 'As well as your sword!'

But the King's son didn't heed him. 'You'll not have my leg!' John yanked his foot from his stirrup as the warrior raised his weapon again.

Forcurse it, John was going to jump from his animal. 'Stay on your mount!' Palmer kicked his horse hard, making for John's defence, blade raised.

But John was off, half-falling from his high seat to stumble on the ground, his panicked horse between him and the warrior.

Palmer swung his weapon, meeting the man's swinging axe in mid-swipe. The force of the colliding blows sent him hard into his wooden saddle pommel.

The man whipped his axe down in a fast crouch, ducking from a clumsy next blow from Palmer.

John had got to his unsteady feet, sword in one hand, his shield lost in his descent.

'Remount, my lord.' Palmer went for another strike.

'I can't! My mail weighs me down and the beast won't stay still!'

The warrior jerked back so Palmer's swipe went wide.

'Try!'

The man brought the axe up again at a poor angle.

No. A perfect angle.

The Irishman sent his blade into the right knee of John's horse and yanked it back out in a vicious strike.

The huge animal squealed and jolted in its agony, its heavy flank thumping John off his feet and flat onto his stomach on the ground.

Eyes rolling, the horse collapsed close to him, blood pulsing from its wound.

'Get up, my lord!' Palmer's destrier heaved under him, his animal spooked and desperate to escape. He knew the perils of dismounting in full armour. But he couldn't defend John from the back of his own animal, not with the injured horse in the way in this tight space.

He clambered from the saddle with an oath. His horse fled as the warrior scrambled over to the still prostrate John, his axe up high again.

Dodging the huge flailing hooves as he followed, Palmer yelled to John. 'My lord! Up!'

The King's son raised his head. Thrust himself to the side as the axe came down.

The warrior bellowed his frustration as his blade sank into mud.

And Palmer was almost on him, his sword raised and ready.

One of the fallen horse's uninjured legs kicked out. Palmer stopped dead to avoid it, skidding on the wet mud and nearly losing his grip on his weapon.

The axeman was ready again, but John had managed to stand. He waved his sword at the Irishman. 'Go to hell, you savage.'

Palmer recovered his hold, stepping round the struggling horse. Fast. Quiet.

The man smiled at John's reaction. 'You can go first.'

John gaped in shock that the man could answer with his own tongue, then howled as the warrior struck his sword from his grasp.

Palmer went for his own strike.

John's glance flicked to Palmer.

The axeman saw it. He whirled with a shout, his vividly painted round shield up.

Palmer's sword bounced off the iron boss at its centre.

The man adjusted the angle of the shield, using its edge to hammer against Palmer's own, then his axe, over and over, driving him backwards, off balance and towards the moving hooves. Palmer's sword angle was too shallow, his grip all wrong. He could only defend against the onslaught of blows that drove the breath from his body and rattled his teeth in his head.

'Use your sword, Palmer!'

'The stripling teaches fighting now, does he?' The towering Irishman laughed as he struck again and again.

A metal-clad hoof missed Palmer's legs by a whisper.

Palmer dropped down and forward to a crouch.

The warrior's strike was off the mark, his own momentum pitching him over Palmer.

Hoof met bone, but Palmer didn't stop to check.

He was on his feet and at John's side, thrusting John's sword back into his hand.

'How can we fight all of them?' John's look was ashen.

Palmer already had the answer. The Irish warriors overran the column of knights and horses, slaughtering all before them. 'We can't. We run.'

He grabbed John by the shoulder and hauled him into the bushes.

Running in chain mail got harder as you got older.

Palmer's breath came in deep gasps, his legs like water as he forced his way through the thick undergrowth. Ropes of ivy snared him and brambles and sharp branches ripped at his face. But he still moved quicker than John.

'Palmer. Stop.'

Palmer did as John ordered. 'My lord, we have to keep going.'

John looked close to collapse as sweat poured down his scarlet face, a face equally as scratched as Palmer's. 'Give me one minute.'

'We only have to get to Ardfinnan.' Palmer pointed forward. 'The river's in that direction. It's not far. Once we get there, we can follow it to your castle. It leads there, the same as the road we were on.'

'How do you know?'

'I spoke to the men who have been there.'

'I need to get rid of this cursed mail. It's too heavy.' John tugged at his helmet's fastening.

Palmer grabbed his hand down. 'No.'

'Do not dare to touch me.' John's face pinched in anger as he shook him off. 'Who do you think you are to order me to do anything?'

Palmer raised his hands. 'I'm sorry, my lord. I'm not trying to order you to do anything. But you need to keep your armour on.'

'We have to move quickly, do we not? So we can get to the safety of Ardfinnan?'

'Yes, my lord.'

'Well, no one saw us go. That bearded monster will have his head cracked by my poor horse's hooves by now. We are not being followed. My gambeson will suffice.' John pulled off his helmet, his red hair plastered wet to his head. 'That will protect me enough, without the weight of—'

Palmer stopped him with a raised hand. 'Listen.'

A flock of wood pigeons clattered through the canopy above.

'Birds.' John ground the word out. 'I thought I told you not to give orders to me.' Then his face paled, despite the heat. He'd heard it too.

The shouts of many Irishmen, men who knew they were in reach of quarry. Men who didn't need to be cautious because they knew they far outnumbered that quarry. Men who knew how to use their axes with devastating effect.

'Palmer.' John began to shake from head to foot. 'What do we do now?'

'We have to make the river.' Palmer took off, faster than ever, crashing through the bushes, John following as he fumbled his helmet back on.

'To fight?'

'To not die.'

'Palmer, I can see it. The castle.' John's words came in panicked, exhausted gasps.

At least he'd learned to keep his voice down. 'I see it too, my lord.'

The barest glimpse through the trees, rising on a high crag above the river. And as Palmer had feared, still too far away. The shouts behind them echoed louder. Nearer.

'Then where are you going?' said John. 'We should be heading straight for it.'

'We're not going to make it,' said Palmer. 'They'll be on us before we get there.' He kept his path through the dense shrubs and bushes.

John's eyes bulged. 'We just keep running around in these woods and wait for them to kill us?'

'No.' Palmer ploughed on, his ears alert for the sound he needed.

'Then what do you suggest?' John's enraged hiss held the threat of violence.

So be it. If what he, Palmer, planned didn't work, he'd need as much fighting blood as possible flowing through John's veins. 'You'll see.'

A drumming broke out. Swords and fists on wooden shields. A beat that readied men for slaughter.

'They want our heads.' John stifled a sound that could have been a sob.

Palmer took a glance back. Still not within sight. 'Hurry.' He picked up his pace in a last push. The beating of the shields got louder, faster.

Then he saw it, through the trees. The rushing waters of the strong, fast river that flowed past Ardfinnan Castle.

He forced his way out onto the bank, praying he'd find what he needed.

John joined him, his gaze moving back and forth to the woods behind. 'We're going to swim for it? Upstream? Have you lost your mind?'

'No, my lord.' Palmer grabbed a handful of John's surcoat. 'And no.' He tore the garment open with a quick slash of his sword.

John stifled a yell. 'But you have!' He took a step back as Palmer yanked the garment from him. He looked ready to flee.

Only the noise of the Irish from the woods, audible above the river, stopped him.

'You're going to have to trust me, my lord.' Palmer shoved the surcoat under his arm and laid his sword against a bush.

'Trust a madman?'

Palmer quickly worked his mail glove off his left hand, Theodosia's bandage still tight on his injured knuckles. 'It's me or the Irish, my lord. And we're running out of time.' He nodded to one of the big piles of debris that lined the riverbank, cast there by winter floods. 'Find me the biggest branch you can.'

'You will build us a boat before the enemy is on us?'

'Now. Please.'

In frowning disbelief, John hurried over to the pile of muddied dead wood and rotting grass and leaves.

Palmer did a quick scan of the woods as John cursed and tugged at a hefty forked tree limb.

No one in sight. Yet. Their calls told him it would be any minute now. He sliced the bandage off with his knife, then angled his blade against the big, healing scabs. He bit down. And cut hard.

'This one's the biggest.' John straightened up, his words stopping as he gaped at Palmer.

The quick flow of new blood was enough. Palmer let it seep onto the ruined surcoat, smearing it out as much as he could.

He stepped over to John, whose mouth curled down at the sight of the bloodied cloth. 'I'm not doing that. I can wait for my blood to be shed.'

Palmer ignored him, snapping off one of the branch's forks, the movement sending more pain through his hand. And more blood. He pierced a wide section of the surcoat with the sharp, jagged branch, then rammed his mail glove onto a bunch of small twigs.

Now he could hear the definite cracking and breaking of branches that meant men forced their way through the woods.

'Palmer.' John's word came through clenched teeth.

'I hear them.' Palmer picked up one end of the branch. 'You take the other end.'

John didn't stop to argue.

'As far into the middle of the current as we can.'

John nodded.

They pulled back the heavy branch, and with a hard, high swing, it sailed over the surface of the river and in with a loud splash.

It turned over, the surcoat submerging.

Palmer's guts coiled. It hadn't worked. At all.

Then the current nudged it, and with a slow, slow roll, it turned over. The bundle of bloodied white cloth showed clear against the rotting wood. The river took it into its brisk flow and it headed off downstream at a steady pace.

'Come on.' Palmer signalled to John. 'We need to get to that.' He pointed a few yards upstream to a tangle of branches and old leaves that had piled up against the roots of a long-dead fallen tree, rotting as they sat trapped at the edge of the water. A few low branches, heavy with leaves, jutted out over it.

John broke into a run, but Palmer halted him. 'Step carefully,' he whispered. 'Stay out of the mud.'

Sweat trickled down Palmer's back as he too forced himself to move with caution. Every inch of him braced to run from the axe-men. But they had to do it this way.

And they were there.

'Get in the water.' Palmer had his sight fixed where he guessed the first men would emerge. 'Use your sword as an anchor. And keep low in those branches.'

Palmer started to wade into the clogged water as he spoke. The angled bank fell away in a steep drop. He slipped, his chain mail a terrifying weight that threatened to pull him under into water that had him gasping with cold. His hands locked on his sword, buried deep in the mud.

John panted like a warm dog as he stared, not moving.

Then past his shoulder, Palmer saw the bushes move.

'My lord,' he whispered. 'In. Now. And hold on.'

John had seen it too. He slid in next to Palmer.

'God's eyes, Palmer. I'm going to drown.'

'Hold on. Stay as low as you can.' Palmer sank, the water rising over his chin and mouth, using his nose to breathe.

The first Irishman stepped out into the open, axe raised and ready. It had the stain of fresh blood on the blade. Several more joined him, their colour high from their battle, their eyes keen for their prey. Last came the huge, hulking warrior that Palmer had thought mortally wounded by the horse. But no. The man had a gash on his head from which blood had drenched one shoulder. Yet he stood as straight as a statue, ready to take on another fight.

The quiver of the water next to him told him John had also witnessed their pursuers.

Palmer offered a brief prayer that he'd done enough. Their dull metal helmets should blend with the colours of decaying nature and the muddy river. The low branches overhead kept them in deep green shade.

The men spoke rapidly to one another, shielding their eyes from the glare of the sun with their shields as they scanned the bank.

Downriver. Just look downriver. The log with the bloodied surcoat, the mail glove. That would surely have them following. Unless it had rolled over again.

A loud order came from one, causing the men to separate, calling to each other as they fanned out along the riverbank.

The injured warrior started to make his way upstream, striding on long, powerful legs, his axe resting on his shoulder, his eyes to the ground. Only one thing for it.

Palmer nudged John with his knee, signalling with his eyes what they had to do.

John's look showed him terrified but that he understood.

Rising enough to take his mouth from the water, Palmer gulped down as many lungfuls of air as he could hold. John did the same.

He sank into the muddy water, the shouts of the Irish becoming thin and faint against the thud of his own heart and the rumble of the river. The murk of the water meant he could make out some of the bank and the branches directly above him, but nothing else.

He wanted to gasp from the cold but held the breath in his lungs.

A moving shadow darkened his vision even more.

The man was here. Right above them.

Then the movement stopped.

The muscles in Palmer's chest, his throat, ached for release, an ache that grew by the second. He couldn't give in to it.

Still, the shadow above.

Palmer's chest tightened more, the desire for air pressing like a hand on his ribs as he strengthened his grip on his sword. He could try a swing. But his sword kept him anchored to the riverbank. If he loosed it, his mail would carry him to the bottom of the river and pin him there while he drowned.

And he had to breathe now. He had to. One more second, he told himself. One more. One more.

His ears buzzed, his chest seared. He had to breathe. He had to. Even if it meant an axe in his skull. He had to.

The shadow disappeared in an abrupt flick.

Palmer shoved his nose to the surface and the sounds of the world broke through again.

The Irishmen shouting. And running. Running downstream, pointing and gesturing at the log bearing John's surcoat.

He pulled hard on John's arm, and he emerged too, coughing and gulping and spitting. 'Ardfinnan?'

Palmer thrust his own face clear from the water. 'Fast as we can,' he gasped. 'It won't be long before they find out what we've done.' He pulled in lungful after lungful of air. It might stink of rotten leaves and mud, but it was the sweetest he'd ever tasted.

Chapter Sixteen

'Nineteen dead. Nineteen.'

Theodosia dug her fingernails into her palms at John's words, repeated so many times.

He sat at the head of the table in his keep at Tibberaghny, his loyal group of young confidantes with him. She had her usual place next to Gerald, tending to his instructions for scribing while every inch of her wished to be elsewhere. This was no feast, no celebration. The sombre group listened to John's account as he veered from simmering rage to boastfulness and back.

'At least you are returned safe to us, my lord,' said Fitzmiles.

Benedict too. Theodosia offered her deepest thanks to God for the thousandth time. The news of the men lost, spreading through the camp like a miasma bringing plague, had brought her a terror that had almost stopped her heart. She had not been able to ask about Benedict, lest she draw attention to herself. All she could do was race to where her brother had entered, craning past those who had gathered, trying with increasing desperation to see if Benedict had returned. She'd wanted to weep in relief when she saw his broad-shouldered frame standing next to a ranting John, but would not allow herself as tears should be for those who had lost their lives.

'That man Palmer lived too, did he not?' another knight asked John. 'The only other to survive with you?'

John snorted. 'Survived because of me, more like. I had to save him from an Irish axeman. Palmer's like a broken-winded old warhorse. Well past his prime.'

The unkind mirth that greeted John's response made her grit her teeth at its injustice. She had not had the opportunity to speak to Benedict yet, though she could hardly eat or sleep until she did so. But she knew in her heart, knew as well as she knew her God was in heaven, that Benedict would not have needed to be saved by John.

'The Irish wield terrible destruction with those axes.' John shook his head. 'Barbarous.'

'Their barbarity is in every inch of their bodies, my lord.' Gerald, sat beside her, raised his voice to get the table's attention. 'And in every one of their customs. Even in the ceremonies to appoint their kings: in so doing, they have carnal knowledge of beasts.'

A mix of disbelieving disgust and a few sniggers greeted his words as Theodosia's stomach rebelled.

'You have knowledge of this?' John looked appalled, yet the spark of unsavoury interest showed in his eyes.

'Indeed I do,' said Gerald. 'A people in the far north of this isle. The ceremony is not a dubbing or any civilised matter. A white mare is brought before the assemblage, and he who is to have kingship conferred on him has intercourse with this animal.'

Theodosia could not bear to be a witness to this revolting discussion. She went to rise. 'Permit me to leave, my lord.'

'Sister.' John's expression hardened. 'You are the one who said you would try to know Eimear O'Connor's heart and soul. This is yet one more example of the darkness that exists within the Irish.'

He jerked a thumb at the door. 'Go and hide from the ugliness of the truth if you wish. Like so many in the Church do.'

Gerald waved her away also, absorbed in the attention of his audience as he continued. 'The mare is then killed immediately and cut up into pieces to be boiled in water. A hideous broth in which the new king then bathes naked, drinking this repulsive brew with open mouth.'

Theodosia made for the door as quickly as she could, willing her ears not to hear this ghastly tale.

'I saw some of those actions myself, Gerald,' said John. 'An axeman landed such a blow to my horse's leg. He knew where to strike and how hard.'

Theodosia opened the door to see a man clattering up the stairwell, still soiled from the road and dressed as a messenger.

He pushed past the guards. 'I must see the Lord John.'

Theodosia halted him with a raised hand. 'He is with his men. He is not to be disturbed.'

'I have come from Lismore.'

She caught her breath. Lismore Castle. John's third fortress, a number of miles away. And she knew some of Gerald's kin had gone there to fight. 'What news?'

The man shook his head. 'So many dead.'

Many. Her stomach knotted. 'The nephew of the King's clerk?'

He shook his head again.

'Then come with me.'

Theodosia re-entered the room, cutting John off in mid-flow. 'My lord.'

'What on earth do you want now?'

'There is terrible news from Lismore.' She ushered the man in.

At first, Palmer thought the howling heralded a fresh attack by the Irish.

Then he recognised the voice: the royal clerk, Gerald.

He hurried to the door of the tent, where he had been discussing with a few of the best remaining men how to deepen the trench that surrounded Tibberaghny.

Theodosia helped the clerk down the steps of the motte, the man's words a stream of blame and anger and grief. Nostrils flaring, John led the way, clutching a rolled letter, his closest group following after.

'What's wrong with Gerald?' asked Simonson.

Palmer spotted a man he didn't recognise in John's group, still wearing the splattered clothes of a rider who has ridden long and fast. 'Bad news would be my guess.'

As if it heard him, the cool stiff breeze gave another strong gust from the low clouds.

'More?' Simonson shivered. 'God's eyes. How long has it been since we have received any good?'

Gerald's shouts continued to draw men from all corners of the camp.

'What man here wants a reward?' John held the letter aloft as he reached the bottom of the steps. 'A reward of many gold crowns.' He marched into the centre of the bailey, waving the letter.

Excited calls broke out as word spread. 'That's right. Go summon your fellows; go and tell every man here what I am offering.'

'I'd quite like a go at that, Palmer,' said Simonson.

'Wait.' Palmer stepped forward with an arm across the chest of the younger man. 'None of us has been paid for weeks. Why does the Lord John have sudden wealth to throw around? I need you here, like I need everyone we have.' He frowned as John carried on shouting his dubious offer of crowns. Tibberaghny's defences were already weak. They shouldn't be losing any more men.

Theodosia had her arm around a quieter Gerald, murmuring words of comfort to him. She gave Palmer a quick glance, which didn't help his doubt.

John now stood in a deep circle of eager faces. 'Yes, you have heard right. I offer great riches. I offer them because we have suffered another grievous loss, this time at Lismore.'

Unease rippled through the crowd.

Palmer shared it. Another defeat for the Lord John.

'Amongst others who have died is the kinsman of the King's own clerk, Gerald of Wales.'

Moans broke from Gerald, Theodosia gently patting his good arm.

'Saints guard us.' Simonson shot Palmer a shocked look, a response shared by many present.

John nodded. 'I see your disbelief. I too could hardly comprehend it.' His voice climbed. 'That these people, these wild dwellers on the edge of the world, could so easily overcome the best of my men. These people who are uncivilised, immoral savages. Defeating my men.' He smacked the letter on his other, open palm. 'But I know how they are doing it. There is only way to explain how these backward brutes are succeeding.'

'It will be the devil guiding their hand.' Gerald put a palm to his face.

'My royal clerk speaks the truth,' said John, to a wave of panicked whispers.

Palmer wondered if he'd heard right.

'A devil that you have all seen.' John pointed to some of the faces that his words held rapt. 'You. And you. And you.'

The whispers loudened to cries.

John nodded. 'A devil who has a name. And that name is Hugh de Lacy, Lord of Meath.'

The cries became angry shouts.

Palmer took a long breath in. Despite John's hysterical description, the King's son was partly right.

'De Lacy has not been seen by any here for over five weeks. It is my solemn belief that he is out there, helping the Irish, guiding them with his wicked talents, using the skills he learned in Henry's armies against his own people. He is the greatest traitor, and I need volunteers to track him down. Our greatest, greatest enemy!' John thrust the letter up in the air to yells of hatred. 'Who will fight for me?'

Palmer caught Theodosia's horrified look. He had to. Not for the money, but to try to stop this tide of defeat. And he could fight with a small band, leave as many as possible to keep Tibberaghny safe. He went to raise his hand.

A grip on his arm halted him.

'Sir Benedict.' One of the guards from the gatehouse had a stricken look. 'You must see this. At once.'

Palmer followed him with rapid steps as the wind whipped across the camp again.

The shouts broke off into exclamations and questions.

'By the love of the Virgin.' John dropped his hand. 'What on earth is that smell?'

Uncaring of his injured hand, Palmer climbed to the top of the ladder so fast his feet barely met each step.

Surely the guard had been wrong. He got to the platform at the top, the terrible stench still filling his nose and throat. A couple of strides got him to the wall. He looked over. And yes, the guard had spoken the truth.

Hugh de Lacy sat astride a huge destrier at the head of a line of mounted men in mail and iron helmets. And behind de Lacy, the source of the smell.

A large cart, filled with severed, decaying heads. The heads of men that had long, flowing hair and beards. The heads of Irishmen.

'Ah, Palmer. I'm glad they found you.' Half of de Lacy's ruined face lifted in his crooked smile. 'May I come in?'

Chapter Seventeen

The huge fires set in the bailey flared high, sending sparks and orange light into the deepening dusk.

Yet their fierce flames were not even close to the anger that burned within John's chest. He kept his smile plastered on. For now. This huge celebration, swelled many times over by de Lacy's men, would have to be borne.

'Some more wine, my lord?' Sat to John's right, in the place of honour, the scarred-faced lord offered him the jug as though he ruled this place.

'Good wine it is too.' If John gritted his teeth any more, they would break. The splash of the wine into his vessel brought him the only tiny comfort.

Raucous, feasting cheer filled the bailey; tables set out again as they had been on the disastrous day of the slinger attack. All of it because of what Hugh de Lacy had done. And no showers of stones, of sharp javelins ruined it. The Irish would be staying far away from this place. De Lacy had seen to that, with his defeat of the men of the north who had dared to try to seize land in Meath from him, and his return with their heads as trophies. Everyone said his name with awe as they drank and cheered him. Even Gerald had taken to wine-bibbing.

'A most wondrous victory, my lord de Lacy!' The clerk's hooked nose shone red in the firelight. 'I shall be writing an account of your great deeds.'

John gripped his goblet stem hard lest he throw the vessel at Gerald's head.

'Thank you, good brother.' De Lacy gave him a gracious bow. 'Though I see your arm still is not healed?'

Gerald slipped into his usual whine. 'No, my lord. The sister here does my bidding though her efforts do not match what my own would be.'

'Not to worry, brother,' said de Lacy. 'Your success at supping wine with one hand is second to none.'

John braced himself for one of Gerald's tirades and for a string of admonishments to be called down on de Lacy's head. But no.

Gerald gave a high peal of laughter, his skinny frame rocking back and forth as all others joined him. 'Very good, my lord.'

By God and all the saints, the clerk was as drunk as an alewife's husband.

'Very good. Oh, very good.' Gerald nodded and nodded to more laughter.

Only the sister didn't laugh. Or even smile. She sat with her eyes lowered as she busied herself with Gerald's plate of untouched food.

Time he, John, drew some mirth from this table. His table. 'Perhaps some wine would cheer you, sister? Make you and Gerald better friends.' He gave her a broad wink. 'Perhaps even the best.'

The only reward he got was a few half-hearted sniggers and the flush that rose in the nun's face.

De Lacy remained impassive, curse him. Instead, he addressed the nun. 'I believe you have already been a constant friend to Gerald, sister. As you have to my wife.'

John tensed at the mention of Eimear. He'd done nothing to that arrogant Irish bitch and here was de Lacy implying that she'd somehow suffered.

'Thank you, my lord.' The sister's flush grew deeper.

'It is I who should be thanking you,' said de Lacy. 'Your health, sister.' He held up his goblet, with a nod to the table that everyone should follow.

Like foolish sheep, they did, some even following de Lacy's bow before they carried on talking and laughing and drinking.

John took a bite of roasted meat. He wouldn't be honouring that Theodosia woman. All she'd done was divert him from his true purpose. And de Lacy looked far too pleased with himself. 'Your wife is not joining us then, de Lacy?' He licked his fingers as he said it.

'No, my lord. Eimear is at prayer tonight.'

'In my keep.'

'In your keep, my lord. Where she tells me she has been kept safe. Secure, one might say.'

John could see the shadow of deep displeasure in the man's one working eye. He was doing a good job of keeping it in check. 'I would have thought she would want to join you here at the feast. It's been weeks since she's seen you.'

'That is why she prays, my lord. She gives thanks to God for my safe return. Once my tent has been cleaned and suitably prepared for my wife, she will return to me there. I will resume my responsibility for her.'

A tall figure emerged from the noisy throng. Palmer.

'My lord de Lacy.' His deep tone held respect, and his face and hair shone with the sweat of exertion.

De Lacy turned to him. 'Have you and your men done what I have asked, Palmer?'

'Yes, my lord. We've finished.'

John looked at the man who'd escaped the Ardfinnan rout with him. Straight-faced as ever. Impossible to tell what lay behind his neutral expression.

'If you'll excuse me, my lord.' De Lacy got to his feet. 'I need to check that Palmer has correctly carried out the task I charged him with.'

'Yes, yes.' John waved him away, keen to see the back of him. Of them both.

With a bow, the two men headed off into the darkness.

Good-humoured shouting and whistling broke out from another table.

A couple of men had struck up a piping tune with a bone whistle and a small drum.

'Let's hear it all!' John clapped his hands along to encourage them, and everyone followed suit.

Good. Let them all be distracted with such a dreadful din.

He filled his goblet once more and settled back in his chair.

De Lacy might think he ruled this night. But John had other plans. He needed time to think.

Palmer led de Lacy up a ladder that led to the wall walk, far more careful in his movements than when he'd rushed up to the gatehouse earlier on.

He stepped onto the wooden platform, de Lacy stepping after.

'All as you ordered, my lord.' He wiped the sweat from his forehead with his forearm, his stomach still rebelling from his labours.

De Lacy looked up at the tall, new spike. Impaled on it was one of the terrible cargo of heads. 'Very good.' He nodded. 'The others?'

Palmer swept his hand to indicate the circle of the wall of the bailey. 'At regular intervals.'

The flames from the enclosure below cast a glow on the many, many heads on spikes. Fixed in their masks of death, the flickering light brought an eerie life back to their faces. The horrible stench remained whenever the breeze eased. The joyful music and singing from below made the sight even more nightmarish.

'What of the head of the king from the north who would steal my land?' asked de Lacy.

'On top of the keep.' Palmer pointed to the Lord John's tower, lit in one narrow window. The head on the long pole made a dark silhouette against the last pale light in the western sky, its lifeless mouth open in a silent scream.

'And the torches?' asked de Lacy. 'They are all in place and ready to be lit?'

'Yes, my lord.'

'Excellent.' De Lacy nodded again. 'I wonder if the Lord John doubts my loyalty to the King now?'

Palmer tensed. He himself had doubted it. Utterly. Not anymore. 'How could anyone, my lord? You taught the enemy a lesson that they won't forget.' *Are teaching John one too: that you can win, while he can't.* De Lacy was openly rubbing John's nose in his victory.

De Lacy smiled as if he had overheard Palmer's thoughts. 'Thank you for your hard work. I'm going to rejoin the feast now. Come with me – I'll find you a place at the Lord John's table. You'll have a great thirst. And you'll want to share in John's approval when he sees this display.'

'You're most generous, my lord.' Palmer had no mind for anything other than getting the chance to talk to Theodosia. Everything was changing and they should be altering their plans.

A burst of laughter came from the bailey.

In the fire's light, the clerk Gerald hopped in an untypical dance.

'Now, there's a sight.' De Lacy shook his head.

Thank the Almighty for a holy man who couldn't hold his drink. 'If you don't mind, I'd far rather go and clean up, my lord.' Palmer held up his bandaged hands, stained from his stomach-turning labours. He grimaced. 'These stink from the rancid flesh, but I fear my own may be turning as well.'

De Lacy's look shifted to concern. 'Then get them seen to, man.' He went to the ladder.

'Thank you, my lord.' He followed de Lacy down. 'Sister Theodosia, the one who looks after the King's clerk. She has seen to my wounds too. I'd be grateful if she could leave the feast. It'll only be for a while.'

His feet met the ground, his heart thumping.

But de Lacy didn't even turn around. 'No need to bother her for such an unpleasant task. I'll send one of my barber-surgeons.' He set off for the Lord John's table with a wave of his hand.

Palmer tipped his head back with a string of soundless curses.

His gaze met the distorted leer of a head above him, as if the dead man mocked him.

'De Lacy.' John greeted the man's return to the table, refilling de Lacy's goblet with a hand that remained steady. Good. He could not show de Lacy so much as a hair-quiver of uncertainty.

'Thank you, my lord. I apologise for having to leave' – De Lacy gestured up to the keep – 'but I wanted to make sure all was complete.'

'All what?' John squinted past the glow of the firelight to the deepening dusk beyond.

'That.'

As if in response to de Lacy, a torch lit the top of the keep. High on a spike, a bearded head adorned it.

John gasped in delight. 'The northern king?'

'Yes, my lord.'

Others took up John's gasp as torches lit up the top of the walls, each one casting a flaring light on another severed head, on and on in a fabulous, dramatic display.

'The sight of victory.' John started to clap, nodding to all his men to follow.

Those present in the bailey joined in, some pointing in wonder, others yelling and whistling their approval.

De Lacy acknowledged it all with a raised hand, not standing to make the most of it. Instead, he went back to his wine.

More fool him. John waved and smiled to all. It was always a good idea to take the praise that one was given. And this was praise from the whole of Tibberaghny. With one exception. The sister had her hands to her cheeks, lips white and eyes wide in shock as she took in the sight. He could swear he caught the smell of terror on her. Serve the self-righteous little bore right. He'd love to make her squirm even more with a few clever quips, but he had no time for that right now.

He clapped de Lacy on the back as the revelry climbed to new heights. 'That will show the Irish who's in charge at Tibberaghny, won't it?'

'I believe so, my lord.' De Lacy gave a sharp nod. 'Firm action is called for at times. It's what I did to secure my lordship of Meath many years ago. I took the head of O'Rourke, a great chieftain, who laid claim there. The head of the son of another – the son of the wily Sinnach, the one they call The Fox.'

'Indeed, one could say you certainly outfoxed him.' John enjoyed his own clever jest.

'You could, my lord.' De Lacy didn't smile. 'Such an approach has made me many enemies. I'm glad to say that less drastic options work very effectively too.'

'Such as?' John took another look at what adorned his walls. 'I doubt there's anything more effective than this.'

'Truces and alliances can work wonders, my lord.' De Lacy nodded. 'And they're easier work.'

'De Lacy! Such a wonderful display of your trophies.' Gerald collapsed into a seat next to him, breathless from his ridiculous dancing.

'Thank you, brother.'

'More wine.' The clerk grabbed for the jug.

'Your head will be sore in the morning, Gerald.' John tried to be rid of him with a warning look.

The infernal man was far too drunk to notice.

'And for you, de Lacy' – Gerald slopped wine into goblets and onto the tabletop – 'we are brothers, you and I.' He pointed at de Lacy, then at himself. 'A brother. Who is a brother.' He pealed out his high-pitched laugh again, de Lacy humouring him with a grin and a clap on the back.

As Gerald launched into a rambling account of the sins of the Irish, John wished the drunken clerk would choke. He didn't need any distractions. Not now. His sight lit on the sister. Finally, she could be of some real use. 'You.' He snapped his fingers. 'Sister Theodosia.'

'Yes, my lord?'

He jerked a thumb at Gerald.

The clerk now seemed to believe that de Lacy would take greater heed of his tales if he delivered them less than an inch from de Lacy's face and with a firm hold of his cloak.

The sister got to her feet at once to approach the small group, carrying the clerk's plate of food.

'See to him,' said John. 'For God's sake.' He took a deep drink as she gently detached Gerald from the Lord of Meath.

'Brother,' she said.

'It's Sister Theodosia!' The oaf grabbed hold of her instead.

'I have your meal,' she said. 'I think you should come and eat with me. Perhaps in your tent?'

'No, no, no.' Gerald patted the seat next to him. 'No. Sit with me.' He swayed as he pointed to de Lacy. 'With the great Hugh de Lacy. He killed Irish savages. Same as me.' He gave another sweeping point, a hair's breadth from overbalancing off his seat.

'You did?' De Lacy seemed very interested all of a sudden.

'I did.' Gerald nodded hard. 'I saved the sister. Saved her from a savage.'

'Some food, brother. I implore you.' The nun scooped a mouthful of soft fish into the clerk's mouth.

John's jaw tightened. It didn't stop the man. He merely chewed and blathered at the same time.

'I saved the sister from your wife too, de Lacy.' Gerald held up a finger. 'Who is also a savage.'

The nun shushed him.

'Gerald.' John's sharp order managed to pierce even the man's wine-filled ears. 'Enough. De Lacy, I cannot apologise enough for my clerk's drunken nonsense. I will get some of my men to take him back to his tent. Immediately.'

'Let him be.' De Lacy shrugged. 'The wine has his tongue, I'm sure.'

'Then apologise for what you said about the Lord of Meath's wife.'

'Eh?' Gerald chewed on another mouthful, with, it seemed, no recollection of what he'd been saying.

'You see, my lord?' De Lacy shook his head. 'It's always worst with those who usually steer clear of it.'

'Nevertheless.' John frowned as if displeased. Inside, he rejoiced. Gerald had brought them to what he wanted to say. 'How dare the clerk compare your magnificent deeds for the crown with his own paltry actions.'

'Each man does what he can, my lord.'

'That is my hope. And you have shown just what that means to the traitors of the north.' He sighed. 'Unfortunately, I have not fared so well here. The onslaught has been relentless.'

'So I've heard,' said de Lacy. 'But God has spared you, and Tibberaghny is safe now. I give you my word I will defend it.'

Gerald made a loud demand to Sister Theodosia for more fish.

John caught back an oath. If the clerk interrupted again, he would squeeze the man's neck until his eyes bulged. He shot the nun his fiercest look, and she distracted Gerald once more with another large mouthful.

'Which is precisely what I need you to do, de Lacy.' John savoured the glorious anticipation anew. 'I need you to take control of this castle. On my behalf.'

'Of course, my lord.'

'Because I am moving my entourage on to the city of Dublin. I need to direct my campaign from its superior security and even greater resources.'

'Again, you have my word that I will defend Henry's lands here.'

'I will have your loyalty.'

'That is what I just said, my lord.' The first question crept into de Lacy's voice.

'I will have it, because I will have your wife as a hostage.' John smiled as if it were a polite request, not an order.

The shock on de Lacy's half-face was worth every moment John had spent in this cesspit of a country. 'You have my promise whether—'

John held a hand up to silence him. 'It is a means of a civilised guarantee. That is all.'

'But the journey to Dublin will not be easy, my lord. Or safe.'

'Which is why I will take most of your men with me.' John refilled his goblet, relaxed. In control. 'Excellent fighters. The ones here?' He snorted. 'Useless. Lazy. Which is why you will remain here.'

Gerald's goblet spilled with a clatter.

'Sorry, my lord.' The nun set to quickly mopping it up.

De Lacy didn't even look round. 'I do not wish any harm to come to wife, my lord.'

'Of course, of course.' John nodded as if considering a good point. In truth, he savoured the note of uncertainty that had entered de Lacy's voice. 'And neither do I. Hence surrounding her with so many protectors.' His voice, his hands – all remained steady. His skills at changing his plans were as swift and unexpected as those he used in his favourite board game. His pegs now sat precisely where he wanted them. And de Lacy couldn't move them. He leaned forward and put a hand on de Lacy's shoulder. 'My hostages are my guests. She will be treated as the King's guest. With her noble Irish birth and her marriage to you, how could I do anything else?'

A yelp and a crash stopped de Lacy from answering.

Gerald had fallen off his chair. The drunken fool.

Chapter Eighteen

'You have made it to your tent and you are in one piece, brother.' Theodosia's heart thudded. Her rash act of tipping him from his chair in the first place, the effort of propelling the drunken Gerald back here – both would have been enough to send her pulse racing. But not as much as hearing that John intended to take leave for Dublin, with Eimear as a hostage. She, Theodosia, would be going too. John would never dare leave the King's clerk behind. And where Gerald went, so did she.

The clerk swayed on his feet as he surveyed his tent, looking as if he viewed it for the first time. 'I have had a terrible shock. I should like more wine.'

'Indeed you have had a fright, falling like that.' She guided him to his bed, thanking God he had not realised it had been her quick elbow that had tipped him over. 'Praise God you did not hurt your arm anew.'

'Praise Him, indeed,' he slurred as she sat him down. 'Praise Him higher for the gift of the grape. I should like some more.'

'Perhaps you should rest instead, brother.' If she could get him laid down, he might soon fall asleep. She needed to seize the opportunity that the whole camp celebrating afforded her. She had to find

Benedict and tell him what John had planned. There had to be a way for Benedict to go too.

'I don't want to rest.' Gerald frowned. 'I want more wine.' He pointed with a wavering finger. 'There. On that chest.'

Easier not to antagonise him. 'Very well.' She hurried over and poured him a small cup from the jug. 'There you are.' She handed it to him with care lest he drop it all over himself. 'But you should get some rest when you are finished. You will need your energy for the long journey to Dublin.'

'Who is going to Dublin?'

'The Lord John, brother.'

'So he is.' Gerald took a swig of his drink. 'I thought I dreamt that.'

'No, brother.' *Oh, please let him finish.*

'He is taking the savage woman with him?'

'Yes, brother. But I do not think it is a good idea to call her that again. Eimear is a noblewoman, and she will be under the Lord John's protection.'

To her surprise, Gerald went off into one of his peals of laughter again. 'His protection? Oh, that's good.'

'What do you mean?' Unease grew within Theodosia.

'John likes a noblewoman.' His shoulders shook with his drunken mirth. 'Likes all women, but they don't always like him back. Which he enjoys most of all.' He hiccupped. 'When they fight him.'

Dread enclosed Theodosia's heart like a cold fist. Perhaps, as Hugh de Lacy had said, this was merely the wine on Gerald's tongue. 'I cannot imagine that is the case. The King—'

'The King? Henry despairs of his youngest son, with John's lewd, unnatural conduct. So many willing pairs of legs open for the stripling, yet he wants the unwilling. Takes them.' Gerald fixed her with unfocused, bloodshot eyes. 'All that fuss from that woman at

John's dubbing. He'd ravished her in the very house of the Knights Hospitallers. The wife of one of Henry's court. Imagine!' He shook his head hard. 'By the blood of the Virgin, I am seeing two of you. I think I must have struck my head when I fell.'

'Honestly, brother, you did not.' Theodosia's breath came fast and shallow. Of course she could imagine. The woman at Windsor, her cries of despair a puzzle to all at the time. But not to her father, the King. Nor her brother, the rapist. And not to her, Theodosia, now. Worse than imagining, she knew. And Eimear would be at John's mercy.

'Perhaps not.' Gerald lay back on his bed in a sudden movement, empty cup tight in his grasp. 'I do not know.' He yawned. 'But I tell you what I do know, sister.'

'What, brother?'

'I know I want some more wine.'

'I will fetch it, brother.' She went back to the jug. 'There is none left. I will go out and get this filled.' He would never be able to tell it still contained plenty, not in his state.

'Go on, then.' He waved her away with a limp hand. 'You know what else?'

Theodosia was halfway to the door. 'No, brother?'

His slack face shifted into an unkind smile. 'The Lord John will tame that Irish savage. You mark my words.' His eyes began to close.

Theodosia fled. Benedict – she had to find Benedict.

Sitting before an abandoned cooking fire that had sunk to embers, Palmer ripped the stained and filthy bandages from his hands. He threw them onto the glowing wood, where they caught and leapt into hissing flame. His wounds weren't too bad; he'd only used them as an excuse for de Lacy. He moved his shoulders to ease the tiredness out of them. Tonight, for the first night in many weeks, he would sleep, and sleep soundly. De Lacy and his men would keep this place secure. For once, he, Palmer, didn't have to. Then he would find a way to get to speak to Theodosia. With calm returned to the camp, he should soon get a chance to meet her at the water barrel.

A new wave of raucous cheers came from the celebrations, and he caught de Lacy's name in the shouts.

De Lacy. How wrong Henry had been. How wrong John had been. And how wrong he, Palmer, had been.

The burning bandages twisted and curled as the fire consumed them, fuelled by the fluids from dead flesh that had soaked them.

Yet he'd had his doubts about de Lacy's treachery before the scarred lord reappeared.

The wearing down of the camp with unseen, relentless noise. The attacks from the trees with darts and slingshot. The speed and stealth of the un-armoured men in the trees. The skill at ambush and the deft wielding of the battleaxes. All showed the Irish to be masters of their own country. Faced with defeat, John could only claim that de Lacy had been helping the natives. The King's son should have been looking at his own methods and weapons, which were suited to a different land, a different enemy. As should he have been.

But with such unskilled fighters and so many deserters, every moment Palmer had had been taken up with defence. He rubbed tiredly at his thick stubble. Deserters. Of course. No wonder the Irish could predict John's moves. Many men had abandoned John because of their empty purses. The Irish had wealth too. A coin could loosen a man's tongue easier than drink.

'Benedict!'

Palmer caught his breath at a whisper from the shadows. *Theodosia.*

He was on his feet and drawing her farther into the darkness in seconds, where he could still make out the curve of her pale face. His tiredness fell away as he drank in the sight of her. He gripped her hands hard with his. 'Finally.'

She clung to him too. 'When the word came from Ardfinnan about the massacre of John's men, I feared you were dead,' came her swift, quiet reply. 'That you would never return to me.'

'Ardfinnan was a close call.' He wouldn't share how close it had been. 'Nothing more. And now de Lacy's back, we must change our—'

'Listen to me. We haven't much time.'

'Time for what?'

Panicked whispers flew from her lips. John, heading for Dublin. Theodosia would have to go too. De Lacy, staying here, under oath to John, with just a few men. Including him, Palmer. Eimear O'Connor, who'd saved her life, as John's hostage. And what John did to women. 'Benedict, you have to get Eimear away. Before it's too late.'

'Slow down.' He broke in as she paused for breath, his heart racing at the truth of Theodosia's encounter with the axeman. 'I'll find a way to travel to Dublin with you. I won't leave you alone. Of course you want to help Eimear. As do I, from what you've just told me.' He took a quick look round to make sure they were still alone. 'I'll do that by going to de Lacy. I'll persuade him. Theodosia, she's his wife. He'll be at John's throat in a heartbeat if he thinks the woman he loves is in danger.'

'No, he will not.' Her tone sharpened in greater urgency. 'De Lacy has no love for Eimear. Their marriage, the one that so angers Henry, is in name only. De Lacy and her father forced her into it to seal a truce between them. Eimear gave de Lacy a son, and that is all that matters to him. He doesn't care what happens to her now.'

Her words shocked but did not surprise. It all fitted. The cold argument he'd overheard between de Lacy and Eimear in their tent.

And de Lacy's slaying of the men from the north spoke of his ruthlessness. 'You're sure this isn't more of Gerald's idle gossip?'

'No!' Her whisper whipped back. 'Eimear told me herself. She gave me her trust, as she sees me as a woman of God.' Theodosia's hand tightened on his, her nails digging into his flesh. 'Benedict, I owe Eimear my life. If you do not act, I will.'

'Steady.' His turn to answer – fast, sharp. 'We'll get her out of here. You and I. You can't stay here alone. Eimear will be able to get the protection of her own people. Then we need to go quickly to Henry and tell him about John. He is bringing nothing but disaster here.'

'Agreed.' She gave a firm nod.

He let out a relieved breath. 'Come on.'

As they hurried off towards the keep, a rough plan formed in his mind. Theodosia was a frequent visitor to Eimear in the keep. That would give them reason to enter. Leaving with Eimear would be a lot harder. They'd have to walk down the steps of the motte, with the risk of being seen by any of those feasting below. But if Eimear kept low behind him and Theodosia, they might do it.

A call from a nearby tent. 'Sister! Where are you?'

'Gerald.' Theodosia stopped dead.

Palmer halted too. 'Forget about him. We have to keep going.'

'Sister Theodosia! My drink!' Louder, in the clerk's piercing whine. He was on his way out.

Worse, a guard emerged from his cross-legged seat before a small, lively fire, peering over into the darkness for the source of the commotion.

'I have to quieten Gerald.' Theodosia loosed her hold on Palmer.

'No!' He whispered a desperate order.

'Yes. Otherwise, he will bring the whole camp here. You must carry on. Eimear is on the top floor.' She thrust Palmer from her.

'I know you will find me.' She raised her voice. 'I am here, brother. I have your wine.'

The guard lost interest and sat back down.

Palmer could only watch as Theodosia scooped a jug from the ground beside the entrance to the tent. She raised her hand in the briefest gesture of goodbye.

Then she was gone.

Chapter Nineteen

Palmer headed for the keep, skirting the very edge of the bailey. For now, the sooner he got Eimear to safety, the sooner he could come back for Theodosia. If any kind of harm had come to her in his absence, he would make sure that he brought a very special kind of hell for the royal clerk. And for John. The Lord of Ireland brought out a deep rage in him now.

Moving quickly, Palmer stayed in the shadows. He doubted if anyone would care if they saw him. He was a known and trusted figure who had spent two months defending this place. But he didn't want to attract the attention of one person: de Lacy, still sitting with John. De Lacy missed nothing, even one-eyed as he was. Palmer's hands had not been re-bandaged, despite him giving that as a reason not to go to the feast.

Palmer climbed the steps of the motte, and one of the guards at the top gave him a wave, which he returned. Again, his familiar face worked in his favour. About the only advantage he had left. How to release Eimear O'Connor now? Palmer's reputation was for his fighting for John and Tibberaghny. Not for frequenting the keep. Theodosia would have provided a much more credible reason. Between the two of them, they might have been able to screen Eimear from view.

Doing it on his own would be near impossible. He, Palmer, had had no dealings with the woman other than the day he summoned her from her tent to go before John. She'd made it quite clear that he should not approach her again. She'd probably have to be carried out. Wait. He tried that thought again. Maybe . . . Just maybe.

'Good evening to you.' Palmer greeted the solitary guard as he got to the open gate at the top. De Lacy's extra troops had brought an ease to Tibberaghny.

'Good evening to you, Sir Benedict,' said the guard. 'What brings you up here? The whole place is feasting. Save me and one other.'

'Is that my call to join the celebrations?' Another guard came to the door of the keep. 'No. Thought not.' He spat in disappointment as he walked over to join them.

'You might be better off,' said Palmer. 'Some people will wish they'd never started. Especially the fellow who's spewed his vomit all over the inside of the clerk Gerald's tent.'

Both men laughed long and hard, Palmer shaking his head. He wanted to be out of here. Now. But he couldn't rush it.

'That'll have gone down well,' said the first man.

'He's about as happy as a pig at a slaughterhouse,' said Palmer. 'There's folk scrubbing it out as we speak. But his rugs have had to be taken out for a proper clean, and now he claims he can't sleep with a damp, bare floor, that it'll put a chill in his bones.'

The second man rolled his eyes. 'Sounds like the clerk.'

Palmer went on. 'The Lord John told me to come up and get one from his hall.'

The first guard sucked his teeth. 'Lot of stairs.'

'It'll be heavy to cart out too,' came the grumble from the second.

'Don't trouble yourselves. You've enough to do on your watch.' Palmer offered up a prayer to the saint of laziness, if there was one. 'It'll be far easier for me to do it.'

'Thanks, Sir Benedict,' said the first man as the second nodded and yawned.

Careful to appear in no rush, Palmer walked to the doorway.

Then sprinted up the stairs.

The weight of a large tapestry, collected from the hall and rolled to carry it on one shoulder, slowed Palmer down.

He climbed the next flight as fast as his burden would allow, headed for Eimear's room. Laying it down in relief, he gave a soft knock on the door, whispering close to it. 'My lady?'

'Who dares to disturb me at this time?'

Right room. He tried the handle. Good. Not locked. Yet. John would be sending new orders any minute. 'Quiet, my lady. Please.' Palmer turned the handle and swung the door open to be met with her enraged gaze.

'You. What are you doing here?' Eimear strode right up to him. 'Have you come to string me up from a tree?' She smacked him hard across one cheek, her heavy gold rings catching his skin. 'For my head to put on one of your spikes?' She went to backhand the other.

He grabbed her wrist. 'Sister Theodosia has sent me.'

'Liar.' She landed another strike with her free hand. 'She would have come herself.'

Face smarting, he stopped another deft blow. 'Listen to what I have to say. And then you can decide if I lie.'

'Told you those rugs were heavy, Palmer.' The second guard stood at the bottom of the narrow stairwell as Palmer made his careful way down, his shoulder and back straining under the weight of Eimear hidden in the rolled wool.

'You did. And you were right.'

'Let me give you a lift with that.' The guard put a foot on the bottom step and held his arms up. 'Pass me that front bit.'

'No.' Palmer shot his free hand up. 'I'm fine. Got it balanced.'

'Please yourself.' The guard stepped back as Palmer reached the small vestibule, and they walked outside.

The other man cast him an uninterested glance. 'Hope the clerk appreciates it.'

'I doubt it.' Palmer went to step towards the top step of the motte. And froze. Something had bumped against the back of his leg and bounced to the ground. He glanced down. A narrow calf-skin shoe. One of Eimear's shoes. He stomped his own boot on top of it. 'Good view of the heads on the wall from up here, eh?'

The guards nodded.

'Been trying to count 'em,' said one.

'A hundred altogether.' Palmer held his breathing in check as though he carried his burden with ease. 'Took me and the others hours to get them all up there. The torches too.' He pointed with his free hand, frowning. 'Has that one fallen onto the wall? Those flames look high.'

'Hell's teeth.' Both men looked to where he indicated.

Palmer ground the shoe into the mud. Impossible to duck down and pick it up. 'No, my mistake.'

One of the guards sighed in relief. 'Praise the saints. Bad enough the Irish tried to burn it down. We don't need to do it ourselves.'

'Very true. Goodnight to you both.' Palmer set off towards the steps. 'And thank you again.'

Palmer made the deep shadow of an empty tent as his shoulder threatened to give out. His back wasn't far behind. He dropped his burden to the ground less gently than he would have liked.

To Eimear's credit, she didn't make a sound.

In a few quick movements, he loosened it enough to give her some air, but kept her concealed in it for now.

'Are you all right, my lady?'

She nodded, her breathing fast, her long hair tangled around her face from her slipped head cover. 'This thing is full of dust. I thought I was going to sneeze. So many times. Did anyone see you come down?'

'I don't think so.'

'That's not as good as "no".'

'It's all we have.'

'My shoe?'

'They didn't see it.'

'How do you propose to get me out of the gate? No one will believe you want to carpet the woods.'

Still recovering his own breath, Palmer nodded to where a small barrow rested nearby, loaded with upright barrels.

'A night soil cart?'

'Do you have a better idea, my lady?'

'No.' She went to clamber out of the woollen cover. 'And if you're lying to me, I'll have you drowned in one of those barrels. That is my solemn oath.'

Palmer didn't doubt her for a second.

'We're almost there.' With his cloak pulled over his face and neck in a rough, concealing hood, Palmer kept his voice low as he shoved the rumbling cart along the rutted track that led to the gate. 'Keep very still.'

Of the three barrels, two had been empty and he'd wrested those off. One was full almost to the brim and far too heavy to shift. He'd got the lid as tight as he could, but the sharp, sour reek clogged his nose and throat.

The cart held none too clean straw also, put there to catch the many spills and leaks. Eimear lay beneath the straw, which he'd piled over her to hide her.

He whistled up to the guard at the gatehouse.

'Bit soon for taking that out?' came the shout down.

'The privies are overflowing already,' called Palmer. 'All that feasting has to go somewhere.'

'Fine for some.' The guard shrugged. But he dropped the gate.

'At least you haven't got this lot,' replied Palmer, increasing his pace to send the filthy, thick liquid slopping down the sides in the cart's bounce over the ruts. 'I'll be as quick as I can, but it'll take me a good while. Close the gate up behind me. Too risky to leave it open.'

He was on the smooth planks of the bridge, his shoulders hunched with effort as he pushed.

He didn't care about the stink, about the weight. Right now, he and Eimear were at their most exposed.

Then with another hard bounce, he was on the roadway, moving as fast as he could, uncaring of spills and oozing, wet lumps, making for the darkness beyond the light of Tibberaghny. The trees, his enemy for so much of this campaign, were his friends tonight. 'We're out, my lady.'

The straw stirred.

'Keep down. Another few minutes. Then we're gone.'

He'd done it. With Eimear safely delivered to her people, he'd remove Theodosia from John's entourage. It would take skill and timing, but he knew he'd be able to do it. Like the Irish, he knew how John worked.

Chapter Twenty

'Brother, we need to go to the keep. Please.' Theodosia urged the clerk as much as she dared without becoming openly rude.

'My wine will have been poisoned, sister.' Gerald sat on the edge of his bed, his head resting in his one good hand. 'Poisoned.'

'I am sure if it had been, we would have been told.'

Gerald gave a plaintive wail. 'And what if there is no word because everyone lies dead?'

'Brother.' Theodosia put a firm hand to his shoulder. 'We have had word. Not of wine that has been tampered with, but a summons from the Lord John. An immediate summons. He wants his clerk. We have to go now.' She fought down the demons who whispered that the call related to Benedict. She'd sat up all night, wide awake, as she listened out for any sign that their flight had been discovered. Even when Gerald had eventually passed out, far too late for her to flee with Benedict, she had not closed an eye, praying without cease as she had in her cell at Canterbury.

As the first light of dawn had shown through the walls of the tent, calls and shouts had begun. Not the slow rhythm of a camp awakening after a night's revelry, but urgent sounds that grew quickly louder. In the midst of those, the summons had come from John.

'Oh, God help a poor, tired man.' Gerald got to his feet, oblivious to anything except his own pounding head.

'The fresh air will help to lift your tiredness.'

The gust of the dawn wind that met them as they stepped outside had Gerald complaining again, though Theodosia welcomed its coolness on her face after the staleness of the tent. Her stomach tightened further. It was as she had feared. Men rushed to and fro, involved in rapid exchanges, with purposeful haste.

She made her way towards the steps of the motte with Gerald, rehearsing how she would look, what she would say, when she was in John's presence. Lying did not come to her with ease, did not even come to her with practice. She would have to, for Benedict. For Eimear.

'Watch where you're going, you simpleton.' Gerald staggered as a man bumped into him.

'Sorry, brother.' The man carried a heavy saddle over his arm. 'I'm in a hurry. Getting the search party ready.'

'A search party?' The urgency of his tone caught even the wine-suffering Gerald's interest. 'For whom?'

Theodosia tensed.

'Eimear O'Connor, brother.' The man kept walking, his steps speeding up.

'The savage has gone missing?' Gerald's eyebrows shot up.

The man nodded. 'With Sir Benedict Palmer.' The man headed off towards the area where the horses were kept.

His answer quickened her breath. Benedict's part in this discovered so soon.

'No wonder the Lord John summons us,' said Gerald. 'Imagine: that Palmer fellow and de Lacy's wife. I never thought he'd have such an unnatural lust.'

'Hurry up, brother.' Theodosia almost yanked him off his feet for his instant, lying gossip.

'Careful, careful.' He staggered hard.

Had he gone over into the mud, she would have preferred it. 'My apologies, brother.' Her pretence at sincerity surprised her. Perhaps she was better at lying than she'd thought.

She prayed that it were so: she still had to face John.

As Theodosia and Gerald entered John's private solar in his keep, he stood alone, looking out of the window, observing the busy preparations below.

'My lord.' Gerald bowed, Theodosia too. 'We have heard the news about O'Connor's daughter and Sir Benedict Palmer.'

John turned to face them.

Theodosia quailed inside afresh.

As expected, John's face was set in a grim mask. 'It's a pity that sight of their escape did not travel as quickly as the talk about it now.'

'Deeply regrettable, my lord.' Gerald sniffed. 'Deeply. Such sinful adultery.'

Theodosia kept her eyes lowered in outward respect, hands clasped, to contain the response she wanted to give to the clerk.

'You know something about these outrageous events, Gerald?' said John.

'No, my lord.' He held up a warning finger. 'But I believe it to be a reasonable assumption.'

Theodosia fought to keep her expression unchanged as Gerald carried on.

'I say this because the Church has had to fight a long battle in this land over the most unusual practices in marriage.'

'Perhaps.' John's face darkened. 'But I have been considering a far more serious possibility: that Palmer has taken the woman to satisfy a different desire. She has great worth in this country. Alive or dead.'

Theodosia gasped at his words before she could prevent herself.

John's frowning gaze came back to her. 'Sister?'

'My lord. Forgive me for my boldness. That my lady could be dead is a terrible shock.' She stammered over her words, not under his appraisal, as he would certainly think, but with her deep anger that John would dare suggest that Benedict, saviour of his life, his camp, would betray him. 'I – I only wondered how you came to such an opinion.'

'When the call went out that she had disappeared, I ordered a search of the camp.' John's mouth curled in controlled rage. 'De Lacy found her shoe, crushed in the mud by the keep. It didn't take him long to extract from our so-called guards that Palmer has taken her out. And as I say, alive or dead.'

'God's eyes.' Gerald shook his head.

Theodosia would not, could not let John see her relief, her triumph. They had done it. Eimear, alive. Benedict too. Both now far away from John and harm.

'De Lacy will not be best pleased,' said Gerald.

'Indeed he is not.' John returned to the window. 'There he goes now.'

A loud clatter of hooves echoed up from the bailey.

'Going?' Gerald hurried over to the window, Theodosia following, her tension returned in cold, sudden shock.

'Yes, going.' John clenched the window frame. Hard.

'Breaking his oath to you, my lord?' Gerald's mouth stayed open.

John nodded.

De Lacy's shout to his small group of men led them across the bridge and out of Tibberaghny in an eager, fast trot.

Theodosia had trouble breathing. De Lacy did not care for his wife. Yet now he led a hunt for her. For Benedict too.

'A matter of honour, apparently.' John's tone came tight, strained. 'Or so de Lacy says.'

Theodosia stepped back. Gerald too.

John was about to let fly.

They were right.

The King's son thrust himself away from the window. 'The treacherous Lord of Meath has broken his oath to me!' His shout echoed in the room.

But it was followed by another.

'And I have never been so happy!'

'You're sure we're going in the right direction?' Palmer asked Eimear with laboured breaths as they ran along the muddy, deserted, narrow roadway. Her smooth face had the barest sheen of sweat, whereas he knew his hair and face were soaked.

'Are you doubting me or looking for a rest?' she said.

'Neither. We can't afford to make any mistakes. That's all.' He looked back with every few strides, checking for riders on the road, as he kept up the fast pace that had his leg muscles burning. Running through the dark had been much safer. Daylight had them exposed now.

'I won't put us wrong. The castle of the King of Thomond might be many miles away, but I know how to get there.'

'I thought you said we'd likely find Irish help before then. Help that would get us moving faster.'

'I did. And we should.'

'"Should" isn't good enough.'

'I'll pardon your rude tongue' – she shot him an annoyed look – 'this time.'

'I've done what Theodosia asked and got you away from the Lord John and what he intended to do to you.' Palmer picked up his pace. 'And if my tongue's too rude, then I'll leave any time you like. I need to get back to her as soon as I can.'

'Don't you mean *Sister* Theodosia?' Her question came with a shrewd glance.

'Doesn't matter what I mean. I serve King Henry. Theodosia does too. We share anything we know in our service to our king. We're loyal to him. What I told you at the keep is all you need to know.' He caught her small frown. 'Yes, more of my rude tongue. I haven't the breath to flower my words.'

'Then I'll permit it. For I'm sure you are loyal. But I wouldn't advise leaving. I am your only guarantee of getting through these lands safely. Any Irish warrior that saw you on your own would slay you in an instant. You'd make a wonderful prize.'

'I can fight the Irish. You know that. You saw it at Tibberaghny.'

'But every fight is a new one. I certainly know that. And what if you lose, Sir Benedict Palmer? Who will go back for Theodosia then?'

He had no answer. The thought of her left alone because he failed threatened to unman him.

'I won't abandon her, Sir Benedict.' Eimear's jaw set firm. 'No matter what happens. I reward loyalty and I—'

Palmer grabbed at her arm and hauled her into the cover of the bushes. 'Listen.'

'What?' came her breath of a whisper.

Palmer frowned. 'I could swear I heard a shout,' he murmured.

They both listened intently. All he could hear now was the rustle of the breeze in the trees. The chirping choruses of birds. The quiet ripple of a nearby stream.

Eimear shook her head. 'I can't hear anything untoward.'

'I still think I heard something.' He moved forward again. 'We have to stay off the road. We can make our way along near it.'

'It'll be much, much slower that way.'

'I know. But the road is too exposed. John will send men out looking for us. I know he will.'

He offered a brief prayer of thanks that Hugh de Lacy had given an oath to guard Tibberaghny. Whoever came after them, at least it wouldn't be the scarred Lord of Meath.

Theodosia dug her nails into her palms to test whether she dreamt. De Lacy gone. Yet John rejoiced. Her flesh stung back, told her she was awake.

John's laughing fit had turned him an alarming hue from lack of breath. 'Your faces.' He gasped the words out. 'Oh, your faces. My jest worked wonderfully. You truly believed my rage.' He brought himself back under control. 'I will treasure those expressions for the rest of my life.'

'My lord, I fear you do not grasp the seriousness of what has taken place,' said Gerald. 'Mirthful though you may find it, de Lacy has broken an oath to you. A worrying and important betrayal.'

'His promise before God Himself, my lord.' Theodosia pressed the point, knowing John's temper to be as fragile as the thinnest glass, but her fear for Benedict was too urgent. 'I believe you cannot tolerate it.'

'What you both fail to grasp is that I am happy for him to leave.' John's lips still twitched in a smile. 'I let him.'

His words made no sense to her.

Gerald's face showed the same incomprehension.

John continued. 'De Lacy's rash actions in breaking his oath have unexpectedly helped my plans. You see, it suited me far better when it appeared that he was fighting alongside the Irish and against me, against the English crown.' The smile disappeared in his scowl. 'But then he came back with the heads of the treacherous Irish.'

'Yet a loyal gesture, my lord,' said Gerald. 'Loyal to his king.'

Theodosia nodded.

'Indeed. Henry's hero.' John almost spat. 'De Lacy's return made things very difficult very suddenly. Complicating matters when I had everything under control.'

'Indeed you had, my lord,' said Gerald, keen as always for favour.

Not control. Theodosia ached to challenge his lie. *A vicious, unnecessary conflict. Defeat.*

'Then, a gift from God.' John threw up his hands, his good humour returned. 'Palmer makes off with de Lacy's strumpet of a wife.'

Out of your reach. Theodosia allowed herself the tiny consolation even as her unease whispered within her.

'De Lacy, hero to his boots, has to chase after her for his honour,' said John. 'He couldn't have moved faster if I'd chased him out with an army of ten thousand men.' He shook his head to himself. 'Marvellous. Simply marvellous.'

'My lord, I doubt if King Henry will see it as marvellous,' said Gerald. 'He needs to know of this treachery by de Lacy, though it will be some time before word reaches—'

John held up a hand. 'There will be no letters to Henry.' He went over to his table on which a locked chest rested.

Gerald gave Theodosia a bewildered look.

Her unease grew.

'No word to Henry until I order it.' Pulling a small gold key from his belt pouch, John opened the chest. 'I have far more important work for you and the sister now.' He removed a rolled manuscript and opened it out to reveal its contents. 'Far more important.'

Theodosia stared at what her half-brother held in his hands. All she had believed about this disastrous mission began to crumble,

crumble as quickly as the stones of the Sonning chapel had the day the earth moved.

Though heavily decorated, the attempts at illustration and colour on the borders of the manuscript showed a hand with little skill. The large lettering at its centre lacked sure lines and consisted only of four words. But what words.

John, King of Ireland.

Even Gerald was silenced.

'Now do you understand?' John beamed like the vellum was made of gold and inlaid with diamonds.

'No, my lord.' Gerald looked genuinely perplexed.

'Nor I, my lord.' Theodosia forced the words out through dry lips. Not fully. But enough that a terrible realisation went through her as swiftly as poison surges through a vein.

John's smile wavered. A little. 'I forgive you both for your slowness. Most minds lag behind mine.' He laid the manuscript on the table with careful reverence. 'This will be included in the great history that you will write for me. My acquisition of a crown. My ascension to a throne.' He gave the clumsy work a gentle pat. 'I have drawn this myself. It has taken me many hours.' Another pat. 'The throne of Ireland, just as it says.'

'But – but Henry sent you here in his name, my lord,' said the stunned-sounding clerk.

'Oh, yes.' John's smile returned. 'My father's name. Under his superior lordship. An old man, hanging on to everything for himself, as old men do. Henry. The Pope. But this says otherwise.' He tapped the manuscript hard with a fingernail, the declaration of himself as king in the poor lettering like a crude bellow from the page. 'Do you see, both of you?'

'Yes, my lord,' whispered Theodosia. She saw it all. But too late.

'Of course, my lord, of course.' Gerald gave a fawning bow. 'Or should I say "your Grace"?' His high-pitched laugh. 'Not all men of mature years are set in their ways. I for one can see the benefits of a new path.' He nodded hard. 'Change. I must say, yours is a remarkable work. Such a wonderful record for posterity.'

The speed of the clerk's self-serving capitulation had Theodosia clenching her fists.

'It is, isn't it?' John looked at it fondly once more.

'May I ask, my lord, how is your' – Gerald cleared his throat – 'ascension to the Irish throne going to come to pass?'

'De Lacy's delivery of the heads of the Irish brutes gave me a wonderful idea,' replied John. 'He defeated one Irish king, one Irish tribe. Yet there are so many others. I shall summon them all here and show them what de Lacy has done.'

'A gathering of the Irish kings, my lord? Are you sure that's wise?' Gerald gave a nervous titter. 'After Waterford, I mean.'

'I have de Lacy's men of Meath at my side to ensure my safety, Gerald. And my plan to bring the Irish kings here is more than wise; it is brilliant. Oh, how I will grieve at his terrible actions. Oh, how I shall proclaim he should be stopped. I will call it "the murder of your fair people". That, by the way, would be a wonderful title for one of the chapters in my history.' John nodded to himself as his eyes went to his manuscript again. 'Eimear O'Connor has helped my cause too.' He gave a long, satisfied sigh. 'Now I can claim that even she fled from her own husband because of his slaughter of the Irish.'

Theodosia closed her eyes, opened them, in a long, slow blink. Her doing.

'I shall of course agree a new treaty with the Irish kings,' said John.

'With respect, my lord, King Henry already has a treaty in place. The one that made Rory O'Connor High King,' said Gerald.

'That treaty is with my father,' said John.

And my *father. A man who has given you so much. Yet you grasp for even more. You seek to steal a whole land from him.*

John carried on. 'The old, slow-footed English king. It has been weak and useless since the day it was agreed. The time has come for change. My treaty will be to agree a brand new settlement. I will divide up de Lacy's lands amongst them. Land, you see – that's what they all want. And de Lacy will be left with none of it.' He pulled in a long breath of delight. 'Same as Henry.'

'My lord. I am not trying to cast gloom.' Gerald wore his best obsequious smile. 'But Henry has always had the greatest of difficulty getting them to hold the peace. And many times they have not.'

'That is because my father is limited, Gerald. Limited.' John jabbed a finger at him. 'I, however, am not. I might have lost one hostage today, thanks to that scoundrel Palmer. But I will have many, many more. I will ask the Irish for their children as part of their land deal. Same as my father has done in the past.'

Theodosia's breath stalled. She knew what John had desired to do to Eimear as a hostage. What of these children?

'They'll be a messy, noisy handful, my lord.' Gerald grimaced. 'Are you sure you want a royal court full of Irish whelps?'

'They won't be a handful.' John shook his head at his own thoughts. 'They'll be wonderful decoration. At least the girls will. I will adorn the walls of my castle with their little heads. I have de Lacy to thank for such wonderful inspiration.'

Theodosia clamped a hand to her mouth to stifle a cry as Gerald gasped.

'I will tell the Irish kings that the boys will follow unless they serve me with absolute loyalty. The howls of protest are depressingly predictable. But they will bow down to me.' John gestured to the window, to the green below, the curve of mountain beyond. 'Then all this land will be mine. I may be a king's youngest son, but I will have a crown.' He nodded. 'John, King of Ireland.' He brought his triumphant gaze back to Gerald and Theodosia. 'You see? Lackland no more.' He held a hand out to his manuscript again. 'Now, shall we begin?'

Chapter Twenty-One

Theodosia sat at the table in John's solar, scribing with her usual diligence even as she wanted to hurl herself at John and tear at his eyes.

The King's son had spoken for almost two hours about the very beginning of his conquest of the country, Gerald chiming in with equally lengthy embellishments. They ordered her to pause frequently while they encouraged each other in increasingly elaborate suggestions of how events should be described. Their current debate concerned John's clothing on the day of his arrival at the port of Waterford. If John had worn as much gold, as many jewels as he claimed, he would have been unable to stand upright.

She cared not. Her head thumped in a horrified rhythm, her heart matching it so hard that she thought it would break apart.

The children. The children of the Irish kings. Bile rose in her throat again in her shock, her disgust, as John's intended plans for them hung in a revolting picture before her. Plans that she had no doubt would work. She put her hand to her mouth lest she lose control. Nothing mattered now. Nothing. No lands, no wealth, no kingdoms. Nothing. Nothing, except the delivery of those so young from this hideous fate.

'Sister, put down that I wore the emerald ring that the Pope sent to my father many years ago,' said John, wine goblet in hand, despite the early hour. 'The one that is for the King of Ireland.'

The ring Theodosia had herself seen, the one Dymphna had brought to Sonning. She bent to the manuscript again to reluctantly comply with another untruth. If only Benedict were still here. He would know what to do. But she had sent him away with Eimear. And now the murderous de Lacy pursued them. Her head pounded afresh.

'Ah. Hold one moment, sister.' Enthroned in a large, carved chair, Gerald bared his long teeth in a wide, indulgent smile at John. 'King Henry keeps that under secure lock and key, my lord. We must have accuracy.'

She paused, her hand to her forehead to ease the pain that coursed through it. Her attempts to save Eimear had condemned others so much more in need of protection. She knew the agony of a child's life being put under threat. She had to – *had to* – stop it. But, God forgive her, she did not know how.

'But who will be lauded as the King of Ireland?' John grinned back at Gerald, his face aglow with his triumph. 'Accuracy!'

'Of course.' Gerald raised his hands in exaggerated delight. 'As the Lord John says, sister.' He glanced in her direction. 'Are you feeling unwell?'

'Only a headache, brother.' The ink flowed from her quill, with her script neat, orderly, mocking the terrible disorder that raged within her. She tried to calm her upset. She had to think.

'Good.' Gerald already had his attention back on John. 'We should turn to the arrival of the Irish at Waterford, should we not?'

'Oh, yes.' John flung himself into a low chair opposite Gerald, legs dangling over the arm. 'The men of the three Irish kings. Imagine if the three kings who visited the stable in Bethlehem had been as hideous in their appearance as those fellows, eh? Armed with axes to visit the Christ child?'

Theodosia finished the words about the emerald ring, gripping the quill so hard she thought it would snap in her fingers. She would not record blasphemy.

'Oh, very good, my lord.' Gerald gave his high-pitched laugh. 'They were indeed a sight. I had a mortal fear of an axe shattering your royal skull.'

'As had I. But I held my nerve.' John exhaled a long, proud breath. 'Sister, those words: shattering my skull. I like those. Very dramatic.'

His words jolted through her even as she nodded. *Shattering a skull.* Of course. The person to whom she should turn for help. The man she had seen murdered in precisely that brutal manner before her very eyes at Canterbury, even as he had saved her life. Saint Thomas Becket, Saint Thomas the Martyr. She began her prayer to him even as she wrote, begging him to the depths of her soul for an answer.

'You must name whose treacherous courts they came from,' said Gerald. 'McCarthy of Desmond. O'Brien of Thomond. O'Connor of Connacht.'

I beseech you, my Lord Becket. Please come to the aid of the blameless, the innocent.

'O'Connor.' John scowled as he gestured for Gerald to refill his cup. 'Sounds like a coward. With his truce with de Lacy so he wouldn't have to fight him.'

Answer those who cry to you for your intercession.

'I don't think I would want to fight the scarred lord.' Gerald shuddered. 'I see those heads on spikes outside in my dreams. And yet he makes such a show of being a devout supporter of the Church.'

Oh, blessed, oh, merciful, Saint Thomas: hear my prayer.

'De Lacy?' John looked askance at Gerald.

I beseech you with humble and contrite heart: hear my prayer.

'Oh, yes, my lord.' Gerald nodded. 'Difficult to countenance, but he has made extensive ecclesiastical benefices over the years, especially to the abbey in Dublin where he buried his first wife.'

I beseech you: hear my prayer.

John grunted. 'Unexpected. The Church has enough wealth, if you ask me.'

Hear my prayer.

Gerald's smile became more fixed. 'De Lacy's first wife, Rose of Monmouth, was a fine woman, by all accounts.'

Amen.

The clerk went on. 'Her tomb at the abbey of Saint Thomas the Martyr is a fitting memorial to her.'

Theodosia's mouth dried at his words, but she forced herself to speak. 'Should I write of this holy abbey, my lord?'

'No.' John waved her question aside. 'The hideous men. Where was I?'

'I have written their names only,' she said.

'Then we will describe them. This will be good sport.' John settled back, his good humour returned.

Theodosia waited, her hands folded in her lap so no one could see them shaking in anticipation.

Her Lord Becket had answered her as he always did. Now the rest was up to her. She had to find a way out of here.

And find Hugh de Lacy.

'A brief stop, my lady. Nothing more.' Palmer pushed his way through the high fronds of vivid green ferns, making for what he craved. He hunkered down on his protesting calf muscles at the edge of the shallow stream and plunged his hands into the clear water, sluicing its cooling relief over his head.

Eimear pulled her veil off to do likewise, releasing a long, twisted plait the colour of dark copper. 'You'll have to forgive my shameless appearance for a few minutes, Sir Benedict.' She soaked her long hair with many handfuls.

'How you look doesn't matter, my lady.' He drank mouthful after mouthful of water, with cupped hands, in grateful slurps. 'It might be better to leave your veil off until we get to safety. White catches the eye far more easily than your hair colour in these woods.'

'A good point.' She bundled the veil into her leather belt pouch. 'And I will look more like a savage.'

Palmer glanced at the gold Eimear wore on every finger and thumb. 'You're no savage, my lady.'

'That is Gerald the clerk's word for me.' She grimaced. 'I'd love to string him up by his sinewy neck.'

'You and me both. If nothing else, it would be a relief to stop him talking for once.' He took another mouthful. 'My lady.'

Eimear laughed, the first time he'd seen her do so.

'A better point,' she said. 'And I give you permission to use my name. It's only one word, and not the two you currently address me with. Who knows when we might need that extra second?'

'Then I'm Palmer. Two seconds gained.'

Her smile left her eyes in one alert blink. 'Hooves. I swear it.'

She was right. Distant. With the unmistakeable rumble made by several horses. Their rhythm was too constant, too regular to come from the woods. 'The roadway.'

Eimear stood up. 'We should run.' She prepared to act with her words.

Palmer halted her. 'No. We need to see who they are.'

'And if they're John's men? What good will that do?'

'We'll make sure they don't see us.'

'Then use some of this.' Eimear bent to scoop a couple of handfuls of wet mud from the stream bed. Passing one to Palmer, she smeared the other over her forehead as he did likewise.

'If it's a group of Irishmen,' he said, 'we don't want to miss this chance. Now, hurry. We haven't much time.'

They swiftly shadowed their faces in wet mud, and Palmer led Eimear with rapid steps to a dense stand of shrubs near to the roadway.

The echo of the hooves grew louder. Purposeful. Relentless.

He forced his way into its centre, the tall nettles that clogged the ground prickling any exposed flesh with their soft leaves worse than any sharp branches or thorns.

'They're getting closer, Palmer.' Eimear kept her voice low, but he heard her doubt.

'They won't see us in here. Not unless we show ourselves. And we don't know who they—'

'Normans.' Her whisper reached his ears at the same moment he saw the dull gleam of a metal helmet through the thick leaves.

'Then we keep absolutely still. No noise.'

'Of course.'

A quick glance showed her melted into the shadowed, dappled green. Her hair, the mud, her darker clothing. Nothing showed. He'd be the same. Good.

The first riders drew level, men with ill-fitting mail and nervous faces at being out here. Men whom he recognised. On horses he recognised. All from Tibberaghny. John's men. Men he, Palmer, had led. And now they hunted him.

Then, their leader. On his huge destrier: the Lord of Meath. In charge of these men of Tibberaghny. Not his own. This made no sense.

Eimear's arm against Palmer's tensed no more than a leaf quiver as his own stomach tightened.

De Lacy spoke to the men nearest him, his quiet words lost under the thump of the hooves. But even as he did so, his half-gaze went left, right, scanning every inch of the woods on either side, flattened nose up as if the man sniffed the air too.

Palmer let loose a string of silent curses even as he stayed as still as stone, heart leaping in his chest. One lucky glance, one shaft of sunlight that caught the gleam of the white of an eye: that was all de Lacy needed. He'd be on them, calling the others down on them too. He, Palmer, had one sword. He might as well have held one of the nettles for all the chance he would have. This was not supposed to happen. Not from what Theodosia had told him.

Palmer didn't know how such a big horse seemed to move so slowly. Slowly. Until, finally, de Lacy passed from view. It mattered not. Palmer remained taut as a bowstring as the others went by in a close group. Even Simonson had been brought along, God help him. The big young man looked ready to faint, eyes darting from one spot to the next.

The thud of hooves and the jangle and clink of metal bits lessened, finally died away, and the sounds of leaves in the wind, and birds and flies and bees, claimed the day again.

Eimear turned to speak to him, but he put a finger to his lips. Waited. And waited.

Palmer pulled in a long breath. 'They've gone.'

'He didn't see us. Thank God.' Eimear's muddy face beaded with sweat where it had stayed dry as she ran.

Palmer brought his focus back now that the threat had passed. 'But I'm sure he wouldn't harm you, my la— Eimear. If you were to be swift, you could catch de Lacy up. Tell him what John planned to do to you. He could protect you far better than I.'

'And risk my head being atop a spike too, to keep company with the other dead Irish warriors?' She bent to grab at a handful of dock leaves and crushed them in her hands, releasing their moisture. 'My so-called husband is interested in one thing only:

land. Who knows what deal he has struck with the Lord John?' She rubbed her nettle-reddened hands with the leaves.

'We don't know.' Palmer frowned. None of this made sense. 'But he has John's men. Why not his own?'

'Hugh de Lacy makes deals and alliances every day he's on this earth.' Her calves were next. 'I will only trust my life with an Irishman now.' She flung the used leaves away. 'And you. Sister Theodosia is lucky to have an ally like you.'

'I'm not much of an ally to Theodosia right now.' His anxiety for her gnawed at him more sharply than ever. 'She's still with John.' He pushed his way back out through the bushes, Eimear after him. 'I have to get her out of there.'

'Then we make for Thomond as fast as we can,' said Eimear. 'Should we go back to the roadway? They've all gone past.'

'Too risky now we know they're on the road.' Palmer pointed ahead. 'The trees look clearer that way. We'll make the best speed we can.'

Eimear cast him a frowning look. 'Doing that will take us so much longer.'

'Better longer than without our heads,' said Palmer. 'Come on.'

The men sent by the Irish kings were the source of much merriment for John and Gerald, with their descriptions becoming wilder and wilder as they egged each other on.

Theodosia kept her counsel, although she struggled to keep up with their demands to write this way, then that way. She had a plan. She was not sure if it would work. But she had to try. All she needed was for them to be distracted. If only for a few moments.

'I must say,' said John, 'I never thought I'd be holding McCarthy's severed hand in mine so soon after looking into his man's ugly face. Write that, sister.'

'Oh, keep the severed hand as a surprise, my lord,' said Gerald.

John sighed. 'Yes, it was rather delicious, wasn't it? Very well: we shall leave that for now. We have discussed the man from Connacht, with his craggy face like an ancient dragon. O'Brien of Thomond's messenger?'

'The big, damp one? More stupid than the other two put together?'

Now came her chance. 'Brother, if I may make a suggestion.'

One annoyed and one surprised face met her words, but she ploughed on with haste.

'Brother, you told me the most amusing story about the court of the King of Thomond.'

'Did I?' said Gerald.

Oh, please do not be as much a teller of untruths as I think you are. 'The woman he keeps at his court?' she prompted.

'Oh, yes!' Gerald turned to John. 'My lord, this is utterly, utterly choice.'

'Go on.' John's pursed lips moistened. 'Is it a story about his lust?'

'Even better, my lord. The King of Thomond keeps a woman covered in hair as a pet.' Gerald slapped his thigh.

John's jaw dropped as he stared at Gerald. 'No.'

'It is true, he does. She has a beard down to her waist, and a crest from her neck down her spine.'

Now or never. They were both rapt: Gerald in the telling, John in the listening. Theodosia put her hand over John's letter seal and slid it back towards her.

'But this unnatural creature must be a man.' John's gaze remained locked on Gerald.

She scooped the seal onto her lap.

'Not at all, my lord. Not even a hermaphrodite. In all other respects she is sufficiently feminine.'

Next, some wax. Again: cover, slide, scoop.

John's face distorted in revolted fascination. 'You mean she has a cunny?'

Gerald shot Theodosia a look as she replaced her hands in full view, sweat breaking out over her whole body. The objects were still on her lap. If they were seen, her attempted theft would be discovered.

'I apologise for this talk, sister,' said the clerk.

'Oh, shut up, Gerald.' John took a drink. 'The sister is always a disapproving mope. Tell me more about the hairy woman.'

'Well, she follows the court.' Gerald embarked on a more lengthy description.

Theodosia quickly hid her treasures in her belt pouch, waiting for her chance.

'Do many men have sex with her?' John again.

Theodosia gave an exclamation of disgust she barely stifled. She put a hand to her forehead as she drew fresh looks of disapproval. 'I am sorry, my lord. But my head aches so.'

John jerked a thumb at the door. 'Out with you. Your constant interruptions are ruining this.'

'You do look peaky,' said Gerald. 'I said so earlier.'

With a swift bow, Theodosia left, the men's attention back on the hair-covered woman of the Irish court of O'Brien of Thomond. The court to which she was headed.

Theodosia approached the fenced area of the bailey that held the horses, her stride purposeful, though she could not allow herself to run. She knew she had little time. If John were to see her, see what she held in her right hand, she would be dead within the hour.

She was not even sure that she had guessed this right. But Benedict's words had come back to her, clear as if he stood beside her: *Eimear can seek sanctuary with her own people.*

He and Eimear would be making for the nearest court to do so. Of the three kings that had sent men to Waterford, McCarthy was dead. O'Connor's lands were farther away. That left O'Brien of Thomond. And where Benedict and Eimear went, so de Lacy would follow. This she had surmised. She swallowed hard. She hoped.

She would go there too.

One of the grooms, a man whom she did not recognise, shovelled manure onto a cart. He must be one of de Lacy's fighters. So many of them were here now. None of them knew her, as many of John's men did from her ministrations to the wounded.

'Good sir, I need the services of a messenger.' She spoke with authority as she walked up to him. 'At once.'

The groom took in her habit and bowed in respect. He whistled to a group of men who sat relaxing and dozing in the breezy sunshine.

One rose, yawning and scratching his thick, fair hair as he walked over. 'I'm needed?'

'The sister here.' The groom went back to his work.

The messenger also gave her his respect. 'What can I do for you, sister?' He could not have been much older than her own son.

She held up the object she had in her grasp. 'This letter has to go to the court of the King of Thomond. Immediately and with all haste. It is from the Lord John.'

The messenger looked at the seal and extended his hand. 'Of course, sister.'

Theodosia kept it in her grasp. 'I have to deliver it personally. I will need to ride with you.'

'Sister, I don't wish to be disrespectful, but you will not be able to ride as fast as I. Also, it's a very risky journey.' The man shook his head. 'I'll go to the Lord John and ask him to rethink his decision.' He went to take the letter from her.

Pulling it back from his grasp, she gave him her fiercest look. 'Good sir: I have been tasked with this message because it is of the utmost importance and concerns urgent matters that relate to the business of the Church.' She stepped aside. 'If you want to question the decision of the King's son, then please feel free to do so. While you do, I will seek out another messenger. One who responds to orders. I am sure the Lord John will have a view on your loyalty.'

The young man glanced up at the motte, then back at Theodosia.

Her heart pounded. The blank parchment she held came from a store Gerald kept in his tent. Applying the seal to satisfactory neatness had taken her four attempts, such was the trembling of her hands.

Another look back at the motte.

She clicked loudly with her tongue in displeasure. 'Very well.' She started for the group of men.

'Wait, sister. Wait.'

She halted. 'What is it?'

'May I please check the seal?' The man held out his hand again.

With an elaborate sigh, she handed the letter over. Now she glanced repeatedly at the motte as the man made a close examination of the imprinted wax. John, Gerald: either could arrive out of the keep at any moment.

The man nodded. 'It's as it should be.'

'Well, of course it is as it should be. The—'

He held up a placating hand. 'I have to check seals are intact before I set off. We can go.'

'Then I thank you.'

The man bowed. 'The name is Nagle, sister.'

'Sister Theodosia. We must make all haste.'

Nagle hurried off, calling to the groom to prepare two horses.

Theodosia slid the fake letter into her belt pouch, her eyes still drawn to the motte. A few minutes, a few more minutes. That was all she needed.

'Stop,' said Palmer to Eimear. 'One moment.'

She halted in the quiet of the dense woods as he pounded his cramping leg muscles with his fists yet again.

'Remind me to run away with a young man in future,' she said.

'I might not be young but I got you out, didn't I?'

His testy reply got a grin. 'You're so easy to rile, Palmer.'

He grunted in reply as he pushed his way through thorny bushes to the next clearing.

And came face to face with the mounted Simonson.

The big young man was at the far side of the clearing, relieving himself from the back of his horse. But he saw Palmer. 'Hey!'

Palmer thrust Eimear back into the bushes. 'Stay in there.'

He drew his sword. And charged.

The horse reared in fright.

Simonson clung to the pommel with one hand, uncaring of his disordered clothing as he fumbled for his sword with the other. 'Get away, you Irish devil!'

Palmer lunged for the reins, but Simonson's shouting startled the beast even more.

'Away, I said!' He swished his sword at Palmer's head.

'Stop!' Palmer ducked. 'It's me, Simonson. Have you no eyes?'

'Palmer?' Simonson's voice squeaked up in shock. 'But you look like one of them. And you've taken one of them.'

Palmer grabbed at the reins again and missed, cursing as the horse stood on his foot. 'No time to explain.' He held up his sword. 'Give me your horse.'

'No, Palmer. No way.'

Palmer's hand got the reins this time, pulling the horse's head down. But the leather slipped through his muddy fingers as the animal jerked back at Simonson's shriek. 'Forcurse it, Simonson. The horse.'

'No! De Lacy will kill me!' The sword again, this time nicking the horse's ear.

The animal wheeled in shock and pain, and Palmer dodged a swift, hard kick.

He weighed up his sword. 'And I'll kill you if you don't give me that animal.'

'No, no.' Simonson hauled the horse's head down and kicked hard at its sides, forcing it forward and on.

About to be trampled, Palmer jumped back.

Simon's yell and fall happened at the same second.

He crashed to the ground next to Palmer, blood pouring from his lip, eyes and mouth gaping as the wind drove from his big body.

'The horse!'

Palmer looked to the source of the female call.

Eimear ran from the bushes, gesturing at him to catch the animal. 'It's all right. Your man Simonson's not dead.' She trailed her long, braided belt on the ground, the makeshift sling with which she'd delivered such a fast, accurate shot.

Palmer corralled the horse in a corner, judging when best to grab the reins again, as Eimear stood over Simonson, refastening her belt on her tunic. 'I didn't use a big stone.'

Pleas for help from the Virgin gasped from the fallen Simonson, his breath returned.

'See?' She gave Palmer a quick grin. 'Now let's get on that animal. We'll make Thomond in no time.' Her face changed. 'Down!'

Palmer dropped to the ground.

The bushes next to him broke open in a shower of snapping twigs and torn leaves as de Lacy's huge destrier charged out, the lord swinging his broadsword in a deadly arc where Palmer's head had been the moment before.

'Damn you, Palmer!' De Lacy roared his frustration and went for a lower strike.

Palmer parried with his own sword as Eimear, hidden now from his sight on the other side of de Lacy, screamed at him to stop.

'Listen to your wife, man!' Palmer fended off another strike.

'You know my wife, do you?'

'I haven't touched your wife!' And another.

'You're dead.'

Palmer landed a perfect heavy strike that blasted the sword from the lord's hands. The weapon flew into the bushes in a high arc. He raised his hands, still holding his sword in one, to show he meant de Lacy no harm. 'My lord.'

'You're still dead.' His hand went to the side of the saddle Palmer couldn't see.

'Palmer, go!' came Eimear's unseen scream. 'Now!'

She was right.

De Lacy held a mace, and murder showed in his half-face.

Palmer shoved his sword back in his scabbard, running for the abandoned horse. He mounted in a fast scramble, shouting the animal into a panicked bolt. He took off through the trees.

But de Lacy was right behind him.

Chapter Twenty-Two

'Palmer! You're a dead man!' De Lacy's shout rang through the trees.

Palmer kept his head down, dodging low branches that whipped at his face and eyes, tore at his skin, as he slapped hard on the horse's rump with one hand to keep up his speed. He had only one stirrup, so his balance was bad. He gripped the pommel with his free hand. If he came off now, de Lacy would get his wish.

'I know you heard me!'

Palmer thrust for the empty swinging stirrup with his foot, swearing hard. He had to get it, had to ride this mount properly. He glanced over his shoulder.

Mace in hand, de Lacy gained ground, in full control of his animal, its huge head and hooves smashing through the thick undergrowth like it was a soft haystack.

Come on. Palmer's furious order to himself and a hard jab with his foot got the stirrup. He steered his horse off to the side. Forget the trees – he needed the road now, needed it to outrun de Lacy, to get him back to Tibberaghny. To Theodosia. He'd use Henry's name to protect them, get them both out of there. Make sure Eimear was safe. If de Lacy didn't get hold of him first.

And he was out, the narrow, muddy rutted road opening up before him. 'Get on.' His horse responded, its stride going from a jerky bolt to a smoother canter.

But the crash from the bushes told him de Lacy had emerged too, the second set of bigger hooves thudding fast behind him.

'I've got you now!'

Palmer drew his sword again, urging his horse to a gallop. The air rushed fast into his face, mud splattering up in a sticky spray with each strike of hoof on ground.

The chasing hooves came louder.

Palmer bent low, kicking his animal to greater speed, its surging, sweating neck and mane inches from his face.

Then de Lacy rode beside him, higher in the saddle than Palmer on his smaller mount, mace already in a wide swing.

Palmer ducked down and to the side, half off his saddle with an oath.

De Lacy met air, then the flank of Palmer's horse.

His animal shrilled in fear and pain, gained greater speed from the strike. Palmer clung on, no way to use his sword as he fought to retake his seat.

'Next one, Palmer.' De Lacy drew almost level again.

Palmer pushed his horse on harder, but the animal tired now, every breath a snort. It couldn't outrun the destrier. Not for much longer. The mace connected with Palmer's shoulder as he ducked away again. Pain. But bearable. 'That all you can do, de Lacy?'

An angry bellow answered him.

Then he saw what he needed a few yards ahead. A huge fallen tree. Lying off one side of the road. He kicked his horse on, pulling its head at the last minute so they made straight for it.

'Get up!' His yell and his kick got his mount to rise. Hooves left the ground in the right moment of weightlessness as he crouched low over the horse's neck. One hard strike, front hooves down. Another – the back. They'd made it.

His horse surged on ahead.

A yelled curse and a crash rang out from behind him.

Palmer looked back to see de Lacy still rolling across the muddy road from his fall, the destrier spinning and snorting from its refusal. 'So you've got me, de Lacy?' He faced forward again with another kick for greater speed.

And a low-hanging branch slammed him from the saddle.

John shifted in his chair and yawned long and hard. His many hours spent on his great history had worn him out. He stretched his tired shoulders to give them some relief. 'I think my history is going to eclipse all others. Don't you, Gerald?'

'I don't merely think so, my lord.' The clerk held up a finger yet again. 'I know so. Wondrous words you have recorded today. Truly wondrous.'

God, the man was so annoying. 'You know, you couldn't be more obsequious if you lay on your back with your legs in the air and asked me to tickle your stomach.'

'My apologies, my lord.' Fear flickered across his eyes.

Good. Always good to keep people on their toes. 'The work we did today wasn't wondrous at all. It was a start, Gerald. No more.'

'Of course, my lord.'

'But I tire now.' John poured himself another goblet of wine. 'I shall relate no more today, and I shall relax with a leisurely meal.' He nodded at the many items used by the nun that remained on the table. 'Tidy all that up. I cannot abide such disorder.'

Gerald held up his bandaged arm, about to plead injury, then obviously thought better of it. 'Of course, my lord.'

The clerk went to the table, making a great show of picking things up with one hand.

Definitely annoying. John took another mouthful.

The man fiddled with parchment, picked up a quill, put down another, moved inkpots around with a sharp sigh.

And slow. John drained his cup. He didn't care. The clerk could spend all night here doing this one simple task if he so desired. He got to his feet. 'I'll assume that you prefer to fool with this task rather than come to the feast tonight.'

But Gerald no longer had the look of a fawning puppy or a put-upon servant. He looked worried. 'It's not that, my lord.'

'Then what?'

'It's just that – that . . .' The clerk's one-handed rummaging through the objects on the table took on an abrupt urgency. 'I – I can't find your seal, my lord.'

'Do I have to perform every task in this place?' John got to his feet and stamped over. He sifted through the items with the greatest of efficiency, waiting for the moment when his fingers closed on his metal seal. He would rap it on the clerk's long teeth when he did. No. He'd missed it. He searched again, as Gerald peered between the fine barbs of a quill feather in useless endeavour. 'The floor, man. Check the floor.'

Gerald bobbed down like he'd been struck.

John rifled through the contents of the table yet again, looked in the chest. Still nowhere to be seen. A strange thought took hold of him.

'Not down here, my lord.' Gerald stood up, scarlet in the face with effort.

'No.' John stared at the lumps of wax. 'I don't believe it would be.' The thought grew, tightened its grip on him, spawned others, then others, all linking into a neat chain. He looked to Gerald. 'Tell me, how long have you known Sister Theodosia?'

'Oh, let me see. It must be a couple of months now, maybe more, probably nearer th—'

'Stop meandering!' John's scream filled the room. 'Where did she come from?'

'I met her on my ship, my lord.'

'With?' John grabbed for the front of the man's robe, twisting it hard. 'Tell me everything you know. With as few words as possible.'

The clerk's words came out in a tremulous torrent. 'She was on the ship, with the Abbess of Godstow. The Abbess is Irish by birth, but the sister wasn't – isn't – she told me of her holy pilgrimage to Jerpoint, to take instructions on manuscripts, so when I was ambushed – no, injured – I thought she would do to assist me. That's all.'

'All?' John twisted harder.

'Yes. Yes.'

He shoved Gerald from him, the clerk clutching his chest and half-sobbing in some air.

'You know I have long suspected I have a spy in this camp, Gerald?'

'Yes, my lord.' Now he did weep. Openly.

'And now I know I have a spy. And you brought her to me.'

Gerald sobbed on. 'I am sorry, my lord.'

'You're a fool, Gerald. A fool.' John marched to the door. 'I am now going to find Sister Theodosia. I will brand her body all over with my stolen seal.' He jabbed a finger at Gerald. 'And then you will put her head on a spike.'

Gerald sank to the floor in noisy, weeping anguish.

John made for the stairs, fury driving his steps even harder.

The little whore would rue the day she'd ever tried to best him.

Palmer dragged his breath back into his protesting chest, forced his legs to move, his arms to raise. Get up – he had to get up. He staggered to his feet, his sword a miracle in one hand. His horse was gone. Not de Lacy's. The destrier still stood nearby on the road, nostrils flaring, ears alert, eyes rolling.

He staggered to the log to look over.

De Lacy lay prostrate on the ground, unmoving. He'd taken a huge fall, thank the saints.

Palmer hauled himself back over the log, every muscle in his back and legs screaming as he did so. He didn't care. The destrier. He had to get the destrier.

The horse eyed him with mistrust, skittering as he approached.

'Easy, fellow, easy.' He kept his voice calm, low. Not only could this beast flee at a second's notice, but it could also decide in a heartbeat to kick him or trample him into the next life. Stepping with as much caution as his protesting limbs would allow, he made it to a couple of feet away.

The horse snorted hard.

'Good fellow.' Another step. Closer.

His hand went to the reins.

And his legs were hit from under him.

Palmer pitched onto the stony mud of the road with a yell, sword falling from his hand as de Lacy went to slam the mace into him again.

He rolled to avoid the strike, landing on his back.

'Mistake.' De Lacy's metal boot was on Palmer's throat, mace raised ready to strike as the lord stared down at him, framed against the blue sky.

Palmer held his hands up, squinting into the light. 'I can explain all this.' His words came out hard as the crush on his windpipe.

'Oh, you'll explain, Palmer. You'll explain everything. I'll smash every single finger and toe you possess as you explain.'

Swift hoof beats echoed along the road again.

'Here's my men now. And when you're done explaining, if I don't like the explanation, I'll get the men of Tibberaghny to hang you.' De Lacy smiled. 'I suspect I won't like it. Any of it.' He looked up as the hooves got louder, opened his mouth to call out.

Palmer curled a fist. Swung it up at de Lacy's groin.

The lord collapsed, retching.

Palmer grabbed the mace from him, rose to his knees. He'd fight them off with this – he'd have to. Then get hold of the destrier.

'Benedict! Stop!'

He dreamt. Or he was dead.

It wasn't the men of Tibberaghny. For riding hard towards him with another male rider close behind her: *Theodosia.*

The groom hung from the gibbet, the man's legs kicking and flailing as the life was slowly strangled from him.

'Cut him down.' John gave the order with a click of his fingers. Still too quick an end. The idiot had let the nun ride from this camp with a letter that bore his seal, a messenger at her side. Without so much as a glimmer of suspicion.

The soldiers at Tibberaghny, de Lacy's men, acted at once on John's order. Excellent. De Lacy had trained them well. They had strung up one of their own without turning a hair.

'Leave him for now.'

They stepped away as the groom writhed on the ground, hands tied behind his back, still trying to gulp for air like a reddened, beached fish.

'You see this?' John pointed to him.

The solemn-faced assembly at the camp murmured that they did.

Gerald, standing close by and looking near collapse, nodded too.

John continued. 'This is what happens to people who betray me. This man did. He failed to stop a spy leaving this camp. Yes, the meek and mild Sister Theodosia. He could not even stop a nun.'

Low rumbles of laughter and a few grins rewarded his witty words.

'I know. Incredible as it may seem.' John shared a smiling nod. 'Of course, you, all of you, as a band of loyal fighting men, brought me the heads of Irishmen. A swift end, losing a head.' He dropped his smile. 'No such mercy for traitors to me. You understand?'

Again a murmur of acquiescence, serious this time. From this large group of trained, armed men. Yet he held power over them with only his words. His presence.

'Like your one-time lord, the Lord of Meath. Hugh de Lacy.' John walked up the line of focused faces, every one of the hard eyes beneath nose-plated helmets on him. 'A lord made by King Henry. Well, I have unmade him.' Turned, walked back. 'For he swore an oath to me to protect this place. An oath which he broke in a heartbeat. From now on, you serve me, the Lord of Ireland. Is that clear?'

'Yes, my lord.' The answer came loud, definite.

'Good.' John nodded to the wriggling groom. 'Put him back up.' He directed his order at a couple of men at the end of the row.

One acted at once, the other hung back for a half-step.

John clicked his fingers at two others. 'Put that man up too.'

'My lord.' The shirker's words came iced in shock.

But no one hesitated this time.

The half-dead groom was dangling again in a moment, legs feebler as he kicked, but he continued to strain for any breath.

'My lord!' The other one fought hard against those who would bind him. 'Please. I am loyal to you.'

John walked on again, ignoring him. 'I hope I am making my point with clarity.'

'Mercy, I beg you, my lord!'

The man's arms were secure, the noose being prepared.

'Now our task is to find that spy.' John paused, watched with pleasure as the man was hoisted next to the groom, legs thrashing like a newborn foal's.

John went on. 'The spy who caused me so many, many losses on this campaign. But no more.' John raised a fist. 'No more. We will find this woman who would dare to don a habit to do her evil work. By the time I am finished with her, she will welcome death. Anyone who hides her, shelters her in any way, will end their days on the end of your blades. They will learn that guile is no match for an honest sword. We start the hunt for her at first light.

A steady chant for him rose up. 'The Lord of Ireland! The Lord of Ireland!'

He basked in their acclaim. Wonderful. So many voices raised to praise him, even as he saw looks slide towards the dying jerks of the men on the gibbet.

Wonderful. But, strangely, not as wonderful as the fear in every man's eyes.

And even that would be a shadow compared to what he would see in those belonging to the Sister Theodosia when he got his hands on her.

Palmer straightened up. He didn't dream; he definitely lived. Theodosia was here. Here, along with one of de Lacy's messengers. How, he didn't know, didn't care. She was here. Back with him. But looking as if she faced a wolf pack.

'Benedict, stop.' Theodosia flung herself from her horse and ran to him as the young man hung back, still mounted. 'Do not use that mace. Please. No.' She grabbed for his arm.

'What's wrong?' His heart quailed. 'Are you hurt?'

She shook her head. 'No.'

Relief surged through him.

'It is worse than that.'

'God's eyes.' De Lacy got to his hands and knees, coughing hard. 'You're in league with a nun now, Palmer?'

'Shut up, you.' Palmer tried to raise the mace.

'No!' Theodosia pulled it down with a cry. 'We need his help. We truly do.'

'Whatever you're playing at, sister' – de Lacy wheezed to his feet – 'I thank you.'

'I told you to shut up.' Palmer took a quick look up, down the road. No riders. Yet. 'Theodosia, de Lacy isn't alone. We need to get out of here. You can tell me what's wrong as we ride.'

The bushes rustled.

Palmer wheeled round with the mace.

Eimear stepped out, breathless from running, her tunic torn and muddy, but with de Lacy's dropped broadsword in hand.

A puce-faced, bloody-lipped Simonson staggered out after her.

'Sister,' said Eimear. 'Oh, thank every saint you got away.' She looked at de Lacy. 'Husband.'

De Lacy scowled. 'Palmer, if I had my mace right now.'

'You don't, and I told—' began Palmer as Eimear spoke over him.

'Hugh, there is much you should—'

'Stop it!' Theodosia's scream cut through it all. 'Stop it, all of you! None of you know the truth.'

Palmer looked at her, at her eyes wide in horror.

'Listen,' she said. 'Just listen.'

'And I swear to you, that every word I have spoken is the truth. John wants the throne of Ireland for himself and will use the lives of children to get it.' Theodosia's own words brought fresh terror to her heart.

'You have no need to swear on anything.' Benedict's mud-plastered jaw set. 'I believe every word.'

'As do I.' Eimear tested the broadsword. 'That I had the little turd of Satan before me right now.'

'That I had my men of Meath.' De Lacy spat hard.

Guilt panged through Theodosia. 'I am to blame that you do not, my lord.'

'You thought it best,' came Benedict's deep murmur to Eimear's nod. 'Faith, look what you discovered as a result.'

De Lacy too waved her protest away. 'You sought to protect my wife from John.' He blew a sharp whistle to the still-mounted Nagle. 'You're with me, lad? If not, turn around and go and serve the Lord John in his slaughter of children. My mace in the back of your head will help you on your way.'

Benedict nodded, smacking the heavy weapon against his other, open palm.

'I'm with you, my lord,' replied Nagle. 'As always.'

De Lacy nodded. 'Then go and find the only band I have and bring them to me. They won't have got far.'

'Wait,' said Eimear to the messenger. She looked at her husband. 'You have no band.' She jerked a thumb at Simonson. 'Only this one here. They all fled when they saw me coming towards them with a sword and him with blood all over his face.'

'Terrified, they were,' nodded the heavy-set young man, his words indistinct through his cut lip.

Benedict and de Lacy swore as one man.

But Theodosia could imagine how the untrained, nervous men would have viewed the armed, mud-visaged Eimear.

'Nagle,' said de Lacy. 'Take Simonson and go and see if you can track any of them down.' He scowled. 'You might find one hidden under a bush somewhere.'

'Yes, my lord.' Nagle heaved Simonson up behind him and they set off in a clatter of hooves.

'And find your animal, Simonson,' called Palmer. 'We need it!'

'I will! I swear!'

They were gone. De Lacy shook his head. 'Our odds against John's castle at Tibberaghny aren't even slim. They're non-existent. Palmer, you built a fine mottte and bailey, curse you. My best troops are guarding it. John has my most efficient messengers with which to summon the Irish kings. The lure of my land will bring them running to him.'

'The offer of land never tempted you to make an immoral alliance, husband?' Eimear fixed him with a steely gaze.

Benedict cut off de Lacy's tetchy reply. 'Then we'll act as messengers. Go to warn the kings.'

'Or warn them as they approach Tibberaghny.' Theodosia already knew from the look on de Lacy's face that both suggestions were futile.

'There are six of us. And one is Simonson.' De Lacy snorted. 'We have three horses between us; four if by some miracle that boy finds his. We won't be able to intercept every king, every chieftain that might be making his way to Tibberaghny.'

'And, Theodosia,' said Benedict, 'we cannot risk you falling into John's hands.'

Eimear's mouth turned down in a grim arc. 'He will be out for your blood, Theodosia.'

'He can have it.' Her reply came steady. 'Any mother would do as I have done.'

'As any father would. Of course they would.' Benedict's dark eyes lit with sudden hope. 'So that is who we have to tell.'

De Lacy scowled afresh. 'Palmer, that's what we've just said we can't do. We can't find a way to warn all the kings.'

'No.' Benedict shook his head. 'Not the kings. At least, not us. The Irish will tell them themselves. Through Eimear.'

Eimear mirrored Theodosia's bewilderment as de Lacy answered in disdain.

'Palmer, Eimear is one woman. Are you sure you didn't hit your head when you fell off that horse?'

'Everything else. But not that. Yes, Eimear is one woman. I'm not suggesting she travel alone. We head with her for the nearest village. Eimear can tell them that the Lord John is out for the blood of Irish children. That they should leave, hide, do anything they can to protect their own from him, spreading the word to as many as they can as they go.'

'It will be very slow, Palmer.' Eimear's voice held doubt. 'Too slow. People may not believe this news, not second- or third-hand. As Hugh says, there's only one of me.'

Benedict stepped over and grasping one of her wrists, raised it. 'Yes, but you have ten digits. So many rings on each. A gold ring to each of their fastest men, so they have your authority.' Benedict released Eimear. 'Your word will spread and spread.'

'A way to stop this.' Theodosia looked at him with deep, grateful pride.

De Lacy nodded. 'A good plan.' Then he was on Eimear in an eye-blink, his broadsword out of her hand as he moved it between Benedict and Theodosia. 'But you'll not use my wife for whatever scheme you are planning. Not until you tell me the whole truth.'

'What are you talking about?' Benedict had the mace.

'Your slip, sister.' De Lacy pointed the broadsword right at her. 'Since when has a nun known the heart of a mother?'

Theodosia took a step back. Her foolish words.

'The whole truth. Now. Or we're gone. You can carry on with your own lies.'

She exchanged a glance with Benedict.

He gave an unhappy shrug but nodded. 'We have to tell them, Theodosia.'

She hated to do it, yet she had no other choice. 'You have a devotion to Saint Thomas Becket, my lord?'

'I do.'

'Then I swear on his life that I speak the whole truth.' Theodosia took a deep breath. 'A life that Benedict and I saw taken before our very eyes. My account will not take long.'

Hugh de Lacy, Lord of Meath, never expected to see a wife of his squatting before a stream to clean the dirt of fighting from her face and clothes like a foot soldier. 'Make sure you get as clean as possible: even I hardly recognised you.' Next to her on the bank, he filled his leather water bottle. 'There is a lot riding on this plan of Palmer's.'

'I don't need you to tell me that.' She scrubbed hard at her cheeks.

He ignored her sharp retort, looking instead to where Palmer and the woman they claimed to be his wife, the daughter of King Henry himself, sat on an old tree stump. Theodosia cleaned his face with water-soaked linen, absorbed in a quiet conversation with him.

Farther along the bank, the bushes parted.

De Lacy reached for his sword as he saw Palmer did too.

'Hold,' said Eimear. 'It's only Nagle and Simonson.'

De Lacy raised his voice. 'Anyone, Nagle?'

'No, my lord.'

Simonson beamed. 'But I found my horse!'

Palmer met de Lacy's look with a shrug.

'Then have a drink,' said de Lacy to the messenger and Simonson. 'You'll need it.' His gaze returned to Eimear. 'Do you believe them?'

'Nagle and Simonson? Of course.' Her pale, smooth skin revealed itself once more.

'No, I mean Palmer and Theodosia. Do you believe what they've told us – that she is the daughter of the King?'

'I do.' Eimear undid her long plait, sluiced dirt and scraps of leaves from her hair, returning it to its deep, deep red. 'Theodosia's actions to me have been without question.' She gave a humourless laugh. 'Though it astonishes me that she has sprung from the same parentage as John, even if only partly. But no, I have no doubts. Nor do I have any about Palmer. You?'

'Unless he's a much better liar than I think he is.' De Lacy shook his head. 'But no. It makes sense now. I knew there was something not right about his choosing to stay close to Tibberaghny, about his whole demeanour.' He drank a mouthful from the bottle. 'I was correct in my suspicion.' He cursed inwardly for not having paid it more attention.

'It looked to me like you were more concerned that he and I might have run away as lovers.' Eimear reached into her belt pouch and took out a carved horn comb.

De Lacy drank again. 'Palmer is clearly a knight of great prowess. And when he disappeared with you, I didn't know what he was doing with you – or to you. He fully understood your noble birth, how important you are in this land.' He filled the bottle up again. 'As I told the Lord John, it was a matter of honour, plain and simple. You are still my wife, as I am your husband. We are still married.'

'Married? Bound to each other more like.' Eimear pulled the comb through her hair with hard tugs, sending it free and shining over her shoulders, same as it had fallen on the night he'd had her.

A night five years before. Impossible to believe. The time had flowed as swiftly as the stream before him.

'Now I see it.' Eimear pinned him with a look. 'You were more worried about your truce with my father. If I were gone, that would be shattered. That's what you broke an oath to John for.' She pointed the comb at him. 'Land. That is all you care about. I swear you would pick it up, sod by sod, and carry it in your cloak if you could.'

'That's not true, Eimear.' *It was once.* He met her accusing look, as he stoppered the bottle with a swift smack. *Not anymore.* 'Only this land.'

'I have never understood it.' She combed on. 'Why this one? Why Ireland? You had your lordship in England; you were Lord of Weobley. It came to you through noble birth. Yet you came here, even let Henry take your castle at Ludlow so you could remain.'

Lord of Weobley. But not the first lord. His heart constricted at who that had been. He scowled at Eimear to hide his pain. 'Who's been talking of my past?'

Combing complete, she braided her hair now with quick twists. 'You've left me on my own in your castle at Trim for much of our so-called marriage. The servants are the same as those who looked after your first wife. They gossip.'

'They have no business gossiping. Especially not about Rose. Neither have you.'

'I have few others to talk to.' Her veil was back on, white, with a circle of gold to keep it there.

'It's not becoming. Not for a woman who is the wife of the Lord of Meath.'

'Oh, isn't it? I am no wife to you.' Her dark blue eyes, angry as a storm cloud, bored into his. 'You told me, the day William was born: "You are done." Those were your very words.'

'That's right. I did say you were done. You agreed to our marriage and gave me our son. You did everything that was asked of you.' De Lacy fastened his water bottle to his belt. 'But, in doing so, you put me in your debt. I came after you because I owed you a debt, Eimear. Now I've paid it. We are both done.'

'We need to get going,' called Palmer, hand to Theodosia's shoulder.

Nagle and Simonson reacted to his order at once.

'Certainly,' Eimear called back as she also rose to her feet. 'I am glad we are even. Husband.'

De Lacy stood too. He should feel relieved that he no longer owed Eimear anything, nor she him. Not the flicker of envy he felt of Palmer. He pushed it away.

He'd made his choices long ago.

The fear on the faces of the mothers was the worst. Theodosia remembered it so vividly, the visceral, overwhelming terror that threatened to stop her heart when she thought her children's lives were in danger. For the men, it was anger, shouting. The children themselves looked bewildered, at least the little ones, who could not understand what was taking place in their peaceful little village. They could only cry and wail at the frightening noise, the commotion, the entreaties to pull on cloaks, hoods, to hurry, to be quick, quick, quick. The solemn-faced older ones locked hands together, ordered to do so tightly – even tighter – and not to let go.

She did not need to understand the words that Eimear spoke in loud, clear tones from the back of the horse she'd taken from Simonson. Their impact hit like a stone thrown into a still pond, the ripples spreading in all and every direction at once. She did not need to understand the responses either.

The men who took rings from Eimear were the youngest, the strongest. The angriest. A few small horses were brought. No saddles, and men shared each animal as they raced from the village with the briefest goodbyes.

She met Benedict's dark eyes as he sat behind her on the mount they shared. She was so lucky – *they* were so lucky. They were still together. Their children had been saved from murder, were safe now.

Then a terrible, screaming, wailing cry as a woman of around her own age was pulled from her tiny, thatched, wattle-sided home by her husband and older children.

'What is happening?' she asked Benedict.

'I don't know.'

Eimear glanced over. 'Her mother is still inside,' she explained. 'The old woman is dying. Too sick to move. They have to leave her.'

'Benedict. There must be something we can do. Anything.'

He shook his head.

Theodosia swallowed down her sadness. She had no right to be upset when this family before her had their hearts broken. All she could do was pray for the soul of the dying woman being left behind and for the consolation of the daughter who'd had to abandon her.

The inhabitants of the small settlement streamed away now, some walking fast, some running, a few driving protesting cattle. But none of them chose the road. They made for the nearby fields, and from there to the woods, the sounds of their leaving fading by the moment.

'A wise choice,' said de Lacy. 'John would have a hard time tracking them down in there. Even with my men.'

'Indeed, my lord,' said Nagle.

Clinging to the messenger on the back of his horse, Simonson only stared in sombre silence.

One small knot of people went more slowly than the rest, the sounds of weeping still carrying fitfully on the warm breeze as they crossed the pale gold of a ripening barley field. The dying woman's daughter, in her anguish, was being half-carried by her family.

To Theodosia's surprise, de Lacy swung himself from his horse and went quickly to the low wooden door of the cottage, bending to disappear inside before coming out a few moments later. 'Eimear.'

She looked over. 'Husband?'

'Tell that woman that she need not fear for her mother any longer,' said de Lacy. 'Then we need to leave.'

Eimear nodded, commanding her horse to a fast trot to catch them up, its hooves leaving a dark scar behind her in the smooth crop.

'Has that poor sick woman been granted the merciful release of death?' asked Theodosia.

Quiet had fallen over the barley field, and the little family had picked up pace.

De Lacy nodded. 'A merciful release indeed.' He climbed back onto his horse.

Theodosia crossed herself, her heart filled with thanks.

Benedict gave de Lacy a long look, before turning to Theodosia. 'We can't be found either, especially not you.' Unseen by the others, he gave her wrist a comforting squeeze. 'We've done what we can for now. We have to ride on.'

'We do.' De Lacy looked up at the sky. 'We won't make Thomond today. But we can still cover a few miles with the light we have left.' He kicked his horse to lead them off.

Chapter Twenty-Three

The last time the bridge at Tibberaghny had dropped behind John as he left on horseback, his insides had threatened to humiliate him. Every tree, every bush, every leaf looked like it concealed a murdering Irishman, ready to bury a hefty blade in his face. How right he had been. The attack on the road to Ardfinnan still came to him in nightmares. But that was all in the past. Things were different now. On this fine, clear morning, he rode with the men of Meath. The ones who had defeated the king of the north.

John took a quick glance back over his shoulder and caught his breath. He'd not seen Tibberaghny's decoration with the severed heads of traitors from outside before. The effect was stunning, even now in the light of day. Flocks of shiny black rooks and jackdaws fluttered around the rotting skulls, pecking, squabbling, calling, bringing a strange life to the horrible tableau even as they consumed it. He faced forward again. What a day, what a night, when the head of the Church's spy would join them.

He snorted to himself. Such a brazen disguise to present herself as a nun, with her modest habit and cowed gaze. When he found her, she'd wear that habit no more. Whipping her naked body would make a good start to her protracted death.

By the end, she'd be begging him to take her head from her shoulders.

And it would not be long. The men of Meath would help him to make sure of it. Fully armed in shining mail and helms, swords ready in scabbards, polished shields slung across their backs: they would devour any resistance from the bearded savages. Male or female. He recalled the clerk's description of the woman at the court of Thomond, with a smile at the idea of her.

Gerald rode with them, silent and morose, his broken arm stuck out at an angle.

John gave a sigh to himself at the idiot clerk. The man really was a hindrance. As soon as he, John, had his own court properly established, he would send the man packing. Back to Henry. Perhaps with his hands missing. Now, that would be amusing. A scribe with no hands. Shame there was no one to tell. John rolled his shoulders, relaxing fully into the glorious sunshine of the day and what it would bring. Once they returned, he might just tell Gerald what he was going to do with him. That would make for an interesting couple of weeks.

A great thrill passed through him. Yes, weeks. Days, really. Not much more than that. Before he got his throne. Maybe a bit less. Had it not been for this bloody woman, Theodosia, he would be able to count the days. Damn her, damn her. A tiny white cloud blocked out the sun, a shadow on this perfect day in the same way that she had created a wrinkle in his smooth, perfect plans. His hands tightened on the reins. It would not be long before they would reach the first village. The serjeant, Aylward, had told him that it was only one of the places the woman might have hidden, that each settlement, however small, should be searched thoroughly. John would do more than that. A few carefully chosen slit throats would be far more efficient in getting people to reveal whether they hid a fugitive.

'Pick up the pace! All of you!'

They responded immediately to his shout, and as one. So immediately John was nearly unseated trying to match them. It didn't matter. He made a quick, sure recovery. *Quick. Sure.* Like his mind.

The sun came back out, its rays piercingly hot as it climbed towards midday.

So similar to how he ascended towards his throne.

He basked in its fierce glare, riding hard, until finally – the call he awaited.

'Settlement ahead!'

He thrilled again inside even as wariness nudged him. It was one thing to suspect that the enemy hid in the trees. Quite another that he would come face to face with them. Any minute now. The roofs of straw and dried heather lay but a short distance away. He took in the broad mailed backs and shoulders ahead. Such muscle reassured him. He had the superior force. Of course he had.

'Searchers, dismount.' The order came from Aylward as the party clattered up the narrow street. 'Not you, my lord.'

John nodded as if he understood completely, many of the knights reacting, others staying mounted. He had actually started to respond, quailing inside at being on foot and vulnerable when the Irish were here. Or somewhere. No sign of life greeted them, only wretched, rounded dwellings set close to the earth, with tightly shut doors. Deserted enclosures, surrounded by wicker fences, added to the eerie quiet.

'Where is everybody?' he asked Aylward, also still on horseback.

Gerald of course hadn't budged, clung to his pommel like a drowning man clinging to a plank.

'Shut inside, having seen our approach.' Aylward shrugged. 'It's what people do. Waste of time.'

'Indeed.'

The men on foot made for the doors of the hovels, shouting, pounding on them with fists, hilts, then breaking them down with blows from weapons and hard boot strikes.

John squared his shoulders, anticipating the moment that the first brute would be pulled before him. 'I will show the first villager mercy,' he said to Aylward. 'That will encourage others who might be hiding to show themselves.'

'My lord.' Aylward kept his eyes on his men.

John's jaw tightened. That man had ignored his excellent suggestion. Then to hell with mercy. More straightforward without it. The first one found could be made an example of, exactly as he had decided.

Blood flowing eagerly in his veins again, he scanned the loud, heaving mass of men, seeking out the long hair and beards and woollen robes he had so come to despise. He frowned. Nothing.

'Nothing?' Aylward's reply echoed John's reaction to those who'd smashed their way into the nearest dwellings and were coming out again empty-handed.

'Empty.'

The same findings were reported, over and over.

'Empty.'

'Nothing, sir!'

'Not here.'

'Nobody in this one, sir.'

'Nobody?' John could only utter the word in bewilderment. 'Not only is this woman I need to get my hands on not here, there is no one else either.' He pointed at Aylward with his whip. 'Have you brought me on a fool's errand, fool?'

'No, my lord. This is the first village. It's unusual to find a place completely deserted. Usually that only happens when there's been a plague.'

'You mean to tell me there is plague here?' Heart thudding in abrupt panic, John readied himself to ride out of here as fast as his beast could take him, even if he had to trample the soldiers that milled around the street.

'No, my lord. There would be other signs. Everything here is tidy, in order. It's just . . . empty.'

Another man spoke up. 'My lord, it could be that there is a wedding taking place in a nearby settlement, or people are making a pilgrimage.'

'You mean the lazy hounds have simply gone gadding off somewhere?' John's heart still raced at the fright he'd had at the suggestion of plague.

'It may be, my lord,' said Aylward.

'Then we have wasted time because of their idleness. God save me from this country.' He pointed his whip at Aylward again. 'We go now. Now. And heaven help this group of shirkers when I catch up with them.'

'Yes, my lord. To your saddles!'

The men responded at once to the order and moved off again in smooth efficiency.

John's heart refused to calm. His task today was starting to frustrate him. Deeply.

'A bigger village this time, my lord,' Aylward shouted back to him. 'It may be that is where the others have travelled.'

A muted cheer met the man's words.

John's mood improved too at the good news. He was eager to proceed; that was all. Always his curse, his whole life: he wanted to move on, to get things done. And always held back by laggards and those too slow to keep up with him.

He smiled his approval at those men who met his glance, even briefly. All of them together in this noble endeavour. He increased his animal's pace so he would arrive at a brisk trot, as if that was how he rode all day. And arrive he did.

It was like a bad dream.

Aylward calling for the men to dismount, and then their swift responses.

Dismounting onto a deserted street. Smashing the doors and twisted twig walls of the mean little dwellings. Mailed men in. Mailed men out. No one else.

The sun reddening his skin as he sat on his mount.

The only difference was the stink from a nearby manure pile, clouded with hundreds of buzzing flies that set on him too, their fat, swollen bodies eager for his sweat as well as his horse's.

'The same, my lord.' Aylward looked concerned now.

'The same?' John's furious yell brought an instant silence. 'The same wedding? The same pilgrimage?' His gaze met uncertain looks. 'The same plague?'

'I don't think it's any of those things, my lord,' said Aylward.

'Then what do you think?'

'I don't know yet, my lord.'

'Limited!' John's scream tore through the empty hovels. 'You're so bloody limited!' He flung an accusatory finger at the oaf. 'They should be here. Should be present to answer my questions about where this woman Theodosia has gone. So burn the place. All of it. Now. Make sure there isn't so much as a twig for them to return to.'

'Yes, my lord.'

'And then we make for the next. At the fastest speed.'

A horsefly bit him hard on the hand, and he swiped it away with an oath.

'Take some of this water. You look as if you need it.' Palmer offered his water bottle to Theodosia.

Their horse had slowed to a plod as the ground rose steeply, the trees giving way to bare grey rock and patches of thin soil with huge stands of spiny, yellow-flowered gorse that threw its sweet scent into the shimmering air of the hot afternoon.

'I will have a little.' She took it from him, eyes shadowed with a worrying exhaustion, her usually pale face a painful-looking red from the long day under the sun's rays.

'Don't expect refreshment,' he said. 'It's very warm.'

She took a drink. 'It is still better than nothing.'

Palmer glanced back. Eimear had her head down as she watched the track for loose stones under her horse's hooves.

'Palmer.' He looked up at the call from above him. Framed against the sky, a silent Nagle and Simonson next to him, de Lacy pointed over at the distant lowlands. 'Smoke.'

'Let me through.' John forced his own animal through the group of riders to take the lead as they entered yet another Irish village that showed no signs of life.

'My lord, please, let us go first.' Aylward's plea came polite, yet forceful. 'We don't know what to expect.

He ignored Aylward's request. 'Oh, don't you?'

'There could be an ambush.'

John pulled up sharply and jumped off his horse. 'An ambush from whom? That cat over there, lying in the sun? The Irish have gone, same as from the other two places. Gone because they know I am hunting my spy, my traitor from the Church.'

Aylward exchanged looks with Gerald. 'My lord, we don't know that. I have been fighting in this country for many years. All sorts of feuds and battles rage all the time between the different families and their followers. Even amongst the settlers.'

'Then you are a fool.' John flung out an arm. 'Use your eyes, man! If it were a bloody feud, there'd be bodies. The injured. The ravished. There is nothing except a cat. A sleeping, bloody cat!' He saw the careful looks in many faces now. For a second, he saw himself through their eyes. Face burned by the sun. Covered in fly bites. Standing alone on the hot street, claiming that one nun could somehow have done all this in only a day. Maybe he was losing his mind. He swallowed down some of his rage. 'Perhaps I shall sit in the shade. While you carry out the usual search.'

'My lord.' Aylward brought his men forward with a whistle.

'I shall sit with you, my lord.' Gerald dismounted too.

John staggered to the shade of a tall ash tree as a man took his horse, and Gerald brought him a leather bottle containing wine. He took a long draught of the sweetness, warm as his own blood.

'Good to rest, my lord.'

John ignored him. The wine made his head spin even more. He palmed at his face, hating the unrelenting heat. Hating today.

Mailed figures, smashing empty hovels. The same hovels that would yield to flames as they left. On and on. Futile.

'I've found someone!' A shout from one poor cottage.

John was on his feet, wine splashing onto the dust, arriving at the low door at the same time as Aylward and Gerald.

A faint, foul stench met him. More flies.

'Who?' John crouched low to push his way in first, eager for someone he could question. He tripped, with an oath, on the rough cobbles of the threshold, his eyes readjusting to the dimness inside as the clerk and the serjeant followed him in.

The man already present yanked down one of the animal skins that lined the wall. Slender shafts of afternoon light found their way through the hazel weave, buzzing insects as well as dust dancing in the beams. 'This old woman. But I think she's dead.'

A small, emaciated figure lay on one of the two straw beds set against opposite walls.

Aylward put a hand on her, much to John's disgust. 'She is.'

'God rest her soul.' Gerald crossed himself.

'What killed her?' John fought the urge to flee, the spectre of plague haunting him once more.

'I'd guess a wasting disease,' said Aylward. 'She has no flesh on her at all.' He crossed himself quickly. 'She's not long dead. Her body is still stiff.'

John frowned. 'Then she has been dead for about a day?'

'Yes, my lord. I would think so.' Aylward stood up. 'Unfortunate. She might have been able to tell us what happened here.'

The man who'd found her nodded. 'We'd have got it out of her.'

'Maybe she still can.' John pushed past him, landing on his knees on the wicker-covered floor beside the bed. His stomach turned over at the stronger stench of death and of flesh that had decayed even while this hag still lived. It had to be done. He ripped the veil that surrounded the woman's thin, toothless face with her spike of a nose.

'My lord.' Aylward's voice sounded disturbed and he saw Gerald's shocked face out of the corner of his eye.

'I thought you had the stomachs of men.' John searched through her sparse, grey hair in a moment. Nothing there. He put his hand to the thin, rough wool of her tunic. And pulled. Hard.

'My lord.' This time Gerald's hand was on his arm, daring to pull him off.

John shoved him away. 'Look, damn you. Look.'

And there it was. His proof. A deep red stain bloomed on the darned greyish linen of the woman's shift.

Gerald moaned in terror, brought his hands to his head. 'They have slain this defenceless wretch.'

'Lest you still doubt me.' John put his hand to her shift.

'My lord, I do not. Spare her her modesty. Please.'

John ignored Aylward, tore that garment open too, his rage now mounting anew within him. He stared at the neat wound, a handspan below where a crude, wooden cross hung around the woman's neck.

'Oh, may God help us now.' Gerald wailed afresh. 'If the Irish can slay an old dying woman, then we can all end up martyred in this terrible country. Martyred like Saint Thomas Becket himself!'

Now John knew. Knew what he had to do. 'You thought I was sun-maddened,' he hissed at Aylward, before clambering back outside through the low doorway.

'A blade has pierced this woman's heart!'

Frowns and a rumble of surprise met John's words.

Aylward, Gerald and the soldier emerged, eyes downcast.

John went on. 'Someone made sure she couldn't talk. Which means someone knew that there would be people arriving who might want her to.' He clenched his fist. 'Us.' He clenched it harder. 'Me.' Harder. 'I have no doubt it is the spy. I have no doubt that this woman, Theodosia, has woven this web of deceit, which allows her to command these villages of traitors. Which has made for so many losses on this campaign.'

The surprise shifted to aggression.

'But this place will be burned too. The houses, the fields. All of it. And the next. And the next. Anywhere that is loyal to an Irish king. I will carve a burning path all the way to Dublin if I have to. No mercy for anyone who gets in its way.'

A great roar went up.

'Once at Dublin, the greatest of resources in the whole of this land will be devoted to making sure that this spy of the Church, this Sister Theodosia, is hunted down and killed. Along with every treacherous knave who has dared to act with her and defy me, the Lord of Ireland!'

The cheers rose up at the same moment as the flames.

He grabbed one of the torches and flung it in the door of the hovel where the corpse of the woman lay. Such a shame she wasn't still alive. Death by fire was a wonderful spectacle.

Palmer arrived beside de Lacy, the horse beneath him and Theodosia breathing hard from the quickened climb and from bearing its double load.

'Smoke.' De Lacy's mouth set in a hard line. 'And lots of it.'

'So much smoke,' whispered Simonson as he clung to Nagle.

'Oh, those poor people.' Theodosia put a hand to her mouth.

'What's happening?' Eimear kicked her horse up the last stretch.

'See for yourself.' Palmer shook his head. 'John's handiwork.'

Spread out below them, the land in its many shades of green and gold sat hazed in the heat of the afternoon sun. But smoke thickened the haze in many places. In so many, many places.

'The whoreson.' Eimear ground out the word.

'I could think of a few more words for him,' said Palmer.

'But are you sure it is John, Benedict?' Theodosia turned to challenge him with her gaze even as her voice came hoarse. 'Could it not be something else?'

'Oh, it's him, Theodosia.' Eimear's disgusted reply came over his. 'You can see it from up here. A line of death and destruction, leading from Tibberaghny.'

'Because of me,' came Theodosia's low, angry whisper.

Palmer wouldn't allow it. 'No, Theodosia.' The horse jigged beneath them at his sharp response. 'Because of John. All of it, because of him. You can't forget that.'

Even as he spoke, a fresh plume rose up in the distance, thin, strong. New.

She went to reply. But no words came out as she slumped forward.

Heart thudding, Palmer halted her fall with his arm. 'De Lacy.'

The lord was off his animal, holding the unconscious Theodosia as Palmer's boots met the ground, his own legs weak now. It would be a faint, a faint. That's all.

'I've got her.' He pulled Theodosia to him and off their mount, laying her gently on the hot, hard ground, cradling her head and shoulders in one bent arm. God smiled on him – she still breathed. 'Open your eyes, my love,' he murmured. 'Come on.'

Eimear joined him with a stifled oath.

'We'll stop for a rest here while Sister Theodosia recovers,' said de Lacy to Nagle and Simonson. 'Make sure you tether your horse.'

'What ails her?' Eimear's dark gaze met Palmer's, her face with its healthy glow a sharp contrast to Theodosia's flushed one.

'Too much.' He tightened his grip on her. His Theodosia. His brave, brave Theodosia. *All I want is her.* His words to Henry, as true now as all those years ago. He swallowed down the sudden knot of tears that rose in his throat as he put a palm to her cheek, her forehead. Dry, despite the heat.

'By which you mean?' came Eimear's question.

'She's exhausted. Her escape from yesterday. Little sleep. These long, hot hours in the saddle. Too much.'

Palmer saw the realisation in Eimear's eyes even as he heard the crackle of movement in the gorse, saw de Lacy's head turn too, Nagle and Simonson stop their tired stretching dead.

A band of Irish warriors rose from the thick bushes, axes in hand, surrounding them completely. He'd seen them before, he would swear to it. Then his eyes lit on the huge axe-wielding man he'd so narrowly fought off in the woods near Ardfinnan.

Palmer clutched Theodosia, his hand going for his sword. Now he prayed she didn't open her eyes. Best she didn't know the end.

Chapter Twenty-Four

Theodosia's head hurt. Not so much hurt, as pounded. Lying on this bed gave her no relief, only discomfort, its hard lumps and bumps pushing into her back. She forced her eyes open, her lids sticky and heavy. All she could see were green spiked leaves, yellow flowers. Specks of blue through them. Her palms found hard ground. Not a bed. She forced herself upright, her recall of what had happened restored. She should be on a horse with Benedict. Not falling from it in weakness and delaying their progress.

'Easy, easy.' Benedict sat next to her, sheltered in the shade of tall gorse bushes. 'Thank the saints you've come round.' He put a hand to her shoulder. 'Don't try to do anything. Just drink.' He brought a leather water pouch to her lips.

'We have little water.' She remembered that. Remembered the tormenting thirst. Her exhaustion. The unaccustomed heat she had not been able to bear.

'No, we have plenty. Thanks to them.'

Theodosia followed the direction of his nod. She pulled in a deep breath of fear.

A group of around a dozen Irish warriors stood with de Lacy. With Eimear. With the wary-looking Nagle and a petrified-looking Simonson.

She tried to scramble to her feet. 'We have to run! We have to go—'

'Easy, I said.' Benedict kept his hold on her. 'They haven't come to do us harm. Now drink.'

Despite her whirling head, she took a grateful mouthful. 'Then why are they here?' And another and another.

'They tracked us down using the news that is being spread. That Eimear started.'

'News of murder, of death?' Her head cleared. She braced for his reply.

'No.' His dark eyes shone with quiet pride. 'Settlements are being burned, destroyed. But John's men have not found an Irish life to take yet.'

'Then the fires we saw, they *were* John's doing.' She looked at him with a fierce hope that she had not misunderstood. 'Yet he has not managed to kill?'

'No. Not that these men have heard.' Benedict shook his head. 'He's very angry, it would seem, with the spy that he had in his midst. Getting angrier by the hour as he travels farther from here. From you.'

'Oh, God be praised.' Relief surged through her, bringing her to greater strength as she drank again.

He flashed her a grin. 'God has my thanks that the little swine is angry too.'

She smacked him on the shoulder. 'You know precisely what I meant.'

'Of course I do. It's the best news you could have had.' He caressed her cheek. 'I saw your despair, though you were shouldering blame for things that were not your fault.'

'I acted rashly.'

'Foolhardy?' His dark eyes had a tease now.

'If you insist, sir knight,' she teased back.

He offered her another drink, but she shook her head. 'I am feeling much better.' She stood up, the last of her dizziness clearing.

Benedict continued. 'The Almighty also has my thanks that he puts more miles between you and John by the hour.' His face became the serious mask she dreaded. 'Because there's been a change of plan.'

'What change?'

'You and Eimear are to travel to the seat of the nearest Archbishop. It's at Cashel, a place called Saint Patrick's Rock. You will be able to seek sanctuary there. It's a lot closer than the court of the king of Thomond. Nagle and a couple of the Irish warriors will go with you to keep you both safe on the journey.'

Her mouth dried again, but not from thirst this time. 'You?'

'Theodosia, I'm going after John. And de Lacy is coming with me.'

Palmer stretched his aching back as much as he could in the confines of his saddle. He already had his fair share of bruises and cuts from fighting for the Lord John. Getting knocked off his horse as de Lacy chased him had only added to them. As always, the battle aches got worse as he came to the end of the day. The sun beginning to sink towards the dense canopy of the thick forest should be a sign that he could slide his weary body from the saddle and lie in welcome rest.

There'd be no rest tonight. No rest any night, until he had his hands on John.

I'm going after John. Palmer had said those words so easily to Theodosia, knowing in his heart it was going to be far more difficult to make happen. First, they had to find the man. Then they'd have to wrest him from de Lacy's trained force.

He looked ahead to where his own unlikely fighters rode.

The men of Thomond used no saddles on their horses, had no stirrups. But then they wore no mail either. Not even boots on their feet.

If he didn't know better, he'd say that they wouldn't stand a chance against the armour that he and de Lacy wore.

Simonson too, wobbling without a saddle on the small, sturdy horse given to him by the Irish. As if sensing Palmer's attention on him, he looked back, clutching his mount's mane for balance.

'Are we really going to try to arrest the Lord John, Palmer?' Simonson's eyes were wider than a player in a mystery play beholding the wrath of a vengeful God. 'Us?'

'Yes, Simonson.' Palmer caught the grin of the huge warrior, Uinseann, to his fellow warriors.

He said something to them in his own tongue, and they bellowed with laughter.

Simonson's look shifted to wary. Worried. Again.

Palmer shook his head at Uinseann. 'I need as much heart in this fight as I can.'

Uinseann made a massive fist and flexed a powerful arm. 'This is all the heart I need.' He leaned over to slap Simonson hard on his podgy back, almost sending the young man from his unstable perch. 'You need some muscle, lad. That's what works.' He slapped him again. Harder.

The air huffed from Simonson as Uinseann's friends roared their approval.

'Like at the riverbank near Ardfinnan, Uinseann.' Palmer gave him a sage nod. 'Worked for you then, did it?'

Uinseann snorted hard. 'It would have if I'd found you.'

'But you didn't,' said Palmer. 'You see, Simonson? Uinseann might have hands the size of shovels. Still couldn't find his backside with both of them.' He winked at the younger man.

He got a ghost of a smile back as Uinseann's friends guffawed, the warrior taking a swipe at Palmer with a good-humoured oath.

'Come on, lads.' The big warrior brought his horse in beside Simonson, gesturing to his friends to draw near too. 'Now, let me tell you a few things about fighting. First, don't piss yourself. That's always a good start.'

'Says the man with the wettest trousers in Munster.'

More laughs, hoots.

Palmer left them to it. He had no mind for sport. Sending Theodosia on her way had pained him deep in his heart, with her increasingly angry, desperate pleas to stay with him. For him not to go, that he'd had to refuse over and over. Eimear had helped, holding his side of the argument: now that the men of Thomond had joined them, they had to go after John. No Irish lives had been lost so far. But the fires showed the depths of John's rage. He had to be stopped before he succeeded in murder.

Theodosia had clung to him with a fierce strength in their last embrace, and he had been the one to break it, with his promise that he'd be back by her side soon. He pulled in a deep, long breath. And he would. Once he'd dealt with John. But first, he had to deal with de Lacy.

He glanced back. The lord rode alone at the rear of the group.

Palmer dropped back to move alongside him. 'I've got a question for you, de Lacy.'

'If it's about tracking John, then you need to ask Uinseann.' De Lacy faced ahead, wouldn't meet Palmer's stare. 'John's trail of fire is a lot harder to follow now that we're on lower ground.'

'No,' said Palmer. 'It's a question I've been waiting to ask for a while.'

'Then ask away.' De Lacy still looked ahead.

'You killed that old woman. Didn't you?'

'I did not expect the seat of an archbishop to look like this,' said Theodosia. Despite her grief at being parted from Benedict and her overwhelming, sickening dread at what might happen to him in his pursuit of John, she looked in wonder at what lay ahead as the tired horse she and Eimear shared plodded on.

Eimear nodded. 'The Rock of Cashel. A marvel of our land.'

'A sight I've never tired of, my lady,' added Nagle, close behind.

All around, the land lay in low, undulating green curves, with the only mountains blue in the distance against the clear sky. Yet right in the middle of the gentle vale sat a huge craggy outcrop. Atop it, a group of stone buildings that soared even higher into the sky, with a rounded tower the tallest of all, spearing the evening light with its pointed tip.

'Now I see why you made the decision to come here,' said Theodosia. 'I did not expect a cathedral that looks like a fortress.'

'It wasn't always in the hands of the Church,' said Eimear. 'It was the ancient seat of the Irish kings of Munster. One of them gave it to the Church almost a hundred years ago. He called it a gift to God's Church that no king had ever given before him.'

'I very much doubt if any king has given one like it since.'

'Certainly not either of our fathers.' Eimear gave Theodosia one of her rare smiles. 'But thanks to the generosity of King Murtagh O'Brien, we have a place where we can claim the sanctuary of the Church.'

As if in response to her words, a bell rang out from the tower on the Rock, calling the monks to prayer.

Theodosia took some comfort from the familiar sound. They would be safe there in God's protection. She would implore her God, day and night in this holy place, for Benedict's safe return.

The magnificence of the sight before her did not diminish as they neared it. She could make out several different buildings, many of the type typical of religious houses. Most were built of grey stone and located at the lower levels. At the height of the Rock, the most spectacular, where every building spoke of design and craftsmanship that strove to bring man closer to the heavens and to God.

A church that must be the cathedral, simple in form, with no transepts or tower, but of considerable size. A smaller, more elaborate chapel with two towers and a steeply pitched roof of pale yellow stone that shone almost gold in the late evening sun. Between cathedral and chapel, what she supposed to be the Archbishop's Palace. Highest of all, the Round Tower with its pointed roof.

As they approached the gate set into the high surrounding walls, Eimear halted their animal to speak in her own language to the two silent but alert warriors who'd accompanied them here.

Nods and bows greeted her words.

'I've given them the thanks of the High King's daughter. We're safe now, so they can leave.' She nodded to Nagle. 'You need to go as well. You can all do more good elsewhere.'

Do more good – that would mean the fight against John.

'As you have already done,' said Theodosia to Nagle. 'I thank you from the bottom of my heart.'

'God be with you both.' Nagle set off to catch up with the departing warriors as the gates of Cashel opened.

Theodosia gave silent thanks for their safe arrival. But her worry for Benedict surged back afresh.

Palmer waited for de Lacy's answer.

But the Lord of Meath said nothing.

Ahead, the other men still discussed battles. The tales that floated back on the soft evening air would keep a troubadour in gold.

Palmer didn't care. 'You did, didn't you? Killed her?' He wasn't going to let this pass.

De Lacy shrugged. 'She was nearing the point of death, Palmer. I saw it for myself.' He fixed Palmer with his one-eyed look, his face lit with anger as well as the flare of the setting sun. 'I know what John is capable of. My men too: they will do what they are ordered to do. If they'd found her alive, they could have done anything to her. Anything,' he repeated. 'And probably would. So I put my dagger straight through her heart. She didn't know a thing – gone between one breath and the next.'

'You call that a merciful release.' Palmer shook his head. 'If she was that close to death, she'd have been gone long before John got there.' He jabbed a finger at him. 'You'd no right to do it, de Lacy.'

'The release wasn't for her.'

'Who else did you murder in that house?'

'No one. The merciful release was for her family. Regret is a poison, Palmer.' He gave a short, bitter laugh. 'I should know.'

'You think you're the only man to know that?' came Palmer's retort, sharp from his own conscience.

'I carry the scars of it every day of my life, for all the world to see.'

Palmer wouldn't allow him that. 'There's no shame in battle scars, de Lacy. Many brave men carry those. But not from killing defenceless old women.'

'How about those that have acquired them through killing their brothers?'

Palmer missed a breath in disbelief. 'You killed your own brother?' Treacherous: Henry had been so clear in his fears about de Lacy. And here the Lord of Meath admitted to one of the greatest betrayals a man could commit.

'Robert, Lord of Weobley before me. Yes. I did.'

Palmer took in de Lacy's powerful shoulders, the man's sword ready for use and one that Palmer knew had such deadly effect. 'That must have been some fight,' he said drily.

'Me against Robert?' replied de Lacy. 'Robert, with his shortness of breath the fear of our mother's life, always needing to be kept warm, to be nursed. Me, with my muscles that outpaced my stature in growth, and so much thick, dark hair all over my body that Robert said I could have been a wolf leader.' He gave a brief smile to himself. 'Yes. Some fight.'

'I thought you more of a man than that.' Palmer eyed him in disgust.

'Steady down, Palmer. It's not what you might think. I didn't kill with a sword or a knife.'

'Poison, then. Or smothering. Kind, were you?' He knew he sneered. He couldn't help it.

'No.' De Lacy's voice dropped. 'There was no kindness. I killed him with my own stupid, selfish behaviour.'

'How?'

'It doesn't matter.'

'Yes, it does.' Palmer looked to the hooting, jostling group ahead.

They were getting Simonson to practise whistles now.

He went on. 'You pulled my secrets, Theodosia's past, pulled them from us with the point of a sword, threatening to help no more if we didn't tell you everything. You at least owe me the same courtesy.'

'Or you'll leave?'

'No.' Palmer's jaw set. 'The Lord John needs to be stopped. But that won't be easy. I fight best when I have men alongside me who I can trust. Doubt makes for mistakes.'

De Lacy rode in silence.

Palmer waited.

Still nothing.

'Well, at least I know who I have on my side.' He went to kick his mount on to join the others.

'You have a man who made the biggest mistake of his life.'

Palmer eased back in the saddle. Waited again.

'I loved my brother. When we were boys. It was simple, everything was simple.' De Lacy's words came clipped, careful. 'As the eldest, Robert would get the lordship. Didn't bother me, the second son. By God, I think I came out of my mother's womb ready for war. As I was near enough the age John is now, preparing to seize my part of the world. The larger the better. For myself. When our father told me I had to stay.'

'Serving your father isn't a mistake.'

'If only my service had been to him.' De Lacy gave an impatient shake of his head. 'My father announced he would be resigning his lands to Robert and joining the Templars. I would have to stay, to serve and protect Robert. I railed against my father, day and night. He wouldn't budge. Robert became our lord in his stead.'

'There are worse fates, de Lacy.' Palmer couldn't help his terse barb. His own father had died unable to put food on the table.

'I know that now, Palmer. I should have been glad for Robert. This was not his doing.' His voice tightened. 'But I was more jealous than Cain was of Abel. My meek and mild brother, a lord while our father lived. My father, a glorious Templar. Me, the fighter: nothing, except a prop to my older brother. To my young mind, I suffered the greatest injustice. I was being penalised for my strength. Robert got rewarded for weakness. But I was angry with the wrong person. Robert had not asked for any of this either. Father had abandoned him, same as he did me. It broke Robert's heart when I forsook him too. I did as little as I could to help him. Found my solace in the bottom of a wine barrel as I carried on fighting, waiting for my time. I was surly, vicious.'

'Like thwarted young men are. But being thwarted is a poor excuse for murder.'

De Lacy shook his head. 'The night I killed Robert, I had been drinking and riding with lances all day. It was a winter's day: iron cold, with a hard, hard frost. I felt nothing. The exercise kept me warm, as did the wine flowing through my veins. All the others gave up early from the cold and made for the castle. I mocked their weakness and carried on. When dusk fell, I couldn't be bothered to go to the castle. I was too tired. Too wine-soaked, more like. A nearby barn gave me all the shelter I needed. I often slept there when I was too drunk to go any farther. I collapsed onto the straw.'

Palmer nodded but said nothing. He could definitely guess the fate of de Lacy's older brother now. A drunk, angry young man with a sword. They made mistakes often. And with mistakes came regret. But de Lacy's next words had nothing to do with a blade.

'A kick woke me,' said the scarred lord. 'Not the kick of another man, like a watchman. But a huge hoof into my back. I opened my eyes, not to a barn, but to hell. Blazing flames. Heat that was making my skin bubble. Bellowing, panicking cattle. Smoke filling my lungs.' He took a sharp breath. 'I scrambled for the door, but it was bolted from the outside. The screams of the burning animals drowned me out as I hammered on it, screamed too. A chunk of burning thatch came down from the ceiling, then another. Caught my hair. So fast. I was howling, beating at it – then my cloak caught too. Fire was eating up the right side of my face. Someone finally got the door open. I fell out, the dousing with water hurting even more. I lay on the ground, still howling like a beast in my agony. Faces bent towards me, their mouths moving. I could hear nothing above my own voice. Then the only face that mattered. Robert. He'd come for me.'

'Then you regret the fire?' Palmer looked at de Lacy, shocked by the man's unexpected, horrific account. No wonder de Lacy had flinched at his offer of sizzling beef the night they'd sat by the fire at Tibberaghny.

'No, Palmer.' De Lacy shook his head. 'I regret that Robert had to come running to save me. He'd heard the commotion that a barn was on fire. Then the panic when word spread that that was where the drunkard brother often lay.' He gave a taut smile. 'They all knew me better than I realised.'

Ahead, Uinseann was the butt of another joke; the laughter and the last of the birdsong in the darkening woods another world from what de Lacy related of his early life. And from the lord's actions in murdering a dying woman.

'He did what any brother would do,' said Palmer. 'You can't regret that.'

'Oh, no?' De Lacy's voice deepened. 'He breathed smoke and frigid air for hours on that icy night. And with me back in the castle, he sat with me while my burns were bandaged and I writhed and howled, my right eye a bloody mess and my skin peeling off. Sat with me the day after. Then the night after that, as I slipped into a fever from my wounds. Sat urging me to life, uncaring of his own fragile health.'

'A good man.'

'He was.' De Lacy's voice came quieter than Palmer had ever heard it. 'Robert died a month later. No one dared say it, but I could see in everyone's eyes that they blamed me. I blamed myself. The cold, the exhaustion: his chest filled with a fluid that drowned him slowly. His meagre strength ebbed like a tide that never washed back in, leaving me, alone. Alone, and Lord of Weobley.'

'You've said he wasn't strong. You can't know that it was your fault.' Palmer knew his words reached de Lacy in the same way that an arrow reaches the centre of a rock.

'Keep your pity, Palmer. If I hadn't been a jealous, drunken oaf, then I would have known that Robert had a tenant that bore him deep ill will. It was he who set the fire in the barn. The man hadn't even realised I lay in there. He was screaming that at me when I hanged him from its ruins.' De Lacy nodded to himself in satisfaction before he went on.

'All I know is that I had power, wealth – everything I'd always prayed for, wished for. Resented my brother for. I was twenty and I was a lord, an important tenant-in-chief of the Crown. But I only had it because my beloved brother was dead. I came to despise every stone of the castle, every blade of grass of that cursed place.' De Lacy spat hard. 'It was like it had been poisoned. By me. I couldn't stay there.'

'Which is why you're in this country. Which is why you took Eimear in marriage.'

De Lacy nodded. 'When Henry asked me to come to Ireland, I didn't hesitate for a second. It was a land unstained by my brother's blood. A land I will do anything to keep, one I never want to leave.' He drew in a long, shuddering breath. 'And you're correct. I had no right to kill that poor woman.'

'It doesn't matter if I'm correct. Yours is the hand that took her life. The hand of the Lord of Meath.'

'But at least her daughter, her family, can come home. Can rebuild their cottage, sow their fields. Without being haunted at every turn that their mother was tortured in her last moments, abandoned by them.'

Palmer looked at de Lacy, his scars. Despair carved forever into his flesh.

De Lacy didn't drop his certain stare. 'I kept the poison from them, Palmer. For that, I will never be sorry.'

'You are so welcome to the Rock of Saint Patrick. Every blessing to you, every blessing.' The voice came from the far end of the hall in the Archbishop's Palace at Cashel, but Theodosia could not make out anyone in the gloom of dusk in the high-ceilinged room.

The clean-shaven young monk who had escorted her and Eimear in here had not appeared perturbed by their dishevelled appearance. Now he left their sides with a patient sigh. 'My Lord Archbishop, you forgot to summon someone to light your lamps again.'

'Did I? Oh, dear. Is it that time already, Brother Fintan?'

'It is, my lord.' The monk set about his task, his height reaching the tallest lamps with ease as pools of light pierced the darkness. 'Your visitors are here.' He added his prompt as silence had descended again.

Eyebrows raised, Eimear exchanged a glance with Theodosia.

'Oh, yes. Indeed.'

The monk lit a tall, wrought-iron candlestick, revealing Archbishop Matthew O'Heney sat at a huge desk, surrounded by piles of documents and manuscripts. He squinted hard, waving them forward. 'Come closer, my lady, closer.'

Brother Fintan cleared his throat. 'Eimear O'Connor, wife of the Lord of Meath, Hugh de Lacy, is accompanied by Sister Theodosia from the court of King Henry.'

The Archbishop's face lit in a delighted smile. 'Why, two visitors. Why didn't you say?'

'He can see nothing that isn't in front of his face,' murmured the monk as Theodosia went forward with Eimear. 'Even when he can, his head is always in his books.'

'My Lord Archbishop.' Eimear gave him a deep bow, Theodosia matching her.

'Every blessing of Saint Patrick be on you both.' The plump Archbishop, his tonsured hair the colour of bleached straw in messy tufts, made a swift sign of the cross with ink-stained fingers. His pale blue eyes, large in his small head, moved in their direction, and he squinted again. 'So honoured. The daughter of the Irish High King and a servant of King Henry. Brother, go and have us some food and drink prepared. Bless you.'

'My lord.' The monk left, closing the door behind him.

O'Heney peered at Theodosia. 'He's gone, sister?'

'Yes, my lord.'

'Good. Young Fintan is my staunch and loyal servant. But he and the rest of them treat me like I've lost my wits sometimes. That's what bad eyes and a love of the written word will do for you, eh?' His face lit with his smile again, a smile which had a genuine kindness in it. 'Now, sit, please.' He gestured at the long table, lit with a line of three-footed iron candlesticks.

'Thank you, my lord.' Theodosia sank onto the padded tapestry chair, her aching body relieved at finally being able to rest but still consumed with worry over Benedict's pursuit of John.

'You are most gracious, my lord,' said Eimear from the seat opposite as the Archbishop joined them at the head of the table.

'Your meal will not take long.' O'Heney pulled a tall jug towards him and filled three goblets. 'First, you will need a drink after your journey.' He passed the full goblets over. 'Our well water works miracles on a day such as this.'

Theodosia took a drink, the cold, pure water a delicious freshness.

The Archbishop went on. 'Now, I have been told that you have come here to seek sanctuary, which worries me greatly. Only those in grave danger would do so.' He folded his hands, his badly focused gaze seeking out Theodosia and Eimear in the flickering candlelight. 'There must be terrible devilment afoot if two noblewomen are fleeing for their lives. So unburden your hearts to me. Then we can decide how to proceed.'

Palmer moved forward through the dark woods, men to the left, the right, Irish warriors all.

De Lacy led the way, his hand raised for absolute silence.

The night breeze carried the sound of the trees, an owl, the distant shriek of a vixen to her cubs.

Then, on the wind came the sound of voices. The whiff of smoke. And a flicker ahead: the very faintest glow of campfires.

A shadow moved against a shadow as Uinseann appeared at de Lacy's side. For such a huge man, he moved quieter than a field mouse. Not like Simonson, noisier than a charging boar. He'd been left to look after the horses in a clearing a hundred yards back.

De Lacy gestured for every man to gather round to hear Uinseann's report.

The warrior's deep rumble of a whisper: 'We've found them.'

De Lacy nodded. 'Layout?'

'Four fires. Looks like John is at the farthest one.'

'Looks like?' Palmer was too tense for doubt.

'Wears that woman's fur,' said Uinseann. 'White.'

John's favourite ermine.

Palmer's fists clenched. John was in their grasp now.

'His big destrier is tethered near him.'

De Lacy snorted. 'A plague on him. Ready for a quick getaway as always.'

'Then that's our chance,' said Palmer.

'How?' said de Lacy.

'We only want him,' said Palmer, careful to keep his voice low. 'We can stir up the camp, make them think the whole place is under attack.'

'Been learning lessons from Tibberaghny, Palmer?' Uinseann grinned, his teeth a white flash in the shadows.

'Maybe I have. But John will run. When he does, he's ours for the taking. Simple.'

'And what if he doesn't?' said Uinseann.

'I've seen him close up in several fights now,' said Palmer. 'He panics. And he's a coward. Saving his skin will be the first thing on his mind.'

'The men of Meath aren't like the shambles at Tibberaghny, Palmer,' said de Lacy. 'They're well trained. They know what they're doing.' He snorted again. 'Trained them myself.'

'Exactly,' said Palmer. 'They're used to a lord who leads them, who knows about battle. That's what they'll be expecting John to do. They can't know him well enough yet. I do.'

'God help you,' said Uinseann.

'Then we'll do it,' said de Lacy. 'The cover of darkness gives us a big advantage.'

'And if we fail?' asked Uinseann.

'Well, I won't.' Palmer checked his belt, his sword. 'That just leaves you.'

Chapter Twenty-Five

Palmer had forgotten the frustration of watching a battle from a distance. Every inch of him itched to draw his weapon, to wade in. Right now.

From his vantage point on the gently sloped higher ground above John's camp, screened by a thin group of trees as he waited on horseback with de Lacy, he could see so much.

The blaze of the fires in the clearing of the thicker woods below. The groups of men, a few sitting, many more lying on the ground, fast asleep at this late hour.

'Exactly as Uinseann described,' he said to de Lacy.

'Mm. Pity about the moon. Could do with rain for once.'

Palmer shrugged. 'Helps with John's robe.'

The pale fur gleamed in the moon's blank light as its owner lay stretched out on the ground.

'You mean his woman's robe?' De Lacy shifted in his saddle with a twitch of a smile. 'Bet the little turd gave them terrible grief about having to sleep outside.'

Palmer held in a laugh. He could sense de Lacy's eagerness too.

De Lacy sat bolt upright in his saddle. 'Here they come. Our men.'

And they did.

Palmer watched, rapt. Terrifying to be the victim of, the Irish attack was a thrill to see let loose onto his enemy.

There was no warning. The first sign the camp got was a horse, running through the camp, trailing a bunch of burning grass, terrified, fleeing, trampling.

The men that jumped to their feet, some awake, many more who'd been roused from sound sleep, leapt into a shower of javelins, stones, all from an unseen enemy hidden in the trees. The familiar chaos could be Tibberaghny.

'Is John up?' said de Lacy.

'I can't see him.' Palmer tried to fix on the white robe. But so many figures ran, sought shelter.

'There he is.'

Palmer followed de Lacy's point to a crouching figure that stayed low even as he scrambled along with fast steps. He swore.

'What?' said de Lacy.

'Your men aren't the men of Tibberaghny.'

Despite the onslaught, shields were being grouped in a protective shell. A few archers had already started to return fire.

The white-robed figure made for the shelter of the shields.

Palmer reached for his crossbow.

'Palmer. No. You'll give our position away.'

Palmer raised his bow. 'I can get a shield-holder. Send John the other way.'

John had almost made it to the safety of the metal shell.

He brought his fingers to the trigger.

'No.'

Then, from below, a bellowing roar and a thunder of hooves.

Uinseann broke from the trees, his horse at full gallop, axe swinging in hand.

The warrior got the first head off without his mount breaking stride. Then another, and another man was down, his right arm no longer on his body.

Even the men of Meath didn't stay in formation faced with that.

They fled.

Many fell as a hollering Uinseann delivered blow after blow with his axe. The other Irish rushed into the camp to join him, their axes bringing mayhem and death.

And then Palmer saw. 'De Lacy, John's away.'

Headed up the slope on horseback, in a straight path parallel to where they were, crouched low over the saddle.

De Lacy smiled. 'He's off like the devil's after him.'

'He's not wrong.' Palmer slung his crossbow on his back again. 'Come on.'

'Most troubling that Henry's youngest son would behave in such a treacherous way.' The Archbishop shook his head at Theodosia and Eimear. 'The King has had many problems with his other sons. Even his wife.'

Theodosia kept her face a mask of serenity. She had first-hand experience of the problems of which O'Heney spoke. Problems that had almost cost her, Benedict and their children their lives. Had cost many others theirs.

O'Heney continued. 'But this plan of his to use the children of the Irish.' He crossed himself once, twice. 'Terrible. God be praised that you have prevented him so far.'

'God smiled on us.' Eimear nodded at Theodosia. 'He gave us the bravery and quick mind of the sister here.'

'I only did the right thing.' She took a draught of her water, embarrassed by Eimear's praise. 'I have my reward of being safely delivered here. There are others still out there putting their lives in danger to bring John to account.'

Sounds came from the door, and Brother Fintan re-entered with several others bearing covered dishes. 'Your meal is ready for you, my lord.'

'Excellent.' O'Heney paused in their conversation as the meal was served to the table, Theodosia following his lead as Eimear, silent too, eyed the arrival of food with a pleased look.

They had given the Archbishop an account of everything he needed to know about John's plan to take the throne of Ireland, including de Lacy's pursuit along with others loyal to King Henry, but with no mention of Theodosia's and Benedict's real identities.

Once the door closed on them again, the Archbishop said a swift grace and waved for them to start.

'Thank you, my lord.' Eimear already had a large piece of bread halfway to her mouth.

'And my thanks too, my lord.' Theodosia took a spoon of oat pottage, thick and rich with butter and herbs.

'I shall write to Henry on the morrow and explain what has come to pass.' O'Heney broke off a piece of his bread to dip it in his bowl.

'Forgive my rude question, my lord,' said Theodosia, 'but why would the King accept your word on this?'

'Not rude at all, my dear sister.' The Archbishop beamed his poor-sighted smile at her again. 'For to question is what makes us alive. Questioning shows a lively mind.' He waved his bread at her, sending a blob of sauce to land on the table. 'Lively. Henry has a long association with Cashel. He visited here the year after Saint Thomas Becket was murdered; I was a mere cleric then. He played a part in the reform of the Irish Church.' His smile was for Eimear now. 'One of those who accompanied him was your husband, my lady. Of course, he was not yet the Lord of Meath then.' He chewed hard on his bread. 'God save us, but he wanted to be. Henry complained to my predecessor that de Lacy had him plagued every minute of the day with his requests and representation for it.'

'Well, my husband got his wish,' said Eimear with a polite smile.

'Indeed, he did, my lady. Not only that, he secured a wonderful truce through his sacred marriage to you.'

Theodosia met Eimear's knowing glance as the Archbishop dunked his bread again.

'My, this is tasty,' he said. 'I think I forgot to break my fast this morning.' He gestured over at his papers, sending more pottage across the table. 'Got caught up in those, you see. Happens all the time.' He gave his desk a wistful look. 'Never enough time.' He hauled his attention back to Eimear. 'As for your husband, I am sure he will have John under his hand well before my letter even reaches Henry. I am sure his reputation and his skill in negotiating truces will be as effective as ever.'

'I hope so, my lord,' said Eimear, 'but of course he does not have his troops with him to help his case, remember.'

'Only a small group, my lord,' said Theodosia. *Including my husband.* 'Which is why it is so important that Henry is quickly informed.' She met Eimear's glance again. They would have to make sure that the Archbishop did not get distracted with his studies. Henry had to know. With all haste.

'Of course, of course.' O'Heney nodded hard. 'I will pray, pray with all my might that there will be no bloodshed.' His voice quietened. 'For which my heart always grieves, as well as my soul.'

'As does mine,' said Eimear.

Theodosia could only cross herself, unable to trust that she could speak without distress. *Bloodshed. Please God, let it not be Benedict's.*

The Archbishop nodded to himself. 'Which is why it was such a wise decision for you both to come to Cashel.' He looked from one to the other with his unfocused eyes. 'I can keep you both from warfare, protect you under *Lex Innocentium*, the ancient law that keeps the innocents from harm. Give you the sanctuary of the Church.' A small, proud smile came back. 'I have the greatest of authority in this land. Authority which has given me the great privilege of having been able to save so many lives. And now I can guarantee the safety of yours until this latest time of turmoil is over.' He gave a deep sigh of satisfaction.

'Thank you once again, my lord,' said Eimear.

'My heartfelt thanks to you too, my lord,' said Theodosia.

The Archbishop waved their replies away. 'Once you have finished your meal, I will get Fintan to show you to your accommodation.' He waved a hand at his hall. 'This is a fine building. But that is your refuge under God's law.' He pointed out of one of the tall windows where the moon had long risen to light the sky, a tall shadow soaring into it. 'Cashel's Round Tower.'

They had him. They almost had him.

Palmer had made a vow not to kill John, only to arrest him. Stop him. He wished that were different. His own fighting blood was up. Without that vow, the Lord of Ireland wouldn't be long for this world.

It was as if John heard his thoughts. His animal picked up greater speed as he drew ahead up the hill, a pale splash of movement against the darkness of the rising land.

Palmer was ahead of de Lacy by half a length as his lighter horse did better on the rising ground.

'Keep on him.'

Palmer kicked his animal on faster at de Lacy's order as the lord increased his pace too.

The drum of another set of hooves came close behind.

Palmer glanced back.

Uinseann, leaving the mayhem in the camp to his capable fellow warriors.

He drew alongside. 'Saw him take off.'

'You can't kill him,' said de Lacy

'I'll try not to.' Uinseann still had his bloodstained axe.

'You might scare him to—' Palmer thought his own eyes failed him. 'Forcurse it. Where's he gone?'

'He was right there.' De Lacy flung up a hand in a bewildered gesture.

A string of Irish words burst from Uinseann.

Palmer knew each one was an oath.

'I hope I'm wrong,' went on Uinseann, in Palmer's tongue again, 'but I think I know exactly where we are. Follow me.'

He made for the spot where John had disappeared.

After not many yards, Palmer saw.

Before them, the ground opened up in a huge scar in the earth, a sheer grey wall of rock facing them. The ground beneath their feet fell away in a steep, steep slope. Covered in loose shards of rock and stunted bushes that gave way to ferns, the slope led down to the black mouth of a huge cavern at the foot of the cliff, open like a beast about to devour the moon overhead.

John's abandoned horse stood nearby, nosing at the ground, its sides still heaving after the fast ride. A few stones rolled down the slope, following the path of crushed fern leaves and disappearing into the darkness, confirming where the rider had gone.

Uinseann let loose another stream of curses as Palmer swung off his horse, de Lacy dismounting quickly too.

'If he's gone in there, we'll get him.' Palmer peered down, trying to make out any kind of movement.

'That we will.' De Lacy stepped on a stone that gave way beneath his boot, rolling and bouncing down with a clatter.

Palmer grabbed at his arm to stop him following.

De Lacy steadied himself as Uinseann got down from his horse, eyes locked on the silent opening of the cave. 'We might not be the only thing to get him. We could be got ourselves.' He pointed his axe at it. 'This is the cave of the Luchthighearn.'

'One of your Irish ghosts?' Palmer couldn't help his rude response. The big man had just taken heads from men's bodies. Yet now he looked ready to flee when facing some sort of imaginary creature.

'No ghost.' Uinseann shook his head.

'Let's get down there, de Lacy.'

'Not so fast, Palmer. Rushing in without thinking is a poor strategy.'

The lord could have been Palmer's squire master. Same lesson. He bit another rude retort back.

De Lacy turned to Uinseann. 'What do we face if we go in there?'

'The Luchthighearn is a monstrous cat. That cave is its lair.'

'A big cat?' Palmer's stomach tightened. 'Like a leopard?'

De Lacy looked at him askance. 'Leopards are exotic creatures, Palmer. You won't find them in these lands.'

'You'd be amazed where you can find them.'

'You're not honestly trying to tell me that you think there's a leopard running loose in Ireland?' came de Lacy's testy response.

'If there was in England, then why not Ireland?' Palmer knew he asked the question of himself, the memory of dappled, muscled fur and razor-sharp teeth and claws forever in his nightmares. 'Look, I'm not saying it's a leopard. All I know is a big cat is cunning. Fast. Jaws that can open a skull like an egg. Believe me. I've seen it. First-hand.'

'Oh, God between us and all harm.' Uinseann had the spooked look of a horse about to bolt.

'That's as may be, Palmer.' De Lacy frowned. 'But if there is a lethal creature living in that cave, then it might decide to make a meal of the Lord John. We need to go in there after him.'

'You could smoke him out,' said Uinseann. 'Much safer. You'd be able to stay out of the blasted place.'

'Bad idea.' Palmer shook his head, though he'd give a bag of gold coins for it to be an option. 'Look at the size of that cave mouth. It would take us hours to set fires big enough for that.'

'Agreed,' said de Lacy. 'Worse, it would signal to the camp below that there's something afoot up here. As things stand, we're hidden. At least for now. But every moment is another where we could be discovered. And our chance to catch John would be lost.' He gave his reins to Uinseann. 'Somebody has to stay here to hold the horses. It might as well be you. Palmer, you're with me?'

'I am.' Palmer thrust his reins at the big warrior, who gave them both a salute.

'Good luck. I'll be right here.'

Palmer paused to grab a coil of rope from his saddle pommel. 'Torches.' He went to rummage in his saddlebag. 'Let me get my flint and tinder.'

'Don't waste time. Mine's in my belt pouch.' De Lacy broke off a few of the bigger branches from a nearby bush as he took a cautious step to where the slope sharply steepened. He took a first step down. His foot slid again and he cursed.

Palmer stepped forward next to him, slinging the rope across his chest to keep his hands free. His feet threatened to go from under him too, tipping him forward at an angle that could snap his neck. Only one thing for it. He dropped to his backside, leant right back and pushed hard with the flat of one hand. He did a fast slide down the first ten feet, slowing himself with his heels.

Stones pinged at his back as de Lacy followed him.

He turned to tell him to move to the side.

'Can't stop, Palmer!' De Lacy clawed at fern fronds that snapped off in his hands, sending a growing pile of rocks and stones bumping into Palmer as de Lacy descended too fast.

Palmer pushed off again.

But de Lacy careered down, out of control, cannoning into Palmer's back in a burst of pain and sending him rolling, spinning, in a slide of rocks and stones that struck his face and hands as he fought to slow his fall.

He landed at the bottom. Stopped. Breathless. Flat on his back. On stone that oozed wet. At least five times the height of a man above him, the black of the roof of the cave blocked out the light of the night sky.

De Lacy's body slammed into him again as the lord ended his descent, driving more breath he didn't have from his body and flipping him onto his face.

'Well, we're down.' De Lacy levered himself up with a hand to Palmer's back, his voice low. 'You make a good cushion, Palmer. Wouldn't think it to look at you.'

Palmer gasped in a painful lungful of air. 'And you have a kick like a mule.' He climbed upright and spat a piece of fern leaf mixed with bloodied spittle from his mouth. 'But yes, we're down.'

The air was cooler, damper than it had been up where Uinseann waited with the horses, and little of the moonlight reached down here. 'But we made enough noise to warn the Lord John.' Or attract the interest of the big cat. He could see nothing in the blackness of the cave but could swear eyes were on him. Amber eyes. Fixed. Before the creature leapt. He shook the thought away.

'Can't be helped.' De Lacy handed him the sticks he held. 'Let's get some light.'

Palmer fastened lengths of rope round the sticks in tight twists as de Lacy got to work with his flint and tinder.

The rope took hold in a smoking sulk but yielded a small flame.

'That'll have to do.' De Lacy handed one to Palmer. 'God's eyes.' He held his torch aloft. 'This place is huge.'

'I thought we'd reached the bottom,' said Palmer. 'But it carries on down.' He moved his feeble light, caught a glimpse of a huge column of stone like human hands had carved it. A gleam of something reflecting his flame. He paused. 'Water.'

'Is it flooded? If it is, that's good news. Nowhere to go.'

Palmer moved closer. The water shone black. Still. Nothing to stir its surface. He hoped. 'No. It's just a pool.'

'Pity.' De Lacy moved away, his tread deliberate as he planted each step. 'Watch your feet. Lot of moss on these rocks.'

Palmer followed.

With the ground beneath them still sloping down, they walked farther from the entrance.

Palmer had thought the light there poor. Now the weight of total darkness had them in its grip. The flames they held barely pierced it, made shadows on the grey stone that gave it faces, movement at the edge of sight, yet showed cold and dead when Palmer fixed on it.

It grew colder. Water dripped from above, in a relentless, sparse seep.

Palmer could sense a vast emptiness over him, but his lungs insisted the ceiling pressed down inches from his head, robbing him of air.

Then.

The rattle of a stone.

Not from his boot, not from de Lacy's.

The lord looked back at him, the half-smile on his scarred face near demonic in the faint, flickering light against the black. 'My Lord John!'

Palmer started, expecting silence where he got a shout.

No echo. The ancient rock deadened the sound as well as it did the light.

De Lacy shouted again. 'My lord! It's Hugh de Lacy. Sir Benedict Palmer is with me.'

Silence except for the drip, drip, and the hiss of the meagre flames when a drop struck them.

Palmer turned slowly, his gaze trying to find any shift in the black.

'We mean you no harm, my lord.' De Lacy again. 'But we need you to come with us.'

Another tiny clatter. Palmer could swear it. He poked de Lacy on the arm, nodded to the part of the cave the sound had come from. He put his mouth close to de Lacy's ear, slipped his own torch into the man's free hand. 'Keep talking. I'll use the dark.'

'I am loyal to King Henry,' called de Lacy, 'as is Palmer.'

The bounce of a stone. Harder this time. Something stirred in the darkness farther back in the depths of the cavern.

Palmer made for it as quickly as he dared. He could see nothing. Nothing. He raised a hand in front of his face to protect it; in the utter blackness he could run nose first into rock and not see it.

De Lacy kept his words flowing. Meaningless words. About loyalty. Forgiveness. Words that John would rarely have uttered in his life. But they covered Palmer's movements.

Another clatter.

Palmer didn't pause. He could only pray that whatever made the noise had two legs and not four. And that the owner of the two legs couldn't see him enough to gut him with a sword.

A yell from de Lacy. 'Palmer!'

He whirled round.

De Lacy was on the ground, yelling, John's shadowy form landing a hard kick in his ribs as he wrenched one of the torches from him.

With a flick of his white robe, he was off, running, running for the blackness beyond. Running deeper into the cave.

Palmer was at de Lacy's side in a few strides. De Lacy thrust the remaining torch at him. 'After him. I'll get another one lit and follow you.'

Palmer took off after John. 'Stop!'

But the King's son ran on, glimpses of him disappearing, reappearing as he rounded rocks, ducked behind others. Panic gave him reckless speed.

Palmer followed close behind. 'There's no way out!' He'd no idea if there was or not. For all he knew there could be an easy tunnel around the next corner, leading out into the night air.

A skittering sound and a strangled oath. John had fallen.

He had him now. Palmer rushed forward. An unseen rock sticking out from the wall of the cave caught the side of his head in an agonising thump and scrape. Staggering hard, it was his turn to swear now. He put his hand to his head, and the warm wet of his own blood soaked his fingers.

He forced his steps straight again.

No sign of John.

He picked up speed, waiting for the flash of movement in the poor light to reappear.

It didn't.

Palmer paused, his hard breaths fogging in the glow of his own flame, making the only sound other than his heartbeat in his ears.

Still no sign.

He moved forward again, more cautious this time.

The little swine could be waiting to jump him. Or had been eaten. He cursed himself for a fool. A big cat consuming a live person wasn't quiet. The whole place would ring with the horrible sounds.

His boot clumped into something. Not rock. Something soft.

Palmer crouched down, ready for an attack, hand out. It met fur.

Chapter Twenty-Six

Palmer jerked his hand back with a yell, his paltry flame lighting up the skin of the animal he'd felt.

Ermine. John's robe.

His heart still raced like it wanted to leave his chest, and he swallowed hard to steady its fool's rattle.

John's robe. But no John.

Now Palmer didn't even have the paleness of the fur to follow.

All he could do was press on, keep his eyes focused on the gloom, look for any movement, any sign of the tiny flame of the other torch. And where was the Lord of Meath?

'De Lacy!' His shout went unanswered. 'Are you with me?'

Silence.

Palmer frowned. The King's son couldn't have gone past him. But he'd been dazed for a few seconds when he'd struck that rock with his head. John might have slipped past him then.

He hesitated. Back or forward?

One of his feet skidded on another wet rock. Recovering his balance, he saw a better path to the side, with the rocks less jagged. He'd follow that for as long as he could. Then he'd turn round and make for the entrance. He stepped over, stepped again onto a shadowed rock. His boot met air. He was falling.

His light blinked out, fell from his grasp.

Falling.

He was dead.

The crash of stone against his head and back told him he wasn't. The groan of his own voice in his ears told him he wasn't. The sparks of pain through him told him he wasn't. But his eyes told him nothing. Not which way was up, down.

Whether he lay on a sloping, narrow ledge, where any movement would send him plunging down, down to where his bones would shatter. He was moving, sliding.

He pulled in a cry. No. He wasn't. His head spun. From the blow as he landed. Not his body. Instinct had him crush his eyes shut to halt it. No difference. Of course. He opened them again. He had to get his bearings.

He stretched out a cautious right palm, flat from his body. Rubble. Loose, cold stones. Big, small. He swept his hand farther. More. He did the same with his left. The same. His legs. More rocks, loose debris. Good.

'De Lacy!' His shout came hollow. Contained.

He must have fallen into another cave. He should move, try to find a way out. But what if he couldn't? Who would know he was down here?

De Lacy hadn't answered his shout before he fell, could be lying dead with John's sword through his heart.

Uinseann might come looking. But when? Fighting raged outside. And the warrior was terrified of this place. Even if he did come to search, he might never come across this place into which he, Palmer, had fallen. He'd chased John for a long way, and who knew how many tunnels and caverns were in here?

So he, Palmer, would stay in here, in the smothering black, calling, shouting, as he grew weaker and weaker until thirst would take him in a slow agony . . .

Sweat broke out over his whole body. He cursed himself for a witless churl. He had a sword, a knife. He wouldn't wait for an end like that. What he needed to do was to get out of here.

Hands and knees first. He knew he had that amount of space. He moved one hand, one leg. His other limbs. Turned over with small, careful movements. And he was there. Ready to crawl. Like Tom had. Matilde had. While his heart surged with pride and he and Theodosia had laughed in joy together at their healthy, beautiful children.

He saw them for a second in the blackness. Now his sight played tricks. He didn't care. He was getting out of here.

'De Lacy!' His call bounced back into his own ears again.

He edged forwards, checking every inch was solid before he put any weight on it. So slow, so slow. But he couldn't risk going any faster. An impatient move could have him put most of his weight onto empty space, toppling, with no way of seeing what to grab to save himself.

But what if he edged away from the hole he'd fallen down? What if that was at his back and before him lay an endless tunnel, one that brought him deeper and deeper underground, where he would no longer be able to hear the cries of any rescuers, nor they him. He paused, sweat pooling on his back. He should turn around. Yet a cave side could be just a few feet away, the hole above it. A side he could climb up. And out.

He balled his fists in frustration and ground out a long, long oath. All he could do was go on.

He put his right palm flat on the ground once again. Loose rocks, but solid beneath. Good. His left. The same. Right knee. Left knee. All good. Right hand.

No rock. Something smooth. Leather.

His mind made that much.

Then his jaw exploded in pain as the boot cracked up and into it.

But Palmer had hold of the mail-wearing leg that wore the boot, yanking it down towards him. Mail. It had to be John.

A punch landed on his shoulder.

'Have some of that back.' Palmer swung in response, met air. Swung again, got the smack and sting of his knuckles on flesh. His hand closed on cloth, pulled hard at it, keeping his hold on his attacker as he returned kicks, punches.

Then his hand found a face, a face that yelled into his own as his nails dug into the flesh even as his other hand fumbled for the throat.

A knee in his stomach made him loosen his hold. But Palmer didn't let go.

He threw all his weight on his attacker, straddled him to pin him down, received another hard punch to the head.

So hard, light flicked across his vision.

He landed a strike of his own.

Light again. Not from his head.

The faintest of gleams came from above.

Thank the Almighty, there was an above. 'Down here!' He yelled and yelled, even as the man pinned under him landed punches, roaring too.

'Here!'

The light brightened. A little.

Dazed as much from darkness as the blows to his skull, Palmer could make out the edge of the hole he'd fallen into; then the unmistakable shape of Hugh de Lacy's head and shoulders appeared in it.

'De Lacy! It's Palmer!' Palmer shoved his forearm onto his opponent's throat. 'I've got John!'

'You have?' De Lacy thrust the light into the hole as Palmer got off his beaten opponent.

'You. Up.' He forced him to his feet by the scruff of his neck and the light finally fell on him.

Palmer froze.

He knew the bloodied face that glared back at him. But it wasn't the King's son.

'John?' came de Lacy's roar. 'That's not John. That's my bloody serjeant.'

The cold pool in the cave of the Luchthighearn, still black even in the wan light of dawn, might usually be empty. Not anymore.

Palmer pushed the serjeant's head under its surface for the fourth time, held the back of his neck down as the man writhed, trying to escape his firm grip.

'Out again,' came de Lacy's calm order.

Palmer hauled him out, the man gulping in great mouthfuls of air as spittle and water streamed from his mouth, unable to wipe any of it away, his hands secured with rope behind his back.

De Lacy hunkered down next to him. 'Where is he, Aylward? Where's John?'

The serjeant spat, shook his head. 'I don't know. I swear to you, I don't know.'

'Don't know?' Palmer shook him like an errant dog. The man had led him a fool's dance in that cave and had done his best to kill him. 'Won't tell, more like.'

De Lacy had already received word from the group of Irish warriors that John was nowhere to be seen.

'I don't know!' said Aylward. 'I am sworn to the Lord John, the Lord of Ireland, so I did what he ordered, led you away. He took twelve men with him. And the King's clerk.'

De Lacy sighed. 'Aylward, I've trained you well. Very well. Perhaps too well.' His look hardened. 'In.'

Palmer shoved the man's head beneath the surface once more. 'Do you think he knows?'

Aylward held still at first, keeping his breath.

De Lacy frowned. 'I don't think so. Which worries me.'

'And me.' The first twitches began under Palmer's hand. Became squirms. Wriggles. Thrashing.

'Don't drown him, Palmer. At least not yet.'

Palmer hauled him back out.

Aylward sounded like a hoarse bullock as he pulled in gasps of air, coughing and retching. 'I tell you I don't know anything. Whatever you do to me. I can't tell you.'

'We haven't time for this.' De Lacy stood up with an oath. 'We should get going, Palmer. Head for Dublin. We know that John planned to take Eimear there.' His backhand caught Aylward on the side of the head. 'And you'll spend time in my prison for this.'

Palmer looked at de Lacy. 'If you still have a prison.' He stood up, hauling the drenched, shuddering Aylward to his feet. 'So in the meantime, we'll make use of what we've got.' He grabbed the serjeant under one of his bound elbows, hauling him back down the slope that led deeper into the cave, the man stumbling to keep his footing.

'What are you doing?' Aylward's eyes widened in fear. 'I don't know where John is.'

'We're in a hurry to find him. We haven't time to deal with you.' Palmer paused. 'De Lacy. I need your help. And your rope.'

The lord followed.

Palmer fixed his glare on Aylward. 'We can put you back in the hole you led me to. You can lie in there, hoping that we don't take too long to find the Lord John. Because if we do, it might be too late for you by the time we come back.' He started the man walking again, though Aylward twisted in his hold. 'Or we might simply forget. Mightn't we, de Lacy?'

'Indeed we might,' came the mild reply.

'No, Palmer. No. My Lord de Lacy, you know me. I'm a truthful man!'

De Lacy shrugged. 'No one's saying you're lying.' He took hold of Aylward on his other side. 'Only that you will have to wait.'

'Please, my lord.' The serjeant tried to kick out, but Palmer wrenched him forward. 'I don't know anything!'

Palmer stopped. 'The problem is, Aylward, that all men know something. And you know quite a lot. You're just not telling us.'

'I don't, I don't.' Aylward's voice held panic.

'Nothing at all?'

Aylward's glance shot to the darkest depths of the cave.

Palmer recalled his own terror when he thought he'd be buried alive in there. He saw it now in the serjeant's face.

'I don't know where the Lord John went – I swear.'

De Lacy gave a snort of disgust. 'Same tune, Aylward.'

Palmer didn't bother replying, started to haul him off again.

'But I do remember something he said. When we were at the village where we found that old woman's body.'

Palmer stopped again. 'Oh?'

'He explained how he wanted me to lead any pursuers away.'

'You've told us all this,' said de Lacy. 'His robe, his horse, the fires. Your idea to use the cave to keep the deception going when you came upon it, if it were needed.'

'There's more.' Alyward's look went back and forth between Palmer and de Lacy. 'The clerk Gerald was talking – you know how he talks. He was raving on about how if the Irish could slay an old dying woman, then everyone could end up martyred in this terrible country. Martyred, he said, like Saint Thomas Becket himself. On and on.'

'You really think that is enough to save you from your fate?' De Lacy almost smiled. 'I expected more from you, I—'

'Hold.' Palmer's spine prickled at the mention of Becket's name. 'Was there anything else said?'

Aylward nodded. 'John was getting on my horse as I was about to set off on his. I wished him Godspeed, said I prayed he didn't meet the fate of the slain Becket like Gerald so feared. John just laughed, said: "I'm not concerned with any dead archbishop. A live one is much more valuable to me."'

Palmer's hope faded in his disappointment. 'Canterbury's in another land, across a sea. Weeks away.' He went to take hold of Aylward again. 'John-talk. Nothing else.'

'Leave him.' De Lacy. Barely a whisper. 'You're sure that's what he said?'

'Positive. But, my lord, that was all, and it may be nothing and—'

De Lacy held up a hand to cut him off.

Palmer frowned at him. 'De Lacy? What is it?'

'I think I know where John has gone.' His voice came thick with emotion. 'I've been there. With King Henry.'

The prickle was back. But not in a way Palmer liked. 'Where?'

'The seat of an archbishop. But it's not Canterbury. It's much closer than that.' De Lacy swallowed hard. 'Palmer: John is headed for the Rock of Cashel.'

Chapter Twenty-Seven

'I do not think we are permitted to come up here.' Theodosia climbed the steep ladder in Cashel's Round Tower, a few rungs behind Eimear; her hands were slippery with sweat from exertion and from her fear of the shadowed drop that opened up below her feet.

'Of course we are,' came the reply. 'The Archbishop said this tower was our refuge. We're only exploring the rest of it.'

Theodosia had no desire to explore. Brother Fintan had walked every sacred building on the Rock of Saint Patrick with them that morning, his pride obvious. While Theodosia had been awed by its ecclesiastical riches, she'd ached to return to the lower room in the tower that the Archbishop had provided for them. Not for the comfort of the large bed with its clean linen, sweet with rosemary. Nor the well-stocked table with its fresh breads and rich, creamy cheese. Though Eimear had passed a peaceful night's slumber in the bed and had feasted on the food, Theodosia had done neither.

She had spent the hours of the previous night, and so many today, kneeling at the carved faldstool in the room, praying without cease for a stop to John's wickedness. Praying for Benedict's safe return. Until God answered her prayers, she would continue. Sleep could wait.

But Eimear had grown increasingly restless in the confined space, prowling up and down like a caged cat. This scaling of the ladders to reach the top had struck her as an excellent idea, and she had persuaded Theodosia to pause from her devotion for a short while to come with her.

'We're here.' Her much cheered tone rang down.

Theodosia let out a relieved breath. Her skirts were so much longer than Eimear's.

Eimear's tone shifted. 'And, Theodosia, wait until you see what it contains.'

The sudden loud clang of a bell almost sent Theodosia plummeting from her perch. 'I think perhaps it would be too easy to guess now.'

'Not the bell.' Eimear leaned down to offer Theodosia help as she climbed from the last rung. 'This.' She gave a wide sweep of her hand.

Theodosia caught her breath.

The room took up the entire top of the tower, in the same way as their own accommodation did. But up here, high as a bird in flight, four tall, triangular-headed windows, each one at an even space at four points in the rounded walls, gave views for miles. The yellow light of the setting sun poured in from one, illuminating the contents that already gleamed with a life of their own. Altar after altar, every one containing a treasure beyond price. Reliquaries of gold and silver, studded with jewels. Caskets and boxes covered with scenes from the Bible and the lives of the saints, the enamel fine as any paintwork. Statues carved so lifelike, they looked as if they would speak. Missals, psalters, gospel books – their glorious tooled and coloured covers proclaiming the exquisite work that would be found inside.

Eimear's eyes rounded as she took in the sight. 'Have you ever seen such riches?'

'Never.' Theodosia shook her head. 'I have seen great wealth at the court of King Henry. But not like this. Not devoted to the glory of God.'

'Well, the Archbishop has made sure he has put it in the right place, hasn't he?' Eimear went to the far window. 'We're halfway to heaven up here. Come, have a look.'

Theodosia stepped over to join her. The sight of ground so far below made her lightheaded. She put a hand to the reassuring solidity of the stone that surrounded the window.

'Do you see that mountain? The one with the large dip in the centre?' Eimear pointed to a line of distant hills, above which a line of full, low clouds approached. 'That's Devil's Bit. Some people say that the Devil took a bite of the rock but dropped it here when fleeing from Saint Patrick. That's the rock we stand on now.'

'Oh, Eimear.' Theodosia gave a little shake of her head. 'That is not mentioned in the Bible. I am sure it is only an outlandish tale, the type of which Gerald is so fond.'

'I know.' Eimear gave a broad grin. 'Why do you think people keep filling his ears with them? He'd believe anything.'

Theodosia tried and failed to look disapproving. Her own laugh met Eimear's.

Another chime of a bell came, this time from far below.

Theodosia looked out again, still with a firm hold on the stone.

A lone monk walked around the outside wall, ringing a small bell at regular intervals.

'What is he doing?' Theodosia turned to her.

'A blessing for this place.' Eimear's expression grew solemn. 'To ward off evil.' Then every trace of colour left her face. 'Dear God. It's not working. The Devil himself is here.'

Theodosia looked back out to see what so terrified Eimear and gave a loud gasp. 'No.' She gripped the stone even harder as she was sure she would fall. 'No. *No.*'

John. Here. At Cashel. With Gerald. A monk leading the two men up the hill that led from the entrance gate to the group of main buildings. Heading their way.

'Where—?' Theodosia's head whirled, but no longer from the height. 'Where is Benedict?' She willed him to appear, sword drawn, John under his authority. 'Where is your husband?'

'They're not here.' Eimear's voice came tight with shock as the Lord of Ireland strode on. 'Which means John has bested them. Got our location from them.' She swallowed hard. 'I don't think either of them would have given him that without the worst of torture.'

'No.' Theodosia's jaw set. 'Benedict would have gone to his grave rather than betray me.' Her words came fierce in her belief, in the grief that threatened to overwhelm her.

'But look at John,' replied Eimear. 'He has the bearing of a victor, of a—'

The ladder gave a rattle, a shake. Shuddered.

Theodosia's panicked look met Eimear's.

Somebody was climbing up.

Hide. She mouthed the word to Eimear as she scanned the room for anywhere that they could.

But Eimear grabbed hold of one of the larger wooden statues and moved to the hole where the ladder emerged, lifting her weapon high and ready.

'Sister?' A hissed whisper. 'My lady? Are you up there? The Archbishop has sent me with an urgent message.'

Theodosia recognised the voice of the monk who served the Archbishop. She stepped forward to block any strike that Eimear might make. 'Leave him.' She raised her voice a little. 'We are here, brother.'

'Oh, thank the Lord.' The ladder shook again, harder. The face of the young Brother Fintan appeared. 'The Lord John is here. At Cashel.'

'We know.' Eimear lowered her arms but kept her hold on the statue. 'We have seen him.'

'He has come for us, brother.' Theodosia spoke with a composure that belied her terror – a terror not only for her own life, for Eimear's, but that Benedict had already lost his. 'I am sure of it.'

'Please do not fear,' said the monk. 'The Archbishop does not think that John knows you are here. There was no mention of either of you at the gate when the King's son asked for admittance to meet with the Archbishop. He said he was here on campaign in the name of King Henry. He has his clerk with him, and a group of a dozen men for his protection on his travels.'

'A small band of fighters remaining.' Eimear nodded in grim satisfaction to Theodosia. 'Then at least Hugh and Benedict put up a good fight.'

'With respect, my lady,' said Fintan, 'I would question if any of these men has been fighting in the last couple of days. I took a discreet look when they arrived at the gate so I could report to the Archbishop. Yes, they are travel soiled, but that is all.' His calm face matched his tone.

His words brought a tiny comfort to Theodosia. 'Any man who had managed to defeat Benedict would carry severe injuries,' she said. 'But John's sudden proximity bodes the gravest of ills: I am sure of it.

'I can assure you the Lord John made no threats,' said Fintan, 'displayed no violence, showed no force.'

No threats, no violence, no force. His words brought terrible reminders to Theodosia. Not like that freezing cold December evening at Canterbury, when the knights descended to brutally maim and murder Archbishop Thomas Becket. When they came for her. She swallowed hard. 'Then what is his purpose here, brother?'

'To receive the hospitality of the Archbishop of Cashel. That is what he has said.'

'I do not believe him,' said Theodosia.

'Neither do I.' Eimear moved quickly back to the window to look out. 'They're going into the Archbishop's Palace.' She turned back to address Theodosia. 'All seems well.' Her tone lifted in cautious hope.

'Precisely,' said Fintan. 'Archbishop O'Heney knew that if he refused entry, it would only make the Lord of Ireland suspicious. John does not know you are here. The Archbishop says to keep yourselves hidden in the tower and you will be safe. He also asked me to remind you both that you have the full protection of the Church. You are here, within the tower, its refuge. Its sanctuary.' He readjusted his grip on the ladder. 'I must go. I do not want to attract any attention through my absence.'

'Of course,' said Theodosia. 'Bless you, brother.'

Eimear muttered her thanks too as he disappeared from sight.

The ladder stopped moving. He was gone.

Eimear let out a long breath. 'I would not have chosen John's arrival. But, with Cashel's help, we should get through it.'

'I fear the men of Cashel are being naive.' Theodosia's thoughts jumped from one possibility to the next. 'We need to move from here.'

'Perhaps they are. But it's too risky,' said Eimear. 'We're hidden from any prying eyes in here.' She glanced around. 'We're with the Archbishop's wealth. We're in the most secure place on the entire of Saint Patrick's Rock.'

'Secure. You mean like in a cell?' *Like the security of the cell of an anchoress. A cell from which her beloved Thomas Becket ordered her out. To leave. And saved her life.*

Eimear shrugged in incomprehension. 'I would think that secure.'

'Then you are wrong. A hiding place that no one knows of is far more secure.' Theodosia grabbed her hand. 'Come. We have to get out of this tower.'

'But where can we go?'

'I think I know.'

Now, this was disappointing.

John had had such high hopes entering Cashel.

His journey here had been one of painfully slow stealth. Hacking through the densest of woods. Giving a wide berth to any settlement. Hiding at the sounds of any other riders. All to make sure he was not discovered by any of the savages who roamed the many miles he'd travelled.

When he'd finally laid eyes on this place, it had pleased him that the buildings had an impressive, if foreign, grandeur, and their position on the enormous lump of stone looked really quite remarkable. And yet its Archbishop, hurrying to greet him and Gerald as they entered his hall, was neither impressive nor remarkable.

'You are so welcome to the Rock of Saint Patrick, my Lord John. Every blessing to you, every blessing. The King's clerk too! Every blessing.'

In fact, the man was a mess. Covered in ink, hair askew. Eyes like a blind frog's.

Gerald didn't seem to notice, was grinning at the man with every one of his long teeth. 'Archbishop. It is such an honour.' Bowing. 'Such a great honour.'

'The honour is mine. Let me see, let me see.' The fat little man searched for a place to sit free from strewn and piled papers and manuscripts.

John kept his own smile fixed. So very disappointing. He'd imagined that a tall, imposing Irishman ruled over this place. This O'Heney could pass for a friar buying apples on a muddy town street.

'My apologies, my lord.' O'Heney picked up papers, peered at them, put them down again. 'If I had received word, my lord, you would have found my hall waiting to receive your noble presence.'

'No need for apologies, Archbishop,' said John. 'Your hall is most fine, and its contents show your devotion to your work.'

The man looked delighted with the risible platitude.

'Devotion, indeed.' Gerald had an equally pleased mien.

John doubted if the clerk would have noticed if the hall had a roof or not, with his covetous appraisal of the manuscripts.

'Such a magnificent collection, Archbishop.' His teeth again. 'I would declare myself envious if it wasn't a deadly sin.' Now his high-pitched laugh.

'They are yours to view and to examine.' The Archbishop held out a hand. 'A joy to meet another who appreciates their sacred words as well as their beauty.'

A rattle came at the door. 'My lord.' A younger monk entered, breathless as if he'd been running.

'Ah, Fintan.' O'Heney beamed, as if welcoming a visiting nobleman instead of a servant. 'Will you be so kind as to help me put some order on this place?'

John let his smile drop. Imagine asking for help. How this man had ever become an archbishop was beyond him. Clearly, the Irish were even more backward than he'd thought.

'My lords.' The young monk called Fintan bowed to him, to Gerald, as he gathered up papers, answering the Archbishop about how much bread was available, Gerald about the date of one of the manuscripts.

Funny. He did all that, and yet his breath steadied. He must have been exerting himself a great deal to have arrived in the state he had.

'My Lord John. Please.' Fintan bowed, indicated the comfortable-looking, high-backed chair he'd just cleared, the clean lines of his handsome face lifting in a smile.

John settled himself with a nod and clicked his fingers at him. 'Wine.'

A smile that was a little too broad. 'Of course, my lord.'

But John cared not. He had far more important business to which he had to attend. That infernal spy had ensured that word of his intent to take hostages had spread far and wide – he had no doubt of that. So he had had to change strategy yet again. He picked up the full goblet and allowed himself a nod of satisfaction. His new strategy had a boldness to it that had taken his own breath away when he had thought of it.

'This life of Saint Hugh has outstanding lettering.' Gerald held up some dull religious work. 'Wouldn't you agree, my Lord John?'

'I have never seen its equal.' John raised his goblet to it.

That seemed enough to satisfy the clerk, who returned to his huddle with the jabbering Archbishop O'Heney.

John took a long draught of his wine. Yes, the little Irishman's appearance was not a match for the well-known blithe countenance of Thomas Becket. But one had to make do with what one was given.

The murder of an Archbishop was an act that echoed across the whole of Christendom. John had every confidence that O'Heney's would be no exception.

And death by fire always appealed to the popular imagination.

They were too slow.

You fool, Palmer. You fool.

Every beat of the surging horse's hooves beneath him was like a drum that beat out his guilt.

'Clench your jaw any tighter and you'll snap it.' De Lacy, riding beside him in the driving, misty rain.

'And if I do?'

'We'll be one man down. Can't afford that. Especially not you.'

'Don't talk to me like I'm a squire in low spirits.'

'Fine.' De Lacy shrugged. 'But if you plan on doing something stupid, at least tell me.'

'I can't do anything. Not right now. Not until we get to Cashel. Get to John. That's the problem.'

De Lacy glanced behind him. 'Pull your horse up.' He matched his words with his actions. 'We're losing the others.'

Palmer did so with a growled oath, the rain-soaked, sweated horses snorting and blowing hard.

De Lacy was right. The rest of their small band rode a long way behind on the roadway.

Palmer blew a sharp whistle, gestured at them to hurry up. Swore again.

'If you were a squire under my command, you'd feel my fist.' De Lacy fixed him with a look. 'You're acting like a knave, Palmer. Stop it.'

'I might be a fool, de Lacy.' Palmer glared back at him. 'But I'm no knave.'

'A fool, eh?' De Lacy leaned forward to ease his spine. 'Why's that?'

'Because only a fool would've misjudged John so badly. I thought him an arrogant, cowardly youngster that could do nothing without the support of a full court around him.' Palmer shook his head. 'But he's shown that he can think for himself. Act for himself. Henry's words to me: *"He's sharp enough."* John's proved he's more than sharp, throwing us off the scent.' He ground out yet another oath. 'I should've seen it.'

'I agree he's made some clever moves in evading us and making for Cashel. The Church is a great supporter of King Henry. John has figured out that they should protect him in a land where he has few friends left. Help him send word to Henry to get—'

'I don't care what happens to John!' Palmer itched to punch the unruffled de Lacy in the face. 'I only care about my wife! Theodosia's gone to Cashel. Your wife too. And we sent them there. What if John got to Cashel first? What if he found them on the journey? He'd, he'd . . .' Palmer swore instead. He couldn't put his horror into words lest he make it real.

De Lacy shrugged. 'How is any of this helping Theodosia or Eimear?'

'It isn't. And we're too slow.' Now Palmer could punch his own face in frustration. 'I was too slow – I still am.'

The other riders had almost caught them up.

'Whatever has put John in this position is of little consequence. We are where we are, and our energy should be put into our next move.' De Lacy pointed at him. 'Our *next* move. Not the previous one.'

Palmer didn't reply, and de Lacy dropped his hand with a terse sigh. 'I underestimated him too. As did so many others. You're not alone in this, Palmer.' De Lacy raised his voice to the others. 'I know you're all tired, that your horses are too. But we have to push on with all haste. Cashel will soon be in our sights.' He clicked to his animal.

But Palmer was already away.

De Lacy's attempt to lift his anger hadn't worked.

Palmer kicked his horse into greater speed. He should have seen it coming. He was still a fool.

And they were still too slow.

Theodosia descended to the bottom of the lowest ladder in the Round Tower. She had checked for any sign of danger from each of the smaller windows on the way down. So far, nothing, except for the usual order of this holy house and the fast-moving, distant clouds extinguishing the setting sun to bring an early twilight.

Eimear jumped from the last few rungs to land beside her in the simply furnished room.

'Still all quiet.' Theodosia did not know whether she said it to reassure Eimear or herself. She quickly stepped to the door and grasped the iron handle to open it. *Locked.* Her stomach tightened. 'Dear God. They've shut us in.' She yanked at the unyielding metal with all her strength. 'It was all a trap.' Struck it hard. 'All of it.'

'Stay calm, Theodosia. Of course Fintan would have locked it. They're trying to keep us hidden in here, remember?' Eimear dropped to her haunches to check a small altar next to the door. 'I'd wager there's a key somewhere in this room. Start looking.'

Breath fast in her chest, Theodosia complied. She upturned candlesticks, a stool, all the while waiting for the dread sounds at the door. Intruders would not need a key. They would use boots. Axes. 'Do you think Fintan spoke the truth?'

'I'm sure of it. As I've just said.'

'Not about locking us in.' Theodosia pulled up a heavy rug from the stone floor. Still no key. 'About John and his men not having fought. Does that mean our husbands will have been spared a battle?'

'You mean, do I think they are still alive?' Eimear pulled a tapestry out from the wall to peer behind it. 'I have no idea.' She turned to pin Theodosia with her look. 'What I do know is we are. And we should be doing everything we can to stay that way. You and I are mothers. Above all else, I need to stay alive for William. As you do for Tom and Matilde. That is all that matters.' She returned to her search.

Eimear was right. Theodosia nodded, unable to trust speech, and opened a large chest containing folded cloaks, rifling through them without success.

'Oh, where is that cursed thing?' Eimear stretched high to run her hands along the lintel. She drew a sharp breath. 'I have it.' She pulled out a large iron key from a narrow recess above the door. The angle made it look as if she drew it straight from the stone of the wall. 'At least I hope I do.'

'As do I.' Theodosia grabbed a couple of the cloaks and hurried over to her.

With a couple of swift clicks, Eimear unlocked the door and turned the handle, releasing the door from its tight fit in the frame. The cool of the stiff evening breeze blew in.

Theodosia put a hand to the handle, preventing Eimear from pulling the door wide open. 'Wait. We need to look out first.'

Eimear squinted through the crack. 'Nothing of concern,' she murmured.

'Then we go. While we still have the chance. Put this on – it'll help to conceal you.' Theodosia handed a cloak to Eimear while she fastened hers about her head and neck.

They stepped out onto a narrow wooden platform with a flight of steps that led up to the door of the tower, many feet from the ground.

Before them loomed the imposing grey stone walls of the cathedral, its tall windows filled with the jewelled colours of exquisite stained glass.

'Should we go in there?' asked Eimear in a low voice as they descended, their steps swift yet silent on each tread.

'No,' said Theodosia. 'I do not remember seeing many hiding places when Brother Fintan showed us the magnificence of Cashel. We are going to that building.' They moved across the grassy ground. Quickly. Quietly. She pointed to the pale yellow stone chapel with its steep roof, also of stone. 'Cormac's Chapel. We need to keep to the back of these structures. Their entrances face the other way, so we are much less likely to be seen here. Keep as close as you can to the walls. We will crawl beneath windows if necessary.'

'Doors?' said Eimear.

'If they are closed, we move past them as fast as we can.'

'And if they're open?'

'We go faster.'

Crouching low in their concealing robes, they moved quickly past the cathedral now, Theodosia's heart racing as she was sure Eimear's did.

The position of the cathedral's windows, set high in its walls, meant no one would see. A small wooden door that presumably led from a side chapel was shut tight.

They came to the corner of the cathedral.

'Wait,' whispered Theodosia, halting Eimear with a hand. 'This is the most dangerous time. You see that next building? With the lower windows? That is the Archbishop's Palace.'

Eimear's eyes widened. 'Theodosia. John's in there. Gerald. If they even glance out, we're done for.'

'We have to get past.' Theodosia fixed her with her sternest look. 'You must trust me. Stay down, low as you can. Keep close to the walls.'

She did herself as she ordered Eimear to do.

The low clouds overhead deepened the dusk, and dew already soaked the thick grass under her palms.

Moving slowly, carefully, Theodosia kept her sight on the window, too dark for her to see inside. Someone could be looking out, watching them, and they would not know until it was too late. When a shout would come, then men and weapons. And John.

Theodosia swallowed down her terror. They had to do this. She glanced behind her.

Eimear's face showed pale against the darkness of the concealing robe, her eyes fixed on the window too.

Lights flickered, then grew in number at the window. The candles were being lit.

Theodosia stretched out to whisper into Eimear's ear. 'This is better. Brightness inside makes it more difficult to see into the dark outside.'

Eimear nodded, still staring at the window.

Theodosia moved forward again, hugging the wall of the cathedral.

They would have to tackle the palace next: it lay between them and her goal of the yellow stone chapel.

The palace was sited at an angle to the cathedral, a shorter, lower building. They would have to creep past directly under the window.

Theodosia signalled this to Eimear, who shook her head, pointing past the stretch of open grass between them and the chapel, to the stones and crosses that marked the start of the graveyard. Shaking her own head with even greater vehemence, Theodosia pressed her hand to the wall.

Using the cover of the gravestones might feel safer than moving closer to John, but the stones were too widely spaced. Theodosia knew she and Eimear were hopelessly exposed if they did so.

Eimear held up a hand in capitulation.

Theodosia crawled forward again, Eimear with her.

They were directly beneath the window now.

It opened above them.

Theodosia froze, grasping for Eimear, whom she could tell was about to run for it. She could only hope that their stillness would hide them. But it wasn't dark enough. Not yet.

Then a male voice sounded above them, and she held in a cry.

'Are you sure it's not too cold, my lord?'

Brother Fintan.

She risked a look up and met his gaze. His eyes told her he'd seen them.

Another male voice. Irritated. John. 'Yes, it's cold. But this room is stale beyond belief. I need some fresh air.'

Footsteps.

'Get away, you devil!'

Theodosia hung on to Eimear. The bewildering call came from Fintan.

'What are you playing at, man?' John. Even more irritated.

'Only a bat, my lord.' Fintan waved a hand again. 'Away with you!'

Theodosia understood. She yanked Eimear to her and made off in a low, scrambling run.

They made it to the concealing far corner of the palace as John's silhouette appeared in the light of the window next to the monk.

'Sorry, my lord,' said Fintan. 'We're plagued with the creatures.'

Theodosia quietened her breathing as Eimear crouched next to her, shaking hard.

'How revolting.' John leaned out. 'Yet I can't see any.'

'They're too fast, my lord. But they're there. Believe me.' The young monk sounded like he had a smile in his voice.

'Come on,' said Theodosia in Eimear's ear. 'We're almost there.'

They ran – ran round the back of the chapel, the first misty rain buffeting their faces. The raindrops fell heavier as they reached the south door of the quiet chapel.

Theodosia blessed herself as they entered its shelter, her whole body shaking from their closeness to discovery. It mattered not.

They'd made it.

John turned back from the window, the hairs on his neck rising at the idea of unseen bats swooping round him when he couldn't see them. He'd gone to the window for a reason. He'd just have to wait.

That young monk was smiling at him again. He wanted to make him stop. And he would. Soon.

John returned to the table and its dull contents and even duller occupants. Though Cashel served passable wine, the dreadful food could have been peasant fare.

The Archbishop and Gerald didn't even seem to notice, exclaiming over some battered metal box that O'Heney had fished out from under the table.

'You see, Gerald' – the shock-headed fool had it open now – 'it contains some of the soil from the grave of Saint Peter himself.'

'Oh, my.' Gerald must be inhaling it, he had his nose so close to it.

'It is wonderful, isn't it?' said O'Heney. 'A gift from the Holy Father himself.' He sighed in contentment. 'I have used it for the swearing of oaths between warring factions. Such a wonderful gift, it has brought so much peace.'

Holy soil. John despaired as he swallowed a deep mouthful of wine. It would take more than a bit of mud to bring peace to this place tonight. He waited, tense. Waited for the bells, the bells that would ring for the Hour of Compline. The Hour of the Night.

That was the signal to his men who had been given accommodation in the lower buildings at Cashel. Once Compline rang, they knew what to do. It seemed to be taking forever. He'd ordered the window open to make sure he heard them. And then that stupid bat. He felt eyes on him and looked up.

That monk again.

'Some more wine, my lord? Your goblet is empty.'

John was about to demand a jug and silence from him, when he heard the first bell. And the next, and the next.

The hour had come.

The muted sound of many sandal-clad feet met him. The monks were hurrying to assemble in the huge cathedral.

He returned the monk's broad smile. 'I think I will have some more.'

Now, all he had to do was await the tramp of boots.

Any minute now.

Chapter Twenty-Eight

'We did it.' Eimear pushed her robe from her head, her skin shining with sweat and raindrops. The few candles that lit Cormac's Chapel gave her fearful face extra shadows.

Theodosia wiped her own wet skin. 'We did, praise God.' The quiet of the pale stone with its intricately carved pillars and the scenes from the Bible that glowed with such life and colour from the vaulted roof of the chancel helped to steady her racing heart. She pulled in a long breath. 'Not a moment too soon.'

From outside came the peals of Compline's bell and the orderly stirring of the monks making their way to prayer.

Eimear frowned as she took in the space. 'Theodosia, this wasn't a good idea. There's nowhere to hide in here.'

'It is not what is in the chapel.' Theodosia hurried over to a door on the right-hand side. 'Rather, what is above it.' She pulled the door open to reveal a spiral staircase, exactly as Fintan had mentioned. 'This leads to the croft. A far better hiding place. Where nobody knows we've gone.'

Eimear nodded in relieved approval. 'I forgive you. I think.' She stepped over to remove one of the candles. 'Though forgiveness was far from my mind when John was a couple of feet away from us.'

Theodosia shuddered as her own fear clawed afresh at her. 'I think my reason almost left me.' She led the way into the staircase with rapid steps.

With the door closed tight behind them, they mounted the winding stone treads, Eimear holding the candle high in a hand that still shook.

They stepped into the croft.

The steeply pitched stone ceiling arched high above, and a few windows set into it at a lower level gave some air, but only the smallest smudge of faint grey light.

'Plenty of room for us here. And dust.' Eimear sneezed hard.

'Dust that lies undisturbed.' Theodosia allowed herself a small smile of triumph. 'Which means people rarely come up here.'

'That suits our purpose.' Eimear placed the candle on a stone beam as her gaze roved over every corner. She sneezed again.

'Hush,' said Theodosia. 'We need to stay quiet.'

'I know.' Eimear scrubbed at her nose with the back of her hand. 'Sorry.'

'Hush.'

'I said I was—'

'Hush!' Theodosia listened out. Her stomach dropped. The tread of metal boots on stone. Eimear's face told her she heard it too.

'It's from outside.' Heart fast again, Theodosia ran across to one of the windows, her wet shoes and skirt sending clouds of powdery stone silt into the air.

'You're leaving tracks!' came Eimear's furious hiss.

Theodosia cared not. She reached the window and gestured for Eimear. 'Quick.'

Eimear joined her, stifling another sneeze.

A group of a dozen mailed soldiers made their way to the cathedral, following in the footsteps of the monks who had walked there a short while before.

'Why are armed soldiers going to Compline?' whispered Theodosia, meeting Eimear's equally mystified expression.

'Those are John's men.' Eimear gave Theodosia's hand a brief, hard squeeze. 'I am very glad we didn't try to hide in the cathedral.'

The door of the cathedral opened to allow the men's admittance, the spilled light bringing a brief gleam to their mail. It closed behind them, and quiet returned once more.

Eimear pulled in a deep breath of relief. 'Who cares why they're going? It keeps them away from us.'

Relief Theodosia did not share. 'Armed men at a cathedral's door.' She licked some of the powdery dust from her dried lips. 'Same as there were on the night of Becket's murder.'

'But John's not with them. Nor Gerald. Neither is there any disturbance.'

'John is plotting something, Eimear. I know it. Why else is he here?'

'My guess would be that Hugh and Benedict caught up with him and his men. John will have run away, bringing this small group with him.' She snorted. 'We know he's good at fleeing.'

'No.' Theodosia frowned to herself as she stared at the dark outline of the huge cathedral. 'If that were so, Benedict would have been close behind him. None of this is right. None of it.'

'If all is quiet, that's good enough for me.' Eimear glanced over her shoulder. 'What I need to do is smooth out our footprints. They could easily give us away if anyone comes up here.' Eimear pulled off her cloak. 'This will have to do to sweep over it.'

Theodosia remained at the window, unable to shake her deep sense of foreboding.

Eimear sneezed yet again as she set about her task. 'I swear this stuff has been here since the time of King Cormac himself.'

'I would think so.' Theodosia did not move her gaze from the closed cathedral.

'It looks undisturbed again.' Eimear came back to her side and gestured to the still night. 'You see? No disaster, no—'

As if in reaction to her words, the door of the cathedral opened again. Opened to reveal John's men, swords drawn this time, lit torches in hand as they flanked a line of cowering monks.

'Oh, dear God.' Theodosia put a hand to her mouth as Eimear gasped in horror.

'Keep moving!' The shout from one of the guards echoed out.

Hemmed in as they were, the monks could only comply in a rapid shuffle.

'They cannot hurt them.' Theodosia's words came low, fierce as she turned to Eimear. 'They cannot.'

'Theodosia.' Eimear's whisper. Her point with a trembling finger. 'Look!'

Theodosia did. Now she feared she had entered a door to hell.

Exiting the palace was John, the Archbishop firm in his grasp, his sword drawn. His bloodstained sword. An ashen-faced Gerald followed.

'Get a move on!' The arrogant, bullying tone she knew so well.

'I pray, slow down, my lord.' The little Archbishop stumbled hard. 'My eyes. In this light.'

John ignored him, brought him to the head of the column, where he paused to address the holy inhabitants of St Patrick's Rock. 'You will come to no harm if you do as you are ordered. I want you all in the chapel!'

The chapel. Theodosia grasped Eimear's arm. 'We have to go.'

'No,' came Eimear's equally firm response. 'Think, Theodosia. John is putting the men of Cashel into the chapel downstairs. I would like to kill him with my bare hands for how roughly they are being treated, and I pray I'll get the chance. What's more, those bloodstains on his sword concern me greatly. But for now, this is where we should stay. This is the last place anyone will look.'

The monks had set off again, orderly as before but with shocked uncertainty on the torchlit face of every holy man.

Eimear went on. 'Not only are we safe, but we may be able to help. We're invisible to John, remember?'

Her words made sense. 'A great advantage.' Theodosia dropped her hand.

'The best we have at this moment. So we stay put.' Eimear caught back a stifled sneeze. 'Oh, God rot this dust. I swear I shall stay quiet.'

Another shout from outside. 'You'll stay in there until I command otherwise!'

A terrible realisation came to Theodosia. 'What you said. Just now. God be merciful, I think I know what John is planning.' She met her friend's frown.

'How—'

'The dust: you said it was here from the time of King Cormac.'

'Dust? Have you lost your reason?'

'Listen. John wants to be King of Ireland. But we have foiled his ambition. Yet Cashel is the ancient seat of the Irish kings. You told me so. Before one of them gave it to the Church.' Theodosia's fists clenched. 'I think John wants to strike back at being so thwarted. And I fear to the depths of my soul what that means for the Archbishop.'

Eimear stared at her. 'Theodosia, my hope is you've gone mad. But I don't think you have. We need to try to get help.' She glanced out of the window. 'They're almost here.'

'Come on.'

Dust bloomed again in the air as they ran to the stairwell.

Theodosia led the way down the tight spirals of the steep stone staircase as fast as she dared, pausing when she reached the bottom. She opened the door a crack. 'The chapel's still empty,' she whispered. 'Quick.'

They made for the door through which they'd entered, swift, silent, as noises came at the north door.

Theodosia turned the metal handle with careful, sweated hands, anxious that she should make no sound.

'Hurry, Theodosia.' Eimear's anxious whisper. 'They're on their way—' She cut off to stifle another sneeze.

'Out. Before you do another.' The door swung open soundlessly in Theodosia's hands, and they slipped through.

Easing it shut behind them, they stepped outside, breathing hard.

Rough, uncouth commands floated on the rain-spattered night air.

'Where should we go?' said Eimear, her voice low.

'We stay where we are for now,' replied Theodosia. 'There are too many eyes that could see us. We should be sufficiently concealed—' Theodosia froze.

Voices raised in argument. John. Gerald. She crept as close to the corner as she dared.

'You can have your manuscripts, Archbishop. It'll help you to pass the time.' John gave the bewildered-looking little man a wave as his soldiers slammed and locked the door of Cormac's Chapel.

He hunched his cloak tighter. This rain went through him on this filthy night. He went to set off for the warmth of the palace but was halted by a hand on his arm. 'Oh, what is it now, Gerald?'

The clerk wore one of his haunted looks. 'My lord, may I make, with the utmost respect, a suggestion?' He quivered hard.

'Go on.' John knew what was coming, though he was surprised that Gerald dared to say anything.

Only a short while ago in the palace, the clerk had thrown up in shock when John had run the young Brother Fintan through with his sword. John had explained the problem, that Fintan had threatened to prevent him from taking the Archbishop prisoner. That simply could not be allowed. Hence, the running through.

Gerald and the Archbishop had failed to grasp the simplicity of the argument.

Now here the clerk was again. 'My suggestion, my respectful and humble suggestion, is that you do not imprison the Archbishop of Cashel in one of his own chapels.'

'It won't be for long, Gerald.'

'That is good news, my lord.'

John went on. 'It won't be for long because he and the other monks are being held while I find every last item of value that this site holds. It may be that some treasures are hidden, and therefore I will require the help and assistance of those men in the chapel.'

The clerk's face and entire body sagged in relief, and he passed his unsplinted arm over his sweated brow.

John held in his smile. 'Once the looting is complete, I am going to burn the chapel to the ground, and those locked in the chapel will be the seat of the fire.'

A terrible moment passed where John thought the clerk was going to spew again. But the old fool rallied.

'My lord, as a man of God, I am appalled, appalled by the killing of Brother Fintan, a young holy man in God's house, and your plan to kill more.' He flung a hand towards the chapel. 'You would murder the Archbishop of Cashel? Another murder like that of Saint Thomas Becket?'

John tensed at this outrageous challenge to his authority. He was tempted to lock the clerk in there with the rest of them. But he needed Gerald's skills at recording. 'Gerald, I'm sick and tired of you and your drivel. Leave this place if you want. Go out amongst the Irish that you're so afraid of. I'm sure they'll welcome you with open arms. And axes. I'm going back to the comfort of the palace. My palace.'

He set off, then paused. 'You should know, Gerald, that it was your harping on about Becket that gave me the inspiration for this. My thanks to you.'

A ridiculous keening broke from the clerk as John went on his way.

Then he rolled his eyes to himself.

It sounded like the clerk was being sick again.

Theodosia fought her own bile, and Eimear's face showed her rigid with shock.

John's words – so vicious, so casual. His taking of Brother Fintan's life. His intention to take that of Archbishop O'Heney, of others, in such a heinous manner. All terrible echoes of those who had come to take her Lord Becket's life, and what followed after. Never again. If she had to lay her life down to stop it, she would. And she had to do it now, while she had not yet been seen and before Gerald walked away.

She moved right to the corner, peeking with caution around the wet stone wall. 'Brother.' Her urgent whisper. 'Over here.' She beckoned as Eimear pulled at her arm in panic.

'Theodosia, what are you doing?

Another. 'Here.'

Gerald looked over in trepidation. His face changed as he saw her.

'He'll bring the Lord John down on our heads.'

'Trust me.'

'Sister Theodosia.' Gerald's thin face in the shadows looked stunned as he came to her. 'You were a spy for Cashel? And you' – he stared at Eimear in open revulsion – 'the savage.'

Theodosia raised a hand. 'Brother, please. I beg you to listen to me. Neither of us is a spy. I swear on God's name that Archbishop O'Heney himself gave us the Church's sanctuary here.'

'You expect me to believe your word?' Gerald drew breath to call out.

'I saved your life, brother,' said Theodosia as panicked sweat engulfed her. 'As Eimear tried to too.'

He paused.

She continued. Fast. Steady. 'If you doubt me, then make your way to the door of Cormac's Chapel and ask the Archbishop if he received us here. But, in so doing, you will make it impossible to save him, for my presence will then be known.'

Gerald opened his mouth. Closed it again.

'We have to save him. We have to.'

'We must.' Eimear pressed the point.

'I don't think we can.' Gerald raised his injured arm. 'Look at us.'

'But we have to try, brother.'

His face showed the war waging within him. Then he swallowed hard. 'You are right.' He crossed himself several times. 'Such wickedness must be countered.'

Theodosia allowed herself a small breath of hope. 'Brother, John said you were free to leave. If we go down to the gate now, you could go to the stables and get a horse and cart, and we could conceal ourselves in the back. No one is going to question your leaving if the Lord John has given you permission.'

'Once we're out, we can get help,' said Eimear.

'Eimear is held in great esteem by the Irish, brother. You would be quite safe.'

'Very well.' Gerald's anguished look went to the chapel again. 'Let us make all haste.'

'Agreed,' said Theodosia. 'Now, come.' She took his arm in the usual hold to steady his steps, hoping to speed them as she did so. 'Eimear?'

'Quickly, brother.' She took the other arm.

Together they bore Gerald away from the chapel, heading down the rock with the clerk protesting at their pace.

Theodosia's heart jumped in her chest. The darkness, the blustery rain in her face. The ground muddy and slippery under her feet. She should descend with care. They all should. But the deep shouts and raucous calls of the looters floating on the wind made her reckless.

'Pray God they stay occupied in their foul work.' Theodosia steadied her footing as her feet almost went from under her.

'I'm sure they'll be like pigs at a trough,' said Eimear. 'Thanks to their greed, the stables look deserted.'

The low buildings indeed sat in dark quiet, with the ground on which they stood levelling off in a neat, cobbled stable yard that was far easier underfoot.

Her tone hushed, Eimear pointed to a small cart in one puddled corner. 'I'm sure I can hitch that one up.' She let go of Gerald to investigate. 'I can. We don't even need a groom.'

Theodosia gave a quick glance up at the Rock. So many lights. Someone could discover them at any moment.

'I could drive such a tidy cart.' Gerald nodded hard.

'Then let's not delay,' said Theodosia.

'Help me lift it, Theodosia.' Eimear went to pick up the shafts to manoeuvre it out of the corner.

'What are you lot doing?' A male voice. Its owner walked out of the shadow of the stable block. Wearing chain mail. With his hand to the hilt of his sword.

Gerald clutched for Theodosia.

'Eimear, don't!'

Her scream came too late.

Eimear flung herself at the soldier, her nails going for his eyes, her teeth on his hand.

With a surprised oath, the man tried to fend her off.

She grabbed for the handle of his sword. 'I'll have that.'

'Off, bitch!' His iron boot met her kneecap in a sickening crack.

She dropped to the wet, muddied cobbles, grinding out a long, long scream through clenched teeth.

'Dear God, no.' Theodosia went to help her, but the man drew his sword.

'The Lord John will hear of this.'

Theodosia looked for something, anything she could use to stop him. Then froze as Gerald's plaintive wail rose up.

'Do not use your sword on me! It's me, Gerald. The King's clerk. These harridans were forcing me to leave with them as a hostage. And me a poor, defenceless man, with my broken arm.'

The coward. She could kill him herself.

'I know who you are, brother,' said the man. 'Let me deal with these two.' He sucked at the blood from the bite on his hand. 'This one first. Definitely.' He raised his sword to Eimear, who clawed at the ground, trying to escape from his weapon's reach.

'Spare her! I beg you!' Theodosia went to step forward, but the man turned his sword on her.

'Pray stay your hand,' said Gerald. 'The moaning savage on the ground is of royal Irish blood, surprising as it may seem. Too valuable to the Lord John. Put her in the chapel with the rest, and I will stand guard over this nun.' He nodded at Theodosia. 'Secure her to that post. I will watch her until you get back.'

'If that's your order, brother.' The man looked disappointed.

'It is.'

Theodosia tried to back away, but the man held his sword up again. 'Move and I will cut your legs from under you.' He placed it out of her reach on the cart and beckoned for her to come over.

'Let her be.' Eimear hurled a string of oaths.

Theodosia complied, knowing he would carry out his threat. 'I beg you, sir. I only want to leave this place.'

'I'm sure you do.' He took a piece of coiled rope from the cart and bound Theodosia's wrists to the wooden upright in tight, quick knots.

Breathing hard in her pain, Eimear raised herself on one elbow. 'Gerald, hell won't be hot enough for you, you know that?'

'Enough of your noise.' The man grabbed his sword and went back over to Eimear 'Up, you.' He yanked her to her feet and she bit back a howl of agony. He dragged her away at a relentless pace. 'I'll send someone down for the nun.'

Eimear's contained cries of pain tore through Theodosia as she watched the guard haul her off into the darkness. She glared at Gerald. 'How could you? How—'

Her question died.

Gerald held up his knife, the same knife with which he'd slain the Irish warrior in his tent. 'And now. Sister.'

'No, brother. Please. Do not.' Theodosia stared at the knife in Gerald's hand, twisting frantically against the rope that bound her.

'I'm sorry, sister.' He raised the blade.

John flung his wet cape aside and reached for the jug of wine, pouring himself a large goblet. The warmth of the palace was most welcome after the chill outside, a chill that was closer to autumn than midsummer. Even better, all of Archbishop O'Heney's mounds of documents had been cleared. John nodded to himself. He couldn't bear disorder.

The manuscripts would provide such excellent tinder in the chapel. And the holy men would provide reliable tallow.

That was quite a good jest. Pity he had no one to share it with. Never mind. That was the price of bold leadership, of being a rare individual whose mind worked in great leaps, no matter what events came at him.

A respectful knock sounded at the door.

'Enter.'

One of his men, one of the many who plundered Cashel tonight, walked in with a broad smile. The smile disappeared when the man's eyes lit on the cooling body of the late Brother Fintan in a puddle of blood.

Goodness, how easily some folk were distracted. 'Yes?'

'I think there is something you need to see, my lord.'

John sighed. 'I do not want a riddle contest at this time of night. What is it?'

'It's the Round Tower, my lord. There's great wealth on the first few floors.' His smile was back. 'But you should see what's on the top one.'

'You really expect me to go out in the wet and the cold and the dark again to go and see it. Bring it to me, man! That's what I told you to do.'

'But that's just it, my lord. We can't. At least not in one sweep. Or even two, three.' His eyes lit up. 'There's so, so much of it. It's a wonder to behold.'

John kept in the huge cheer that threatened to break from him. Now, this was good news. The very best. He got to his feet. 'Very well. I'll come and have a look.' He picked up his damp cloak again with a grimace and walked to the door.

'Should I send someone to remove the dead brother, my lord?'

John swung his cloak over his shoulders. 'When the task of gathering Cashel's wealth is complete. And make sure they bring me the head. It will make an excellent display high on the Rock.' He nodded to himself. 'I've seen that done elsewhere. I rather like how it looks.'

Chapter Twenty-Nine

Theodosia tried to twist away from Gerald's knife with a cry.

But she could not.

The clerk brought it down on the loops that bound her to the post. 'I am sorry for alarming you.' He sliced through the knots at her wrists and the tight rope fell away.

Her knees felt as if they were about to give, and she could not trust speech, not for a few thudding beats of her heart in the hiss and drip of the rain.

Gerald continued. 'But I had to think fast when we were discovered, and it was the best I could do.'

'You have my heartfelt thanks, brother.' Her voice sounded like another's.

'We can still leave and try to find help. But we'll have to hurry. No time now to attach a cart to a horse.'

'Brother, I am not going.' She swallowed hard. 'I never intended to. I was trying to arrange it so I could get Eimear out of here. I knew she could summon help. With your aid, of course.'

'Sister, you are staying here? With the risk of the Lord John finding you? Are you quite mad? He will tear you limb from limb!'

'Brother, I cannot abandon the Archbishop to his fate. Nor the monks. Eimear's fate now too.' She clenched her fists. 'I will not have that on my conscience.' *Not as Becket's is. Forever will be.* 'I have the best chance while John's men are still occupied with stripping this place of its sacred possessions. Once they are finished, it will be too late.'

'Then you have greater courage than I.' His face fell. 'God help me, I am too afraid. I cannot fight much with one arm, but at least my feet and legs are working. I shall go with all haste to seek help at the nearest monastery. I'm sure they will find those who can come to Cashel's assistance. And I have my knife to defend myself on the way.'

As he flung the shredded rope back into the cart, Theodosia did a quick search of it. Her hands closed in triumph on an intact coil.

Gerald poked around under the seat. 'You might as well have this too.' He held up a small hatchet. 'For all the good it will do.'

'Thank you, brother.' She took it from him. 'Godspeed you.' She set off in a run back up the hill.

'You see, Palmer?' The thick blanket of fine rain deadened de Lacy's call. 'We're here. Nothing appears untoward at Cashel tonight.'

Palmer pushed his wet hair from his face as he stared at the hulking rock. The shadowed buildings above it showed many lights. 'If Theodosia and Eimear are dead, it wouldn't look any different, de Lacy.'

He frowned. Footsteps.

A lone figure ran along the road towards them, knees up, one arm flailing, in the most bizarre gait he had ever seen.

Now de Lacy's brows drew together. 'Is that the royal clerk?'

'Palmer! De Lacy!' The familiar wail floated over to them.

'It is,' said Palmer. 'Something's wrong.' He kicked at his animal to get to Gerald more quickly.

'No, no.' The weird flailing wave again. 'Get off the road. You shouldn't be seen.'

'Hell's teeth,' said de Lacy. 'What's the matter with him?'

'Off the road. I beseech you!'

Very wrong. 'Do as he says.' Palmer gave a sharp whistle to the other riders who followed a short way behind. He urged his horse to trample a path into the darker shelter of the soaked, dripping trees.

De Lacy and the rest of the group abandoned the roadway with him, converging together to share hushed questions in heightened alert.

A loud crashing announced Gerald's arrival through the bushes. As he burst through, his eyes lit on Uinseann and the other Irish warriors. 'Don't let them kill me!' he shrieked. 'I have terrible news!'

Palmer's fear became a knife that might stop his heart. 'They won't touch you, Gerald. What's going on?'

'Palmer. De Lacy.' Gerald sobbed without cease as he staggered over to them. 'Oh, dear God. You must help.'

'Spit it out, man,' said de Lacy.

Palmer swung off his horse and was on the clerk, grabbing his bony shoulders to pull sense from him. 'Is Theodosia hurt?'

'What of Eimear?' De Lacy's horse jigged at his strident question.

'The sister is unharmed.'

Relief surged through Palmer.

'That I know of.'

Stopped. 'What does that mean, Gerald?' He tightened his grip on the clerk.

'And Eimear?' De Lacy again.

'I'll tell you, let me tell you.'

'Let go of him, Palmer,' said de Lacy.

Palmer did as ordered, listening with growing horror.

Gerald didn't take long. Though he delivered a heart-stopping account with sobs and wails, the clerk used no extra words, no flowery words.

The face of every member of their small band told of their shock.

Palmer wanted to grab the clerk by the throat this time. 'Are you trying to tell me you let Theodosia go to try to free the Archbishop?'

'Everyone in the chapel. The wounded lady Eimear too.' Another wail. 'I couldn't stop the sister!'

Forcurse it to hell. Theodosia was trying to fight a war. Single-handed. 'I'll stop her.' Palmer was back at his horse in a few strides.

'Palmer.' De Lacy's order. 'Get back here.'

'Damn you, de Lacy. I'm going for Theodosia.' He went to remount, grabbing hold of his saddle, foot up to one stirrup.

Muscled arms grabbed him.

'You heard the man.' Uinseann hauled him down and back from his horse.

Simonson lunged in to grab hold of one wrist.

'Get off!' Palmer threw Simonson off with ease onto the wet ground, but the warrior held him in an iron grasp.

Palmer strained in his hold, his own balance off in the mud. 'I said, *off*!' He swung a fist, got one of the man's eye sockets.

'Have this, Englishman.' Uinseann hit back, his thumping fist straight in Palmer's stomach.

Palmer's breath grunted out, and he doubled over, swearing with what he had left.

De Lacy shook his head. 'Palmer, have sense. She's gone to the chapel. To the Archbishop's aid. To my wife's. Not the palace.

The Lord of Ireland's in the palace, so she's not near him.' He pointed to the darkness of the Rock. 'John wants the place looted before he starts his murdering fire. Plundering a large site like that is going to take hours.'

'I'm going, de Lacy.' He forced the words out as he straightened up.

'No, you're not. And I'll put a sword through you myself if you don't calm down and listen. We will rescue everyone. Including the sister. I promise you.' He stressed the word *sister*.

Of course. Not everyone here knew Theodosia was Palmer's wife. And it had to stay that way. 'All right. I won't. Now let go.'

De Lacy nodded to Uinseann, who released his hold. 'We need to keep this very simple. Simonson, you stay here and keep watch over the King's clerk.'

Simonson straightened. 'Yes, my lord.'

'As for the rest of us, this,' said de Lacy. 'We get to the palace by scaling the wall beneath it and climbing up the outside of the rock. It's not a difficult climb, but it's steep and it's dark and wet. At the top is a wall the height of more than two men. Try not to break your necks. Once we have John, we have control and we stop it. Stop it all. John is the one we need to get our hands on. In the meantime, you take the innards, the heads from any man in chain mail that says he is loyal to the Lord John. Understood?'

A chorus of agreement met his words.

Palmer added his mumble of agreement.

For now. But he'd follow orders for only so long. First chance he had, he was going for Theodosia.

'These ladders are so steep. Why on earth are there no stairs?' John climbed up what the soldier told him was the last ladder in this tall tower. He prepared his wrath for the fool who said he should come out here. Granted, he'd seen plenty of valuables on the lower floors. But nothing to warrant enduring the Irish rain yet again

'It's how these towers are designed, my lord.' The man's voice from above.

John climbed out from the hole through which the ladder protruded.

And wondered if he'd climbed into a dream world.

Gold. Silver. Ivory. Jewels on the precious metals. So much wealth. Wealth beyond what he'd ever thought possible. And miraculously, he held his dream in his hands once more.

Yes, he'd planned to take whatever he could get from here. Killing the Archbishop would cause terrible problems for Henry. Might even cause him to lose his throne. It would certainly send the Pope into an impotent rage. Both men, both old, stupid men, would realise their profound folly in passing him over.

But that no longer mattered. He had the means to buy a kingdom. An entire kingdom. He had the means to raise an army, seize a crown with what this room contained.

He had, literally, ascended to greatness. *Ascension to greatness.* That would be a chapter in his book.

He bent to look at yet another jewelled reliquary. 'Go and fetch every man I have here. I want all of this brought to my palace. All of it. As quickly as possible.'

John, Lord of Ireland, let out a long, slow breath of triumph. He was lord no more.

Cashel, seat of the ancient Irish kings, had just birthed a new king within its walls.

And the Archbishop served no further purpose.

The time for the flames had come.

Theodosia slowed her pace as she approached Cormac's Chapel, looking right, left in the soaking darkness. She could see no guards. Unless they lurked unseen, like the man at the stables. And she did not know where he had gone.

She tightened her hold on her hatchet. At least she had something, however meagre, to fight someone off with. The rope slung over her right shoulder would surely help her too.

All still seemed without watching eyes, guarding swords. She hurried to the south door. Locked, the planks far too strong for the weapon she held. Quick strides took her to the main entrance at the north. Drips fell from the tall, carved arch that also held a formidably stout door. She put her ear to the wet planks.

Her heart turned over. The monks prayed quietly, calmly. They trusted John, that he'd locked them in there simply to steal their treasures. But no. Eimear had been locked in there too. She would have told them what was happening. So they knew death drew near. That was what their prayers were for. They had no way of knowing that no guards patrolled outside.

A hot anger, strong and fast as a lightning strike, went through her. All this for power, for wealth. That John would inflict such a hideous, agonising end on others for his own gain. On men who had not fought back and who still did not resort to violence as a response. Who simply waited for death to come and take them to their God.

Hurrying back around the corner, she estimated the height of the three windows that were set into the west wall. She could get up there. She had to. Had to climb.

She yanked her veil from her head, then used the sharp hatchet blade to tear off most of her long, soaked wool skirt.

She took the few steps to one of the tall gravestones set into the earth and uncoiled some of the rope. Once she had looped it around the cold, wet stone twice, she secured it in a few swift twists.

Then she returned to the wall below the window, playing the cord out and praying hard that it was long enough. Prayed harder she could do this without being seen.

One prayer was answered: it looked like she had enough length.

Sticking the hatchet into her belt, Theodosia put a hand to the rough wet stone of the chapel's wall and pulled herself up with fingers, toes. Most of her weight hung from her arms, arms that no longer had the full strength of youth. She didn't care. She let her rage carry her, up three feet, four, five, more, more until her hands grasped at the carved arch that surrounded the right-hand window.

Hanging on with one hand, one arm, almost had her fall. She tightened her grip, uncaring of the scream of tendons in her shoulder and of her leg muscles that shook with effort.

Her free fingers sought the hatchet. Found it. Brought it up in a heavy arc. And smashed it through the window.

Cries of fear met the bang and the shower of broken glass.

Theodosia put her face to the gap. 'Brothers, fear not. It's Sister Theodosia.'

'Blessings to you, sister, blessings.' The Archbishop's quavering voice sounded. 'You see, brothers?' She heard it steady and lift in delight. 'God does answer our prayers.'

'Please stand away if you are able. I'm knocking out as much of the window as I can.'

Another blow, more glass and a muted chorus of rejoicing.

She thrust the hatchet back in her belt, then hauled herself to the sill with both hands, pausing to steady her balance as she looked down.

Where earlier the only other faces in the chapel had been those on the carved stone heads that gazed down from the ceiling, now so many live ones looked back at her, suffused with fear and jammed in tightly behind where O'Heney stood. She could make out Eimear's too. She lay at the altar amongst the piles of the Archbishop's manuscripts, her leg at a terrible angle as she lifted a hand in triumph to Theodosia.

Theodosia raised her voice as much as she dared to call again. 'Hurry. I have a rope to help you climb out.' She dropped it down, its coils opening to end a couple of feet from the floor. That didn't matter: it would suffice. 'But let me come in first.'

'Stay out, sister,' called the Archbishop. 'We will be with you shortly.'

'I am coming to get my friend.' Theodosia climbed in over the sill, her linen underskirts tearing on shards of glass and twisted lead. She grasped at the rope to lower herself into the chapel, hand over hand, landing to clasp the Archbishop's outstretched one.

'God has sent you this day, sister.' His soft eyes filled with gratitude.

'Get your brothers out.' She thrust the rope to a strongly built monk. 'You will assist?'

He nodded, taking it from her as O'Heney clapped his hands. 'We have the sacred gift of life, brothers. Take it and run once you are out.'

'You first, Archbishop.'

O'Heney drew breath to protest, but his fellow monks swept him along with them to clamber to freedom.

Theodosia moved past them to kneel at Eimear's side.

'Theodosia.' The sweat of pain beaded her forehead yet she managed a smile. 'You got away from Gerald.'

'He was on our side,' said Theodosia. 'He did what he could.' She drew breath to tell Eimear how she planned to get her out of the chapel, but an urgent sound cut across her.

Bells.

Not a call to prayer. Nothing so orderly.

This was a clamouring jangle. And it came from the Round Tower.

John dropped the reliquary he held, and a fine carved image of the Virgin on its ivory lid snapped off.

The bells, right above his head, had started with no warning, clanging so loudly they could be right inside it, throbbing, vibrating.

He swore long and hard. A small fortune had fallen from his hands. He went to the ladder. 'Wait till I get my hands on the fool that is doing this.'

One of the other men stood up, raising his voice over the din. 'I'll do it, my lord.'

'No, I want to speak to the oaf personally.' John was already climbing down. 'Get a move on. I want everything in here in my palace, with all haste.'

He descended, ladder after ladder, the echoing chorus above him still continuing.

As he arrived at the last, his stomach contracted. One of his own soldiers lay on the floor, clearly dying from the gaping axe wound in his chest, his hand threaded through the rope as he pulled and pulled on it with his last strength.

But it was the man's words that sent a deeper chill still through him.

'My lord, the Irish are here.'

Theodosia squeezed Eimear's hand as the last of the monks climbed the rope, leaving only the hefty man that had helped to speed escape.

He waved a meaty hand at Theodosia. 'I will have you out in minutes, good ladies.' He hurried over.

'The brother here can lift you, Eimear,' she said. 'We will tie the rope around you and pull you out. But it will hurt. I am sorry.'

'It hurts like the devil already.' Eimear's brow creased, but she forced a smile. 'Can't be much worse than that.' She looked up at the monk. 'Do it.'

The monk hunkered down.

Eimear's grip tightened on Theodosia as the man got an arm under her back. 'Sweet God.'

'It will be over soon.' Theodosia held fast.

The clamour of the bells in the tower stopped abruptly.

'The Lord John!' A panicked whisper from the high window. Another monk's stricken face showed through it. 'He's on his way over here.'

The monk froze. Theodosia too.

'Go,' said Eimear. 'Both of you.'

'I am not leaving you,' said Theodosia.

'Nor I.' The monk released his hold on Eimear. He stood up to grab a heavy metal candlestick.

'Take this instead.' Theodosia pulled the hatchet from her belt and handed it to him.

He made the door in fast strides.

'Brother, go.' Eimear's words bounced off his broad back. She ground out an oath. 'Theodosia.' Eimear pulled her hand away. 'Have sense. Even if you did get me out, I can't run.'

'No.'

A noise came at the door, of someone slamming at locks, bolts.

The monk squared his footing. Raised the hatchet.

The door burst open.

The Lord of Ireland stood there, lit torch in one hand, sword in the other. 'Prepare for—'

The monk came at him with the hatchet even as John's furious face changed in shock. But his sword was a blur.

'No!' Theodosia stifled her cry as the monk fell back, his throat carved open and the hatchet dropping from his hand.

John's gaze went to her. 'You?' His scream of rage echoed to the roof of the chapel.

'One motherless child is enough,' gabbled Eimear, with a shove to Theodosia. 'Go! Now!'

Theodosia scrambled to her feet as John ran at her. She made for the window, hurled herself at the rope, climbing with speed that only terror could give her.

'You!' He slashed at her with his blade, his torch. Missed. *'You!'*

She was on the sill, barely out of his range as he swiped again and again. She went to clamber farther from his reach. Could not. Her skirt tangled on a sharp piece of broken lead. She pulled, tugged. Still stuck. But he couldn't get at her.

John spat an oath, backing away from the window to turn to a white-faced Eimear.

'Theodosia, go!' she screamed.

With a desperate wrench, Theodosia got her skirt free. But she would not turn her back on her friend at the moment of death.

John stood over Eimear, his stained sword raised. 'You could try to beg for clemency.'

She did not flinch from his wicked blade, stared him right in the eye. 'I am the daughter of the King of Connacht. I will beg for nothing from you. *Stripling*.'

'Well, perhaps you should have.' His voice came tight in rage. 'The sword would have been more merciful.' He stepped past her. Thrust his torch into the pile of manuscripts. 'Than this.'

Theodosia screamed as the flames sprang up.

John looked up at her. Smiled. 'I haven't forgotten you.'

Theodosia didn't bother with the rope. She leapt for the black, rain-drenched air.

And the ground came up to meet her.

With the driving rain hard in his face, Palmer slid down from the high wall that edged the rock, cursing his slowness. The Irish had swarmed up the ridges of the Rock, then up and over the wall, leaving him and de Lacy clambering in their wake.

Yells and screams from the darkness and the movement of shadows told him the fight had begun.

He scanned the buildings on the Rock, breathing hard, leg and arm muscles jumping. 'What were those bells for, de Lacy? Some kind of warning?'

'Don't know and it doesn't matter.' De Lacy's breath came short too. He pointed to one of the large stone structures, light glowing from inside. 'The palace. The door's round the other side.'

'Let's go.' Palmer set off at a run, sword in hand, de Lacy matching him. A few more strides and he would face John. He couldn't wait. He'd end this.

As he rounded the side of the building, Palmer looked for the chapel where Gerald had said Theodosia had gone. His heart stuttered in his chest.

The glow of fire. The billow of smoke into the sheets of rain. 'De Lacy!'

'I'm here.'

Palmer took off towards it, de Lacy with him.

He could hear female screams from inside as he made the closed entrance of the burning building. This couldn't be. He'd already almost lost Theodosia to the agony of flames once. It couldn't be her fate now.

He belted the stout planks of the high door with his sword as de Lacy struck at the handle.

It held firm to more screams from inside.

'Again,' shouted de Lacy. 'Harder!'

Nothing.

'And again.'

One plank split.

Another scream. 'Somebody! Please!'

'This is too slow.' Palmer yanked at de Lacy's arm. 'With me. Now.'

De Lacy nodded his understanding.

They ran a couple of yards back. Then turned, charged at the door with the full weight of their swords, their bodies, their panicked strength.

The split plank gave, opening a panel through which smoke and heat and sparks roiled out.

Palmer flung an arm up to shield his face. 'Theodosia!' He kicked out another panel.

'Palmer!' It wasn't her.

'Eimear?' De Lacy booted out another panel.

'Theodosia's gone! John's after her!'

God alive. His terror at her words gave Palmer extra strength. He finished off the half of the door with another kick.

De Lacy looked at him as the heat pounded out. 'Go for Theodosia.'

Another scream.

Palmer couldn't. He shook his head. 'Not yet.'

With a nod, de Lacy yelled in through the ruined entrance. 'Eimear, the door's open! Just run through. If the flames catch, it'll only be for seconds.'

'We'll put them out,' shouted Palmer. 'Run!'

'I can't!'

'Eimear, you must try.' De Lacy leaned in closer, put a hand up to shield his own flesh, his scars looking new again in the roar and crackle of the flames. 'Think of our son.'

'I can't.' Her voice came clear, calm. 'My knee's broken, Hugh.' Steady. 'Throw me a knife or a sword. I'd rather go that way.'

De Lacy took a step over the remains of the door.

And Palmer knew what the man was doing. 'De Lacy! No!' He went to grab him back. Missed.

De Lacy flung himself into the flames.

Theodosia fled back around the corner of the chapel, not daring to take a second to look back. John would be mere strides away, armed with a sword.

Terrible shouts, bellows, screams filled the night. She did not know from whom. Horrifying images of the monks, the Archbishop meeting the sharpest of blades in the darkness swam before her. As she might too.

She had to find somewhere – anywhere – to hide. But where?

Pounding steps behind her told her John was almost on her.

Her toes stubbed hard on the slab that covered an old burial, and she stumbled, half-fell with a cry. She ducked behind a gravestone. But the ground under her right foot gave way, wrenching her hip to one side in a stab of pain as her leg slipped into a freshly dug grave. She clawed at the loose earth at its edge, pulling herself from the black pit as the sodden soil crumbled in her panicked grasps.

'I've got you now!'

He'd heard her struggles.

She wrenched a hand up, grabbed for the cold, wet headstone, uncaring of her palms ripping as she hauled herself free.

She took off again, ran faster. But he gained so easily. She could not outpace him. He was so much younger. And the lust for blood drove him.

The cathedral. Her only hope now. She prayed that the door she'd seen was not locked. A door that could keep John out. Keep that blade from slicing through her skin.

Her chest threatened to fail as she gulped in wet air, forcing her legs on. She'd made it. She grasped for the metal clasp so hard her thumbnail snapped off.

Locked.

'Oh, what a shame!' John was mere strides away.

She wrenched the handle with both wounded hands. One way, then another, her breath in gasping sobs.

It turned.

She shoved the door open, flung herself inside and slammed it hard, one hand on the handle as she fumbled for the bolt, the metal slipping in her wet, bloodied grasp.

'Still got you, sister.'

The handle moved, John's strength more than hers.

Theodosia threw all her weight against it as she tried to ram the bolt home.

The door began to give.

'Get away from me!' She kneed it hard, bashing the hard metal of the bolt with the heel of her hand, uncaring of the pain.

The thud of a brutal kick blew the door right open, sending her falling on her back to the floor.

John was in.

'No!' She screamed again, rolled and scrambled from his reach along the cold stone floor. The blood from her damaged hands made livid smears on its blank surface. She staggered upright, making for the altar as if that would somehow save her.

A boot to her back sent her sprawling to the hard floor again with a stinging blow to her jaw.

'Look at me. I want to see your face when I do this.'

She turned over, her stomach heaving in terror and pain.

John's eyes so like her own. 'Finally.' His sword an inch from her face, the shiny metal dulled with the lifeblood of two of the monks of Cashel. 'You have cost me so very dearly. Now you will pay.'

'Please, I beg you. Do not.' She raised a hand as if that could somehow stop it, stop the cruel metal that would plunge into her body, rip her life from her.

'There could be no reason why I should not. And a thousand why I should.' He readjusted his grip.

'Because I am your sister!' Her scream echoed up to the vaulted ceiling.

John gaped at her. Then burst out laughing. 'That is the best reason you could think of?'

'I've got a better one.'

The deep voice came from the darkness of the nave.

'Because I'll have your head.' Benedict stepped forward, sword raised and ready. 'John.'

Chapter Thirty

Palmer advanced on the altar with a deliberate tread.

'You here as well?' John's astonished, furious gaze met his. 'God's eyes.'

At the side of his vision, Palmer saw Theodosia inch away from the sword tip. But not far enough.

'Yes, I'm here,' he said. 'Here to arrest you in the name of King Henry. The Lord of Meath is with me.'

John snorted. A sudden thrust had his sword at Theodosia's throat, and she choked back a scream.

Palmer held in his own. Took another step.

John's weapon stayed steady. 'If you're so loyal to the King, then why do you not care or even look surprised that this woman, this spy, is claiming to have his blood?' He frowned. 'Or do you know something more?'

Terrified gasps came from Theodosia.

But Palmer couldn't take his eyes from John now. He took another small step.

'If I were facing the point of a sword like she is,' said Palmer, 'I'd say anything too. She is no spy.'

'She is responsible for all my defeats!' John's voice rose in a shrill yell. 'She knew all my plans, brought them to the enemy.'

'No, John, she didn't.' Step.

'Of course she did!' John back-heeled Theodosia hard, and she cried out in pain. 'Didn't you?' He kept his eyes on Palmer.

'No, my lord,' she panted, 'no, I swear to you. No.'

Palmer's self-control balanced on an edge sharper than John's sword. He had to hold on. He kept his tone even. 'I know why your plans failed, my lord.'

'I do not want to hear—'

'Your own father told me why they would.' Halt.

'My father sent me to this infernal country because he knew I would deal with it.' John's face reddened. 'It's an important part of his realm.'

'As important as the Holy Land?'

John's high colour darkened even more. 'Yes, it is. More so. In fact.'

Palmer almost had him. But John still had his sword at Theodosia's throat. 'Do you want to know why Henry didn't send you to Jerusalem? The real reason?'

'Gossip, more like.'

'Because, Henry said, the Saracens would have strewn your bones across the desert by Christmas.'

'That's not true.' John's mouth puckered.

Almost had him. But not quite.

'Because, Henry said, you've been too coddled.'

'What?' John's yell had his sword pointed at Palmer now.

Almost there.

'And because, Henry said' – Palmer made his own grip as firm as he could – 'you are not a naturally gifted warrior.' He braced himself. 'Not like your brother, Richard.'

'You lying bastard!' John ran at him, sword swinging hard, fast, incensed. 'I am better than him. Than all of them!'

Palmer parried, landed a blow of his own on John's weapon as Theodosia fled to the side of the altar.

'I'll kill you, Palmer! And then that bitch of a spy! You're a liar, a liar, a liar.' John drove even harder at Palmer, his towering rage giving him strength, skill.

Palmer went back at a wild swipe, his shoulder striking a pillar and sending him off balance.

John's blade was coming at him. Right at his face.

Forcurse it: he'd been bested.

Then the King's son collapsed with a grunt on the floor of the cathedral, his sword clattering from his unconscious grasp.

Theodosia stood there, holding some sort of engraved bronze weapon in her grasp, breathing as hard as he did.

'My love.' He couldn't help a grin, even as his breath, his pulse raced. 'Where did you find a mace in a cathedral?'

'This is no mace.' Theodosia gave him a shaky smile in return. 'My love.' She held it aloft, still clutched in her double-handed, bloodied grip. Designed to represent an arm, it ended in a closed fist. 'This is Saint Lachtin's Arm. One of the sacred reliquaries of the Archbishop of Cashel.' She looked down at John, then back at Palmer. 'I just hope Saint Lachtin hasn't murdered the Lord of Ireland.'

'Benedict, you cannot kill John.' Theodosia saw her words bounce off her furious husband like arrows off a metal shield.

'And why not?' He paced the floor of the hall of the Archbishop's Palace, the pale early sun at the window lighting his exhausted features.

'Because we have all told you why.' She swept a hand to the others who sat with her: the Archbishop, de Lacy, Gerald.

'Telling does not always change hearts, my lady,' said the Archbishop.

'Indeed,' said Gerald.

Both men knew their whole story now. She and Benedict had had to share it with them in the aftermath of the dreadful events that had taken place.

Benedict shook his head at their responses and challenged de Lacy with his stare. 'I'm right, aren't I?'

'It's an act that would make me happy too.' De Lacy shrugged, his long cloak bearing the scorch and holes of flame. 'But it would be an unwise move.'

Benedict pulled his hands through his hair with an exasperated snort. 'If only you'd hit him a bit harder, Theodosia.'

She gave him her best warning look.

He responded with his most innocent one.

'John is still my brother,' she said. 'I was not trying to kill him. Only to stop him.' She cast a grateful look at those present. 'Which we have done.'

'If I may.' The Archbishop peered at Benedict. 'Sir knight, if the King's son were to lose his life here, Henry would exact terrible vengeance on the whole of Ireland. He knows how and is accustomed to make martyrs. I fear to the depths of my soul that Ireland will have its martyrs, just as other countries.' His sad smile was kind. 'But please, do not be the one to hasten that day.'

Theodosia saw the shift in Benedict at the Archbishop's gentle words. She knew the man she loved would do anything to change the role he had played in the martyrdom at Canterbury.

'I bow to your wisdom, my lord.' He matched his words with his actions, then came to Theodosia, his warm, strong hand on her shoulder. 'Then we will have to take a different approach.'

His explanation was met with full agreement.

Once Benedict had finished, de Lacy rose to his feet. 'Now if you'll excuse me, I need to see how Eimear is.'

As Hugh de Lacy walked into the quiet solar in the Archbishop's Palace, his heart almost stopped.

Eimear lay so still on the bed, her eyes closed, one knee swathed in linen bandages.

The elderly monk with her beckoned to him. 'Enter, my lord. Your wife has been sorely injured and has breathed much foul smoke and air. But she will be fine, if God is good.'

Her lids lifted at the sound of voices. 'I feel far from fine.' The effort of speaking made her cough and cough.

'My lady has the strength to argue, which always bodes well.' The monk gave a nod of satisfaction. 'As you are here, my lord, I will go and fetch some supplies, if I may.'

'Of course. Thank you for all you have done.'

The monk bowed and left.

De Lacy went to her side and sat on the stool he'd vacated. 'How much does it hurt?'

Eimear shrugged, coughed again. 'I'm still alive. Still here for William.' She gave the ghost of a smile. 'You?'

'Well, as you can see, my reputation as a comely knight is at an end.'

Her smile turned to a laugh, more coughing.

'A few more marks on a face and body that have plenty.' He hesitated. 'Eimear, I need to tell you what we are doing about John.'

No more smile. 'I'd like to gut him like a fish.'

'As would I. But we can't.' He explained what would be done, and she listened without interruption. 'I hope it isn't too much to ask.' His voice lowered. 'I always seem to be asking something of you.'

'No.' Eimear shook her head, and he was shocked to see the silver beads of tears forming at the corners of her eyes. 'It's not too much.'

'Then why are you crying?'

'I'm not. I'm just grateful.'

'As am I. Your son still has his mother and—'

'I'm grateful for you. You. You came for me.' She raised one hand to his face, put gentle fingertips to where the gouges of his burned flesh began. 'You, who've been almost consumed by fire.'

Her touch called to something deep within him. He could not speak.

The tears slid from her eyes now, flowing slowly and steadily as she went on. 'I thought you had paid your debt to me. I thought we didn't owe each other anything.' Her fingers moved over the sensitive whorls of his scars, tracing each one.

De Lacy pulled in a ragged breath. 'Someone came for me once. With no care for his life. So little care for it, he lost it for me. I have regretted it every day of my life.' He put his hand over hers. 'You've done so much for me. If I had abandoned you to the agony of the flames, I would have regretted it every day for the rest of my life. And regret is a poison. I want no more of it.'

He took her hand from his face.

But she kept it clamped in his. 'Nor I,' she whispered.

He lifted her hand to his lips. Still she didn't remove it.

'Nor I, Hugh.' She held his gaze with a fierce tenderness.

John opened his eyes, and his head pounded in its familiar pattern on waking in the brightness of the morn.

Wait. He closed them again. This was no wine headache. It radiated from the back of his head, sending shooting fire through his skull.

He put a hand to the source of the fire and his fingers met a thick bandage over a poultice. Fire. Of course. The chapel.

He opened his eyes again.

If he could have, he would have sat bolt upright in the bed in which he lay.

Hugh de Lacy stood in the lower circular room of the Round Tower, Gerald with him.

Both were watching him. The mail-clad de Lacy with his one-eyed stare. Gerald in his cleric's robes, with less of a fawning look and more one of accusation. Much more.

'You are here, de Lacy.' John frowned at the croak in his own voice.

'I am, my lord.' A bow. That somehow had no respect in it whatsoever. 'For it is where my wife came to.'

'She came here with that spy. That Sister Theodosia.' His head cleared, though it still banged like the Devil. 'And that spy, that nun, tried to kill me.' He managed to sit up, pushing the coverlet from him, though he wore only a long undershirt. 'I want her hunted down. I want her—'

'My lord.' Gerald held a hand up.

'You dare to—'

'My lord.' Firmer. 'Listen to me. As we speak, the Archbishop of Cashel is making the strongest of representations to your father about recent events. Henry is unlikely to be pleased, which is putting it mildly, as the death of Archbishop Thomas Becket almost cost him his throne.' Gerald drew his mouth down. 'It was a sinful endeavour, my lord.'

'I will find her.' John's fists tightened on the coverlet. 'I will.'

'My lord, you will not be pursuing a nun across Ireland. The Lord of Meath and I have agreed to take you to the relative safety of Dublin to sit out the rest of this miserable mission.'

'For your own protection, my lord.' De Lacy gave him his one-sided smile. 'Of course.'

'But she isn't only a nun.' John drew in a breath, waiting for their stunned response, for their change of heart. 'She claimed to be my sister!'

They said nothing.

Then they laughed. *Laughed.*

John glared from one to another. Sat up in bed like this, listening to their indulgent mirth, he might as well be a small boy relating a dream about dragons to his nurse.

'My lord, you must be confused from the blow to your head when you fell face first into that grave.' Gerald's long-toothed smile went. 'A fall that I believe was God's vengeance.'

John wished he had his strength. He would set about the pair of them. But he couldn't rise. 'She told me. In the cathedral.' And of course. 'Sir Benedict Palmer was there, another traitor, defending her.' He pointed a shaking finger at Gerald, de Lacy. 'You bring me Palmer. I'll get it out of him.'

'Palmer is dead, my lord.' De Lacy smiled no more too. 'He perished in the fight here, alongside so many others. He is buried in the graveyard, as are they all.'

'Now, I suggest you get some rest, my lord,' said Gerald. 'You will need your strength for the journey to Dublin.'

'I have a guard outside. In case you need anything.' De Lacy's meaning was clear.

The two men left.

John knew they were lying, both of them, all of them, which he would deal with another day.

His head felt like it was about to burst with pain as well as anger. He lay down again, wincing as his injured skull met the mound of pillows behind him.

He'd been so close to a throne. The throne of Ireland. But close would never wear a crown. Instead, he lay alone. Shamed. Defeated.

He, John, youngest son of the great Henry. He was still Lackland. *Lackland.* He swore hard to himself for a good minute.

Yet, even injured as it was, his mind still thought ahead.

He would spend his time in Dublin working out a credible story for his father. The old fool would believe anything John told him. He, John, would lay most of the blame at Hugh de Lacy's door. Henry would definitely swallow that. Doubtless an account of the treacherous Irish too. Claim an alliance between the two sides, united against him, John.

Then it hit him.

De Lacy wasn't the only man who could form alliances with the Irish.

As the bell high in the tower above rang out, calling the monks to prayer, John marvelled at his own speed in changing strategy.

That was what came of having a brilliant mind.

Chapter Thirty-One

Cloughbrook, Staffordshire, England
6 September 1186

Palmer rode back to his hall at Cloughbrook, spent from his long day on his land. The last of summer always brought an urgency. Every hour of daylight had to be spent overseeing his tenants, checking yields, taking in harvests and crops, bringing them to store and kitchens. Short yields benefitted no one, and he did everything in his power to make sure that didn't happen. He'd even spent two hours on his haunches helping to mend a broken wagon wheel. It didn't bother him. Hands got jobs like that done, not titles.

He had left his loyal tenants toiling on, though it bothered him to do so. Most had risen before dawn and would work on with little rest until well after nightfall.

Palmer eased his aching shoulders. He would work on tonight too, with Theodosia's help. As lord, he had to record all the workings of his lands. Well, the money that was attached to them. He could add up things with ease in his head but still found the written word more exhausting than pushing a plough. She'd help him, as she always did, with her quick reading and her swift, neat, precise quill.

A first few dead leaves blew across the ground as he approached the hall. Yes, today had brought hours of hot sunshine, and his lands had never looked so reliable, so ordered. But as with all September days, the light was changing. Shortening. The tips on the leaves of many of the trees were turning yellow and brown. After so many months, only a few short weeks remained before the dark and the cold returned. They would all need to be ready for when it did.

As he turned his horse for the stable yard, a groom walked out to take it. 'Good evening, Sir Benedict. Finished with your horse for the day?'

'I am, thank you.' Palmer dismounted, pointing to his animal's hind leg. 'Have a look at that, will you? I'm sure there's a few ticks in there.'

'Benedict!'

Palmer looked over at the source of the call.

Theodosia stood in the front door, face pale, holding something tight in both hands. A letter.

'I need to speak with you,' she said.

Palmer nodded to the groom. 'See to the ticks. Please.'

He hurried over to Theodosia, unease replacing his tired contentment from his day. 'Is it from the King?' He kept his voice low.

'No. It is from his royal clerk.'

'Gerald?' Palmer's own confusion was mirrored in her eyes. 'Why would he write to us?'

'I do not know. I have not opened it yet. I wanted you to be here when I did.' She looked past him to where the groom had disappeared with Palmer's horse. 'No one else.'

Palmer nodded. 'Let's go inside.'

He followed her in, and she halted with a poor attempt at a smile. 'Go and wash from your day,' she said. 'I have waited for many hours; I can wait a little longer.'

'And I can see from your face that you've spent every moment of that wait in a frenzy.' He slipped an arm across her shoulders.

'So you'll have to put up with your mud-splattered husband.' He led her to the peace of the hall. 'Do Tom and Matilde know about this letter?'

'No. I have sent them out on an errand to the far end of the estate. They will be riding for some time.' She sat on the stone window seat to get the best light from the setting sun, Palmer close next to her.

She broke the seal with an unsteady hand and rolled it out.

Palmer recognised his own name. He focused on trying to make out the first lines.

'No.' Theodosia's soft gasp, her hand to her mouth, told him it did not contain good news. 'Oh, no. No.' Sudden tears pooled in her eyes.

'Tell me.' Palmer laid a gentle hand on her arm. 'Please.'

She began to read it to him. And the words of the King's clerk came to Palmer's hall at Cloughbrook.

Every Grace of God and salutation to you, Sir Benedict Palmer. I trust that this finds you and the Lady Theodosia in the best of health, and if it does not, that God will grant you relief from your troubles.

I write, in secret of course, with the most solemn of news. I write of further treachery in Ireland. I write of Hugh de Lacy, the Lord of Meath . . .

Durrow, Co. Offaly, Ireland
26 July 1186
Six weeks earlier

Hugh de Lacy tipped his head back to look up at his new castle, finished and complete on its fresh motte. It soared high into the clear, blue, blue sky, higher even than the towering ancient oak trees that flanked the bailey.

Have to cut down some of those trees. He smiled to himself. His advice to Palmer at Tibberaghny, and yet he hadn't followed it. Not yet. He would. That would be his next task. Then he would plan out a keep of stone, one that would take much longer to build but would last for generations.

Generations. Still to come. He looked over to the lip of the motte, where his son rolled down yet again, shouting his joy.

'Be careful now, William.' Eimear's call to the lad.

He met her gaze and she smiled. Waved.

'I can't climb down after him if he gets stuck.' She brought her hands to her swollen belly. 'You'll have to do it, Hugh.'

'As my lady commands.' He bowed extravagantly, drawing a laugh from her.

He'd never seen her look so beautiful as today, as at this moment, so near to bringing this child into the world. Not even the night they had first lain willingly together, her skin pale and smooth and soft against him, her long hair covering him as she brought her mouth to his, uncaring of his ruined flesh. As they had done for so many nights since. They belonged to each other now.

As he watched William climb up again, the midday bells of the nearby monastery of Saint Colmcille rang out, their deep chimes reminding him as they did every time he heard them.

He'd chosen this place for his Eimear. For them to be together.

Sacred. Blessed. The saint himself making it a holy place many centuries ago. A huge carved high cross, itself fashioned in times long past, stood at the edge of the holy community, facing the castle, a path beside it connecting his motte to the monastery. The cross called to his heart, a tribute to this land that he loved and to his wife who came from it, whom he loved even more.

A shout from the base of the motte, where a group of men from the nearby settlements worked with shovels.

'I think we need to reinforce the ditch, my lord.' Simonson's large face shone from his toil. 'Make sure it holds.'

'Let me take a look.' De Lacy descended the steep slope.

'The ground's boggy, even in this sun,' Simonson explained as others chimed in with opinions.

'My Lord de Lacy.'

They were interrupted by an Irishman who made his way towards them, on the path that led from the cross, fine-robed, bearing a large leather water bottle.

The man smiled, held it aloft as he walked up. 'I came on pilgrimage to the well of the Saint. I heard you were here, so I came to offer my greetings and to offer you this gift of its blessed water for this hot day.'

'And my greetings to you.' De Lacy took the bottle from him. 'I'm most grateful.' Closing his eyes, he tipped his head back to drink deep.

The cold, pure water from the well of Colmcille brought a coolness to his throat.

And more.

A calm to his soul that he hadn't felt since Robert died, maybe that he'd never felt. A peace. True happiness. He opened his eyes again, looked into the endless blue of the sky.

Then a rush of air, a scream that could be his own.

But he could scream no more. Instead he was falling into the blue. The peaceful, peaceful blue. Falling. Falling off the edge of the earth.

The murderer was sent by an Irish chieftain of Meath, a chieftain who claims that he ordered the murder to atone for the wanton destruction of land sacred to the great Saint Colmcille on which de Lacy has built his castle at Durrow.

I believe this to be a sinful lie and that the act was one of treacherous revenge. One of the chieftain's sons was slain by de Lacy some eight years ago, when Hugh de Lacy first took the lands of Meath.

The murderer sent by the chieftain carried out his heinous act with great guile. Those who were present say that the man approached de Lacy as the Lord worked on his motte with some of his household. His wife, Eimear, and their son were nearby.

There was nothing to make anyone suspicious, for the murderer had concealed an axe beneath his cloak. He took de Lacy's head off with one savage blow, and the Lord of Meath's mortal remains, head and body both, fell into the ditch of the castle.

Praise God the Lady Eimear remained unharmed, as was their son. She was safely delivered a few days later of their second child, a daughter. She is said to be bereft at the murder of her bravest of husbands.

'Oh, Benedict.' Theodosia paused, her tears spilling over. 'Such terrible, terrible news.' She leaned against his chest, sobs flooding through her. 'For Hugh to die in such an awful way.'

'That it is,' said Palmer quietly, his own heart sore at the loss of a good man, a man who'd fought so bravely by his side. 'But he knew the risks of conquest. And he got his wish. He told me he never wanted to leave Ireland. Now he'll lie there forever.'

'That is no consolation. Not to Eimear. Nor to him. Never to have seen his child's face.' Her tears carried on but her voice angered. 'He was taken too soon, Benedict. Too soon. What if a similar fate had befallen you?'

'It didn't.' He kissed the top of her head. 'Nor you.' Kissed her again. 'We've had great good fortune.'

'Or we have God's protection. I thank Him every day and night for it.' She looked again at the letter, pulling in a shuddering breath as she scrubbed at her eyes with fury though tears still fell. 'There is a little more. Pray God it is not so shocking.'

She read silently for a moment. Then gasped. 'It is. Oh, truly: it is.' She read aloud again.

The Lord John is said to have rejoiced when the news of de Lacy's savage death reached him at Windsor. Henry also shared in that rejoicing. The King prepares to return John immediately to Ireland.

'Henry's sending John back?' Palmer stared at her. 'To fail again?'

'How can he do this?' Her face flushed in anger. 'What more do we have to do to convince Henry that John is dangerous? Unfit to rule?'

'We tried, Theodosia.' Palmer shook his head at the memory of the guarded letters Theodosia had sent and Henry's terse replies. 'It's clear he believes his own son's account over ours.'

'You mean John's lies about de Lacy's disloyalty?' With an angry shake of her head, her eyes lowered to the letter once more.

Then.

'No. Dear God, no.' Her hands tightened on the letter. 'No. No. *No.*'

The look of horror in her eyes set his heart thudding faster. 'What is it?'

She read with fast breaths:

The Lord of Ireland is to return there, his new opportunity thanks to the hand of the man who killed de Lacy, a man sent by the Chieftain Sinnach Ua Catharnaig. The chieftain is known as The Fox because of his wily ways. It appears the Irish have not lost their love of treachery.

His pulse slackened, the words making sense with what had gone before. 'De Lacy's murder is an act of revenge for an old wrong, Theodosia. One that has fitted in with what John wanted, I admit, but—'

'Benedict, John knew about this chieftain.' Theodosia shook the letter at him. 'The Fox. About The Fox's hatred of Hugh de Lacy for the murder of his son. De Lacy told John himself, at the feast when he'd returned to Tibberaghny. I was there. I heard him.'

'Just because John knew about this Sinnach, this Fox, doesn't mean he was involved in de Lacy's death.' The words sounded hollow even as he spoke them.

'Eight years.' Theodosia shook the letter again. 'Why would The Fox wait eight years to get his revenge on Hugh de Lacy? It makes no sense. Unless you think of who really wanted de Lacy out of the way.'

'John.' Palmer dragged a hand through his hair. 'And he couldn't manage it himself. But he found a way.' He swore long and hard. 'If your brother stood in front of me right now, I'd put a sword through him. No question.'

'It would join mine,' came Theodosia's steely response. 'But hold, let me read the clerk's final words.'

Again, she read in silence. Again, she gasped.

I write this in haste as an addendum as events have changed immeasurably.

Geoffrey, Henry's third son and Duke of Brittany, has been fatally wounded at a tournament in France, may God rest his soul. Henry is recalling John from his progress back to Ireland. The King has only two sons remaining now, so will be reconsidering how he rules his lands.

I believe that you, Sir Benedict, and the lady Theodosia should be on your highest guard.

'There is no more.' Her shocked gaze met his. 'But John is so much nearer the throne of England. His power increases by the day.'

Palmer put his hand over her shaking one, a trembling that was born of fury. 'Your father still has that throne. And Richard succeeds him.' He pulled her to him, held her tightly in his arms. 'We need have no fear of John.'

'Oh, I think we do.'

'He will be far too consumed with his new status to even think of us.'

'And if he is not?'

'He will be,' he repeated. 'I'm always right, remember?'

As the last of the sun's golden light lit the room, Palmer offered up a prayer that he was.

But he would be taking Gerald's advice very seriously.

Palmer would be on his highest guard. As he always was.

List of Characters

The majority of characters' names and Irish place names used in this novel are in their Anglicised form. I have done this to aid clarity for readers who may not be familiar with the Irish language. For those who can read *as Gaeilge*, I hope you will forgive me.

The Normans

Sir Benedict Palmer, Lord of the Manor of Cloughbrook, Staffordshire
Lady Theodosia Palmer, wife of Sir Benedict and secret daughter of Henry II
Henry II, King of England
John, Lord of Ireland, youngest son of Henry II
Hugh de Lacy, Henry's 1st Lord of Meath
Gerald of Wales, Royal Clerk to Henry II and adviser to the court

The Irish

Eimear, second wife of Hugh de Lacy and daughter of Rory O'Connor
Rory O'Connor, King of Connacht and High King of Ireland
Dermot McCarthy, King of Desmond
Donal O'Brien, King of Thomond
Matthew O'Heney, Archbishop of Cashel, Ireland

Historical Note

My story of John's disastrous 1185 campaign in Ireland as *Dominus Hiberniae* is of course fictional, but much of the history and many of the places and events are real.

Theodosia's experience of an earthquake (whilst still in England) might seem odd. But on 15 April 1185, a large earthquake did indeed take place. According to the British Geological Survey report, *The Seismicity of the British Isles to 1600*, sources record that it was felt throughout all of England, and was the worst 'ever known in England'. 'Stones were split, stone houses were thrown down' and Lincoln Cathedral was badly damaged.

Twelfth-century Ireland was indeed viewed as a wild and inhospitable place by those on its neighbouring and larger island. It was genuinely perceived to be at the earth's edge, for of course people had no idea what lay on the other side of the Atlantic. Those views of Ireland were largely reinforced by contemporary chroniclers, as most people in England had never set foot there. Gerald of Wales was one of the most prolific chroniclers, with his *Topography of Ireland* and *The Conquest of Ireland* among his extensive works. He did visit there twice.

Gerald portrayed Ireland as a natural resource in the most positive light, but his accounts of its people are extremely problematic. I have used many of his own views in the novel as, to put it simply, you just couldn't make it up. But it's important to remember that Gerald was on the side of the invaders. And if you make those you seek to conquer less than civilised, less than human, then you have the sword of justification in your hand. It's a very powerful weapon and has never been sheathed for very long in human history. The history of Ireland is no exception.

Hugh de Lacy was also a real historical figure. De Lacy was originally Lord of Weobley in Herefordshire. His father had joined the Knights Templar and had signed his lordship over to Robert, his eldest son. Robert died childless, so Hugh inherited the title, which he had not expected to do, and became an important tenant of the Crown. That wasn't enough to satisfy him. He married Rose of Monmouth, the widow of the powerful Baderon, increasing his prosperity. And he liked to acquire land, whether in England, Wales or Normandy. He also had a rather unfortunate tendency to simply take it. In 1171, de Lacy went with Henry II to Ireland. The kingdom of Mide (Meath) was a particularly attractive prize, and de Lacy made sure he won it.

We know quite a lot about de Lacy as a person, as Gerald wrote extensively of him. He was probably not the most handsome of men. Gerald's description certainly does not flatter: 'What Hugh's complexion and features were like, he was dark, with dark, sunken eyes and flattened nostrils. His face was grossly disfigured down the right side as far as his chin by a burn, the result of an accident. His neck was short, his body hairy and sinewy. He was a short man. His build – misshapen.' Gerald even included a picture of him in his *Conquest of Ireland.* Such detail is a gift to a novelist.

The trouble was, de Lacy was a bit too good at what he did – certainly as far as Henry was concerned. The King tried to clip de Lacy's wings, recalling him to England several times and granting the lordship of Ireland to Henry's own son, John, who was only around eleven years old at the time. But de Lacy was one step ahead. His first wife, Rose, had died around 1180. He married again, but this time he took an Irish wife, a daughter of the High King Rory O'Connor (Ruaidri Ua Conchobair) of Connacht. Some records name this woman as Rose also, but this is likely to be a confusion. I gave her the name Eimear, a warlike heroine from Irish legend.

This marriage was not well received by Henry. He had suspicions that de Lacy was attempting a strategic marriage in the same way that another of his men, Richard FitzGilbert de Clare (Strongbow), had done a decade earlier. Gerald certainly had a dim view of de Lacy's ambitions: 'He was avaricious and greedy for gold and more ambitious for his own advancement and pre-eminence than was proper.'

Henry's solution was to send his son John, now eighteen (or possibly nineteen: there is some debate on the exact date of John's birth), to Ireland in 1185 to assert his authority as Lord of Ireland. John's mission, which started with him pulling the beards of the Irish dignitaries who came to greet him at Waterford, was not a success.

Frustratingly, there isn't a great deal of detail about John's campaign. Gerald is the main source of information. We know John built castles at Tibberaghny, Ardfinnan and Lismore. We know that he made serious errors of judgement, abandoning the prospect of the native Irish and the settlers being equal partners and making huge grants of land to his friends. Gerald also writes of drunkenness, laziness and desertion by John's men as well as their defeat on a number of occasions by the Irish.

John went back to England after nine months, complaining to Henry that de Lacy had been conspiring against him. This is highly unlikely. John was more than capable of failures of his own making.

Whether de Lacy had designs on taking Ireland from Henry, we will never know, for his life was brutally cut short. On 26 July 1186, de Lacy was inspecting his new castle at Durrow when he was murdered by a single assassin. Contemporary accounts tell us that the murderer had concealed an axe beneath his cloak, and he took de Lacy's head off with one savage blow, and his head and body fell into the castle's ditch.

The murderer was sent by a chieftain of Meath, Sinnach 'the Fox' Ua Catharnaig. Sinnach claimed that he ordered the murder to atone for the wanton destruction of land sacred to the great saint Colmcille, on which de Lacy had built his castle at Durrow. It's more likely that it was simple revenge. One of Sinnach's sons had been slain by Henry's men some eight years previously, when Hugh de Lacy was the King's representative in Ireland. Sinnach had always vowed to avenge that death.

I added the fiction of John's involvement in de Lacy's death. Whatever the real motive, it solved a problem for Henry. The powerful threat that was Hugh de Lacy was no more. Chronicler William of Newburgh recorded that 'the news was gladly received by Henry'.

De Lacy was buried at Durrow, but his body was later removed to St Thomas's Abbey to lie buried alongside his first wife. The Archbishop of Cashel, Matthew O'Heney, was instrumental in its removal.

The Rock of Cashel was an obvious choice for the climax of the novel, the events of which are entirely fictional. Henry II had visited there in 1171–72. Some of the buildings that still stand on Saint Patrick's Rock appear in the novel as they would have stood there in 1185. The Round Tower, an architectural design that is unique to Ireland, is the site's oldest building. Originally a bell tower, it dates from around 1100. Cormac's Chapel, built by a king of Desmond (part of Munster) was consecrated in 1134. The ruins of the cathedral are not those of the cathedral that appears in my novel. That cathedral was built in the thirteenth century and added to over the centuries. Some sources claim that a cathedral was built there in 1169, and then replaced.

The mid-ninth-century High Cross is still there at Durrow, and the remains of the motte where de Lacy met his brutal end can be glimpsed through the trees.

Acknowledgements

As ever, there were many people who helped me in getting this novel to publication to whom I owe every thanks. Julia Jewels, the audience member who asked me (at the launch of my first novel, *The Fifth Knight*, at the Irish World Heritage Centre in Manchester) if I would ever write a book about medieval Ireland. I, of course, said no. But the seed was instantly planted, and now here is that book.

It has been in very safe hands. My agent, Josh Getzler, remains my cheerleader for all things medieval. Emile Marneur at Thomas & Mercer received the idea with great enthusiasm and encouragement. Also at Thomas & Mercer, Sana Chebaro has always been on hand to make sure the world gets to know about my novels. A special word of thanks must go to my editor, Katie Green, for her brilliant insights and for her patience that would make Job look twitchy.

There are many historians whose excellent work I have consulted and who are mentioned in the bibliography. Any errors and fictitious accounts are of course mine. But I would like to give sincere thanks to Dr Colin Veach for his answers to my detailed questions about Hugh de Lacy and for his generosity in sharing his knowledge.

Joe Newman-Getzler needs a special mention for the timely Idiot Plot reminder. Kevin McMahon of Manchester Irish Writers provided inspiration for names within my ridiculously restricted brief but came up trumps. Dan FitzEdward and re-enactors from Historia Normannis were utterly generous with their time and sharing of their huge amount of knowledge. Beta-readers Paul Fogarty and Graham Mather reported for duty as always. Stephanie Powell and John Ketch made the Rock of Cashel research extra fun, as well as making arrangements for it not to rain.

And my Jon and my Angela are, as always, my life.

Bibliography

Without the sterling work of historians, historical novelists could not do what they do, and I am no exception. Though I try to ground my fiction firmly in fact, any errors are down to me.

For anyone looking for an overview of the history of medieval Ireland, I recommend:

Seán Duffy, *Ireland in the Middle Ages* (London: Palgrave Macmillan, 1997). Duffy also has an excellent chapter on John and Ireland in S.D. Church's *King John: New Interpretations* (Suffolk: Boydell Press, 1999).

Art Cosgrove (ed.), *A New History of Ireland, Volume II, Medieval Ireland 1169–1534* (Oxford: Oxford University Press, 2008).

Dáibhí Ó Cróinín, *Early Medieval Ireland: 400–1200* (London: Longman, 1995).

Historian Marie Therese Flanagan is a wonderful read for those seeking to go deeper, with her publications *Irish Society, Anglo-Norman Settlers, Angevin Kingship: Interactions in Ireland in the late 12th Century* (Oxford: Clarendon Press, 1998) and *The Transformation of the Irish Church in the Twelfth Century* (Suffolk: Boydell Press, 2010).

She is also the author of the entry on Hugh de Lacy in the *Oxford Dictionary of National Biography*.

Colin Veach's excellent *Lordship in Four Realms: The Lacy Family, 1166–1241* (Manchester: Manchester University Press, 2015) is invaluable for the history of Hugh de Lacy. Two further exemplary articles by Colin Veach on Hugh de Lacy's history are:

'Relentlessly striving for more': Hugh de Lacy in Ireland, *History Ireland: Features*, 15(2) (March/April 2007).
'A Question of Timing: Walter de Lacy's Seisin of Meath 1189–94', Proceedings of the Royal Irish Academy, Vol. 109C, pp. 165–194 (2009).

There are many, many books on King John. Three of my favourites are these:

W.L. Warren, *King John* (New Haven: Yale University Press, 1981).
Frank McLynn, *Lionheart & Lackland: King Richard, King John and the Wars of Conquest* (London: Vintage Books, 2007).
Marc Morris, *King John: Treachery, Tyranny and the Road to Magna Carta* (London: Hutchinson, 2015).

And for those of you who want to hear more from the colourful Gerald of Wales:

Gerald of Wales, *The History and Topography of Ireland* (London: Penguin Classics, 1982).
A.B. Scott and F.X. Martin (eds), *The Conquest of Ireland by Giraldus Cambrensis* (Dublin: Royal Irish Academy, 1978).

About the Author

Photo © 2012 Angela Channell

E.M. Powell's medieval thrillers, *The Fifth Knight* and *The Blood of the Fifth Knight*, have been #1 Amazon bestsellers. She reviews fiction and non-fiction for the Historical Novel Society, blogs for English Historical Fiction Authors and is a contributing editor to International Thriller Writers' *The Big Thrill* magazine.

Born and raised in the Republic of Ireland into the family of Michael Collins, the legendary revolutionary and founder of the Irish Free State, she lives in north-west England with her husband, daughter and a Facebook-friendly dog. Find out more by visiting www.empowell.com.

Made in the USA
Lexington, KY
14 December 2019

58575816R00226